Darcy's Journey

M. A. Sandiford

Cover art from *The Duchess of Richmond's Ball* by Robert Alexander
Hillingford (1870s), downloaded from Wikimedia Commons

Prologue

May 1814

Cannon Street was a prosperous road populated more by businessmen than gentry. As the carriage threaded through traffic towards St Pauls, Mr Gardiner pointed out the residence of a ship-owner he had once dealt with, and later, a cabinet-maker in demand for his fine craftsmanship. Elizabeth answered politely, but her mind was preoccupied with other concerns: her encounter, just a few weeks ago, with Darcy at Hunsford; and a major grievance in their quarrel, the plight of her sister Jane, still despondent after the separation from Bingley.

They dismounted at a narrow terraced house which had been rented by Giuseppe Carandini, a Venetian trader in glass, and long-term business associate of Mr Gardiner's. They had met over a decade ago and collaborated on several ventures before 1806, when Napoleon blockaded all trade between Britain and the continent. With Napoleon exiled to Elba this constraint had at last been lifted, and merchants from all over Europe were racing to London to renew their contacts.

Signor Carandini had not come alone: he had brought his daughter Regina, now in her early twenties and still unmarried—although probably not for long, since if rumours were true she had taken London society by storm, and caught the eye of a baronet. On learning that Mr

Gardiner had a niece of her own age, the sociable Miss Carandini had begged for an introduction. Elizabeth, for her part, was excited to meet the young lady who had made such an impression.

An English servant led them to the drawing room, where they were received by a young woman with thick auburn hair, pinned so that curls framed her face and extended to the shoulders of her silver-blue muslin dress. The contrast of the reddish hair with the pale blue material was striking, and Elizabeth paused in frank admiration before advancing with a smile for the introduction.

'Miss Bennet. Such a pleasure to make your acquaintance.' Regina Carandini spoke precisely, with a musical lilt. She turned to greet Mr Gardiner. 'My father apologises that he is unable to join us downstairs.'

Mr Gardiner frowned. 'Has his condition worsened?'

For an instant Miss Carandini's mask slipped, and Elizabeth saw she was truly afraid. 'The physician called again this morning, and insists he remain in bed. However, he is eager to speak with you. We are assured that his illness is not infectious. It is *idropsia*—how do you say—dropsy? Of the lungs.'

Mr Gardiner faced Elizabeth, his expression grave. 'It would be best if I went up alone, Lizzy.'

Elizabeth agreed, and after the servant returned for Mr Gardiner, was left *tête-à-tête* with Miss Carandini.

'You will take the afternoon tea, yes?' Regina bounced out of the divan, more animated now they were alone, shouted an order in Italian to a maid, and returned smiling. 'We have fresh *frittelle*. I hope you will like.'

Elizabeth smiled back, warmed by such enthusiasm in the face of adversity. 'May I ask what *frittelle* are, or would that spoil the fun?'

'Ha!' Miss Carandini raised her arms dramatically. 'No, definitely you must wait. It is—*meraviglioso*, wonderful, to have your company, Miss Bennet. I have found it so quiet here.'

'Really?' Elizabeth dropped her voice to a whisper. 'I was informed that you had taken to the *ton* like a fish to water.'

Miss Carandini looked up sharply, then laughed. 'You are *teasing* me, Miss Bennet. Yes, my father still has friends in London, in particular a count who, like us, comes from *Venezia*, Venice, and kindly invited us to a musical soirée. This led to a further invitation, to a ball, and a few social calls.' She spread her hands in another dramatic gesture. 'And that is all.'

Elizabeth drew back as a maid entered and placed a tray on the table between them. The tea was served in a traditional English pot, but the cakes were unusual: they looked like small fried dumplings, crisp and light, speckled with raisins and dusted with fine sugar.

'Forgive me for repeating such gossip,' Elizabeth said. 'I am notorious for my impertinence.'

'Impertinence.' Miss Carandini rolled the word around her tongue. '*Impertinenza.* I like it.' She met Elizabeth's eye. 'Both the word and the—how do you say—the attribute? Of course you will now have to permit me to be, ah, *impertinent* in return. But wait!' She pointed to the tray. 'We have the *frittelle*, and I am eager to know whether they please you.'

She poured tea, and offered Elizabeth one of the cakes in a delicate lace napkin. 'Eat like this, so that your fingers are not made sticky.'

Inside its crisp outer layer, the bun was soft and delicious, with hints of brandy and orange zest. Miss Carandini observed Elizabeth as she ate, impatient for her reaction.

'Good?'

With her mouth still full, Elizabeth nodded.

Miss Carandini clapped her hands. 'I am happy. Now, to return your impertinence, I should say that I have also heard certain things about *you*.' She put down her cup and leaned back, freeing her hands for gestures. 'It is told that you are sad because a trip with your uncle and aunt had to be cancelled.'

Elizabeth smiled, then replied more seriously, 'A small matter compared with your father's illness.'

'But is it true?'

'Yes.' She paused. 'I have been upset too over some personal issues, which ought to remain private.'

Miss Carandini studied her. 'Where I come from, such issues normally regard a gentleman.' She grinned. 'See, Miss Bennet, now I am being *very* impertinent.'

Elizabeth grinned back. 'The gentlemen can certainly be troublesome, Miss Carandini, and for all I know, you may also have concerns that should remain private.'

'True.' Miss Carandini raised a finger. 'But consider. If you have enjoyed our conversation, and these cakes, you might call on me again, and in time we might become friends. And once we are friends, I might share some of my secrets with you, and you with me. Is it not possible, Miss Bennet?'

Elizabeth studied her beautiful, crafty face, enjoying her more and more. 'You may call me Elizabeth if you wish.'

'And you may call me Regina.'

'Should we have another cake, Regina?'

'I think we should, Elizabeth.'

They continued talking until Mr Gardiner entered with

a gift from Signor Carandini. Elizabeth opened the little package to find a necklace of a kind she had never seen, made of coloured glass beads in subtle shades of blue, pink and orange.

'Beautiful.' She turned to Regina. 'This is so kind of your father. May I venture upstairs to thank him?'

'I will come with you.' Regina caressed Elizabeth's arm lightly as she passed to lead the way.

PART I

1

December 1814

Fitzwilliam Darcy strode along a path leading from the kitchen garden at Pemberley towards open countryside. The morning was crisp, rime glazing the hedgerows, and he longed for exercise. The last half-hour had been spent examining the progress of his steward's latest experiment in the *forcing of rhubarb*. McBride had learned this technique during a trip to Yorkshire: farmers had begun to keep the crop in the ground for two years to encourage root growth, then replant it in dark warm sheds where it would ripen over the winter to yield sweet crimson stalks. A tour of the sheds by candlelight had shown promising results, but it was a relief to escape McBride's overlong explanations, and exchange dank outbuildings for fresh air.

The fine weather was welcome for another reason: he was awaiting a party from Netherfield, including not only the Bingleys, but Georgiana. They had planned to over-night at Rugby, and with luck should arrive before dusk. As the cold snap set in, there was every chance of snow, with ice thick enough for skating on the lake. Two years ago Darcy would have been contented at the prospect of a white Christmas. He smiled, recalling the confident am-bitions of that 27-year-old who had never loved—and never lost.

He had met Elizabeth Bennet in the autumn of 1813. She was the second daughter of a country gentleman, a lively, impudent girl with bewitching brown eyes. From the start, there had never been any question of courting her. Whatever her charms, the family was simply insupportable, from vulgar mother to eccentric father to flirtatious younger sisters—not to mention an uncle and aunt in trade in Cheapside.

But the workings of the heart defied logic, and within six weeks he had acknowledged his predicament, quit Hertfordshire, and persuaded Charles Bingley (who was besotted with her sister Jane) to leave as well. The matter should have ended there, but no: in March the lovely lady turned up again, at his aunt's estate in Rosings, and this time he had gone overboard and actually proposed to her. The manner of her rejection still stung. *Impolite* hardly covered it. He was accused of arrogance, and disdain for others. He had ruined Wickham's career and her sister's happiness. His proposal had been insulting. He was the last man in the world that she would ever marry.

To cap it all, on the following day, she had refused to accept a letter explaining the misconceptions on which her rejection was based! His sins, already many, were now compounded with another: that of improperly seeking to correspond with a single lady.

He could see her now, in his mind's eye, her intelligent face flushed with embarrassment and anger as he pleaded with her to read his explanation. The final shake of the head (*No, it is impossible*), and she span away, walking so fast that she stumbled in her eagerness to remove herself from his presence.

And that was the last time they had met.

As time passed he realised that her bitterness was understandable. He *had* treated her rudely, both at the ball where they first met, and during his proposal. It had been underhand to separate Charles from her sister. Anyone could be misled by Wickham. There seemed no point in attempting a further meeting, but he could at least address his own mistakes. So it was that he had spoken to Bingley when they were next in town, and confessed his connivance with Caroline Bingley in concealing Jane's presence in London during the winter. This initiative had at least turned out well. Charles had forgiven him, and returned to Netherfield to resume the courtship.

Unfortunately, Elizabeth was no longer around to receive this news. Over the summer she had befriended an Italian woman, recently married to a baronet, and accompanied the couple to Venice. Jane, according to Bingley, had sent several letters, but only the first had received a reply; with communications still unreliable, there was no guarantee that the others had arrived.

Darcy had never met Elizabeth's Italian friend, but was acquainted with her husband, Sir Ambrose Havers, through his younger brother Edward. Darcy and Edward Havers were not close, but they had overlapped at Cambridge University and kept in touch. The family was respectable, but no longer wealthy owing to unwise investments by the former baronet, Edward's late father.

It was hardly surprising that Elizabeth had accepted the opportunity of a trip to Italy. Since their early conversations in the drawing room at Netherfield, Darcy had known of her interest in art and architecture. The war in Europe had ended, with Napoleon exiled and King Louis XVIII restored to the French throne. Young Englishmen again ventured to the great cities of the continent, including the poet Percy Shelley, who had scandalously abandoned his pregnant wife and run off with Mary Godwin, the 16-year-old daughter of the author Mary Wollstonecraft.

Since Elizabeth was in reliable company, there was no reason to doubt her safety. What he sought was confirmation that she had heard the latest news, not only about Bingley and Jane, but about Wickham, whose character had now been exposed in all its venality by his elopement with Lydia Bennet. Had Jane's letter announcing the catastrophe arrived? More importantly, had Elizabeth seen Jane's *next* letter, recounting that the couple were now discovered, married, and dispatched to the North of England, where Wickham had taken up a commission in the regular army?

If only they had a reply from Italy to reassure them that Elizabeth was well, and had received their latest reports …

Darcy deflected along a track leading to his favourite spot by the river. The cold weather had firmed up the ground, leaving only a few muddy patches that he easily side-stepped. He tried to calm down. Elizabeth was staying with a wealthy family and accompanied by a trustworthy English gentlemen—moreover, a *recently married* one. Sooner or later she would learn the truth about Wickham. Bingley would be arriving shortly, perhaps with good tidings from Longbourn.

He sat on a tree stump and absorbed the view, allowing himself once again to dream.

2

December 1814

At dawn the canal was already a hubbub of shouting and banging as bargees competed for space on the *Rio di San Luca*, which joined the Grand Canal directly under Elizabeth's bedroom window. They carried all manner of goods, from apples and potatoes stacked in boxes, to coal and wood, to piles of discarded furniture and other junk. Still in her nightdress, Elizabeth eased the window open a fraction and unfastened the shutters, steeling herself for the rank smell from the canal: the custom was to dump all sewage into the water, and let the tides carry it into the sea. She leaned far enough out to see the Rialto Bridge, a hundred yards away, already coming to life as moneylenders and jewellers opened their stalls.

It was beautiful, romantic—and her prison.

In the other bed Céline rubbed her eyes, and sat up.

'Is it morning?'

Elizabeth crossed the room and sat beside the child, resting a hand on her shoulder. Céline was Sir Ambrose's daughter from his first marriage, a rosy-cheeked girl with pale fair hair which she wore in braids. Now approaching her 12th birthday, she was practical and mature for her years, but with her father remarried, and the family whisked off to a foreign city, it was hardly surprising that she had become anxious—a plight recently aggravated by her father's illness.

'Sleep a little,' Elizabeth said. 'Sofia has not yet come with water for our pitcher. Shall I reclose the shutters?'

'No.' Céline withdrew under the blanket. 'Will it be sunny?'

'When the haze lifts.'

The girl fell silent, and Elizabeth returned to her own bed, hoping to doze a little longer. But sleep would not come, and she found herself reliving the twists and turns of the last months.

How could a venture that started so promisingly have led her into this predicament?

The trip out had been arduous, but also inspiriting. They crossed the channel to Calais, where Sir Ambrose bought a coach. As well as Elizabeth and Céline, the party included Regina, in mourning after her father's death, a maid to be shared by the ladies, two manservants, and a retired schoolmaster named Mr Theodore Avery who was earning his passage to Italy by serving as their 'bear-leader', or cultural guide. A French driver helped plan their route, and interceded with innkeepers along the way.

Paris was their first call, now returning to normal after a peace treaty signed in the spring. To Elizabeth's delight they had stayed a full week, before embarking on the long leg through Dijon to Geneva, in the south-west corner of Switzerland. From there it was a short trip to the Alps, where the coach was taken to pieces and they proceeded in a mule train, helped by hired guides, and carriers who lifted the ladies over rough spots in sedans. The scenery was astonishing, and more than once Elizabeth smiled at her disappointment, earlier in the year, at missing a trip to the Lakes.

In the reassembled carriage they turned south to Turin

before crossing the northern plain of Italy to Milan, Verona, Padua, and the port of Mestre, where Sir Ambrose sold his carriage to a returning traveller. Over the lagoon, Elizabeth espied for the first time the spires and pink roofs of the city her father had called the most beautiful in the world, now just an hour away on the ferry.

Nothing had prepared Elizabeth for the thrill of the final gondola ride from the opening of the Grand Canal to the Carandini residence. They first said farewell to Mr Avery; she then joined Regina, Sir Ambrose, and Céline, in a curved boat made luxurious by flowers and cushions, and gazed in amazement as they passed palaces that had been restored to grandeur on the interior while their ancient facades crumbled. Regina pointed out one landmark after another—a gallery here, a fish market there—but Elizabeth was too spellbound to pay attention.

If only Jane were here to see this ...

By habit, the household split in two at the breakfast table. At one end, Regina's brother Gabriele sat close to their mother Claudia; they spoke in Italian in hushed voices. At the other sat Elizabeth and Céline, eating mostly in silence. Regina often took a tray to her husband, now bedridden, leaving her younger sister Maddalena in between the two groups, next to Céline.

The meal, called *prima colazione*, consisted mostly of pastries brought fresh each day from the market. They reminded Elizabeth of delicacies she had enjoyed in Paris, but took a variety of forms including the *cornetto*, a cream-filled cone, and *brioches* shaped like croissants, but speckled with coarse sugar and sometimes filled with almond or chocolate paste. They were washed down with coffee, which could be diluted with hot milk, although Regina's mother and brother preferred a syrup of black coffee and sugar which they drank from small cups. Fruit was also provided: pineapple rings and baked apples and pears—sprinkled again with sugar, from which there was no escape.

Maddalena was a year younger than Céline, and made Elizabeth think of a pixie with her thin face, dark hair, and faraway eyes. The girls shared lessons and played together, learning each other's languages. Since Regina tended her husband, Elizabeth was often left alone during meals. She did not mind: it was interesting to listen to the others and try to work out what they were saying—and a relief to escape the attentions of Gabriele.

Regina's older brother was a very serious young man of 25, and the impression he first gave was *non-descript*. He was Bingley's height—not especially tall—and had the thin features of Maddalena, but without her charm. His reddish hair, sparse compared with Regina's, was worn short with sideburns. His voice was thin, and he compensated by forcing the tone so that he seemed perpetually anxious. Elizabeth, wary of first impressions, had tried not to judge him harshly. She smiled, listened attentively, tried to draw him out. But by doing so, she unwittingly became a focus of his attention, a *project* to which he now dedicated himself.

There was nothing that she could rebuke him for. He never teased, flirted, or took liberties. What rankled was his view of her as the clay from which he would sculpt a masterpiece. In every gesture, every utterance, he defined himself as a paragon of refinement, as if placed on earth to judge others and find them wanting. Practical life meant nothing to him. He revered painting, literature, but above all music, especially the Germanic tradition: Mozart, Haydn, and now Beethoven, whose violin sonatas he saw as the pinnacle of culture.

Gabriele approached her, as usual, while the maid cleared up after breakfast.

'*Cominciamo*?' Shall we begin?

'*Subito*?' Right now? Elizabeth could maintain a simple conversation in Italian, or at least the Tuscan variety favoured by the Venice elite; confusingly, the language of the market place was the local Veneto dialect. But for the most part they talked in English, which Gabriele, like Regina, had learned from an early age.

'We will go through the first movement again, and this time play it rhythmically, as Beethoven intended.'

'If you wish.'

Thrown on the defensive, Elizabeth wondered why she accepted her role so meekly. Gabriele's subtext was plain: the unsatisfactory rhythm was not *his* fault, but entirely hers. Why did she not puncture his arrogance with a rebuttal? She had managed with Darcy, even Lady Catherine, so why not this far less eminent Italian?

The trouble with Gabriele, and also his mother, was that they showed no sign of *understanding* humour—or at least, not Elizabeth's brand of it. She might have asked how he was so well-informed of Beethoven's intentions: had he perhaps consulted the composer himself? It would not have worked. He would stare back at her as if she were deranged. It would be like asserting that two plus two equalled five, or the moon was made of gorgonzola. He was right, everyone who disagreed with him was wrong, so what was there to laugh at?

She followed him to the music room and seated herself at the pianoforte, where the score of Beethoven's most recent violin sonata awaited her.

3

With Bingley at his side, Darcy rode along a bridle path to Longbourn. It was another cold day, turning the puddles to ice, and he took care to restrain his horse even though the turmoil of his feelings demanded haste.

They had left Netherfield immediately after breakfast, after a gruelling journey completed in a single day, the last part by moonlight. Such a disruption of their plans upset Georgiana and perplexed Caroline and Louisa, who wondered why their brother should come up to Pemberley one day only to return the next. The reason could not be explained without revealing Darcy's special concern for Elizabeth, and this was of course out of the question. Bingley had insisted on coming too, and after brief resistance Darcy had been grateful for his support; at least his friend would be rewarded by the prospect of further time with Jane.

Their arrival occasioned a typical brouhaha. They were shown to the parlour, to be received by Mary and Kitty, both obviously surprised by Bingley's presence and overawed by Darcy. Jane had been whisked upstairs by Mrs Bennet for alterations to her hair—as if Bingley's ardour might be cooled if a curl was discovered out of place. Not for the first time, Darcy was grateful for Bingley's poise as he chatted to the Bennet girls. Finally the squawking ('Hill!') and clatter of footsteps died down, and a demur-looking Jane entered, followed by her mother.

'Mr Bingley!' Mrs Bennet gushed. Her voice muted as she turned to Darcy. 'And Mr Darcy. You are welcome too.'

Bingley bowed. 'Good morning Mrs Bennet.' A smile to Jane. 'Miss Bennet.' He extended an arm towards Darcy. 'Excuse our unexpected visit. A matter has arisen over which we would like to confer with Mr Bennet.'

A sharp intake of breath by Mrs Bennet suggested that this utterance had been misconstrued. 'Of course! You may see him directly in his study. Kitty, inform your father!'

A bewildered Kitty led the way, and they heard Mrs Bennet whisper to Jane: 'See, he is back already, but what has Mr Darcy to do with it?'

In the sanctuary of Mr Bennet's study, coffee was ordered, and at last they could get down to business.

'Let me get straight to the point,' Bingley said. 'I have informed Mr Darcy of the letter recently arrived from Italy, and he may be able to help.'

Frowning, Mr Bennet turned to Darcy. 'Any friend of Mr Bingley's has my full trust. However, I do not wish the contents of this letter generally known. It would distress my wife and younger daughters.'

'You have my word.' Darcy leaned forward and spoke more quietly. 'Has there been further news?'

'None.'

'Just this short note, dated four weeks ago?'

'Correct.' Mr Bennet sighed. 'Probably nothing is seriously amiss, and we may hope for better tidings before long. But I *am* concerned. The newspapers confirm that cholera is spreading in Austria and northern Italy. We had been relying on Sir Ambrose Havers to ensure my daughter's safety; he is now gravely ill. What is more, we find no evidence, in Lizzy's note, that she has received any of Jane's letters apart from the first. I expected at least *some* reaction to our news about my youngest daughter Lydia, who is now married to Mr Wickham.' He pressed his lips together. 'I assume Mr Bingley informed you?'

Darcy nodded, with a slight smile. 'I have known Mr Wickham since we were boys, and cannot pretend surprise at what has occurred. However, I am glad that the problem has been resolved, and wish your daughter every happiness.'

Mr Bennet snorted. 'I would rather wish her some *sense*, but there is little prospect of that.' He leaned back in his leather chair, shaking his head. 'How my brother-in-law achieved this outcome remains mysterious to me, but we are much relieved. If only we had equally reassuring tidings of Lizzy ...' He regarded Darcy quizzically before continuing: 'I am still unclear, Mr Darcy, of your interest in the matter.'

'It is twofold.' Darcy took a deep breath. 'First, as you will be aware, I have met Miss Elizabeth on a number of occasions, and found her a most pleasant and intelligent young woman. I cannot say we are close friends, but I would hate any harm to come to her. Second, I know the Havers family, through Sir Ambrose's younger brother Edward, whom I met while we were up at Cambridge. It is through this contact that I may be of assistance. What I suggest is this. I will visit Edward Havers in London, pass on your news of his brother, and find out whether any communications from Venice have reached *him*. Perhaps through this channel we can obtain the reassurance that you seek.'

'Capital, sir!' Mr Bennet sipped coffee, before continuing: 'I am not, like you, acquainted with Sir Ambrose's family. I sent a letter to his London address, but have had no reply, so I assume it was not opened by his brother.'

'Probably forwarded to Venice,' Bingley mused.

Mr Bennet spread his hands in frustration. 'In which case it will have ended up God knows where.'

'I'm surprised communications have proved so poor,' Darcy said. 'They were reliable before the war; why not now?' He looked first at Bingley, then at Mr Bennet. 'Are we agreed? I will go to town today, consult Edward, then report back, either in person or by express.'

'You have my gratitude.' Mr Bennet looked away sadly, perhaps upset that he could take no useful role himself. 'It is asking a lot that you should continue your travels in such haste. Why not take a day to recuperate?'

'I fear we might soon be snowbound.' Darcy paused. 'Before I leave, may I have a private word with Miss Bennet?'

Mr Bennet looked surprised, but raised no objection. 'Since you are at your ease, I will ask her to join you. Mr Bingley, it falls to us to attend the other ladies.'

Jane sat opposite him, hands folded in lap, her expression as usual unreadable. Despite the anxiety over her sister, she looked well, buoyed no doubt by the renewal of Bingley's attentions. With her blonde curls and angelic countenance she was the equal of any society beauty: no wonder Bingley was smitten.

'You wished to ask about Lizzy's letters?' She drew out two sheets, one a scrap, the other a folding letter with tiny handwriting filling every space.

'Not only.' Darcy lowered his voice. 'I wondered whether there might be pointers that Miss Elizabeth had told you, ah, in *confidence*.'

Jane smiled. 'Matters that could not be shared with my father?' Her expression sobered as she sought the right words. 'Lizzy *did* mention some of what passed between you in Kent.'

'Yes?' He tried to hide his alarm, intrigued to know what Elizabeth had said, but also wondering how this was relevant to the issue.

'She said you had quarrelled over Mr Wickham.' Jane reddened. 'I should tell you also, Mr Darcy, that I am aware of the role you played in helping poor Lydia. It was Lydia herself who let slip your presence at her wedding, after which I applied to my Aunt Gardiner for the particulars.' Tears pricked her eyes. 'Unfortunately by then Lizzy had already reached Venice, where she received my first letter, written in August, with the news that Lydia had eloped—or so we supposed. Nearly two months passed before I received a reply.' Jane held up the folded sheet. 'Most of it is about her summer in Venice. She describes the beauty of the city, the family's hospitality, a visit to their glass factory on the island of Murano. She is glad to hear that Mr Bingley has returned to Netherfield, but shocked at Lydia's folly; she begs me to confirm that a marriage has truly taken place.'

Darcy was silent a moment, digesting this momentous report. 'Which you had already done, in your next?'

'Just so.' Jane struggled to keep her composure. 'But that letter was sent in September, and from then we heard nothing, until a few days ago, when this arrived.' She held up the scrap of paper. 'In Lizzy's handwriting. But in an envelope addressed by another hand.'

'Are the contents private?'

'No.'

Jane handed the sheet over, and Darcy saw that it was brief, and written in a hurry.

```
Dear Jane, There is cholera in Venice, Sir Am-
brose has been taken ill, and I cannot leave
```

```
the house. Please please write with news of
poor Lydia. I know not when I will escape from
this trap, and feel sick with foreboding. E.
```

And that was all.

Darcy asked, very gently, 'Miss Bennet, you mentioned my, ah, encounter with Miss Elizabeth at Hunsford. Did she give details on what she accused me of?'

Jane considered. 'The main item was mistreatment of Mr Wickham.' She looked up. 'I gather from my aunt that she was in error.'

'Wickham lied to her.'

'Apart from that, only general comments on your, ah, character.' Jane's face turned pink. 'I'm so sorry, Mr Darcy. If Lizzy knew what you had done for us, she would bitterly regret her words.'

So Jane was unaware of his connivance in separating her from Bingley. Darcy sighed with relief. 'I trust we both regret what passed that day. But thank you for your kindness.'

They parted on this amicable note, and as Darcy followed Jane out of the study he saw Bingley hovering at the end of the passage.

'Miss Bennet!' Bingley confronted Jane with mock outrage. 'You have spent far too much time with my tall friend, and made me exceedingly jealous! There is a question I have been meaning to ask you, and your father has kindly loaned us his study for the purpose.'

Darcy left them alone, with a wink at his friend as they passed.

4

Darcy left his Mayfair house early, skipping breakfast, in hope of finding Edward Havers still at home. The family was more respectable than wealthy; Edward made do with a flat in Marylebone Road, near a park now being redesigned under the patronage of the Prince Regent. Except for a brief flurry the snow had held off, so Darcy, weary of riding, went on foot.

A maid-of-all-work led him to a drawing room occupied by an owlish young man named Algernon Hare who shared the diggings with Edward. The interior was genteel but falling into disrepair, with the fading wallpaper mostly concealed by a pair of huge bookcases—evidently for use by Mr Hare, since Edward had never been studious. A little probing revealed that Edward was dressing, having been abed when Darcy rang. From the kitchen came the appetizing aroma of sizzling bacon, and Darcy was glad to accept two rashers on a buttered roll, washed down with a mug of tea.

Mr Hare tactfully left them alone, and when they had eaten, and Edward had fully woken up, Darcy imparted the grave news. At first, Edward was too shocked to respond. He had received no word that his brother was ill, and of course had no reason to expect such tidings from a man he had scarcely met since university.

'I must leave for Venice directly.' He paced the room. 'But how is such a journey to be planned? Or financed?'

'I can help on both points.' Darcy pointed to the chair. 'Calm down, Edward. We must first visit your brother's London house, to find out if post has arrived there. Or have you already checked?'

Edward returned mechanically to his armchair. 'I haven't passed by Montagu Square for months. The servant should have informed me of any urgent messages.'

'Shall we go right away? We can flag down a hackney on the Marylebone road.'

'Or walk it in ten minutes.'

Edward Havers cheered up once they were on the move. He was tall, the same height as Darcy, but carried himself loosely, like a puppet, slightly stooped, with his arms flapping. At Cambridge he had been seen as one of the brightest men of his year, but through indolence had left with a mediocre degree in classics, and after that subsisted on an allowance. Perhaps for this reason he had never married, although he could charm the ladies when he made the effort.

'Have you other kin who might have received post from Italy?' Darcy asked, as they turned off Marylebone Road into a quieter side-street.

Edward shook his head. 'My mother died shortly after I was born; father never remarried. We have cousins, but I doubt Ambrose would inform *them* at such a time. He would write to me, at my apartment.'

'Who else was in the party?'

'Lady Regina, Miss Bennet, and Ambrose's daughter.' Edward's face softened. 'Céline. You see, he married a Frenchwoman, Paulette Le Bon, when they were both in their early twenties. Her family had fled from Paris after the revolution and lost most of their fortune. Paulette sickened and died when Céline was two years old. It was a love match, and my brother was devastated. During those years Céline was the consolation of his life, as he took over the baronetcy and struggled to rebuild the family fortunes. During the summer, he met the most entrancing Italian woman at a soirée. The Carandinis are wealthy through manufacturing, and their daughter Regina is a classic auburn-haired Venetian beauty. My brother was bowled over. Within two months they were married.'

Darcy nodded—he had heard some of this from Mr Gardiner, while negotiating Lydia Bennet's marriage to Wickham. 'Even though her father was seriously ill?'

'Signor Carandini was delighted with the match, and urged them to proceed directly by special license.' Edward halted his loping walk, as if to emphasize the point. 'He was concerned, you see, with Regina's safety, so far from home. He saw that my brother was not only titled, but a trustworthy man who would never let his wife come to harm.'

At Montagu Square, an elderly footman showed them to the parlour, and brought a carafe of wine and box of mail. Edward, still distressed, drank a glass straight off as he sorted through the letters; Darcy took only token sips. There was no correspondence from the continent, but Darcy noticed an envelope addressed in Mr Bennet's hand, confirming that the enquiry had not been forward-ed to Venice.

Edward refilled his glass with a sigh. 'There is nothing further to be done in London. My brother is sick; Céline is left in the care of a woman she has known just a few weeks. I must go to Venice.'

Darcy nodded gravely. 'It is painful, Edward, but have you considered the consequences if your brother dies?'

'I would inherit the title.'

'And Céline would return to this country under your guardianship. The Carandinis have no claim, nor any motive to keep her.'

'Another reason I must go to Italy.'

He sounded desperate, and Darcy took pains to respond calmly.

'It is a terrible situation, but I believe we can make the best of it. First, I have every confidence in Miss Elizabeth Bennet, and feel sure she will give support both to Lady Regina and Céline. Second, I can help you with the practical arrangements.' Darcy drank a little more wine as he thought the matter through. 'My cousin Colonel Fitzwilliam has travelled extensively in Europe, and I was able to pick his brains at dinner last night. Venice can be reached most quickly by sea. Merchant ships leave often from London to Gibraltar, which is firmly in British control and a hub in the trading networks. From there you should find ships sailing to the Adriatic. Given luck and reasonable weather, you could be there within three weeks.'

Edward brightened for a moment, then slumped back in his chair. 'There remains the question of finance.'

Darcy was silent for several seconds. *He had to decide now.* Leaning forward, he said quietly, 'What if I offered to fund the venture, and came with you?'

5

January 1815

The physician was a neat man with hair that must have silvered prematurely, since he seemed in his early thirties. He spoke with exaggerated clarity, as if explaining complexities to a child. His name was Orsini, and he had attended the family regularly during Sir Ambrose Havers's illness.

'*Un poco più alto, signorina.*' A bit higher. Elizabeth raised the black veil, exposing her neck. He walked round, examining her from every angle but not touching. '*Va bene.*' Okay.

From the edge of the parlour, Signora Carandini and Regina observed. Orsini gestured that he had finished, and turned to report to Regina's mother. Favoured by his meticulous speech, Elizabeth understood most of it. She was still *pallida*, pale, but there were no signs of sickness. It was safe for her to leave the house but she should be accompanied by someone who knew the city well, so that she would not stray into the poorer areas where there might remain pockets of the *miasmas*, or bad air, that were responsible for cholera.

Elizabeth offered to pay—she had brought a bag of ducats—but Claudia Carandini waved this away: she was their guest, and the fee would be added to the family account.

Regina took her arm as the physician was shown out, and led her to a divan in the drawing room. 'So, my dear *Elisabetta*, it appears that you are not sick, so let us try to cheer you up.'

Elizabeth sighed. 'I'm supposed to be joining Gabriele in the music room.'

'Ha! Always he wants to practise.' She drew closer and whispered, 'You understand how he admires you?'

Elizabeth forced a smile. 'I try, Regina, but if I rehearsed day and night I would never meet his standards.'

'Oh, that is just his way. Yes, he is shy, he cannot express his feelings. But inside …' She touched her heart. 'Surely you understand.'

Elizabeth made a moue. 'He shows no shyness in expressing his *critical* feelings.'

Regina laughed. 'There! Already your spirit returns.'

Elizabeth recalled the camaraderie they had once enjoyed, but as the moment passed, the darkness overtook her. 'It is you who have cause to sorrow, not I.'

Regina looked away. 'I am, how do you say, *adjusting* to the loss. My husband suffers no more, and we must thank God for that.'

'Have you heard from his family?'

'Not yet. Ambrose left an address in London where his brother lives, and I sent two letters. I hope one at least gets through, but according to Gabriele, the post is still in confusion.'

Elizabeth fell silent. She had written repeatedly to Jane and her father since the onset of the cholera scare, but received not a single reply. The last communication had arrived in September, bringing the alarming news of Lydia's supposed *elopement* with Mr Wickham. Her instinct had been to return immediately, but how could this be arranged without obliging Sir Ambrose to curtail his visit?

So she had held off a few more weeks, hoping for reassuring news; then the cholera had struck, and Sir Ambrose had been confined to his bed with distressing symptoms.

Although irked by the regime imposed by Gabriele, with Orsini's support, Elizabeth had not feared for her own safety, nor that of Regina or Céline. They were assured that cholera was not infectious. It was caused by evil miasmas that gathered in poor areas of the city, where people lived in squalor. Orsini had dealt with dozens of cases among his wealthy clientele, without contracting the disease himself. He had treated Sir Ambrose with opium and regular bleeding, and recommended a restricted diet of beef tea and diluted wine. But the disease had proved too virulent, and in early December Regina's husband had passed away, leaving the family again in mourning, and Céline distraught.

Gabriele came into the drawing room, wearing his habitual frown.

'*Signorina?* I am awaiting you in the music room nearly half an hour.'

Elizabeth rose slowly to her feet. Gabriele's attentions were becoming suffocating, but at least the music helped pass the time …

'No, no, no!' Gabriele Carandini deposited his violin and bow on a divan and joined Elizabeth at the piano. 'It is marked *rallentando*.' He pointed at the sheet music, his elbow coming so close to her ear that Elizabeth had to lean away.

'I *did* slow down,' she said.

'Not enough! Look, we are reaching the end of the development section, and the main theme is about to return. Do you not see?'

There was a tap on the door, and the maid Sofia entered timidly.

'*Scusatemi.*' Excuse me. She edged towards Elizabeth, and whispered in Italian, 'Lady Regina requests your presence in the parlour. Two gentlemen have arrived. From England.'

Elizabeth gasped, and turned to Gabriele, who glared at the maid in irritation.

'We are not finished.' He ran to the divan and picked up his violin. 'Miss Bennet will come later.'

'No!' Elizabeth faced him, hands on hips, amazed at his unfeeling reaction. *Could this be Mr Gardiner, or even her father?* She wanted to ask Sofia, but in her excitement the Italian words escaped her. 'We will continue later.'

As they entered the parlour, she heard Regina talking in English, her voice hushed; her mother sat beside her on the window seat, intent as she struggled to follow. The visitors had been seated in the library chairs. Elizabeth recognised a gangling young man as Sir Ambrose's brother, Edward. They had met briefly at the wedding, where he had chatted to her with a relaxed charm that reminded her of Bingley; now he sat rigidly as Regina described Sir Ambrose's final days, and their efforts to inform the family in England.

The other gentleman had his back to her. She realised straight away that he could not be Mr Gardiner, nor her father; he was too tall and strongly built. In fact he reminded her of ...

Regina ran over to enfold her hands and usher her into the room. '*Elisabetta*, come and meet our visitors. You know Mr Edward, my brother-in-law. And this gentleman—' The other man turned, giving Elizabeth such a shock that her legs nearly gave way, and she clung to Regina for support. '—is his friend, Mr Darcy. With whom I believe you are already acquainted?'

'Miss Bennet.' Darcy bowed stiffly, his unease as great as her own. 'Excuse such an unexpected intrusion.'

Elizabeth managed a token curtsy. 'But why ...'

Darcy held an arm towards Edward. 'I am accompanying Mr Havers, a friend from university. It seems we are too late, since sadly his brother has passed away. Lady Havers is kindly bringing us up-to-date. Afterwards, he would like to see his niece ...'

Elizabeth asked Regina, 'Where is Céline?'

'Playing with Maddalena,' Regina said. 'I thought it better to leave her there for the moment.'

Elizabeth addressed the whole room. 'I'm sorry for interrupting. We should allow Lady Havers to continue her narrative.'

'I wonder ...' Darcy said to Regina. 'Is there another reception room where I could have a word in private with Miss Bennet?'

The *salotto* was across the hallway. Elizabeth heard echoes of Gabriele's violin as he played the sonata on his own. She grimaced: this stubborn refusal to greet the visitors was typical of Regina's brother. He had to *finish his practice* first, as if to underline the importance of what he was doing.

She asked Sofia in Italian to bring coffee and cake, and left the door ajar so that they would remain in open view.

'I did not know you were acquainted with the Havers family,' Elizabeth said, offering Darcy the divan. He sat near her armchair, so that they were just a yard apart and could speak quietly.

'Only Edward really.'

'I'm sorry that he has come so far, only to learn such tragic news.'

Darcy nodded, as if unsure how to reply, then drew a bundle of papers from his coat pocket.

'Miss Bennet, having heard from Mr Bingley that you were in Venice, I took the liberty of bringing letters from your family.'

Elizabeth accepted the package with a trembling hand. 'But how ...'

She paused, blushing at their mutual disquiet, and after a pause he said, 'You will no doubt prefer to read them in the privacy of your room. Would you allow me, however, to assure you that all is well? I visited Bingley at Netherfield shortly before leaving England, and was glad to find all your family in excellent health.'

Elizabeth stared at him. 'Including ... my youngest sister?'

'You have heard no news?'

'Only ...' Her eyes moistened. 'Excuse me, Mr Darcy. I cannot say.'

He extended a hand, as if to comfort her, then caught himself and withdrew. 'Miss Lydia is now married to Mr Wickham, and living in the north, where her husband has accepted a commission in the army.'

'Oh!' Elizabeth shuddered with relief, and this time there was no holding back tears. *If only he would leave her now!* She buried face in hands, emerging to find him waiting patiently; a clean handkerchief had appeared on the arm of her chair.

'Excuse me.' She dried her eyes, glancing towards the doorway to check that this intimate gesture had not been observed, then hesitated, unsure what to do with the used handkerchief.

'Keep it,' Darcy said. 'I have plenty more.'

She muttered her thanks, and after a short pause continued: 'Mr Darcy, you should return to your friend. I am unfit for company.'

He looked disappointed. 'But think, is there anything you wish to ask me urgently?'

'I'm surprised to hear that Mr Bingley has returned to Netherfield. I thought …' She sighed. 'I never expected to meet either of you again.'

Darcy smiled, not ironically but with what appeared genuine pleasure. 'He has indeed returned, and is now a happy man, as you will learn when you read your letters.'

Bedrooms had been reallocated after the funeral. Céline now shared with Maddalena, and Elizabeth with Regina, who had preferred to leave the chamber where her husband had lain. Grateful for solitude, Elizabeth sank into a soft corner chair that she used for reading, and opened her letters.

Everyone had written except Lydia: there was even a sarcastic note from Caroline Bingley, praising her enterprise in travelling so far away, and congratulating the family on its new in-law. Kitty bemoaned the loss of the militia; Mary listed the piano pieces she had recently learned; Mrs Bennet fretted over Elizabeth's wardrobe; Mr Bennet affectionately hoped she was well, and asked her to return as soon as possible so that he might have some sensible conversation. All of them referred her to Jane for an account of what had transpired.

Jane's letter, filling four sheets front and back, opened with an appeal for confidentiality: the truth of how Wickham had been found, and persuaded to marry Lydia, had been withheld from everyone else, even Mr Bennet. In her impatience Elizabeth raced through this section, her stomach aflutter, occasionally murmuring out loud in disbelief: *This cannot be! Jane must surely have misunderstood.* But the letter included verbatim citations from Mrs Gardiner, and Elizabeth recognized her aunt's clear, rational style. The story also made sense, for who else but Darcy had the resources to locate the fugitives, and proffer £10,000 to pay off Wickham's debts and induce him to marry?

Having re-read Jane's narrative more carefully, Elizabeth put the letter aside. If this were true, as it must be, her entire dealings with Wickham and Darcy had to be re-evaluated. Wickham's allegation against Darcy was false: he had not been *deprived* of the living, but had *renounced* it in return for the generous sum of £3,000. And it was this allegation that she had hurled in Darcy's face after his proposal at Hunsford. Another point immediately struck her. *Darcy's letter!* If she had only put sense above convention and *accepted* his explanation, none of this would have happened. She could have informed her father, he would have acted promptly, and Lydia would have been protected. *It was she, Elizabeth, who was the villain.* She had rejected and abused a good man, refused to heed his warnings, and put her sister in grave danger. She had been so confident in her own judgement, so cavalier in exposing Darcy's faults and cutting him down to size. And she had accused *him* of pride! How he must despise her …

In which case, *why had he done all this?* What could possibly have spurred him to go to such trouble and expense, merely to save Lydia, a foolish girl who was not his responsibility? Could it have been for *herself?* Was it conceivable that he still loved her?

No. It was inconceivable. Her own follies apart, Darcy would never contemplate a match that made him brother-in-law of Wickham.

In that case, *why come to Italy?* Was he concerned for her safety? So concerned that he would cross a whole continent to assist a woman who had treated him so ill?

Again, no. He must have other reasons. It would be

entirely in character for him to accompany his impecunious friend. As a cultured man he would be eager to tour Europe—an experience blocked for over a decade by the war. He could have no special interest in her …

Except, perhaps, to reassure Jane, now to become the wife of his best friend. And perhaps most of all, to relieve his resentment at being insulted and falsely accused by one whom he had loved.

As she wallowed in shame, Elizabeth felt no warmth towards Darcy. He was an honourable man, no doubt, but he could not love her now, nor could she feel comfortable with him. It was as if all his actions had been designed to highlight her inadequacies. She had accused him of separating Jane from Bingley; now they were engaged. She had accused him of casting off the companion of his youth; now Wickham was exposed as a scoundrel who had risked the reputation of her family. It was only through Darcy's selfless intervention that they had been saved.

If only he would leave her be, return to England, and let her drown in shame!

6

The dining room was designed to impress, with its long oval table, chandeliers, and windows overlooking the Grand Canal. Darcy waited while the family assembled, hoping that Elizabeth had been reassured by the letters from Longbourn. When she arrived, looking dazed but composed, he followed her to the table, only to find his path blocked by Gabriele Carandini, who pushed in with a muttered apology to claim the place at her side.

Frustrated, Darcy seated himself next to Gabriele, who threw him an irritated glance before resuming a conversation in Italian with Elizabeth. Two footmen served broth with rice. By listening carefully Darcy could follow the gist of what Gabriele was saying, a classical education in Latin proving useful for once by allowing him to guess words. It seemed that now that the danger from cholera had abated, Elizabeth was to embark on a voyage of cultural discovery, including visits to art galleries and the opera—and all under Gabriele's tutelage.

It was simple fare, warming and filling. With Gabriele monopolising Elizabeth, and Regina captivating Edward, Darcy was left to himself. He ate in silence, trying to divine Elizabeth's response to Gabriele. There was something relentless, even obsessional, in the Italian's manner; his nasal voice grated the nerves. Elizabeth, when able to get a word in, replied politely, but Darcy could find no trace of her usual sparkle, except for one or two attempts at gentle irony which seemed to go over Gabriel's head—indeed, he paid little attention to anything she said, treating her interjections as an opportunity to catch his breath before resuming his own lecture.

As he surveyed the gathering, Darcy noted that he was not the only person eavesdropping this conversation. Signora Carandini was too subtle to stare, but every few seconds her gaze flicked to Elizabeth, as if to assess her son's progress; she also glanced often at Edward, a hint of a smile forming as she saw him falling under Regina's spell.

As the soup plates were cleared away, Signora Carandini clapped her hands, gaining the attention of everyone except Gabriele, who continued his addresses to Elizabeth as if they were the only people in the room. A louder clap from his mother silenced him, and she began what Darcy guessed was a welcoming speech.

'My mother is honoured,' Regina translated, 'to receive our distinguished visitors. She hopes that despite our sad bereavement Sir Edward will accept the family's hospitality and spend some time in Venice. We regret we cannot accommodate his friend Mr Darcy.' Regina reddened as she faced Darcy. 'You are welcome to visit any time. But no doubt you will be eager to continue your tour and see Florence and Rome as well as Venice.'

Aware of Signora Carandini's alert gaze, Darcy replied with relaxed composure. 'I perfectly understand. For the time being I will find a hotel and remain in Venice.'

He glanced at Elizabeth, but could not tell whether her expression was anxious or relieved. As if alarmed by his scrutiny she looked away, and to cover her embarrassment he addressed Gabriele. 'While I am here, Signor Carandini, there is a business matter we should discuss. Before his untimely death, your father was eager to renew his trading arrangement with Mr Gardiner. On learning of my plan to visit Italy, Mr Gardiner entrusted me with a document proposing terms for a regular order of glass beads, for sale to jewellers in London. If you can propose a convenient time we can go over the details ...'

He broke off, disconcerted by Carandini's strained expression. It was as if he were listening to Darcy under duress, while seeking the earliest opportunity to resume his conversation with Elizabeth—who, by contrast, was giving Darcy her full attention.

There was an awkward pause, before Gabriele replied wearily: 'I regret you have been misinformed. I have never played any part in the running of the, ah, *business*.'

Darcy frowned. 'I assumed that as eldest son ...'

'I am owner.' He took a deep breath, his chest swelling. 'Not manager. I am interested only in music and other cultural pursuits.'

'Then with whom should I speak?'

'My cousin. Mario. Also Carandini.'

It was like squeezing liquid from stone. 'And how do I find Signor Mario? Does he live nearby?'

'Murano, near the factory. You must take a boat.'

'I visited once,' Elizabeth put in. 'Signor Mario showed us round the factory and was most kind ...'

'So you can take your proposal to him,' Gabriele interrupted. 'Excuse me, I was talking with Miss Bennet.'

Darcy struggled to hide his anger at this further display of rudeness. Had a similar remark been made at his club he would have asserted himself, by fisticuffs if necessary, but here he was a guest, and there were ladies present. He was also unsure where Elizabeth stood: could it be that she welcomed Carandini's attentions? He turned away as the next course was served.

Accompanied by his manservant Burgess, Darcy set off after lunch to make practical arrangements for his stay. He began by calling on the British consul, a man of his own age named Richard Hoppner. They got on well, and Hoppner advised him to stay at the Gritti residence, a *palazzo* on the Grand Canal between Rialto and St Mark's Square. Although still living there, the Grittis accepted paying guests, and on reading the consul's letter of recommendation their housekeeper allotted Darcy a comfortable room on the second floor, and found accommodation nearby for Burgess.

Leaving Burgess to arrange the transfer of his luggage, Darcy next sought a bank, recommended by the invaluable Hoppner, where a letter of credit from his own bank in London could be produced to acquire silver *lire* and Venetian gold ducats. He went on foot, through the warren of narrow alleys, welcoming the exertion as a remedy for his frustration. How galling to have crossed a continent, only to find his way blocked by the proprietorial Gabriele Carandini—whose attentions Elizabeth seemed to accept, if not with delight, then with resignation …

He recalled how, after lunch, Carandini had shepherded her directly to the music room. It had to be admitted that Gabriele played well, with such frantic attack in the faster movements that his fair accompanist struggled to keep up. In the Beethoven slow movement they sounded almost professional, confirming that Elizabeth had progressed under his hectoring guidance.

Before leaving, Darcy had had another word with Edward. A programme for the week was taking shape. The afternoon would be spent with Céline. Next morning they would visit a cemetery to leave flowers at Sir Ambrose's tomb and the memorial to Giuseppe Carandini. For the following evening a box was reserved at the new opera house *La Fenice*, for a performance of Mozart's *The Magic Flute*. As if to compensate for her mother's coldness, Lady Havers pressed Darcy to accompany them—an offer he was glad to accept.

Installed at *Palazzo Gritti*, Darcy had time to rest before meeting the consul again at Florian's café for drinks before dinner. Hoppner was now joined by his wife, and they spoke of their disappointment at being posted to Venice instead of Milan, which was closer to her family in Switzerland. The party proceeded by gondola to a restaurant near the Rialto fish market, where Mrs Hoppner was eloquent in praise of her husband's prowess in art, and his interest in poetry; this led to a discussion of the notorious Lord Byron. It was a fascinating dinner, and for Darcy a relief to be distracted, if only for a few hours, from his anxieties over Elizabeth and the Carandinis.

7

The Carandini's box was located on the second tier, near the edge of the stage. The auditorium was both imposing and intimate, comprising 150 boxes ringed in five tiers beneath an ornate ceiling. Guided to a seat at the front, Elizabeth was so overwhelmed that she could ignore, at least for a moment, Gabriele Carandini's continual presence at her side.

The location of *La Fenice* could not have been more convenient: a short gondola ride along the *Rio di San Luca* brought them to a water-level entrance. The party included Edward Havers but not Darcy, who had found rooms near St Mark's.

As the overture began she fancied she heard movement from the back of the box, but did not turn. To hear a full orchestra was a rare experience; the beauty of the music took her breath away. Gabriele's incessant flow of conversation at last ceased. He sat motionless, entirely absorbed: with all his faults, his love of music could not be gainsaid.

By the end of Act I Elizabeth had given up trying to understand the plot, and her thoughts turned again to Darcy. Why had he not come? Did he resent his cool reception from the Carandini family? One thing was certain: he could have no further interest in *her*. He had satisfied his sense of duty by accompanying his friend to Venice, bringing her letters, and delivering Mr Gardiner's order for beads; since lunch on the first day he had said not a word.

The curtain fell, and she rose to stretch her legs. Gabriele launched a critique of the orchestra. Edward Havers, sandwiched between Regina and her mother, was trying to escape to the back ...

Where Darcy now sat, talking with a man whom she recognised as Mario Carandini.

Self-consciously Elizabeth picked her way through the chairs, Gabriele's commentary going in one ear and out the other. She exchanged a quizzical glance with Darcy, but Regina took her arm and led her towards the hubbub of the ladies' room.

'You like?' Regina asked.

'*La musica*, yes. The story is silly.'

'In *opera lirica* the story is always silly. It is a tradition. Did you see the woman in the next box? Never have I seen so many feathers. Do you think she is really a bird?'

'She aspires to be Papagena perhaps.'

'She might spread her wings and fly away.'

Elizabeth smiled. She wished her friend was not *always* flippant, but at least the light chatter was a change from Gabriele's lecturing. 'Or maybe lay an egg.'

They laughed, and carried on talking.

When a bell announced the start of the second act, one of Regina's tresses came loose; by the time they reached the box the scene had started. Regina pushed through to join Edward Havers, while Gabriele irritably beckoned Elizabeth to the front. No Darcy: she wondered if after completing his business with Mario he had left. Ignoring Gabriele's frantic signals, she sat at the back.

Quietly the door opened, and the dark shape of Darcy

took the chair next to hers.

For a while they said nothing, but during a *crescendo* he whispered, 'Are you not eager to view the stage?'

'You seem content here.'

'I prefer the side-lines.' He smiled. 'As you may have noticed at the Meryton ball.'

Her eyes moistened at this reminder of home. 'I see now that I mistook reserve for arrogance.'

'Join the others if you prefer.'

Elizabeth shook her head. 'Here, every eccentricity is explained by my being *English*, so I do whatever I please.'

'Ah.'

He fell silent, so Elizabeth continued: 'Any progress with Signor Mario?'

'It was a relief to find him so approachable. He has accepted your uncle's terms, and a consignment will leave next month. I was wondering ...' He dropped his voice. 'About the letters you sent your family. Only two arrived, one a hastily written note. May I ask how many were sent?'

'Perhaps ten.'

'Your sister showed me the note you wrote on scrap paper. The envelope was not addressed in your hand.'

His solemn manner reminded her of her father's interrogations when she had misbehaved as a small girl, but in his face she saw only concern.

'I was desperate.' She looked away, to hide her distress. 'Venice was cut off. No letters arrived, none left. A visitor who knew Giuseppe Carandini called to give his condolences. He impressed me as an honest man. Just as he was leaving, I scribbled a note with the address on the back, and asked him to post it once he reached a city well away from the cholera.'

'Were the family aware of this?'

She moved closer and whispered, 'I told him the note was private, and begged him to show it to no-one.'

'And this was the only letter that got through,' Darcy mused. He waited for the music to louden before adding, still in a whisper, 'Miss Bennet, did you wonder whether your post was being intercepted?'

She tensed, disturbed by his question but also relieved to hear her fears expressed by a man whose sense was not in doubt. 'I confess I did. You see ...' She spread her arms. 'I was confined to the house. Signor Carandini and his physician both insisted. My letters were taken to the post office by a servant ...'

'Who might have been told to dispose of them.'

Elizabeth sighed. 'But this is speculation, Mr Darcy. We ought not speak thus of a family that has given me hospitality. There are, after all, other explanations. In any case, what motive could they possibly have?'

She stopped, fearful of rebuke, but after thinking for a moment he replied: 'You're right. The situation is odd, but we have no reason to suspect the family.' He paused, before continuing, 'I was impressed by your performance on the pianoforte.'

Her lips twisted into a smile. 'How gratifying that *some-one* approves.'

'Signor Carandini is an exacting master?'

She leaned away, thinking this over, as the audience applauded an aria. 'He is a man unlike any I have met. He has no lightness, no frivolity. For the first time in my life, any charms that I possess count for nothing. At home, my efforts at singing and playing were applauded; here, they are exposed as mediocre, and I am not allowed to escape with a joke. I am inadequate, and must improve.'

He fell silent, and she realised her words must have af-fected him in some way. Eventually he smiled sadly and said, 'That is a sentiment I know well.'

Her hand flew to her mouth. 'I hope you are not re-calling …'

'Yes?'

She whispered, 'You know. Hunsford.'

'In my case the censure was deserved.'

She swivelled to face him, forgetting for a moment where they were. 'Mr Darcy, it was not! The folly was all mine.' She put head in hands, before recollecting herself and dropping her voice again. 'It is pointless to re-open old wounds, but if I could wind back time and recant every word, I would. Please understand that.'

He regarded her a few seconds, before murmuring, 'You are kind, Miss Elizabeth, but I have long accepted that much of what you said was true. Not the part about Wickham, but the rest.'

She yearned to contest this, but saw that he really believed it, and marvelled at such humility. There was a long pause, in which she felt strangely at ease. Both had admitted fault; both had sought to forgive. She asked, changing the subject, 'What are your plans?'

'For the present, to remain in Venice.'

'But having come so far, you must see the rest of Italy. Florence, Rome, Verona. It is the opportunity of a lifetime.'

'And yourself? How will you return to England?'

'With Sir Edward and Céline, in the spring. Regina too, if she accept his offer of a dower.'

He thought awhile before saying awkwardly, 'I have no wish to intrude, Miss Bennet, but should you ever require assistance, of any kind, I beg you to ask me. Whatever has passed between us, I hope you can see me now as a friend of your family.' He smiled. 'Indeed, the best friend of the man now engaged to your sister.'

A shadow passed over her heart. This was a kind man, honourable, even good company. She had been given a precious opportunity, and had thrown it away. She nodded, unable to speak; he too turned his attention to the music. His dignified presence, so different from the passionate demanding Gabriele, felt safe, comfortable, homelike. She sat contentedly, wishing the moment would never end.

8

March 1815

Spring had come, and fruit trees were in blossom. In his hired carriage, Darcy sat opposite Theodore Avery, whom Lady Regina Havers had recommended as cultural guide. They had set off from Mantua after lunch, and would shortly enter Verona, the final leg of his tour.

Leaving Elizabeth behind in Venice had been hard: all his protective instincts rebelled, and he had gone only under the conviction that this was her wish. He understood now that in helping her family he had increased her feelings of guilt. It upset her deeply that he had borne the main cost of rescuing Lydia, and she was obviously afraid that he had come to Italy mostly in order to rescue *her*—establishing a comparison that was hardly flattering. What had finally decided him was his trust in Edward Havers, who planned to return to Verona in March, and thence to Switzerland, where they would wait for an opportunity to cross the Alps.

Leaning out of the window, Darcy recognised the pink roofs of the ancient Roman city centre, with the Lamberti tower just visible in silhouette. Impatiently he called out to Avery, who was dozing. 'Nearly there!'

The guide roused himself for a token glance. 'Twenty minutes should see us through the city gate.'

In which case, all going well, he would see Elizabeth

within the hour. Edward's party was to have arrived the day before, and should be installed at the Hotel Leoncino, chosen for its proximity to the Roman amphitheatre.

And what then?

He hoped, of course, to accompany them to England: Edward, scarcely the most practical of men, had begged him to do so. But what of Elizabeth? In Venice he had sensed a change in her feelings. First suspicious, then embarrassed by guilt, she had relaxed and started to confide in him. How would she respond to the prospect of a long journey in his company? Did she fear he would renew his attentions?

But there were reasons for optimism. Whatever Elizabeth thought of him, she would surely value the security of a second Englishman joining the group. After all, they would not be thrown together constantly: he would spend time with Edward, and she with Céline—and perhaps also Lady Havers if Sir Ambrose's widow had accepted the dower and decided to settle in England ...

Or was it Regina's plan to entice Edward to the altar, once a proper period had elapsed?

Darcy relaxed, recalling the beauty of Florence and the grandeur and fascination of Rome.

Edward ran into the foyer of the Leoncino exactly as the clocks struck seven, the time of their rendezvous.

'Darcy! Thank God you're here.'

His agitation alerted Darcy. 'What has happened?'

'Let's get a drink.' Edward led him to a lounge where a sideboard held two decanters.

'Is everyone well?' Darcy demanded. 'Where is Miss Bennet? Céline?'

Breathlessly Edward poured two glasses and took a hasty swig, dribbling red wine down his chin. 'Céline is upstairs with the maid. Miss Bennet ...'

'Yes?'

He sank into a divan, head in hands. 'I've made an unholy mess of things.'

Darcy sat beside Edward and tried to keep his voice calm. 'Where is she?'

He spread his palms. 'I don't know.'

A jolt ran through Darcy's body. 'Was she lost during the journey?'

'She never *began* the journey.' He took a deep breath. 'It happened the day before we planned to leave Venice. I had been on an excursion to Castello with Céline and our English maid. Returning, we found the house abandoned except for a footman. Communication was difficult since he spoke little English, but it seemed there had been a change of plan: the Carandinis had gone to visit friends and were not expected back for two weeks.'

'And Miss Bennet?'

'Went with them.' Edward looked up, his face reddening. 'According to Céline he said that Miss Elizabeth was to remain *permanently* in Venice, and that a *happy announcement* was imminent.'

'An engagement to Carandini?'

'I assume.'

Darcy swallowed. 'And their destination?'

'I pressed him repeatedly but learned only that they had gone to the region north of Venice where Prosecco wine is made.'

'What did you do next?'

'What *could* I do?' Edward took out a handkerchief and mopped his brow. 'I'm sorry, Darcy, but I had to stick to my original plan. Our crossing to Mestre was booked, as well as our carriage to Verona. We stayed overnight at the house, and left the next morning.'

'Did you speak to Carandini's cousin Mario?'

'No time.'

'Surely …' Darcy broke off, realizing that Edward had done his best in a difficult situation. He refilled their wine glasses, struggling to collect his thoughts. His impulse was to find a horse and leave for Venice, but a night-time gallop through unfamiliar countryside was pointless. No, he would remain in Verona overnight, hire a local driver, and leave in the morning.

He put a reassuring hand on Edward's shoulder. 'You acted for the best. Let us dine now and discuss further.'

They found a corner table in the Leoncino's elegant dining room and ordered platters of polenta, lentils and sausage meat. While they waited, Edward outlined the events of the last two months, which had seen some oddly shifting alliances.

'It began with Lady Havers.' Edward met Darcy's eye. 'Did you notice how she sought my company?'

'A most alluring woman,' Darcy said with a grim smile.

'I can concede that she formed a sincere attachment to my brother. But myself? I think not. Or rather, only because I am now baronet.'

'You gave her no encouragement?'

'I was charmed at first, but wearied of her. Noticing this, Lady Regina redoubled her efforts for a day or two and then suddenly dropped me. I was upset that she also ignored Céline.'

'And her brother?'

Edward raised his eyebrows. 'Continued his attentions to Miss Bennet, but with one alteration. For the first time he began to compliment her. It was embarrassing in its clumsiness, but also a relief. Rehearsals were *requested* rather than demanded. He even found aspects of her performance that he could praise.'

'Was Miss Bennet impressed?'

Edward looked away as a waiter approached with their food. 'Hard to say.' He raised a finger. 'You remember the younger sister, Maddalena?'

Darcy nodded. 'A sweet child.'

'Clever too, and not an admirer of her brother. I overheard her once whispering a warning to Miss Bennet. *Be careful of Gabriele, he is bad man.* I think she became attached to Miss Bennet. As did Céline.'

After eating in silence for a while, Edward asked, 'And your own plans?'

'My duty is clear: to find Miss Bennet, confirm she is well, and ascertain what she truly wants. I don't trust the servant's account.'

'This will take time, Darcy. Weeks, perhaps months.'

'Indeed.' Darcy looked up. 'If you felt able to wait, we could return together.'

Edward thought for a moment, then shook his head. 'Have you heard the news about Bonaparte?'

'That he has escaped from Elba?'

'Worse.' Edward leaned forward. 'It is said that he will soon arrive in Paris, and that his former generals have pledged their support. The war may start up again.'

'In which case you must hurry Céline to safety.' Darcy nodded approval. 'You are right, Edward, I should have thought of that. Let me know if I can help in any way.'

9

'*Elisabetta.*' A hand touched her shoulder.

Elizabeth blinked. She must have fallen asleep again. With an effort she pulled herself up a little and turned to face Regina. 'What time is it?'

'Early afternoon.' Regina pointed to the bedside table. 'I've brought broth and a glass of wine. The doctor says you are to drink it all. It will make you stronger.'

'Oh. *Grazie.*' Elizabeth struggled to sit up. Why were her limbs so heavy? Regina balanced the tray on her knees and she took a few sips of the appetizing broth. She had been sleeping alone in the tiny bedroom since they had come here—when? A week ago? Two? Time passed in a blur; she could no longer remember how they had moved out of Venice, or why.

'Where are we?'

'This is our holiday home. The air is fresher than in Venice. It will help you get better.'

Elizabeth sipped the broth, which helped soothe a dry sensation in her mouth. So they had moved here on her account, because she was ill. Yet she felt no symptoms except a languor that was not uncomfortable; if anything it was pleasant, as if her mind were floating in the clouds, removed from the niggling problems of everyday life.

'Drink your wine,' Regina said.

Elizabeth reached obediently for the glass. The wine

tasted strong and sweet but with an edge of bitterness. 'It seems a bit off.'

'The physician prescribed a few drops of medicine.'

'Oh.' She drank the rest.

'*Signorina.*'

Regina had left, her place taken by Gabriele. He handed her a document, clipped to a board, and pointed to a quill on the bedside table. 'You must sign this. Here, next to the cross.'

The document was in Italian. She tried to read it, but the language was too formal. 'What does it say?'

'That you agree to place yourself under my care.'

She put the board down, her head swimming. 'If I am under someone's care, why not Sir Edward Havers?'

'Sir Edward is no longer here. He left for England with Céline. Do you not recall?'

Now that he mentioned it, she did remember. Around the time she fell ill. Something about Bonaparte.

He gave her back the document. 'Here.'

An image of her father came into her head, warning her to exercise care when signing legal papers. She shook her head. 'I don't understand what it means.'

'I have just explained.'

'Even so.'

'You do not trust me?'

She sighed and made no reply.

A petulant look flashed across his face. 'Dearest Miss Elizabeth, do you not realize that you already signed this document two days ago? This is just a formality. We need a second copy for the *comune*, the local authority.'

Elizabeth reached for the quill, but a spasm of unease made her withdraw. 'Perhaps later.'

He slapped the table with frustration, and launched into a tirade reminiscent of their rehearsals. The whining voice made her cringe. She closed her eyes and clenched her fists, digging her nails into her hands as a distraction.

He had gone. She unfurled, allowing the tiredness to seep through her limbs and carry her away.

In the distance, she thought she heard the sea.

10

After a three-day journey Darcy had at last crossed into Venice, to find the city abuzz with gossip about Napoleon. The Corsican had sneaked past his guards, evaded a British ship patrolling the island, and made his way to France. French police sent to arrest him kneeled in fealty. At the Congress of Vienna, delegates planning the aftermath of the war pronounced him an outlaw—an empty gesture when French generals and their troops were rallying to his support.

Rising early in his former room at the *Palazzo Gritti*, Darcy lost no time hiring a boatman recommended by the Gritti family, a bronzed man of few words named Luca. Leaving Mr Avery to resume his scholarly pursuits in Academia, he set sail for Murano with his manservant Burgess, and they made their way to the glassworks.

Luckily Mario Carandini was on site, and Darcy joined him for coffee. The reception was cordial, with no hint of any crisis. As Darcy recounted what he had learned from Edward, the manager fidgeted nervously.

'It is … preoccupying,' he said finally.

'You were unaware of Sir Edward's departure?'

'Oh, that was planned long ago. No, I had not realised that Miss Bennet had remained behind with my family.'

'And left Venice?'

Mario Carandini chose his words with care. 'Such outings are common in the spring.'

'You mean, outings to the wine-growing regions in the north?'

Another pause, then Mario shook his head. 'I would be surprised if they had gone north.'

Darcy sensed his embarrassment, and tried to control his own impatience. 'Where then?'

'Gabriele owns a villa on Lido which the family uses for vacations. Since he does not always inform me of his plans, I cannot guarantee they are there. Still, it is probable.'

'You can give me exact directions?'

'Yes.' He frowned. 'You are concerned for *la signorina inglese*? Miss Bennet?'

'I am concerned about your cousin, and his intentions towards her. Have you heard anything in that regard?'

Mario bit his lip, as if engaged in an internal struggle. Finally he said, 'Mr Darcy, I know you as an honourable man. I would like to help. You must appreciate, however, that my position here is insecure. Since my uncle's unfortunate passing, I have been in sole charge of the business. It is important for our family that I continue in this role. But as you know, I am not the proprietor. My cousin Gabriele owns almost all the shares, and I am thus dependent on him. He can dismiss me any time he pleases.'

Darcy nodded slowly. 'You would not wish to cross him.'

Mario Carandini grimaced. 'Nobody would. These are times in which political and legal authority are in flux, and consequently money talks. So you are right, it would not be in my interests to provoke conflict. Still, like you, I am concerned.' He checked the door, and dropped his voice. 'In confidence, I cannot altogether trust my cousin.'

Darcy leaned forward. 'Go on.'

'You will have noticed that he is influenced by his mother, my aunt, who has always longed to secure for our family a social status commensurate with our wealth. It was for this reason that she urged Regina to set her sights on the English aristocracy. With Gabriele she has a harder task. As you will have observed, he is neither handsome nor socially adept. People find him intellectually intimidating or even absurd. Over the years he has attracted no young women except for fortune hunters from the lower orders. Now, all of a sudden, his sister brings from England the daughter of a gentleman. Not titled, nor rich, but a lovely personable woman who would grace any *salotto*. What is more, this young lady shares many of his cultural interests, and treats him politely and with respect. He sees her as his destiny, his grand opportunity. He cannot bear the idea that one day she might leave. You follow?'

Darcy frowned. 'Let us speak plainly. You fear some kind of—abduction?'

Mario recoiled a little. 'That would depend on whether Miss Bennet shares his ... hopes.'

'And if she does not?'

He sighed. 'I cannot be sure. All I can say is this. My cousin, for all his gifts, is not a *reasonable* man. He is like a child who becomes obsessed with something he wants, and pursues it to the exclusion of all else. Even if others suffer, even if he brings destruction on himself, he will not relent. He must have the thing he desires.' He looked up, trembling. 'It is not easy for me to say this.'

'It will not be repeated.'

'I wish you well Mr Darcy. By the way, I have sent the first consignment to Mr Gardiner, as agreed. For the second there may be some delay. We are all in fear that the war with France will begin again.'

'And the house in Lido?'

'I will show you now.'

As Darcy left, carrying an annotated map, another reason for Mario's helpfulness struck him. Honourable Mario might be, but Elizabeth was not just *any* young woman.

She was Mr Gardiner's niece.

11

The villa was located midway along the narrow island of Lido. Having decided to reconnoitre, they sailed down the west coast, bringing bread and salt cod to eat on the way. Lido seemed to go on for ever; luckily a tiny island just off the coast provided a landmark, and they easily found the wharf that Mario had highlighted on his sketch. From there the villa was a short walk inland.

It was a fair-sized square building of recent construction, set away from the older terraces and ringed by a garden planted with Mediterranean pine, cypress, and lemon trees. Observing from nearby scrubland, which provided good shelter, Darcy remarked to Burgess that the shutters were open; however, during a ten-minute surveillance, no-one came or went. Burgess pointed to movement in the back yard, and with his pocket telescope Darcy saw a maid enter a chicken run, perhaps to collect eggs.

'I must get closer,' he said to Burgess. 'Run back to Luca and make sure he is ready for a fast getaway. Then return here, and wait for me.'

'Are you planning to enter the house, sir?'

'I see no alternative. We must find out whether Miss Bennet is here.'

'Begging your pardon, sir, might it not be better to come back later with reinforcements?'

Darcy sighed. Burgess was correct: they had not even

troubled to bring pistols. But he had to find out whether Elizabeth was truly in danger. Even if common sense advised caution, it ran against all his instincts to retreat, when for all he knew she might be inside those walls, just a few yards away.

His knock was answered by a footman, whom he recognised from the residence in Venice.

The man bowed. 'Signor Darcy.'

'*Buon giorno*. Is Signor Carandini here?'

There was a frantic hiss from the passageway and the servant shook his head. '*Mi dispiace*. He is unavailable.'

'And the others? Lady Havers? Miss Bennet?'

'Unavailable.' The footman reached for the door, but Darcy held up a hand.

'When are they expected back?'

The door slammed shut. Angry at not inserting a boot, Darcy retreated past the gate, and waited a moment before circling round to the side of the plot. Using a convenient overhanging branch he pulled himself back into the garden, and began a cautious circuit.

There were two main floors, and an attic. All ground floor windows had iron bars. Above, the windows were shuttered but unbarred; some had terraces. He sought a tree that would provide access, but found none. Scanning the upstairs windows, he saw no sign of Elizabeth or anyone else. Round the back, near the chicken run, he came on a back door, and breaking cover, gave it an exploratory tug.

The door held firm, probably bolted on the inside.

Darcy looked both ways before returning to the shelter of the bushes. He watched, wondering whether he had been seen.

On the floor above, a window opened and a small face peeped out.

Maddalena. The younger daughter.

She waved, and he moved out a little and waved back. Fearing she might cry out, he lifted a finger to his lips.

The little girl nodded, held up a hand as if telling him to wait, and ducked beneath the window sill.

He held his breath. Would she find a way of opening the door for him? Or summon Elizabeth to the window?

Maddalena returned, holding a cloth doll, which she launched into the garden not far from where he stood. Could there be a note attached? He stepped forward to examine the doll. No message. He looked up questioningly, and she pointed down to the back door.

He thought he understood.

She could not come herself, but had found a pretext for causing a *servant* to open the door.

Darcy dropped the doll and crept to the side of the house, where a rose bush beside the door offered shelter. Minutes passed. A bolt was drawn, and out trotted the maid whom Darcy had seen earlier with his telescope. He dodged round the bush as her back was turned, and found himself in a scullery. In the kitchen, a cook stared at him open-mouthed as he passed through to the hall. There was a cry as the maid returned. A door swung open and the footman appeared, followed by Gabriele Carandini. They froze, then Carandini stepped forward, bristling with outrage.

'Signor Darcy, you have no right …'

'My entrance was unconventional, but I might also ask why I was so rudely excluded.' Darcy turned as another door opened and Signora Carandini joined her son, with Regina at her flank. 'I have been told that Miss Bennet is still residing with you. May I see her?'

Carandini shook his head. 'Impossible. Mr Darcy, you must leave now.'

'Is Miss Bennet here or not?'

'She is unavailable.'

From the top of the stairs a tiny voice cried out, '*Non è vero*. She is here.'

The maid scampered up with the cloth doll, as Darcy turned back to Carandini. 'Enough. I will see her now.'

'Miss Bennet is sick, and not to be disturbed. I must insist that you leave.'

Darcy looked at Regina. 'Is this true, Lady Havers?'

Regina threw an anxious glance at her mother, then at Carandini, before responding in a whisper, 'My brother is right. *Elisabetta* has not been well.'

There was no point appealing to the mother. Darcy span round and mounted the stairs, ignoring the outraged cries of the family. He found nobody in the upper passage, only six doors, all closed. From the stairs came a frantic clatter as Carandini and the footman gave chase. He saw the cloth doll again, on the floor, with its arm extended towards a door. Coincidence, or a pointer? He ran to the door, pulled, and discovered it had been locked with the key left on the outside. Quickly he entered, slammed the door shut, and relocked it.

The room was tiny, with a clammy atmosphere. Elizabeth was levering herself into a sitting position, blinking in confusion as if awoken by the rumpus. She gasped as he approached, but said nothing.

'My dear Miss Bennet …' He sat beside her and took her hand. 'You are ill?'

She met his eye, and he flinched to see the pallor on her face. 'Tired.'

There was a rap on the door, which he tried to ignore. He leaned close to her and whispered, 'What is happening? Why did you not leave with Sir Edward?'

The banging intensified. 'Signor Darcy!' Carandini's

voice. 'I have sent for the police. Unlock this door!'

Elizabeth touched his arm, her brow creased. 'I cannot remember …' The door shuddered as a shoulder was applied, and she fell back in a swoon.

'Stop!' Darcy yelled. 'I will unlock the door.' He made a quick survey of the room, spotted an empty wine glass on the bedside table, and sniffed it. Replacing it with a grimace, he turned the key, returning to Elizabeth's side as Carandini and the footman rushed in.

'Leave now,' Carandini said. 'Or you will be arrested.'

'I will leave when Miss Bennet is ready to accompany me,' Darcy said.

Carandini took up his familiar bristling stance, his face beaded with sweat. 'The *signorina* is too sick to travel, and you are not responsible for her.'

'As a friend of her family it is both my right and my duty to assist her.'

'On the contrary.' Carandini waved a piece of paper. 'As her *fidanzato*, betrothed, it is *I* who am responsible.'

Darcy took the document, which held a lengthy text in Italian followed by an illegible signature. 'This is meaningless to me and proves nothing.'

'I can call my lawyer if you wish.'

Darcy turned to Elizabeth, who had opened her eyes and was following the conversation with a curious apathy. 'Is this true? Did you sign this document?'

She blinked. 'It seems I did.' She looked away dreamily. 'My father warned me …'

'Miss Elizabeth, listen carefully. What do you wish to do? Remain in Italy and marry Signor Carandini? Or return to England?'

Carandini stepped forward. 'Miss Bennet is too sick to travel. Do you not see, she can scarcely follow what you say? She is receiving the best possible care from my physician, and must stay here.'

Darcy held out a palm to ward him off. 'Elizabeth?'

Her eyes moistened. 'I would like to see my family ...'

The crowd attending at the door parted, and a man in dark blue uniform entered. He recognised Carandini, and there was an exchange too rapid for Darcy to follow. The man turned to Darcy, and spoke very slowly in Italian:

'Signor, you must leave now. The English lady will stay because she is sick and under the care of a physician.'

There was a whimper from Elizabeth, who looked imploringly at Darcy before burying head in hands.

'See, you are distressing her,' Carandini said.

There was no point resisting. Darcy bowed to the policeman and followed him from the house.

12

Seated at his desk, Richard Hoppner attended impassively while Darcy concluded his story. Through the open window at the consulate a clock tower chimed four. The consul nodded slowly.

'So what would you have me do?'

'You tell me. I have reason to think that an Englishwoman has been abducted, and is about to become the victim of a forced marriage. What redress do we have? Can we count on the authorities to investigate honestly?' Darcy threw up his hands. 'Who are the relevant authorities in any case?'

'Well may you ask.' Hoppner opened a box of cigars and pushed it across the desk. 'Smoke?'

Darcy shook his head. Hoppner clipped a cigar, lit it, and leaned back. 'It is like musical chairs. For centuries, this region was administered by the Republic of Venice. This ended with the French invasion at the end of the last century, and Napoleon later included the Veneto in his Kingdom of Italy, and appointed French officers to look after the police. Last year, just a few months ago, this was changed again when the Congress of Vienna re-assigned control to the Austrian Empire. Now Bonaparte is back in France, and who knows what will happen. The prefect is trustworthy, but he remains a French appointee, now answerable to an Austrian commander. In such times, the

abduction of an Englishwoman will command little attention—even assuming that we can provide proof.'

'So how is law and order maintained?'

'Poorly. Much depends on the local captains, who are
Venetians, not foreigners, and likely to favour their own
kind. They are also susceptible to bribery.'

'They would stoop so low as to support abduction and
forced marriage?'

The consul blew a smoke ring. 'It would depend on
the official. The trouble is that we have two rival interpre-
tations of the facts. Miss Bennet has resided in Venice for
months as a friend of the family. An attachment with Carandini is not implausible. His lawyer is willing to attest to
an engagement. She is plainly sick, and under the care of
his doctor. Against this weight of evidence, I fear you
have no case.'

Darcy clenched his fists in frustration. 'I'm convinced,
Hoppner, that Miss Bennet is being held under duress,
probably through the use of drugs.' He recalled the smell
of the empty wine glass at her bedside. 'If I am not mistaken, they are dosing her with laudanum.'

Hoppner rested his cigar on an ashtray and leaned
forward. 'I'm sorry, but it will not do. We have no proof.
Laudanum is often prescribed as a medicine. I see no way
to proceed by official channels.'

Darcy lowered his voice. 'And what of *unofficial* channels?'

The consul studied him. 'You care for this woman?
You would risk your life for her?'

'Certainly.'

'You have resources,' the consul mused. 'Money. Skill
with a rapier, I would wager. Did you bring a pistol?'

'Two, to defend against brigands.'

Hoppner continued in a whisper, 'I speak now as a

friend, not as an official. Yes, in your place I would seek reinforcements and attempt a rescue. The administrative chaos of recent months will work in your favour. But remember, Carandini has resources too. If you have drawn his character correctly, he will not take this lying down. He will employ agents of his own and come after you.'

Darcy recalled Mario Carandini's warning. 'I will be ready.'

'One thing I can do.' Hoppner took a key from his pocket and unlocked a drawer. 'Again in confidence.' He withdrew a wad of documents. 'As a precaution I keep false letters of safe conduct for use by my wife and myself in an emergency. They may prove useful if officials have been ordered to detain anyone named Darcy or Bennet.'

Darcy glanced at the letters, which related to a certain Mr Giles Ashley from Cambridge, and his wife Rebecca. 'Do you not need these yourself?'

'I can make two more sets.'

'This is a kindness I will not forget.'

Hoppner rose and offered his hand.

13

The night was clear, the moon almost full. Their vessel, a *caorlina*, resembled a rudimentary gondola, but had a longer interior with space for six rowers. Darcy had taken an oar, leaning back against a small trunk holding their possessions. In front were two sailors, Angus and Dougal, whom he had found hanging around the port in hope of earning their passage to Scotland. Having enjoyed no success that day, the sailors were glad of the opportunity to earn a ducat apiece. They had co-opted two drinking companions, Italian fishermen mostly drawn by adventure, but with an eye to the flagon of wine that Darcy had brought along as an incentive.

It was an hour past midnight, Darcy estimated, yet traffic still moved over the lagoon, the dark shapes pinpointed by oil lamps. As well as manpower, Angus and Dougal provided equipment: ropes, a grappling hook, an iron lever, a hammock. For weaponry they carried knives; Darcy had sword and pistols—a necessary precaution, but he knew in his heart that if it came to a battle, their chances of escape were slight.

They found the dock near the villa, and Darcy checked the coast was clear before passing through to the scrubland.

'Burgess?' he hissed.

'Over here, sir.' The servant was seated on a tree trunk

shielded from the villa by oleander bushes. He pointed to the gate.

'Is the family still here?' Darcy asked.

Burgess nodded. 'They've posted two guards.'

Darcy peered through the bushes. 'I see no-one.'

Burgess pointed to a hut that adjoined the villa. 'One is inside. The other is round the back, patrolling.'

They waited until a man walked stiffly into view, carrying a musket. Darcy sighed. Some kind of defence he had expected, but to neutralise two armed men without a fracas would take time, if it could be done at all. He thought for a while, before leaving Burgess on watch and returning to the dock.

'Nae a problem,' Dougal said. 'Creep aside them, one two wi' the hilt of ma wee knife, and it's gudnicht to baith of them.'

'Or goodnight to both of *you* if they hear you coming,' Darcy said. 'I have a better idea.' He took a small bottle from his pocket, and whispered to the fishermen to bring the stoneware flagon of wine from the boat.

'I'm hoping that our friends outside the villa will be bored, and not amiss to a little refreshment.' He uncorked the phial and held it to Angus's nose. 'Recognise this?'

'Boggin 'ell, tha's bitter.'

Darcy up-ended the phial into the flagon. It was laudanum, the mixture of opium and alcohol he had smelled in Elizabeth's wine glass. He had brought it in case she craved the drug; now it had found a better use.

'Waste of gud buckie,' Angus complained.

Darcy shook the flagon and tested the wine with a finger. Yes, it was bitter, but still drinkable. He gestured to the fishermen to join them, and in broken Italian issued his instructions.

An hour or so later, Burgess joined them at the boat.

'It's working,' he whispered. 'One of the guards managed a wobbly patrol ten minutes ago, but his mate hasn't come out. They're both in the shed now.'

'Excellent. Tell us if anything changes.'

Darcy gave the thumbs up to the fishermen, who had hoodwinked the guards by pretending to be local revellers willing to share a flagon of *vino rosso*. The guards were ex-militiamen who offered their skills to anyone willing to pay. Weary and bored, they were easily tempted to try one swig, then another, until eventually they traded a pinch of tobacco for the whole flagon.

'They winna be out cold,' Angus warned. 'Nae on laudanum.'

Darcy nodded. 'But we have them drinking in the shed now, and their reactions will be sluggish.'

They sent the fishermen back to the shed. One guard was now snoring; the other, recalling his job, staggered around the villa until he reached a tree, where Angus and Dougal jumped him and stuffed a rag in his mouth to keep him quiet.

Able to move freely at last, with both guards bound and gagged, Darcy unlatched the gate and led the sailors to a cypress that he had spotted from Elizabeth's window. He looked up at the small stone balcony and rickety wooden shutters. *Had they moved her?* But why go to such trouble with two guards outside?

The tree was too far from the balcony to provide access. Angus and Dougal conferred by gesture; then Angus leaned against the wall while Dougal climbed on his back. Dougal's fingers reached for the balustrade, but it was too high. Angus pointed to a rope, which Darcy passed up; Dougal managed to lob the end over the balustrade and thread it back. Looking down with a grin, he fashioned a noose to grip the top of the wall, and jumped down.

Darcy pulled on the rope. It held firm.

Lower down the rope, the sailors had tied thick knots to serve as footrests. Angus shimmied up, the iron lever in his teeth, and was probing the shutters as Darcy joined him. He pointed to a gap, where a fastener on the inside was visible, wiggled the blade of his knife through, and lifted it. With a creak the shutter opened to reveal a sash window slightly ajar.

Carefully, Darcy raised the window and climbed inside. He recalled the clammy air and the faint odour of opium. A woman stirred, then rolled on to her side, asleep. Darcy leaned over the bed and saw the familiar dark curls, now unpinned, and the pale skin shiny with sweat.

It was Elizabeth. She was here.

14

Someone was whispering her name. A man's voice, familiar, like a dream of home.

'Miss Bennet. Elizabeth. Wake up.'

She twitched, and nearly cried out, but the reassuring voice hushed her. 'Don't be alarmed. You are safe, but we must speak softly.'

She saw the outline of his face, just a few inches away. 'Mr Darcy! But how ...'

'Shh.' He held a finger to his lips. 'We must go now, and take care not to alert the household. Do you understand?'

'Go? But it is impossible ...' Frantic images came into her mind, of Regina urging her to take her medicine, and Gabriele waving a document that she had to sign—or had she already signed it?

Darcy rested a hand on the blanket, near her shoulder. 'I am going to take you back to your family in England, if that is what you want.'

Her heart jumped. 'They say I am too sick to travel.'

His voice was quiet, but firm. 'You are not sick, Miss Elizabeth. You feel tired and confused because you have been drugged, with an opiate.'

'It is a medicine ...' A wave of drowsiness overcame her, and she bit her lip, struggling to focus.

'The physician is in the pay of Signor Carandini, who

seeks to lock you away until you consent to marry him.'

'They say I have signed a document.' She recalled her father's advice. 'Although I should not have.'

'Do you wish to marry him?'

'Marry?' She shivered. 'No. But they say I have given my word ...'

'Miss Bennet, listen carefully. I have seen the document. The signature is illegible. Either it has been falsified, or you wrote it when you were half asleep and had no idea what you were agreeing to. The document *does not matter*. All that matters is whether you prefer to stay here, or return to England.'

She felt a familiar annoyance at the way he assumed command. But she was too weak to retaliate now; it was a relief to submit and give herself into his care.

'I will come with you.'

'Then let us make haste. Can you walk?'

She tried to lever herself up, but her limbs were so heavy that she trembled with the effort.

'Never mind, I will carry you. Now your clothes ...'

She pointed at a wardrobe. 'How can I dress?'

'No time for that.' He quickly made up a bundle and handed it to someone on the balcony.

She managed to sit up, and pointed to her nightgown. 'I cannot travel in this.'

'We'll use the bedclothes. Permit me.' She gasped as he pulled back the blankets, and he raised a hand. 'This is no time for delicacy. Relax, and try not to make a sound.'

His arms came around her and he lifted her on top of the bedclothes, then wrapped her like a parcel. The sensation of his hands through the thin cotton nightdress took her breath away, but with his warning fresh in her mind she remained compliant. A wave of fresh air hit her as he handed her through the window to another pair of hands;

a moment later she found herself on the balcony floor. She probed under the blankets and felt rough canvas.

A hand touched her arm, and Darcy whispered, 'Keep still. We're lowering you in a hammock.'

The canvas enfolded her and she was swinging back and forth. There was a muffled oath from above as the hammock bumped against the outside of the balcony, but she was unhurt, and did not cry out. Another pair of hands guided her to the ground. Light footsteps sounded behind her as Darcy and another man descended, then the hammock rose again, twisting her into a bow shape as her head and feet were pulled up.

She heard a rattle from the villa followed by the bang of a shutter, and a shriek of *'Intrusi!'*

'Confound it!' Darcy growled, no longer keeping his voice down. The hammock swayed as the men rushed her through the gate. In the corner of her eye she saw Darcy alongside, shouting at the men to stop.

'Too slow! I will take her. Run ahead and alert the others.'

She felt his arms enfold her body, still wrapped in the bedclothes, and they set off again, now at running pace. The cries from the villa receded, then they were alone, in a woodland, with Darcy breathing heavily as he picked his way between the trees.

A cold breeze woke her. She was in a boat, leaning against the hard edge of a platform at the rear. In front of her she recognised Darcy, silhouetted against the moonlight as he pulled on an oar; beyond him she counted five other men. As she sat up a headwind caught her hair, which streamed behind. The men grunted with exertion. She reached back and tried to fold her hair into the blankets, but it flew out again as soon as she released it.

Darcy stopped rowing, and pointed. 'There! Another boat, from the same dock.'

'A gud half-mile ahint,' a man replied.

Darcy applied himself again to his oar, and smiled as he realised she was awake. 'Comfortable?'

Not very, she thought, but at least the blankets were keeping her warm. 'Who is following us?'

'I fear Carandini has found reinforcements.' He pointed over his shoulder. 'Do you see an opening inland from the lagoon?'

She leaned over, and squinted into the distance. 'I see two openings. No, three.'

They passed between a pair of tiny islands, and a man at the front shouted, '*Fusina*.'

Elizabeth looked back at Darcy. 'Is that our target?'

He nodded.

'And after that?'

He frowned. 'We shall see.'

Unaccountably she felt a lightening of spirits, and met his eye with a smile. 'Mr Darcy, am I to understand that you have no idea what to do next?'

He smiled back. 'My plans are flexible.'

'In other words, non-existent.'

'Miss Bennet, we have a two-mile row ahead of us into a stiff wind. Lie back and try to sleep. Perhaps when you wake, my plans will have evolved to your satisfaction.'

She laughed—when had she last done that?—and tried to find a comfortable angle to rest her head.

15

When they reached Fusina it was still dark, but the wharf was already busy as goods from Venice were loaded on to barges, to be drawn by horse power along the river towards the Brenta canal. Looking back across the lagoon Darcy could no longer discern which of the boats had been pursuing them from Lido. He had wondered whether to dock first elsewhere, as a decoy, but decided that the priority was speed: they had only half an hour on Carandini and his men, and must put it to good use.

Facing him at the back of the boat, Elizabeth had slept through the latter part of the journey, and he felt a twinge of guilt at the pleasure of having her so close, curled up in the warm blankets with her hair spilling in all directions.

Angus and Dougal moored the boat, and helped Burgess unload Darcy's trunk, which now held some of Elizabeth's clothes as well as his own. He puzzled what to do with Elizabeth herself, still dressed in her nightgown and probably too drowsy to walk. Eventually he awoke her, then simply carried her up the steps to the wharf and sat her on the trunk, where she drew the blankets across her shoulders and awaited events in silence.

It was time for a parting of the ways. Darcy extracted two gold ducats from his belt for Angus and Dougal, and gave the Italian fishermen a silver lira each to compensate them for the missing wine, sacrificed in order to drug the guards. The men set off in excellent spirits. Without them Darcy felt a knot of anxiety: if Carandini and company caught up, it would no longer be possible to resist. He hoped that his pursuers would see the *caorlina* boat depart, and divide their forces in case Darcy and Elizabeth were still on it.

Burgess returned with the welcome news that a barge was about to leave, and could take them along the Brenta to Padua. Even better, when tempted by another coin, the bargee sent two men to carry their luggage.

It was a low thin vessel with the decks at both ends laden with barrels, and a covered sitting area recessed in the middle. As Darcy boarded, the bargee left to talk with a boy who was harnessing two horses to the side of the boat. On deck there were open boxes of fresh fish, which Darcy had to side-step as he carried Elizabeth inside. Two other passengers, dressed like farm workers, watched with interest as he set her down on one of two wooden bench-es which ran along the sides. Their presence obviously disturbed Elizabeth, who had woken up sufficiently to worry about her hair, but she managed to coil it beneath a blanket, after which she again closed her eyes.

As the barge moved slowly off, Burgess joined them.

'Any sign of Carandini?' Darcy asked.

Burgess shook his head. 'Won't be long though, sir. An hour at most, probably less.'

'What would you do in his place?'

'Ask at the wharf. Then hire a horse and gallop after the barge.'

'Just so.' Darcy thought for a moment. 'Which means we have a problem. We cannot hope to reach Padua by barge, because in an hour's time we will be overtaken. We must disembark earlier, at a place they won't expect.'

'We'll be seen leaving the barge,' Burgess pointed out.

'As soon as Carandini's men catch up, they will question the bargee, who will set them back on our trail.'

Darcy nodded pensively. Of course he had no proof that Carandini was *on their trail* at all; the boat following them out of Lido might have been a fishing craft. But he trusted Mario Carandini's account of his cousin's character. Gabriele would not relinquish his obsession so easily. He would go to any lengths, spend any amount of money, to get Elizabeth back ...

Darcy woke with a jolt, to discover that the farm workers had left. He cursed himself for giving way to his weariness and dropping off. How much time had passed? Had they been overtaken? He shook Burgess, who was also dozing, and ran up on deck, where the farm workers were exchanging pleasantries with the bargee as they waited to disembark.

'Where are we?' Darcy asked in Italian, joining them.

The bargee pointed to a villa with a facade made up of triangles and columns, beautifully composed in the style of a Greek temple. 'Villa Foscari.'

In the dawn light the villa seemed a fantasy, too good to be true. Darcy looked back along the river bank for evidence of pursuit, but saw no riders.

'We will disembark now.'

The bargee regarded him strangely. 'You won't find anyone here from the family.'

'I want to see the villa.'

The bargee shrugged and shouted instructions. By the time Darcy returned, with Elizabeth in his arms, Burgess was standing on the grassy bank, next to their luggage, and communicating in a mixture of gesture and Venetian dialect with the farm workers. Darcy seated Elizabeth on the trunk, and she stretched and rubbed her eyes.

'Where are we?'

He pointed to the villa, and she gasped.

'Oh my goodness, what a lovely place!'

'How are you feeling?'

'Not unwell, but so tired! I could sleep forever.'

'Don't be alarmed. It will wear off.' He turned to Burgess. 'We need to move quickly from the riverside.'

Burgess pointed to the farm workers. 'They say we can go to the house. They work for a man named Boscolo, who may be the owner.'

'Not Foscari?' Darcy queried.

Burgess threw up his hands. 'That's how it seems. But they will help with the luggage if we want.'

'Well done.' Darcy nodded to the Italians, asked their names, and helped Elizabeth to stand so that they could carry the trunk. Although impeded by the blankets she tried a few steps, but their progress was too slow, and he gathered her in his arms again; it was in any case a walk of only a hundred yards.

Reaching the villa, he was surprised to find two rustic carts parked outside, with chickens and geese running freely. The centre of the facade extended in a wide balcony, with six columns in front and a room underneath. It could be reached by external L-shaped staircases on either side, and since this seemed the main entrance, Darcy carried Elizabeth up the steps, and motioned to the others to follow.

On the balcony, a low wall helped conceal them from any observers on the river bank. At the back a door was left open, and Darcy found himself in what must have once been a grand hall. Its condition was a shock. Instead of divans, carpets, a formal dinner table, he found only a few rickety benches, several dozen sacks of grain, and a huge open pile of dried maize.

He seated Elizabeth gently on a bench, and they both looked around in wonder.

The interior was arranged in a cross shape, with four corridors leading out from the hall. Over their heads was a vaulted ceiling which, like the walls, was covered in the most amazing frescos of classical themes from Greek mythology. One could have spent days studying the paintings. They were plainly the work of great artists, on a par with the magnificent architecture.

Yet the villa had been abandoned.

Wondering who was in charge, Darcy turned his attention to the other occupants. A few were sleeping on straw pallets. A woman was filling a basket with cobs of maize, perhaps for feeding to chickens. In a corner he spotted a man dressed in breeches and a light jacket, leaning against a sack of grain while he drew in a sketchbook with a stick of charcoal. After a reassuring word to Elizabeth, Darcy crossed the hall to approach him.

'*Buon giorno.*'

The man looked up with raised eyebrows, threw down his sketchbook, and jumped to his feet. 'And good-day to you too, sir!'

Darcy was momentarily lost for words as he stared at a fresh-faced young man with flowing fair hair and a confident manner. 'You are English?'

The young man bowed. 'Gerard Hanson, from Woodstock, near Oxford. Of which I am an undistinguished alumnus.'

'Then I fear we will never get on, since my *alma mater* is Cambridge.' Darcy wondered whether to give a false name, but decided to risk it. 'Fitzwilliam Darcy, from Derbyshire.' He stepped forward and dropped his voice. 'Are you by any chance on terms with the owner? I find myself in a quandry, and would appreciate some help.'

'The estate has been rented to a man named Boscolo who owns most of the farmland around here. As you see, the villa has been left to decay, but this floor and the one beneath are used for storage, while the upper rooms are let out for a pittance to itinerant labourers or anyone else passing by.' He paused. 'What help do you need?'

'I'm travelling with an Englishwoman who has been ill. She needs privacy to wash and change. We have not eaten for a long time.'

'I suggest in that case that you bring your, ah, companion upstairs, where I have one of the chambers. The furniture is dilapidated, but includes a dresser with a jug of water, which she is welcome to use.'

Darcy introduced Mr Hanson to Elizabeth, and he led them through a domed side-room to a staircase. Reaching one of the smaller upper chambers, he held up a hand.

'Excuse me a moment.' He opened the door a crack and poked his head inside. 'Alice?'

There was a moan from within, and with an impudent smile he beckoned Darcy to follow him through. 'As you see, I also have a lady friend. Don't worry, she's still abed. Alice, we have visitors from England!'

Darcy frowned. 'This is not what I expected, Mr Hanson. Is there not another room?'

Hanson laughed. 'This is all I can offer, but don't hesitate on our account. We can leave the ladies in privacy and go in search of breakfast.'

Darcy looked down at Elizabeth, who was observing him with an amused smile. 'Miss Bennet?'

'I will stay, if Mrs Hanson permits.'

'Very well.' Darcy stepped into the room, where a pale young woman lay in an ornate four-poster that looked as if it might collapse at any moment. He found a similarly regal and dilapidated armchair for Elizabeth.

'Will you be alright here?' he asked softly.
'Fine. Thank you.'
'What clothes shall I bring?'
'All of them.'
He turned, with relief, and followed Hanson out.

16

Elizabeth remained seated, adapting to another kaleido-scopic change of scene. She wondered how she could feel so calm after such adventures. To be rescued by Mr Dar-cy, carried in his arms to a boat, rowed across the Venice lagoon, transported by barge to an abandoned villa, and finally to share this room with this stranger, now observ-ing her with puzzlement. It should have been disconcert-ing, but she felt instead a drowsy euphoria.

A hand touched her arm. 'Are you alright?'

Elizabeth blinked. 'I must have dozed off.' She smiled at the woman, who stood at her side still wearing an em-broidered chemise. She was young, no older than Kitty, and pale, with a freckled face and mouse-coloured hair.

'Would you like to wash first, Mrs ...'

'Miss Bennet. Yes, if you like.'

There was a tap on the door. 'Miss Elizabeth?' Darcy's voice. 'I'll leave your clothes outside.'

The girl peeped round the door and returned bearing an assortment of shifts, petticoats and dresses, which she laid on the bed.

'Thank you, Mrs Hanson.'

'Miss.' The girl regarded her with a mixture of embar-rassment and defiance. 'Alice Dill.'

'Miss Dill.' Elizabeth tried to lever herself up so that she could throw off the blankets.

'Let me help you.' Miss Dill took Elizabeth's arm, allowing the bedclothes to fall, and guided her to the washstand. 'There's cold water in the jug, and a flannel.'

Elizabeth watched as the girl poured water, but standing was too much effort. 'Sorry …'

'Let's sit you on the bed.' Elizabeth submitted gratefully as her nightgown was removed and Miss Dill brought a bowl of water. The room was cold, and she shivered as she wiped her face and arms with the flannel. This quick cleansing was deemed sufficient, and Miss Dill, now taking control, chose undergarments and helped her dress.

'My turn,' Miss Dill said cheerfully.

Elizabeth rummaged through her heap of clothes and was rewarded by finding a pair of half-boots to complete her attire. But her hair remained troublesome.

'Miss Dill, I have no brush or pins.'

Her companion handed over an ancient mother-of-pearl hairbrush. 'I found this in a drawer.' She looked in a silver bag with tassels and threw two comb-shaped clasps on to the bed. 'I can spare these.'

'You're very kind.' What a relief to brush her hair! She regarded Miss Dill with grateful affection. 'Where are you from?'

'The rectory at Woodstock, near Oxford. My father is rector at St Mary Magdalene's.'

'And Mr Hanson?'

'Also Woodstock.' She sat beside Elizabeth and said in a whisper, 'Gerard and I are artists. His father owns an estate with £4000 a year, but Gerard has preferred to make his own way and shares a house with friends from his university days. I knew him from church when I was a small girl, and we met again at an exhibition. My father said I should have nothing to do with him, since he had been living with an actress and was not respectable.'

Elizabeth took her hand, in shock. 'Has he persuaded you to elope?'

Miss Dill smiled. 'I cannot honestly claim that much persuasion was required. I am a free thinker, Miss Bennet. To leave home has been a breath of fresh air.'

Tears stung Elizabeth's eyes as she recalled the trauma of Lydia's lapse with Wickham. 'But my dear Miss Dill, to be cut off from your family!'

'I have what I wanted. Freedom. The company of an intelligent man who respects my ambition to be an artist.' She bit her lower lip, and looked away. 'But there is truth in what you say. I do miss England, my home, and yes, also my family.'

'Could you return now?'

Miss Dill shook her head. 'We have still to see Verona and Florence.' She sighed. 'And yourself?'

Revived by the conversation, Elizabeth recognised the implications of this brief query. After all, she too was travelling with a man who was manifestly not her husband. 'Well, I hail from near Meryton in Hertfordshire, where I met Mr Darcy last year. I came to Venice some months ago with an Italian friend and her family, but we, ah, fell out, and I found myself in something of a pickle until Mr Darcy unexpectedly turned up and offered to help.'

'So you are not …'

'Intimate?' Elizabeth smiled. 'No. Unless quarrelling is a form of intimacy, for we do a lot of that. Mind you, these last days I've been too tired to quarrel with anyone.'

Miss Dill touched her arm. 'You've been ill, I think.'

'Yes, but Mr Darcy assures me I will soon recover, and since he is always right, I remain sanguine.'

Miss Dill laughed, and they continued talking.

17

After conferring with Burgess, who was keeping watch at the riverside, Darcy followed Gerard Hanson to a kitchen located in the basement. Here they found a merry group gathered around a farmhouse table, served by two women in black peasant garb. The room was warmed by a brick oven in the corner, where one of the women was grilling polenta over the ashes of a wood fire. The other woman tended a stove where delicious smells of chicken, onion and garlic rose from a huge pot of boiling water.

Darcy sat opposite Hanson and accepted a glass of red wine, followed by a bowl of chicken broth ladled from the pot. The hot food revived him, but his pleasure was marred by guilt at pre-empting the ladies. Still, this was no time for worrying about social niceties: at any moment they might have to flee, and he needed all the sustenance he could get.

A slab of polenta arrived in front of him, seared with black lines from the grill. He thanked the cooks and tried to explain that he needed a tray for two people upstairs.

'They speak only Veneto dialect here,' Hanson said.

Darcy found a tray and handed two mugs to the woman at the stove, who filled them with broth. At this point everyone caught on, and soon the mugs were joined by a jug of wine, a platter of polenta, even half a boiled chicken. He bowed his thanks and placed a lira on the table, to general merriment.

'That should pay your board and lodging for a week,' Hanson laughed as they climbed to the upper floor.

Darcy smiled grimly: if only they could stay that long.

They found the ladies sitting side by side on the bed and talking cheerfully. There was no table, but Hanson found a stool just broad enough to hold the tray if it was balanced carefully. He pulled up two more chairs, while Darcy poured wine and handed out mugs of broth.

'Thank you.' Elizabeth smiled sleepily as she held the mug with both hands and took a sip. 'Miss Dill and I have been comparing notes about Venice.'

'Miss Dill?' Darcy frowned at Hanson. 'I assumed …'

'That we were married?' The young man grinned at Alice Dill, whose cheeks had turned pink. 'Not yet, anyway.'

Darcy studied Elizabeth for signs of shock or embarrassment, but she looked down and avoided his eye.

'You disapprove?' Hanson asked.

Darcy glanced at the ladies before glaring at him. 'This is hardly the moment …'

'I'm sorry.' Hanson sipped wine with a smile which reminded Darcy of Wickham at his most impudent. 'I had also made an assumption, apparently incorrect, regarding yourself and Miss Bennet.'

Darcy nearly dropped his glass. 'How dare you!'

The young man held up a hand, as if to pacify him. 'I apologise again, but what was I to think when you arrived unchaperoned, carrying Miss Bennet in your arms?'

Darcy took a deep breath. 'You have a point there. We do indeed find ourselves in—unusual circumstances.'

Elizabeth gave a little cough. 'You should know, Mr Darcy, that Miss Dill has looked after me with exceptional kindness.'

Darcy turned to Hanson. 'Please excuse my outburst. You have given help when we desperately needed it. For all I know there are special circumstances in your case too.'

'Not really.' Hanson glanced at Miss Dill, and sighed. 'We are artists, Mr Darcy. Most of our friends are also artists, or poets, or musicians. Since I was up at Oxford I have moved in circles where individual freedom matters more than convention. Even so, I would have gladly married Alice, had her father approved the match, and I hope to do so once she has attained her majority.' He smiled at Miss Dill. 'If she will have me of course.'

Darcy shivered as he imagined how this conversation must be upsetting Elizabeth. 'It was not my intention to intrude or pass judgement. I was concerned only for … Miss Dill's reputation.'

Miss Dill regarded him earnestly. 'Pray Mr Darcy, I am not the innocent that you imagine. On the contrary, it was I that had to convince Gerard of the necessity of flight. Of course there are consequences. To lose the esteem of my parents has been a sad blow. But there would have been consequences too if I had bowed to my father's will and married a man I could not love or respect.'

Darcy glanced at Elizabeth, who was listening to Miss Dill with evident admiration. He spread his arms. 'Let us speak of this no more. Pray try the polenta, which is excellent.' He handed them the platter, and turned to face Hanson. 'How are you travelling? Have you a carriage by any chance?'

'We took the stagecoach from Venice.' Hanson pointed to the back of the villa. 'It crossed the river at the lock, and from here runs south down the coast. But our plan is to head west towards Padua, Verona, and then Florence.'

'When?'

'As soon as possible.' Hanson glanced at Miss Dill, as if to confirm her agreement. 'The farmer sold me an old wagon which should get us cross-country to Verona.' He paused. 'Are you in need of transport?'

On impulse, Darcy decided to trust the runaway couple. 'Yes, and with some urgency.' He lowered his voice, as if in a symbolic appeal for secrecy. 'We are being pursued, and may need to hide or flee at short notice.'

Miss Dill gasped, and took Elizabeth's hand. 'But you said nothing! How can you be so calm?'

The opiate, Darcy thought, but the tender moment was interrupted by a rap on the door, at which they all froze.

'Sir?'

Darcy recognised Burgess's voice and ran to open the door. 'News?'

'Begging pardon, sir.' Burgess edged into the room and whispered: 'Carandini's manservant has just galloped past with four constables in his wake.'

'Could they have seen you?'

'Not a chance.' Burgess looked offended.

'Good man.' Darcy moved closer. 'Now listen. They'll catch the barge and race back within the hour. Get some breakfast from the kitchen. Then move our luggage to the back of the villa and wait there.'

18

The wagon was little more than a cart on which a canvas roof had been stretched over wooden hoops. Lying back against the rim, Elizabeth was grateful for the blankets that had accompanied her all the way from Venice. Beside her, Alice Dill sat cross-legged, reading a spiral-bound notebook, with Hanson observing over her shoulder, and Darcy at the back keeping watch.

On Darcy's instructions Burgess was driving the horses at a good lick, even though this meant a bumpy ride. The route was unfathomable—deliberately so, since their pursuers would have reached Villa Foscari and interrogated the farm workers. Leaving the villa, Burgess had taken the obvious road west, but once out of sight they veered south along a smaller track which looped around a vineyard, then turned off again between fields planted with maize and sugar beet.

As she lay half awake, she replayed in her mind their adventures at the villa, and especially the conversation in which Hanson and Miss Dill had admitted their elopement. Why, she wondered, had they not *pretended* to be married? Their lack of artifice could be seen as brazen arrogance, a deliberate flouting of convention. Alternatively it could be seen as admirably honest, or even considerate, given Hanson's assumption that Darcy and Elizabeth were also illicit lovers. Instinctively Elizabeth favoured the latter interpretation, because she *liked* them—or she liked Alice Dill, at least; Hanson's impudent confidence was less appealing. Yet he had helped them, and had remained polite under provocation.

She recalled with a smile Darcy's angry rebuttal (*How dare you?*)—whatever he thought of her now, his protective instincts were keen as ever. Yet Darcy too had exhibited surprising moderation in apologising to a man that he must despise. The reason must be that he needed Hanson's collaboration to secure their escape. She had never thought of Darcy as diplomatic, but on this occasion he had kept his feelings under control and the main objective clearly in view—that is, their safety. Or rather *her* safety, since a man acting from self-interest would scarcely have attempted such a rescue in the first place.

If only he would occasionally act irresponsibly instead of being so consistently admirable. It was insufferable! But in her present state an honourable guardian was what she needed, and she had felt cherished as well as safe as he carried her …

A jolt woke her from a daydream as the wagon passed over a rut. She levered herself up and looked around, first to the front where Burgess sat holding the reins, wearing a farm worker's straw hat for disguise, then to the notebook that Miss Dill had been studying. Or rather, sketchbook, since the pages were filled with delicate drawings of wild flowers.

She leaned over to get a closer look. 'Miss Dill, these are exquisite. Are they your work?'

Miss Dill blushed. 'I found this in a meadow downriver from the villa. The petals are blue, with hairs on the leaves and stem. I believe it is called Blueweed, or Viper's Bugloss.'

'And this one?'

'Sweet violet, also common in early spring. The colour was blue, shading to purple.'

'Do you paint too?'

Miss Dill glanced at Hanson. 'Gerard advises me to concentrate on drawing, but I would like to try with water colours when I am more skilled.'

'Show me some more.'

Miss Dill turned a page, and brought out a tiny guide book that she had been using to identify the flowers. As they passed the time in this pleasant way, Elizabeth was impressed by her companion's determination. Merely to be accomplished would not satisfy her. She aspired to be a serious artist, and also a botanist who could explore mountains and deserts and bring back pictures of little-known species. In no way was she comparable with Lydia. Elopement had allowed her to travel around Europe in the company of an experienced artist. It was not a romantic fancy, but a well-conceived means of achieving her goal.

Elizabeth would have liked to discuss Miss Dill with Jane, or her father. For a moment homesickness overwhelmed her, until she looked up and noticed Darcy in quiet conversation with Hanson. How would the master of Pemberley view Miss Dill's ambitions, and her decision to run away from home? It interested her that she *did not know*. The conventional response would have been abhorrence, but she had come to see Darcy as an independent thinker who might privately hold surprising views. If only she could ask him now …

She leaned back, and drifted into another daydream.

They were no longer moving. Elizabeth blinked, looking for Miss Dill, but the wagon was empty.

She crawled to the back, which faced a narrow track through woodland. A crunch of boots on twigs startled her and she withdrew, only to be reassured as Darcy came into view.

'Miss Bennet! How are you?'

She hesitated. 'Still shaky. But a little better.'

'We've been picnicking with scraps from the villa.' He lifted her gently down. 'Shall I carry you?'

'I'll try to walk.' She took his arm, and he led her to a clearing where one of her blankets had been spread on the dusty ground. Hanson, sitting shoulder to shoulder with Miss Dill, greeted her with a cheeky smile and pointed to a basket holding brown rolls, cheese, apples, and dried figs.

She kneeled on the blanket, feeling queasy at the sight of the food. 'Where are we?'

'I thought it best to hide,' Darcy said. 'So far as I can tell we are near a road that leads north to a small town called Oriago. My plan is to cross the river there after dark.'

'Why not leave now, before our pursuers catch up?'

'Because that is what they will expect. We cannot outrun them, remember. Our only chance is to remain out of sight for such a long period that they have no idea where we are. Then their forces will be dispersed far and wide. They might even conclude that we have got away, and abandon the search.'

Elizabeth regarded Hanson and Miss Dill. 'And how do *you* feel about this? I fear we are delaying you, perhaps even exposing you to danger.'

Hanson shrugged. 'Mr Darcy has contributed to costs, which is welcome since I am short. We are in no hurry, and Carandini's men have no reason to harm us.'

'In any case it is our duty to help,' Miss Dill said. 'It is shocking that you have been treated so ill. I'm sure that if our situations were reversed, you would feel the same.'

Elizabeth threw an anxious glance at Darcy. *Was this true*, she wondered. Darcy had selflessly helped her own family—Lydia, and now herself. But would he moderate his plans in order to save a runaway couple? She feared he would not, and what was more, that he was only accepting their help now *because of her.*

'Where is Burgess?'

Darcy pointed. 'Watching the road. I doubt we are in any danger here, since nobody saw us drive in. Still, it is best to know what they are up to.'

She smiled at Miss Dill. 'I pray that one day I can return your kindness.'

Miss Dill smiled back. 'Waiting here is no hardship, for there are many flowers for me to draw.'

Elizabeth tried to eat, but the uneasiness remained. Why was she on edge? Yes, their situation remained perilous, but so it had been when rowing across the Venice lagoon.

Darcy raised a bottle. 'Wine?'

He poured a little into a cup, and she accepted it gratefully, wishing that she could lie back as before and float into oblivion.

19

As dusk fell Darcy held a council of war with Hanson and Burgess, leaving the ladies to rest before the next leg of their journey. They saw only two choices. The first was to cross the river and follow a direct route to Padua; the second was to stay in the warren of smaller roads below the river and approach Padua from the south-east. Darcy was tempted by the second option because it made capture unlikely. However, he was concerned that they were asking too much of Hanson and Miss Dill; he was also anxious for Elizabeth's health. Her alertness was improving, but she suffered increasing attacks of nausea and sweating. A week wandering around the countryside in a wagon would do her no good: she needed a comfortable bed, and access to a physician in case of emergency.

On balance, then, he favoured the riskier plan. Follow the road straight up to Oriago, cross in the late evening, and head north-west towards one of the main roads. They might run into a constable in Carandini's pay, but so far Burgess had spotted no pursuers; perhaps the search had been called off, or redirected to another area.

As they set off, the skies were clear, with the promise of a moon to light their way. For a while the roads were deserted, but entering the town they found themselves in a crush of carriages all heading for the river. The chaos was in a way reassuring. Walkers joined the procession, some carrying lanterns. Elegant couples strolled along the roadside, with children running here and there, and dogs barking.

'Can you see the river?' Darcy called to Burgess.

'Just coming into view, sir.'

'Stop here!' Darcy turned to face the others. 'I'm going to reconnoitre.' He noticed Elizabeth's frown, and added: 'It will take only a minute.'

Descending the step at the front he felt a prickle of danger, as if a man might be training a musket on him. It was nonsense, he told himself. In this confusion, nobody would notice him. He advanced with the crowd and observed the bridge from the shelter of another parked carriage. It was a swing bridge, hinged so that it could be parted to allow barges to pass. At present pedestrians and carriages were crossing, so river traffic was halted. At the near end, outside a small hut for the attendant, a constable stood next to a man whose face looked familiar. The man was leaning against the railing and peering into every carriage; now and then he also swept his gaze across the pedestrians. Darcy melted back into the crowd, and advanced a few more steps.

There was no doubt. The man was a servant from Carandini's villa on Lido. Not the footman who had opened the door, but another, whom Darcy had seen momentarily when he broke in.

What to do? Their pursuers knew they had left in a two-horse wagon, so hiding inside would not work. Walking Elizabeth across was too risky. Turning round would be difficult when all the traffic was directed towards the river. So many people lined the bank that the routes left and right were impassable.

He went back and explained the situation.

'We can turn,' Hanson said immediately.

Darcy pointed down the road. 'It would be like trying to swim against the tide.'

'We have to try,' Miss Dill said.

'No!' Elizabeth took Miss Dill's arm. 'I cannot bear to be such a liability. You and Mr Hanson need to continue to Padua. If necessary, Mr Darcy and I can get off here.'

'How?' Miss Dill asked. 'You have no carriage of your own, and no way of carrying your luggage.'

Elizabeth looked at Darcy. 'We will find a carriage.'

Darcy sighed: this was not London, where one could hope to flag down a hackney. To unload their trunk and other bags in this confusion would attract attention, and leave them unable to move quickly if spotted.

'I agree with Miss Bennet that we have inconvenienced you enough,' he said to Hanson. 'But we cannot unload here.' He spoke to Burgess. 'Listen carefully. The servant on the bridge is from Lido, and has never seen your face. If Mr Hanson and Miss Dill agree, I suggest you stay with them until Padua, where you can find a boarding house and unload our luggage at your leisure. I will get off now with Miss Bennet, and join you by another route. Once you are settled, stand outside the Basilica of Saint Anthony every day at noon, so that we may find you. Clear?'

Burgess nodded, and Darcy turned to Hanson. 'It's a lot to ask, but can you do this? I can give you some ducats to cover any additional expenses.'

Hanson considered. 'Is it not possible that the constable will detain us anyway? He will have our descriptions from the people at the villa.'

'We can say that we dropped Mr Darcy and Miss Bennet at a village near Villa Foscari,' Miss Dill said.

'That should suffice.' Darcy frowned. 'But your point is well made, since they may wonder why a servant previously in my party is now travelling with you.' He turned to Burgess. 'I have it! When Miss Bennet and I have descended, give the reins to Mr Hanson, then walk across the bridge and wait a little further along. Provided you are not seen with them, you cannot be identified.'

Hanson clapped his hands. 'Excellent.'

Darcy looked at Elizabeth. 'Are you sure you want to go ahead with this?'

A grimace gave away her unease as she shrugged. 'I see no other option.'

Miss Dill took her hand with a crestfallen expression. 'Dear Miss Bennet, you are not well.' She raised her eyes to face Darcy. 'Where will you go?'

'I cannot say. We must improvise.'

Darcy loaded essential items into a leather bag, and handed Hanson two gold coins from his belt. Miss Dill wept, and Elizabeth hugged her briefly before crawling to the front, where Darcy was waiting to help her dismount.

The wagon moved on, and they were alone at the roadside.

20

Darcy's heart beat faster as Elizabeth looked up at him, her eyes huge with panic. He had read once of the symptoms of laudanum withdrawal, after learning that his aunt Lady Catherine de Bourgh had badgered a physician into prescribing the remedy for Anne. As the drug wore off Elizabeth was more alert, and steadier on her feet, but might suffer any of the accompaniments of a cold—fever, headache, sore throat and eyes—as well as attacks of anxiety. The extent of these symptoms would depend on the dose, which must have been substantial enough to keep her compliant, and administered over a period of several weeks.

'What are we to do?' she gasped, breathless from the effort of dismounting.

He took her arm, and led her into the crowd seething towards the river. 'Let us walk along the bank so that we can keep the bridge in view. I want to make sure that our friends cross safely.'

'Might we be seen?'

'I think not, provided we act like everyone else. If we walked away from the river we would be pushing against the crowd and more likely to attract attention.'

'I wish I had a bonnet.' She looked down, as if to hide her profile, but kept pace without difficulty.

'Burgess has crossed.' Darcy slowed to keep the wagon in view as it stopped at the attendant's hut. Carandini's servant was talking to Hanson, who shrugged and pointed back into the wagon. The constable looked carefully, and after a brief conference waved them on.

'It's all right,' Darcy said. 'They are through!'

'Thank God!'

'We must take care now.' Darcy turned sharp left as Carandini's man climbed up the bank and surveyed the crowd. 'Don't look back.' He resisted the temptation to keep the servant under observation, and kept in step with the crowd, which thickened as they approached a cluster of rafts lagged together to form a platform.

Elizabeth tugged his arm. 'What is happening?'

He stood tall for a moment, and saw musicians seated on a crimson carpet ringed with flowers and lanterns.

'Let's get closer to the bank.'

The press was now so dense that they could scarcely move. Squeezing through a gap, Darcy pushed Elizabeth to the front, and she cried out in delight as a silver-haired conductor strode to a makeshift podium. The orchestra struck up an eccentric piece in which violinists became percussionists by banging bows against music stands.

'Rossini,' Elizabeth said. 'I heard it at a concert, while you were away touring Florence and Rome.'

'It's a cheerful piece.'

'Can we stay? Are we safe now?'

Darcy risked a look behind, and saw no sign of pursuit. 'Yes, but let's edge forward when we get the chance.'

They gained twenty paces during the overture, and the crowd began to thin. Elizabeth withdrew her arm to join in the applause, facing him with a radiant smile. Without his support she stumbled, and he caught her as she fell.

'Pardon me.' She looked down, deflated. 'I'm ashamed

to feel so feeble.'

'You're tired.' He pressed a hand to his aching temple, realising that he too was exhausted.

They had to find an inn.

After twenty minutes of painstaking progress they had passed only two unsavoury *locande*, and Elizabeth, making a brave effort, was near to collapse. Two locals had recommended Hotel Petrarca, supposedly a short way along the riverbank. Darcy was wondering whether it existed at all when he saw a villa set further back than the rest, with an ornamental garden at the front and space for carriages to unload.

The foyer was well lit, with a tiled floor and comfortable chairs. Hopeful again, Darcy helped Elizabeth to a divan before speaking to the manager. The words came easily, since he had had many such conversations on his travels. He needed two adjoining rooms for himself and *la signora*. The sentence was scarcely out before the manager shook his head. They were full. Not a single room. Because of the festival.

Darcy tried again. He was willing to double the usual rate. It would only be for one night. The lady was tired after a long journey, and help would be *hugely* appreciated. He produced a bag of ducats from his frock-coat pocket to signal the form such appreciation might take.

The manager was a plump mustachioed man with eyeglasses perched on his nose and a self-important manner. After waving his hands and protesting throughout Darcy's appeal, he fell silent on seeing the bag of coins, and finally raised a hand. There was a suite with two rooms. One with double bed, the other a bathroom. It was reserved permanently for use of a count. It should be empty tonight, but they would have to leave if the count arrived unexpectedly. Of course, by letting the room to someone else, the manager would be placing himself in a most vulnerable position ...

The chamber was on the first floor at the back—which at least meant only one flight of stairs for Elizabeth. It had a wooden floor with Persian rugs, and practical furniture including a four-poster bed, wardrobe, and small table with two chairs. Next door was a washroom with bath and commode: evidently the count valued cleanliness.

'You will have the bed, of course,' Darcy said. 'I asked for a cold supper to be brought up.'

Elizabeth came through to view the washroom, which was narrow and relatively bare.

'Mr Darcy, you cannot sleep in this room.'

Darcy pointed to the copper bathtub. 'I will borrow bedclothes and make myself comfortable here.'

On a marble-topped side-table she found a jug of water, which she poured into a bowl to freshen up her hands and face. 'You are sure there are no other rooms?'

He explained his conversation with the manager. 'I'm afraid I had to give him the impression that we were a married couple.' He retrieved the false papers from his bag and showed them to her. 'The consul gave me these for use in emergencies. I think it safest that we go under the names in the letters of safe conduct. I will be Mr Giles Ashley; you will be my wife Rebecca. This means that if enquiries are made about English persons staying at the hotel, we will not be discovered.'

She nodded vacantly, as if too weary to assimilate this. 'I would like to lie down now.'

'Shall I wake you when supper arrives?'

'No, just leave the food for later.'

He looked decorously away as she removed her boots

and hair clasps and lay fully-clothed on top of the bed.

Having rented out the count's chamber, the Petrarca did not stint on service. A liveried servant brought a huge tray of cold meats, rolls, pickles, and fruit, accompanied by jugs of wine and ale. At the same time a maid carried hot water to the washroom, and lit them a small fire. Elizabeth, still awake, joined him at the table and tried salami and cured ham. They finished with dark purple grapes, and apricots, all washed down with ale, a pleasant change from the ubiquitous red wine. To eat a good meal in comfort had become a luxury, and Darcy noticed that like himself, Elizabeth showed no inclination to hurry. Apart from references to the food, they ate in silence, as if shying away from discussions about their predicament.

Finally every morsel was gone. Their eyes met, and Darcy stood up. 'I will leave you in privacy now.'

She faced him, biting her lower lip as if afraid of what she was about to say. 'This is not right.'

'I know.' He spread his arms. 'If you prefer, I could seek a room elsewhere, but I confess I'm afraid to leave you on your own.'

'That is not what I meant.' She rose, and opened the door to the washroom. 'It is not right that I should sleep in comfort while you make do with *this*. You spent last night rowing across the lagoon, and have had little or no rest today. You must be completely exhausted. These are special circumstances. We are in a foreign land trying to escape a man who would force me to marry against my will, and have you imprisoned or worse. What matters is that we remain strong and alert.' She turned back into the chamber. 'We will find a way of sharing this bed. If that is not to your liking, then *you* will have the bed, and *I* will take the bath.'

He recoiled. 'Out of the question.'

'Indeed?' She faced him, hands on hips. 'And which part of my argument do you dispute?'

He froze, partly lost for an answer, and partly elated to be confronted by the old Elizabeth, the woman who had mocked him at dances in Hertfordshire, and upbraided him after his proposal at Hunsford.

Finally he smiled. 'Do you imagine I'll be able to sleep in this bed, in the knowledge that you are shivering in a hard copper bath in the next room?'

'I might ask you the same question.'

He sighed. 'What do you propose?'

'We will lie side by side. It is not so shocking, after all. We sat together at the table without committing any major impropriety.' She threw up her hands. 'In any case, for all the world knows we are Mr and Mrs Ashley, so our reputations will remain intact whatever we do. Did you bring any suitable attire?'

'Only this.' He pulled her nightgown from his leather bag and shook it out. 'Still damp from the boat, I fear.'

She folded the plain cotton garment over a chair beside the fire. 'And yourself?'

'I will keep my day clothes.'

'Then so shall I.'

She sat on the side of the bed and leaned forward as if to remove her socks, then thought better of it and slipped fully clothed between the sheets. Darcy remained standing, his mind frazzled by weariness. To share a bed with Elizabeth! The moment he had hoped for had been reduced to absurdity, as if fate were mocking his dreams. He blew out the candles, unbuttoned his vest, removed his boots, and in white frilled shirt and breeches sat on the side of the bed, facing away from its other occupant. Swallowing, he lay on top of the blankets.

21

Elizabeth fidgeted, irritated by the weight of the blankets, which were making her too hot. If only she could take her dress off! She had automatically occupied the right half of the bed, a habit from sharing with Jane; as a result she could not sleep in her usual position without facing Darcy. With a sigh of frustration she rolled on to her back, and tried to lever off one of her scratchy socks with the other foot.

'Are you uncomfortable?'

His voice, from so close by, gave her a jolt. She froze, then turned her head to view the dark form at her side, just visible in the fading firelight. He was also on his back, on top of the bed, gazing straight up.

'It's hot with all these layers on.'

'Shall I open a window?'

She wriggled again. 'The problem is really the dress. It would be better if I could take it off.'

'I could go to the washroom while you make the necessary adjustments.'

She smiled, sensing humour behind his grave manner. 'That would help.'

She heard footsteps and the click of the door. Quickly she sat up, pulled off the irritating socks and dress, then hesitated. She was not wearing stays, which Darcy had left behind in the bedroom at Lido, only a petticoat over a shift. But it would feel so good to remove the petticoat too—and really, what difference did it make? *Might as well be hung for a sheep* … With resolution she threw both dress and petticoat over an armchair, checked the door again, and dived back under the covers.

'Ready!'

Her courage still high, she rolled on to her favourite side, and observed as Darcy resumed his former position.

She felt comfortable, freshened by the breeze from the window, now ajar. The feverish sweating was wearing off, and she had no nausea from the meal. But her thoughts remained chaotic and discordant, like an orchestra tuning up. She recalled how drowsy she had felt over the past weeks; now it seemed that sleep would never return. She opened her eyes to observe Darcy, who lay perfectly still, in a rigid posture that signalled his unease. What thoughts might be churning in his head?

'Difficult, isn't it,' she whispered. 'To relax.'

'Are you still uncomfortable?'

'I am well. And thank you for your forbearance. I just wanted to say …' She blinked. 'You need have no fear of my revealing this to *anyone*. Not even Jane.'

He frowned. 'Why raise the point now?'

'To reassure you.'

'That you will not oblige me to wed you?' He smiled. 'From *some* women I might fear such a motive, but in *your* case I am entirely tranquil!'

She blushed at this reference to her dreadful behaviour at Hunsford. Despite his protestation, she believed he must have felt some such fear. To be forced into marrying Wickham's sister-in-law!

'Where will Mr Hanson and Miss Dill be now?'

'Half-way to Padua, I hope. There's a good road all the

way, along the north bank of the river.'

'What do you think of them?'

He reflected. 'What can I say? I'm grateful to Hanson for his help; on the other hand, his behaviour towards Miss Dill is scandalous.'

'Are you sure he is the prime instigator?'

'As an older man, he must accept responsibility.'

Elizabeth conjured an image of the couple—the supercilious convivial young man on one side, the acute determined girl on the other. 'My impression was the opposite. Mr Hanson is all impudence and bluster, but I suspect it is the quiet Miss Dill that holds the reins.'

Again he pondered, and again she feared a critical response. He turned towards her a fraction, and for an electric moment their eyes met. 'You may be right. I found Hanson amiable, but childish. I can believe he would be easily led.'

Elizabeth levered herself up a little. 'When I first got to know Alice, Miss Dill, I thought of my sister. Lydia. But their cases are entirely different. Lydia is a child. Alice is gifted and single-minded. Perhaps she will marry Hanson, but it would not surprise me if in time she discarded him, as being of no further use.'

'A formidable young lady, then?'

'Yet I liked her. She was kind, modest, a good listener. I found myself confiding more than I should, although that was probably the influence of the opiate.'

He nodded, and after a brief silence she went on, 'The trouble is, I have lost confidence in my power to judge. I have been thinking about Regina, whom I believed my friend. She was clever, charming, affectionate, but it seems clear that she connived with her brother in holding me captive, so that he might trick me into marrying him. I even wonder why she married Sir Ambrose. For love, or for his title?'

Darcy's face twisted into a scowl. 'There is something badly amiss with that family, and I suspect it stems from the mother.'

She nodded. 'But do you not see? On a brief acquaintance you have already unmasked the Carandinis. I became friendly with Regina over a period of months and noticed nothing wrong. Once I prided myself as a judge of people; now I have fallen at one hurdle after another. Wickham, Regina, not to mention—' She stopped just in time, cursing her tiredness.

He smiled. 'You were about to add, Miss Dill?'

She could only smile back. 'You know full well what I was about to say. I hope you are suitably embarrassed.'

His eyes softened. 'You did not misjudge *me*. On the contrary, you saw my faults all too clearly.'

It was tempting to apologise yet again, but instinctively she resisted. 'Can we be sure? Perhaps you are even worse than I thought.'

They both laughed, and she was surprised to find tears in her eyes, as if a tension had lifted.

She rolled over, and at last fell asleep.

22

Darcy peered round a bend in the stairwell and checked the foyer. He recognised the waxed moustache and squat figure of the manager, talking with a distinguished silver-haired gentleman. Darcy pulled back, wondering where he had seen the man before. Nothing came to mind, but he could recall no link with Carandini. Trying to appear relaxed, he stood tall and walked confidently down.

The silver-haired gentleman had moved aside to check his bill, and as Darcy approached, the manager raised his arms to greet him. '*Signor Ashley*! *Buon giorno.*' A barrage of questions followed. The chamber was comfortable? *La signora* slept well? The supper was to their satisfaction?

After assuring him all was well, Darcy leaned forward and lowered his voice. 'Has anyone asked for us?'

The manager frowned. 'Late last night a man did ask whether we had English guests. I cannot recall the names he gave, but they were not yours.' He drew Darcy to one side, and whispered: 'In fact he was so impertinent as to demand details of *any* English patrons. However, as I explained yesterday, I would not like it generally known that I rented out the count's room. This was a special favour. I therefore told him that we had no foreign guests, English or otherwise, whereupon he went on his way. I apologise, Signor Ashley, but I had to consider my own position.'

'You did excellently,' Darcy assured him. 'I appreciate that you have protected our privacy; you may also rely on *my* discretion.'

The manager bowed. 'The signor is all politeness. You will take breakfast, yes?' He pointed at the door opposite. 'The *sala* is comfortable and catches the morning sun.'

'I will see whether Signora Ashley is ready.'

The bed was empty, with sounds of whimpering from the washroom. He called softly, 'Miss Bennet? Are you well?'

'I am not!' The door was yanked open and Elizabeth faced him, dressed but in tears, waving two hair grips. 'I am such a mess! These are useless. And my face!' She ran to the mirror. 'I have no powder box, no rouge, nothing!'

'What do you need?'

'I had almond bloom, but it was left behind. Even talcum powder would do. Plus safflower or any pink blush.'

'We can go shopping once we reach Padua.'

She waved this away. 'How can you be so calm? As if all was proceeding smoothly according to plan? Do you not see that our situation is *disastrous*? Trapped in a foreign land where we barely speak the language, separated from our luggage, no proper clothes, pursued by constables who would arrest you for abduction, obliged to travel unchaperoned under false names, not to mention our reputations ruined if this escapade becomes known …'

He could only smile at this accurate summary. 'And to cap it all, no almond bloom.'

'Most amusing!' She took a step forward and he was struck by the pallor of her skin, and the panic in her eyes. No wonder she craved powder and blush. 'Mr Darcy, saunter with your head in the clouds if you must, but try to grasp one point. *I will not marry you.* You may spend a fortune to save my sister, risk your life shepherding me across Europe, sacrifice yourself to duty like a knight of old, and *still* I will not marry you. Foolish and unworthy I may be, but inside there remains a speck of self-respect that will not be denied. Do you follow? Must I make it plainer?'

He took her arm. 'Miss Bennet, do not excite yourself. You are unwell.'

She pulled away. 'I mean what I say!'

'I know. You will not marry me. I am, indeed, the last man in the world whom you could ever be prevailed on to marry. You have expressed yourself with exemplary clarity in the past, and need not remind me now.'

He regarded her, trying to mask the bitter despair in his heart. She met his eye, then turned away with a cry. 'Oh, what is the point? You will never understand.'

'On the contrary, I understand perfectly. Let us not distress ourselves by talking of this further. I came to ask whether you would like breakfast. I have checked downstairs and the coast is clear.'

She turned back to the mirror and struggled to attach a hair clip. 'I look such a fright.' Her hand lingered on her temple. 'And I have a headache.'

'It will pass.' He stepped closer, speaking softly. 'You are recovering from the opiate. In a few days you will feel much better and your cheeks will bloom even without the aid of rouge.'

She threw him a suspicious glance, but with the hint of a smile. 'So you are a physician, Mr Darcy?'

'No, but I have come across cases of laudanum withdrawal.'

'Of course. You know everything. How foolish of me to doubt it.'

'I know I would like breakfast, at any rate.' He walked away, and after a final adjustment of her hair she followed.

The *sala colazione* had filled, but at the window table a man raised his hand and beckoned them to join him. As they approached, Darcy recognised the silver-haired gentleman he had seen earlier at reception.

'*Buon giorno.*' Darcy bowed. 'Giles Ashley.' He extended an arm towards Elizabeth. 'My wife, Rebecca.'

The man rose and bowed to Elizabeth. 'Good morning Mrs, ah, Ashley. Professor Pavoni. Antonio.'

Darcy helped Elizabeth into her chair, admiring her poise as she replied in Italian, 'An honour to meet you sir. We admired your performance of Rossini last night.'

Of course: *that* was why the man was familiar. Yet up close he appeared younger; Darcy wondered whether he was bewigged, or prematurely grey.

'English, please!' demanded Professor Pavoni. 'I'm most impressed, madam, that you should recognise the piece, since we printed no programme.'

'My wife is an accomplished pianist and music-lover,' Darcy said.

She threw him an amused glance, as if enjoying the game. 'My, ah, husband grossly exaggerates my abilities,' she said. 'Everywhere we go he arouses expectations that I cannot possibly fulfil. However, it is true that I love music, and it was a delight to listen to an orchestra in such a setting.'

A maid took their order, and returned with a basket of rolls and pastries, soon followed by a fresh pot of coffee and a bowl of boiled eggs.

'Are you based in Venice?' Darcy asked Pavoni.

The professor shook his head. 'Padua. I hold the chair in musicology. Conducting is not part of my work, more a recreation. I have assembled a small amateur orchestra to perform at festivals and other popular venues.'

'Your musicians are also staying in the Petrarca?'

'The leader only. The others are down the road in a *locanda*.' Pavoni pointed out of the window. 'I hired a barge for the trip.'

Darcy glanced at Elizabeth, and she turned to address Pavoni with an innocent smile. 'Your boat must be full, with so many instruments to carry.'

He hesitated. 'Where are you bound?'

'We have been making our way from Venice to Padua,' Darcy said. 'With so many Palladian villas to admire, our tempo has been more *Lento* than *Allegro*.'

Pavoni smiled. 'You have a carriage?'

'We shared one with friends,' Darcy improvised. 'But they have gone ahead now, so we will have to find an alternative.'

'I see.' Pavoni hesitated again. 'I would offer you a seat on our barge, but perhaps you will need a carriage in order to complete your tour.'

'On the contrary, your offer comes at a most fortunate moment,' Elizabeth said. 'We were remarking only yesterday evening that no matter how exquisite the architecture, one can have too much of a good thing.'

'I concur fully with my wife,' Darcy said.

Pavoni clapped his hands. 'Capital! Your company will light up an otherwise routine journey.'

With relief, Darcy resumed eating.

23

The barge was built to transport people, not goods—and in some luxury. The cabin contained rows of upholstered benches with an aisle down the middle; a spiral stairway at the back led to the roof, where the more enterprising passengers might venture for a longer view. The walls were painted with vines on a pale blue background, and held vases filled with orange-red spring geraniums.

As Professor Pavoni's guests they shared a bench at the back, sheltered from the hubbub up front where the musicians unpacked their instruments and belted out dances and folk songs. Elizabeth had the window seat, but preferred to draw a curtain so that her face could not be seen from the bank; beside her, Darcy conversed with Pavoni about the latest news from France.

The trip would last five hours, which meant that they were safe, provided that they kept their heads down when passing through a lock. It was also hard to feel afraid when surrounded by such jolly company. Liveried servants had brought an ice-box on board, and despite her protests Pavoni pressed a glass of chilled Prosecco into her hand—a treat that soon made her even more light-headed. She glanced at Darcy, his expression typically grave with undercurrents of humour as he defended his view of the political crisis. She regretted that she had harangued him in the washroom that morning.

Why was she so skittish? Perhaps, as he claimed, she was suffering after-effects of the laudanum, but surely the main reason lay elsewhere. *They had shared a bedroom.* What was more, they had done so at her own insistence; Darcy, had she permitted, would gladly have made do with the bath. At the time she had given little thought to the consequences; it mattered only that they had both had a good night's rest. But now it was done, and there *were* consequences. No matter that back in England, no-one would be any the wiser. *Darcy* knew, and in his mind, obsessed by honour and duty, that could mean only one thing: *they must marry.* They must marry despite their difference in rank; they must marry despite her slanderous accusations and general abuse of his character; they must marry despite the ignominy of having Wickham as his brother-in-law.

But she could be stubborn too. She knew what she owed him, and would not allow this to happen.

She smothered a chuckle—the wine, no doubt—as she recalled the scene at breakfast when they had pretended to be man and wife. How *natural* it had felt, and also, what fun. Well, why should she not enjoy it, while it lasted? The more she immersed herself in the role, the better the deception.

A servant brought pineapple ices, and she smiled at Darcy as they accepted another treat.

Darcy leaned forward to admire the grand facade of Villa Pisani, on the outskirts of Padua. He wondered whether to wake Elizabeth, who had dozed off after accepting a second glass of Prosecco with her lunch. On balance he thought better not; she had recovered well from her early-morning panic, but sleep was too precious a restorative to disturb.

'So Mr Ashley, we approach the *city of learning*, as some call it.' Professor Pavoni glanced at Elizabeth's sleeping form, and smiled benignly. 'Before we part, may I tell you a story? It is one I heard last night from a passer-by. Perhaps it is familiar to you, perhaps not.'

Darcy flinched, but managed to reply in an even tone. 'Go ahead.'

The professor lowered his voice. 'It concerns a compatriot of yours, a certain Mr Fitzwilliam Darcy. This man arrived in Venice in the company of a friend, whose older brother had married into the Carandini family, who have made a fortune from glassware.' He regarded Darcy with a twinkle. 'Perhaps you have heard of them.'

'Go on.'

'Well, after touring Italy for some weeks, this Mr Darcy learned on his return that a certain Miss Bennet, an Englishwoman staying with the Carandinis, had become engaged to the head of the family—Signor Gabriele. For reasons unknown, this arrangement was not to Mr Darcy's liking. Indeed, so extreme was his disapproval that he abducted Miss Bennet from under Carandini's nose, and rowed her away into the moonlight. Despite an intensive search, they remain undiscovered to this day.'

'I see.' Darcy frowned. 'And why do you tell me this?'

Pavoni smiled. 'A number of coincidences strike me. First, the descriptions of Mr Darcy and Miss Bennet are a close fit to yourself and Mrs Ashley. Second, given your obvious social standing, it is unusual that you have no carriage, no servants, and no luggage except a single bag.' He met Darcy's eye. 'Need I elaborate?'

Darcy paused. 'And supposing that what you imply turned out to be true, what then?'

'As a responsible citizen I should inform the authorities,' Pavoni said. 'Which is what I *would* do, were it not for one fact. I happen to know Gabriele Carandini.'

Darcy stared at him. 'Yes?'

'It is hardly surprising.' Pavoni spread his arms. 'He is a man obsessed with music. He attends every concert, large or small. I have known him since he was a student at the conservatory, rebelling against his father's wish that he should learn the family business. I have heard him speak up in lectures and symposia. I know him to be passionate and articulate. As a violinist he has attained proficiency in spite of limited talent. His dedication and hard work deserve respect. But there is one further thing I would say of him.' Pavoni leaned closer, speaking softly and very distinctly. 'I have a daughter, named Maria Grazia. She is charming, lovely, the apple of my eye. Signor Ashley, if Carandini wished to marry my daughter, *I would do everything in my power to prevent it.*'

Darcy nodded, wheels spinning in his head. Could this be a trap? But if Pavoni sought to expose him, why not simply call a constable? Why make friendly conversation and then reveal his suspicions privately?

He lowered his voice to a whisper. 'And if it were admitted that I *was* Darcy, and had acted from a similar motive?'

'I would like, if I may, to help.'

24

Elizabeth reclined in the soft leather divan of the *Sartoria Padovana* as a model displayed a cream-gold silk gown with sheer net overlays on the upper arms. Beside her, Signora Pavoni and her daughter Maria Grazia purred approval.

'*Elegantissimo.*'

'Exquisite. The nets are detachable of course?'

Elizabeth sighed. The gown was truly delightful, and she believed the colours would suit her. But the price! Of course Darcy would pay, and he had encouraged her to choose at least one evening gown that could be worn at a ball or concert. He seemed to have forgotten that only two days ago they had been rattling along country roads in a farm wagon.

She had awoken in Padua at a small dock, from where a private gondola had taken them along a tributary to the city centre. They had disembarked at a bridge just outside the city gate, where an official eyed them suspiciously, but waved them through after checking their false papers.

A few yards further along, in Professor Pavoni's regal apartment, they were introduced to her new companions, Signora Pavoni and her daughter Maria Grazia. Their reception was overwhelming. She must take tea and cake; a maid would help her wash and change; how distressing to lose their luggage; so difficult to get competent help in these times; she absolutely must accompany them to the modiste later in the afternoon when the shops would be open. Both women were her own height, or a little taller, with olive skin and deep brown eyes. Before long Elizabeth was left in the daughter's care, and pressed into borrowing powder and a change of dress …

The cream-gold silk gown was added to her order, and a clutch of bonnets brought out. Signora Pavoni had gone away to another section of the emporium, dedicated to hairdressing and cosmetics, with the aim of securing Elizabeth an immediate appointment—a concession that might require a *little push*, or bribe.

'You must order something yourself,' Elizabeth said to Maria Grazia, whose English was fluent.

'My allowance for this month is spent.' Her expression flipped from moue to grin. 'But I shall be back next week for your silk gown, if it can be done in silver.'

Elizabeth pointed to a bonnet with a broad peak, well-suited to hiding her face as well as protecting her from the sun. 'This one please.' She turned to Maria Grazia. 'And that should be all, except that I must choose a wig.'

'*Una parrucca*?' Maria Grazia stroked Elizabeth's hair with a finger. 'But your hair is beautiful *al naturale*.'

'Mr, ah, Ashley insists,' Elizabeth said. She swallowed, having nearly said *Darcy* by mistake. 'He has a fancy to see me with fair hair, while he looks distinguished in grey.'

'What a strange notion!'

'Indeed, but since he is paying, it would be churlish to deny him!'

'I implied no criticism…' Signorina Pavoni blushed. 'Pardon me, Signora, I am all nerves. Father wishes me to perform this evening.'

'Not on our account, surely?'

Maria Grazia sighed. 'We have visitor from Austria, a singer named Hilda Edelmann. Fraulein Edelmann has taken some days off at the hot springs in Abano to recuperate before giving two recitals next week. She will return this evening and asked that we might run through her programme at home ...'

'With yourself as accompanist?'

Maria Grazia covered her face. '*Esattamente.*'

'Why not your father?'

'His instrument is the violin. Not the pianoforte.'

Elizabeth put a hand on her arm. 'If the keyboard part is not too demanding, I could share the burden.'

Her face lit up. 'Would you?'

'I warn you that sight reading is not my *forte*. Still, if I fail horribly, at least you will gain from the comparison.'

In a splendid saloon overlooking *Piazza della Frutta*, Darcy sat opposite Professor Pavoni sampling an aperitif of Prosecco and soda water, served in a wine glass with a slice of orange. In an hour he had achieved several useful goals, starting with a visit to a barber, where after a shave and trim he had invested in a grey wig. With his appearance thus altered he had called at a gentleman's outfitters to be measured for a new coat and boots, and selected a shirt and breeches ready-made for immediate use. In his new clothes and wig he had strolled past Pavoni at their rendezvous without being noticed—an encouraging sign.

It had been agreed that their real identities should not be divulged to the professor's family. If Darcy and Elizabeth wished to circulate in society without alerting Carandini's spies, they would have to preserve the alias, and it was unfair to expect Pavoni's wife and daughter to contribute to the deception. So for the time being they would remain Mr and Mrs Ashley—at least in public. In Pavoni's apartment they could occupy adjacent rooms, designed for a married couple, with a dividing door decreed by Darcy to be as impassable as the walls of Jericho.

In the café, the gossip inevitably centred on Napoleon, who from latest reports had reached Paris, to be welcomed by crowds of admirers. The royalists were in disarray, the king Louis XVIII having already fled. Pavoni was reading a newspaper report on preparations for a further war when his daughter approached arm-in-arm with a lovely blonde-haired woman in a fine muslin dress.

The men stood up and bowed, and Darcy took Elizabeth aside. 'I hardly recognise you, Rebecca dear.'

'Disconcerting, isn't it?' Elizabeth whispered. 'When I look in the mirror I see Jane.'

'And I see my father.'

She sighed. 'The world has gone mad.'

'In more ways than one. We have been discussing the latest reports from France, which may affect our plans for returning to England.'

'It is very disturbing.' She grimaced. 'And you will receive a further shock when the modiste delivers my purchases and you see the size of the bill.'

'It is well spent, Rebecca. We need suitable clothes, and at present, money is the least of our troubles.'

She smiled at this use of her new name, and took his arm saucily. 'Well dearest, shall we return to our friends?'

25

When they reached the apartment, Fraulein Edelmann had arrived, and gone to her room to rest. Elizabeth decided to follow her example, and received another shock when she saw herself in the mirror—she had forgotten about the wig. She spent some time repinning her natural hair, and adjusting the cosmetics applied by the beautician. A maid tapped on the door and carried in packages from the *Sartoria*. Elizabeth did a jig of delight: she could now try on the silk dress, which she planned to wear to dinner.

Thinking back to the embarrassing scene at the hotel that morning, she marvelled at the transformation in her mood. She had woken in a panic; now, one by one, her problems had been solved. They had found transport to Padua, passed inspection at the city gate, bought clothes, and changed their appearances; best of all, they were now comfortably accommodated. Most of this had been due to Darcy, who had befriended Professor Pavoni, as well as procuring all the necessary false papers back in Venice. He had also responded calmly to her rant about *never marrying him*, although he seemed not to understand that her purpose was to reassure him.

The silk dress fitted well, and she changed back into muslin before sitting at the bureau and writing to Jane. Of necessity she glossed over the adventures of the last days; her story would be that she was returning in a *party* that *included* Mr Darcy. With a smile she imagined the effect on her family had she admitted that she was travelling now as Darcy's wife and had shared his bed. More shocking yet was that she had actually *enjoyed* this role. Not the embarrassing sleeping arrangements, but the fun of taking his arm in public, whispering asides, calling him *dearest*.

She put down her quill, and as if to test her feelings, imagined how their lives might have turned out. Suppose her perception had not been poisoned by Wickham, and she had seen Darcy for what he was—not as charming as Bingley, but intelligent, honourable, kind. Suppose she had heeded his warnings about Wickham, not just at Hunsford but before, in Hertfordshire, and passed them on to her father. Minor differences, but what a transformation in outcome! Lydia would still be at home, having had no opportunity to elope. She, Elizabeth, might already be Mrs Darcy. How would *that* feel?

It was hard to say. She had no doubt now that Darcy was a good man. Too good, perhaps. He was not sharply critical like Carandini, but he did set high standards both for himself and others, standards that she would doubtless fail to satisfy. *My good opinion, once lost, is lost forever.*

That was the problem. *She* was not good enough.

Still, how pleasurable to enact the role of his wife …

At dinner, Signora Pavoni was in her element. Not to be outdone by Elizabeth she had also chosen silk—including the fashionable net overlays, which Elizabeth had decided to leave off. In a word she was *attentive*, her eyes flicking from one guest to the next as she checked that every possible step had been taken to assure their comfort. Maria Grazia was timider, but Elizabeth noticed that she backed up her mother unobtrusively. While Signora Pavoni lauded Fraulein Edelmann's dress to the whole gathering, her daughter preferred a whispered compliment. The table was set for eight people, since they were to be joined by the leader of the orchestra and his wife.

Elizabeth had been wary of meeting Hilda Edelmann, imagining an imperious diva with an overpowering voice. Instead she was confronted by a slender, tallish woman of her own age, with a quiet manner and style of dress. Her colouring was pale, with very fair hair that she wore in a coiled braid at the back, and grey eyes set far apart. After the introduction Fraulein Edelmann lingered at her side, and answered questions about Abano in careful English, rather as if she were reading from a book.

'The baths are large enough to swim in, and hold water from underground springs that are naturally hot.' She winced. 'Very hot. Afterwards you lie on a towel and mud is spread over your face. Also hot. It is said to be healthy for the skin. How do you say, the *complexion*.'

'I would like to try it—I think.'

Fraulein Edelmann smiled. 'Have you and your husband travelled in Italy?'

'A little. Most recently we were in Venice.'

'I was staying in Florence with my father. Unfortunately he was called away, since he is an *Oberstleutnant*, a colonel in the Austrian army.'

Elizabeth frowned. 'Was this related to Bonaparte's return to France?'

'It happened earlier, when Bonapartists in the Kingdom of Naples rebelled against the Austrian Empire.' She flushed and lowered her voice. 'It is best not to speak of it, since our intervention is unpopular in Italy.'

'Did this oblige you to return to Austria?'

'I planned to remain in Florence, since the war is not

expected to last many months. However, we received word from my family in Salzburg that my mother is ill, so I am trying to make my way home.' She pointed to Pavoni. 'Antonio is an old friend. He has been so kind as to arrange recitals in Padua and Verona so that I can pay my *vetturino*, how do you say, *driver*, and keep a maid.'

Elizabeth swallowed, awed that this woman was travelling alone, except for servants, and would be performing to discerning audiences. 'I hope your mother soon feels better.'

'I'm not too concerned, since she has had the vapours before and recovered well.' She smiled sadly. 'Sometimes I believe she is simply anxious for my father.'

After dinner Elizabeth joined Hilda Edelmann and Maria Grazia in the music room to look at the piano accompaniments. A few were familiar, including arrangements of arias by Purcell and Mozart, but she was pleased to find Italian folk ditties too. The recital was to close with two unpublished songs by a young composer named Franz Schubert, who had allowed Fraulein Edelmann to write copies when they met in Vienna.

'What do you think?' Maria Grazia asked.

Elizabeth ran a finger along a piano arrangement of Dido's Lament. Compared with the Beethoven sonatas demanded by Carandini, it was straightforward. 'Would you like to play this one, Signorina Pavoni?'

Maria Grazia pointed to a stretch in the right hand. 'Not sure about this bit.'

'Leave out the bottom note,' Fraulein Edelmann said.

Elizabeth grinned in appreciation of this simple solution, which Carandini would never have countenanced.

'I could try the Mozart,' she offered.

They divided the other pieces, Maria Grazia still anxious. 'Should we rehearse them now, before the others come in?'

The singer laughed. '*Nein*. This whole evening is a rehearsal, is it not? It will go splendidly. You will see.'

The music room was the grandest in the apartment, with two rows of chairs upholstered in floral chintz facing a slightly raised platform for the grand piano and other instruments. Overhead hung a ten-candle chandelier in the French style; a matching candelabra on the piano illuminated the musical score.

As a guest, Elizabeth was invited to sit in the front row, with Darcy on one side and the lead violinist's wife on the other. Small ornate tables held brandy for the gentlemen, but Elizabeth opted for coffee in hope of clearing her head.

'Are you not playing, Rebecca?' Darcy asked.

'Be patient, dearest. We're taking turns.'

'You look exquisite in that dress.'

'So I should, considering what you had to spend on it. Still, thank you for the compliment. My good qualities are under your protection, and you are to exaggerate them as much as possible.'

They fell silent as a tentative Maria Grazia played the opening bars of Dido's Lament. Fraulein Edelmann waited calmly, hands loosely clasped, her gaze directed over their heads into the distance. She sang the first line, *When I am laid in earth*, in the original English, and Elizabeth shivered. It was as if the room had been transformed. The voice was magical. It was not the voice of an operatic diva, resonant with vibrato, but thinner, more fragile, with a purity that took the breath away. Elizabeth saw now why Fraulein Edelmann gave recitals to small audiences, rather than concerts in grand halls like *La Fenice*. In a huge auditorium filled with people fidgeting and coughing, her art would be lost. But in a drawing room she was hypnotic.

The piece ended, and during the applause Elizabeth observed that Darcy too was captivated. It was now her turn, and she was surprised by her own confidence as she replaced Maria Grazia at the piano. She knew the aria, a popular duet in which Don Giovanni tries to seduce a peasant girl who is engaged to another man. *Là ci darem la mano*—Give me thy hand. Professor Pavoni, who was to sing the seducer's part, followed her to the platform. This time there was no introduction: Pavoni beat time with his forefinger, met her eye, and they began together.

He sang pleasantly enough, but as she played the simple chord sequences Elizabeth found herself waiting for Fraulein Edelmann's response, and when it came she was again so electrified that her scalp tingled. Somehow she managed to continue the accompaniment, as if her hands and eyes went ahead on automatic while her attention was fully occupied in listening. They finished with a flourish, and Maria Grazia ran to her side.

'Signora Ashley, *bravissima*!'

Elizabeth blinked. 'Did I play it correctly?'

'Every note! You must play the others as well.'

'I would rather take turns.'

She returned to her seat, very aware of Darcy's admiring gaze. He touched her arm gently. 'That sounded truly beautiful, Rebecca.'

'We both know who deserves the credit.'

A servant came to refresh their drinks, and she felt a glow of intense happiness as they chatted before the next piece.

26

Torrential rain woke Darcy. Navigating by the embers in the grate, he opened the shutters and looked down at the water splattering against the roof below. On the horizon lightning flashed, and he counted ten before hearing a rumble, so distant it was almost drowned out by the rain.

Someone screamed. He went to the dividing door, and heard whimpering from the next room.

He pulled on his dressing gown, hesitated a moment, then opened the door half-way. What could it be? An intruder? The thunder? She cried out again and he scanned the chamber before hastening to her bedside.

'Miss Bennet? Are you ill?'

She gripped his arm, and in the dim light he saw sweat gleam on her brow. She was like a trapped animal in panic. He took her hand. 'You're safe. There is no danger, it is only a storm.'

'Mr Darcy?'

She fell back, taking a deep breath, and he took the opportunity to light a candle. 'Do you see now? There is nothing to fear.'

She sat up, shivering. 'It was a nightmare. I was held prisoner in a dungeon. The ceiling fell towards me, so low I was forced to lie down, and still it descended …' She shuddered at the memory. 'I'm sorry. I'm behaving like a child. It was only a dream.'

'Can I bring you a drink? Wine? Brandy?'

'A sip of brandy would be nice. But later.' She mopped her brow with a sleeve, and managed a smile. 'What happened to the walls of Jericho?'

'I scaled them to rescue the damsel in distress.'

'I'm not usually like this. Bad dreams, yes, but not these intense attacks of panic.' She held up a hand. 'No need to play the physician, for I know your diagnosis. It is the opiate. It will pass.' She sighed. 'In truth I thought it had passed *already*, since I felt so well during the evening.'

'It is normal. There are setbacks, but they will become fewer and soon vanish altogether.'

'How fortunate that I have a husband to comfort me.'

'It seems rather that I irritate you, by repeating the obvious. Still, I have scant experience in the role, having been your husband for only two days. I hope to do better in the future.'

'Come come, Mr Darcy. As you may recall, I examined your character long ago and found it without flaw. For one on such a lofty peak, no improvement is possible.'

He felt self-conscious, recalling her teasing manner in Hertfordshire, which he had misinterpreted as flirtatious. 'I will fetch the brandy now, Miss Bennet, since you have obviously recovered.'

'You mean, I am restored to my usual silliness?'

He smiled, disdaining to contradict her, and left the candle at her bedside in case she took fright again. At the door he took a last glance at the lovely apparition in white, still watching him, dark curls hanging loose around her smiling face. *This is not real*, he told himself. *We are acting a part*. But reason be damned: he could still dream.

'Can we try this one?' Fraulein Edelmann turned a page in

her hand-written manuscript book. '*Come raggio di sol.* How do you say? Like a ray of sun?'

'Sunshine.' Elizabeth peered at the piano part. A traditional Italian song, author unknown, slow and relatively simple.

They had been alone in the piano room since luncheon, running through the pieces one more time. At the recital, scheduled for the early evening, the accompanist would be a local *maestro* who had sent a servant to pick up the sheet music, while declaring himself too busy to rehearse—his scribbled note mentioned *teaching engagements.* Fraulein Edelmann took this in her stride: she was used to impecunious musicians who would prefer to give a ragged performance than turn down a fee.

Elizabeth managed well enough until a tricky bar full of accidentals. She had broken down before, and noticed that every time, Fraulein Edelmann carried on as if nothing had happened, rather than stopping to repeat the passage. The accompanist was expected to catch up. At the end, she apologised.

'Doesn't matter.'

'Shall we do it again?'

Fraulein Edelman shook her head. 'Better to stay fresh for the recital.' She turned to a song by her Austrian friend Franz Schubert. 'Try this one.'

There was a tap at the door and Darcy entered.

'Giles!' Elizabeth went to meet him. 'Did all go well?'

He nodded, and replied softly, 'Burgess was waiting at the Basilica, as planned. Our, ah, *friends* from Villa Foscari have continued towards Verona, but left a note for you. Also a present.'

Elizabeth smiled eagerly. 'Show me!'

'Patience, Rebecca. You may view them in your room after rehearsing.' He turned to Fraulein Edelmann. 'Excuse the interruption. Might I listen for a few minutes?'

They tackled the Schubert, and during an easy passage Elizabeth glanced round and noticed that for once, Darcy's gaze was not focussed on herself.

He was watching the singer. Hilda Edelmann.

They had agreed that it was too risky to attend the recital, which might attract Gabriele Carandini's notice if he was searching for Elizabeth in Padua. Professor Pavoni concurred; his wife and daughter, unaware of the deception, were mystified.

'Signora Ashley, you *must* come,' Maria Grazia pleaded.

Elizabeth explained that they were tired, having been kept awake by the thunderstorm—which was true, so far as it went.

Left alone with Darcy, in the *salotto*, she showed him the note from Miss Dill, which gave her address in Oxfordshire with the message: *Hoping to meet you again, and as a memento, please accept these pages from my sketchbook.* Carefully she handed him the drawings of blueweed and sweet violet that she had last glimpsed over the artist's shoulder in the farm wagon.

'Excellent.' He gave them back. 'I admire economy in art. There is not a single unnecessary line.'

She paused, intrigued by this comment. 'I feel uneasy to receive such a gift. After all, these drawings are important to Miss Dill. They record her discoveries during her travels.'

'No doubt she made copies.' He smiled, and Elizabeth felt a quiver of humiliation that she had not drawn this obvious inference herself. He continued, 'Miss Bennet, while we are alone it would be a good moment to plan our next move. The Pavonis have been all generosity, but I would not wish to outstay our welcome.'

She bridled, finding him patronising. 'Indeed, to out-stay one's welcome is rarely advisable.'

He flinched, and continued with forced politeness. 'Of course I am also concerned that you should have time to recover from your ordeal.'

She sighed, feeling ridiculous. 'I'm doing my best.'

'Believe me, I understand how difficult it must be.'

Her eyes flashed. 'Can we drop the subject, Mr Darcy? I realise that in my present state I am even more burden-some than usual. Yes, sooner or later we must continue our journey, presumably to Verona, and then west to Mi-lan and the Alps.'

Darcy raised a finger. 'Just so, and there I have an idea. Fraulein Edelmann will also be leaving Padua in a few days time, and for a while our routes coincide. Why not share a carriage to Verona?'

Elizabeth brightened, feeling a spark of optimism at this clearing of the mist. It would be a relief to remain in comfort for a few more days; she had also enjoyed the company of the Austrian singer. But a shadow crossed her heart as she recalled the way in which Darcy had looked at Fraulein Edelmann in the music room. The contrast between the talented, courageous young woman and herself was all too sharp.

'So?' Darcy pressed. 'What do you think?'

'Oh!' She blinked in confusion. 'It is masterful, like all your ideas.'

He recoiled, and managed a token smile. 'You exag-gerate, of course, but I hope your approval is sincere.'

'Forgive me. I do approve.'

He nodded, and she wondered why their conversation had become so awkward. She recalled wistfully how easily they had managed as Mr and Mrs Ashley. *That was it!* Play-ing the role of a married couple they were relaxed, entertained, confident. As Mr Darcy and Miss Bennet they had a history of misunderstanding and mutual harm …

She remained silent, not wishing to share this observation. Perhaps one day, but not now, with the atmosphere still fraught.

27

April 1815

Darcy strolled alone round the Roman amphitheatre in Verona. In the sunshine he felt warm in his light morning coat; he wore also a hat over the grey wig. The disguise might not deceive Carandini if they met close up, but he dismissed this as unlikely. His earlier visit to Verona had been interrupted by the urgent necessity of returning to Venice; now he had time to tour the sights.

So far all had gone smoothly. Fraulein Edelmann accepted his plan with alacrity, and a *vetturino* recommended by Professor Pavoni provided a carriage with covered seating for four, and extra space outside—sufficient to carry the singer's manservant and maid as well as Burgess. The professor, eager to attend further recitals, came along as well, and introduced them to his friend Signor Alfredo Zamboni, director of the *Accademia Filarmonica*. This was originally a circle of artists and musicians who met every week to talk, and organise exhibitions and concerts; now it ran a magnificent opera theatre that would celebrate its centenary the following year. Zamboni had already offered hospitality to Fraulein Edelmann, and Darcy was quietly delighted when the offer was extended to the Ashleys—a private residence was not only more comfortable than a hotel, but far safer.

They had intended to stop in Verona only two nights before proceeding to Milan, but for several reasons Darcy had preferred to extend their stay. Foremost among these was the convenience of having a companion for Elizabeth—an arrangement that suited Fraulein Edelmann too since Elizabeth (or rather, Rebecca Ashley) had become an invaluable partner for rehearsals. Playing the piano accompaniment had also helped distract Elizabeth from the vexations of laudanum withdrawal. With every day that passed she grew stronger, removing any illusion that her symptoms had been due to an authentic illness.

The other reason for staying was that Darcy was having second thoughts over their itinerary. He had assumed that they would follow the most direct route, via Milan, Switzerland and France. Disadvantages of this plan were now apparent. Napoleon was back in Paris, having regained the loyalty of the French army. This could mean only one thing: within weeks France would be at war with a coalition of states that included Britain. Moreover, after leaving Fraulein Edelmann they would be alone, with no companion for Elizabeth, nor even a maid. Both problems could be allayed by taking the alternative route north through Austria and the German Confederation towards Ostend.

Darcy circled round the amphitheatre to the cobbled road leading to Zamboni's town house. Elizabeth was still probably with Fraulein Edelmann in the music room, rehearsing two new pieces for tomorrow's recital, which she hoped to attend. Since adopting their disguises they had circulated in society with increasing confidence, so her bravura was understandable. He pressed his lips together. It would not do. He would have to persuade her ...

They had been allotted adjoining chambers in a wing of

Zamboni's grand house, this time with no connecting door. To talk in privacy they could use the larger bedroom, Elizabeth's, which had two armchairs facing the fire. They had retired after lunch, announcing their intention of taking a *siesta*.

Seated with an atlas on her knees, Elizabeth traced the line north through the Adige valley towards Innsbruck. 'Is it not longer than the other route?'

'In distance, yes. In time, probably not. Almost certainly we would be delayed in France, even assuming that we are allowed to move freely at all.'

'The Dolomites!' Her eyes sparkled as she traced the route through Bavaria and Prussia. 'So much to see.'

'And in Fraulein Edelmann's company.'

He expected this to be a further inducement, but for a moment her face fell—had he missed something? She recovered and flashed him a smile. 'We could go all the way to her home town. Salzburg.'

'That would be a digression, Rebecca.'

'Rebecca?' She smiled. 'I can be Miss Bennet now that we are alone.'

'If you were Miss Bennet we would not be *tête-à-tête* in your bedroom.'

'True. Anyway, I much prefer Mr Ashley to that awful Mr Darcy.'

'There is an obvious rejoinder to that, madam.'

She thought for a moment, then smiled. 'Concerning the even-more-awful Miss Bennet?'

'Enough nonsense.' Darcy took a deep breath. 'Listen, Rebecca, you are not going to the recital tomorrow.'

She flinched, but managed to maintain a light-hearted tone. 'Come dearest, we are a hundred miles from Venice and have perceived no sign of Carandini or his acolytes for over a week. I will be wearing my wig, new dress and hat, even a veil if you wish. Are you not exaggerating the risk?'

'I would remind you that Carandini is an obsessional devotee of music. Even living a hundred miles away he is known to Zamboni's circle.'

'And *I* would remind *you*, sir, that I have spent many hours this past week helping Hilda prepare for her concerts, and would enjoy just one opportunity to hear the results of my labours.'

'So it's Hilda and Rebecca now?'

'I think of her as a friend, yes. Indeed, that is the main reason I wish to attend. Do you not see? We have made some excuse or other *every time*. How do you think she feels?'

He sighed, seeing the force of this. 'If you are attending, then so will I.'

'Of course.' She grinned, sensing victory. 'I would have it no other way. With my devoted husband at my side, I shall feel entirely safe.'

28

On a balmy evening, Elizabeth crossed *Piazza delle Erbe* arm in arm with Darcy. It was dusk, and the market stalls were closing down. The recital would start in just ten minutes, but as a precaution they had decided to arrive at the last moment and walk straight to their reserved seats.

Wearing her new silk dress, with veil and bonnet over the blonde wig, Elizabeth hoped she would be well disguised; even so, she kept her gaze to the front, resisting the temptation to keep a lookout for Carandini, or agents who might be in his employ. Walking the length of the *piazza* was daunting, but less conspicuous than arriving in a carriage. They reached *Palazzo Maffei*, the location of the recital, and were ushered to seats at the front between Professor Pavoni and the Zambonis.

While Elizabeth greeted Signora Zamboni, she heard Pavoni whisper to Darcy, 'There will be a delay. De Santis is late and a servant has been sent to his house.'

Elizabeth frowned. She had met Giovanni De Santis, a young fop of undoubted talent who had offered to serve as accompanist free of charge—intending, in her view, to exercise his charms on Fraulein Edelmann. A rehearsal in Signor Zamboni's music room had been cut short when De Santis realised, first, that the piano part provided him no scope for displaying virtuosity, and second, that Hilda would be chaperoned by her friend Signora Ashley, and was in any case unmoved by his flattery.

Ten minutes passed, and the small *sala* filled to overflowing. Allowing herself a quick glimpse, Elizabeth took in a hundred seats, all occupied, with latecomers standing at the back. The conversation was so loud that she could scarcely hear herself speak. There was no platform, just a well-lit space at the front for the grand piano, flanked by two small round tables holding vases of dark red roses.

As she leaned to catch a remark by Signora Zamboni, Elizabeth felt a tap on her shoulder.

She turned back to Darcy. 'Yes, dear?'

He pointed to his right. 'Fraulein Edelmann is calling you.'

'*Scusatemi.*' She bowed to Signora Zamboni and joined Hilda Edelmann, who was in animated discussion with Professor Pavoni.

'We can find someone else from the *Accademia*.' Pavoni waved his arm in the direction of the second row.

'Who?' Fraulein Edelmann insisted.

'I don't know. Someone.'

Hilda reached for Elizabeth's arm and pulled her closer. 'Rebecca, we have a problem. De Santis left this morning on a trip to a vineyard and has not returned.' Her grip tightened. 'You know the pieces. You play them perfectly. It is a lot to ask, but could you …'

Elizabeth felt a shiver pass through her body. To perform in public was daunting enough, but she would also become a focus of attention. Carandini, if he were here, would surely see through her disguise, especially since he was familiar with her style of playing. On the other hand, to let Hilda down …

'Just a moment.' She leaned over Darcy and informed him in a frantic whisper what had occurred. 'Giles, what can I do? It's risky, I know, but I see no alternative.'

'No.' Darcy was incisive. 'Make some excuse. You are not a professional musician. You have never performed to such a large gathering. It is far too much to ask of you.'

She stiffened, riled by such a blunt dismissal. 'I remind you, sir, that I will not be playing a concerto, only some simple accompaniments which in Hilda's opinion lie well within my modest capabilities.'

He sighed. 'I was merely trying to suggest the form your excuse might take. It surely goes without saying that my only concern is for your safety.'

She stood up, her fear displaced by indignation at his paternalism. 'I have already admitted that there is risk, but for my part I am willing to run it. If you disagree, you might prefer to leave now.'

He stared at her, aghast. 'Miss B…, I mean, Rebecca, this is folly.'

She swung round and re-joined Fraulein Edelmann, who led her to a side room where they could prepare.

Elizabeth trembled as Hilda Edelmann helped adjust the wig. Her bonnet, with its comfortably anonymous veil, had been set aside on the dressing table.

'These overlays.' Hilda fingered the nets on the upper arms of her dress. 'Will they hamper you?'

'No.' Elizabeth strained to follow proceedings in the *sala*, where Signor Zamboni was introducing the recital, no doubt announcing the change in personnel. She realised now that Darcy was, as usual, correct. Not for the first time, she had allowed his haughty manner to cloud her judgement, and blinded herself to the truth of what he was saying. She *was* a rank amateur. The audience had paid to listen to skilled musicians; instead they would witness the floundering of a woman who through pride had ventured out of her depth.

Hilda dealt her a reassuring smile. 'Ready?'

Elizabeth froze for a moment, then felt herself wilt, as if all energy had drained away. 'I cannot do this.'

Hilda's arm came around her. 'Rebecca. Listen carefully. I have done this many times. Do you know how?'

'I can't imagine.'

'I do it for *myself*. Not for them. It gives me joy to sing, and even more joy when I have a friend to accompany me. When we play tonight, we do it for our own pleasure. The people out there may listen if they wish, but we care not a fig whether the music pleases them. Mistakes do not trouble us. We can make a thousand mistakes and it will count for nothing, so long as we are enjoying ourselves. You see?'

Elizabeth nodded. Was this true? Was it really possible to *ignore* the audience? She brightened, standing tall again. 'Very well. We play for ourselves alone.'

They made their entrance, and she was surprised to find a young man beside the pianoforte. Was this a reprieve? Had they found a more suitable substitute for De Santis? But on spotting an extra chair, she realised he was there only to turn the pages.

Applause greeted them, and she bowed, taking her cue from Hilda, before adjusting the piano seat. Suddenly the nerves were gone, and she felt a strange stillness. Whether she could *enjoy* the experience remained to be seen, but there was a job to be done, and she would simply have to do it. The familiar score of the Purcell faced her on the stand, and after exchanging a glance with Hilda she found herself playing the opening chords. The touch was lighter than she was used to, but she quickly adapted. Hilda hit her entry perfectly, and the magic of her voice took over. Now there really was no audience. It was as if she were being led by an expert dancer, her arms and feet eased into the correct motions.

The piece was over, people were applauding, and Hilda beckoned her forward to take a bow. Glimpsing Darcy still in the front row, she looked down to avoid meeting his eye.

The Mozart began, and the young man at her side revealed a second reason for his presence as he stood up to take on the role of Don Giovanni. Although not acting his part fully, he advanced a few steps towards Hilda, who retreated to suggest the peasant girl's reluctance. Their interplay drew some laughter from the audience, especially when he rushed back to the piano to turn a page. The applause at the end shook the small hall, with cries of *'Bis, bis'* demanding a repeat.

'We will do it again,' Hilda hissed as they took another bow. 'Sorry, I should have introduced you. Signor Rossi, Signora Ashley. Just once, then we will continue.'

Rossi escorted Elizabeth to the piano, and she confidently replayed the duet. Far sooner than she could have imagined, performing had become fun. Her companions were so immaculate, and the audience so noisily appreciative, that she felt invulnerable, as if buoyed along by a current.

Since the recital was a brief one-hour affair, there was no interval. They ended as usual with the Schubert songs, which had more challenging piano parts, but by then Elizabeth was secure enough to bring them off with only minor slips. As a light-hearted encore they tried the Papageno-Papagena duet from Mozart's *The Magic Flute*, which Elizabeth recalled from the performance at *La Fenice* in Venice. More cries of *Bis*, yet another repetition, and at last the ordeal was over.

As the crowd surged to the exit, Elizabeth was aglow with a satisfaction she had never believed possible. She realised that her role had been small, but even so, what a thrill to feel such enthusiastic acclaim. Walking to join Darcy and the others she detected a new grace in her carriage; it was as if her body deemed she was now a person of worth, and should comport herself accordingly.

She wanted to apologise to Darcy for her outburst before the recital, but was immediately surrounded by Zamboni's family, and other members of the *Accademia*. Pavoni too congratulated her—evidently with some relief. She was searching for Darcy when a familiar voice whispered, 'Miss Bennet, can it be you?'

She turned round, open-mouthed. 'Miss Dill!'

Alice Dill faced her, with a smiling Gerard Hanson at her side. 'I'm sorry. I meant, Mrs Ashley.'

'How wonderful to see you again!' Elizabeth dropped her voice. 'It seems my disguise is ineffective.'

'We are artists,' Miss Dill said.

'I received your gift, which I will treasure. Have you enjoyed Verona?'

'Our accommodation is hardly palatial,' Hanson said, 'but there is so much art and architecture that we had to stay a few more days.'

'And happened to attend this recital,' Miss Dill added.

'Have you greeted Mr Ashley? My, ah, husband?' She looked back to the front row, where Darcy was speaking with Professor Pavoni, and froze in horror as an all-too-familiar figure strode towards her, his maniacal eyes impaling her. The short reddish hair, the sideburns, the thin features, there could be no mistake. He confronted her, just a yard away, and behind him she saw the dark blue uniform of a constable.

'*Signorina* Bennet.' Gabriele Carandini bowed. 'A passable performance, marred by wrong notes in the encore. I believe we have matters to discuss with the Prefect of Verona.'

A hand touched her arm, and she saw Darcy at her side. Scarcely able to speak, she whispered, 'I'm sorry.'

'You were wonderful,' he whispered back. He turned to face Carandini. 'On what grounds do you seek to arraign Mrs Ashley?'

'Travelling under false papers, for a start.' He stood aside, to let the constable through, and hissed in Italian, 'Signor Darcy, who abducted my fiancée. Take care, he may resist.'

The constable placed a hand on the hilt of his sword. 'You will accompany us?'

Elizabeth watched the angry workings of Darcy's face as he looked around for possible avenues of escape. He met her eye, with a slight shrug, and replied politely to the constable, 'Of course. We have nothing to hide and will do as you ask.'

29

Flanked by two constables, Darcy tried to affect an air of nonchalance as they walked the short distance to a neighbouring square, the location of the *Prefettura*. At his side Elizabeth stayed close, perhaps disturbed by the antics of Carandini, who was trotting impatiently ahead and occasionally looking round to check she was still there.

They reached a red-brick building sporting a cluster of flags, with ominous gratings on the lower windows, and were led through to a cell furnished with a bare wooden bench and table. Outside they heard Carandini's frantic demand that Elizabeth should be given into *his* custody and not left alone with Darcy. *Più tardi*, later, an official kept telling him. First they would see the *viceprefetto*.

A bolt was drawn and Elizabeth's pretence of dignity collapsed. She leaned forward, head in hands, muttering self-deprecations, until Darcy gently touched her arm.

'We will find a way out of this.'

She sat up abruptly. 'How?'

'We must reason with the vice-prefect. Carandini has no authority here, and not all officials are corrupt.'

She sighed. 'Go on. You may as well say it.'

'Say what?'

'This is entirely my fault. You told me not to agree to Hilda's request. You explained it was too risky. As usual I paid no attention, went my own way, and now I have put us both in great danger.' She faced him with a look of despair. '*Why do you do it?* Why waste time, effort, money, even your own safety, to help an unworthy creature like myself? Your sister needs you. Your estate. Your family. *Why?*'

He said softly, 'You know why.'

She found a handkerchief and impatiently wiped her eyes. 'And now you will be lenient with me. You will tell me I was blameless, that I acted from the best motives.'

'You took a risk to help your friend. Nine times out of ten no harm would have resulted. We were unlucky.'

'There we are. I am exculpated.' Her face wrinkled in disgust. 'But I have not forgotten your words before the recital. *Rebecca, this is folly.*'

She looked so desperate that Darcy instinctively took her hand. 'Dear Miss Elizabeth, let us not waste energy in denigrating ourselves. We are not the villains here.'

She softened, as if moved by his gesture, and squeezed his hand before pulling back. 'You are kind.'

The door jolted open and an official pointed at Darcy.

'*Venga.*' Come.

The vice-prefect Signor Vicario was a tall thin man with a bony pock-marked face, and what appeared a permanent scowl. He waved Darcy to a chair, peered at a document on his desk, and said in Italian:

'Who are you?'

'Fitzwilliam Darcy.'

Vicario waved a wad of papers. 'Yet you were carrying passes in the name of Ashley. Mr and Mrs. This is a serious offence. May I ask how these letters of passage came into your possession?'

Darcy paused, confounded momentarily by Italian officialese. But he had anticipated such a question, and prepared what he hoped was a safe reply.

'They belonged to an English couple whom I met at a hotel in Florence. Mr Ashley left the papers behind. I offered to carry them to Venice, hoping to catch up with him there.'

'A most unlikely story.' Vicario regarded him with contempt. 'So why show these papers rather than your own?'

Darcy explained, as best he could, that he had been forced to use fake identities in order to rescue an English lady from attempted abduction and forced marriage.

Vicario shook his head. 'Again you lie. I have spoken with Signor Carandini, a respected businessman. He can produce witnesses that the Englishwoman was visiting his family and signed a document agreeing to their betrothal. Moreover, his physician testifies that she was ill and under his professional care when you abducted her from Lido.'

'The Englishwoman, Miss Bennet, is here,' Darcy said. 'If you question her you will discover that she was being held prisoner and given laudanum to keep her compliant. You will also observe that her health has improved since she was removed from this physician's so-called *care*.'

Vicario waved this away. 'She will say whatever you have told her to say.'

'How can you make such an assumption without first investigating?'

The vice-prefect glared at him. 'It is not *your* prerogative to ask *me* questions, sir. By your own confession you are guilty of serious infractions; it remains only to determine their full scope.'

'None of this reflects on Miss Bennet,' Darcy said. 'It was I who presented false papers, not she. I implore you, allow her to return to her family in England.'

'You are in no position to bargain.' There was a rap on the door and the vice-prefect grunted. 'What?'

An officer entered. 'Message from the commander, sir. Request to interview the prisoners directly.'

Vicario frowned. 'Strange. Very well. Let them be sent over.'

The *Castelvecchio*, or Old Castle, was a square compound built in red brick with little ornament. Located in the city centre, beside the river Adige, it was a well-known landmark with a violent history still fresh in people's minds. Once a fortress of resistance to Napoleon's armies, it had been damaged during the French conquest, and occupied briefly by Bonaparte himself. Now it served as a barracks from which the Austrian commander and local militia maintained control of the city and its environs.

Having viewed the castle and fortified bridge on his tour of Verona, Darcy was familiar with its high walls and numerous look-out towers. It was not a place from which one could hope to escape.

They were brought in a carriage by two guards from the *Prefettura*, and handed over to an officer at the gate. In the carriage Darcy had summarised his unproductive encounter with the vice-prefect; it seemed now that they were being passed up to the next level, a symptom perhaps of the seriousness of their situation. Elizabeth was calm, but he sensed this was more in resignation than hope.

After a brief wait they were taken to an imposing office with a huge heavy door, richly carved, and patterned marble floor. Behind a long desk sat a tall bulky man in military uniform, with sleek greying hair parted in the middle, moustache, and pince-nez hanging from a cord. Facing him, leather chairs had been arranged in a semi-circle, and as they entered Darcy recognised a nervous-looking Gabriele Carandini at the far right. A woman rose from the next chair, and Elizabeth gasped.

It was Fraulein Edelmann.

The commander came round the desk, and bowed. The contrast with Vicario could not have been acuter. He beamed at them, and said genially, 'Herr Darcy! Fraulein Bennet! *Guten Abend!* My name is Brigade Commander Johann Graf. Let us see whether we can sort out this little misunderstanding.'

Bewildered, Darcy sat next to Elizabeth and nodded to Fraulein Edelmann, who dealt him a steely glare in return.

Commander Graf resumed his place, and continued to address them in painstakingly correct English. 'Before we begin, my interest in this matter should be explained. As you will know, I am a general in the Austrian army and have been assigned responsibility, under the Treaty of Vienna, for overseeing administration in the Republic of Italy. I am also a music lover, and this evening had the pleasure of attending the recital by Fraulein Edelmann—' He extended an arm. 'Whom I have known many years, since her father is both a colleague and a friend.'

Darcy observed Elizabeth as she threw an inquisitive glance at Hilda Edelmann, but the singer refused to meet her eye and remained impassive.

'Duty obliged me to leave early, so that I did not witness what happened afterwards. However, I understand from Fraulein Edelmann that her accompanist, whom she knew as Mrs Ashley, was detained, along with her husband.' He beamed at Elizabeth. 'I should mention, as an aside, how much I enjoyed your performance.'

Elizabeth reddened, but made no reply.

'Now, to specifics. Fraulein, I suggest you wait outside now.'

Graf waited for Hilda Edelmann to leave before raising a sheath of papers. 'Vice-prefect Vicario has forwarded these letters of passage in the name of Ashley, which are admitted to be false. Signor Carandini alleges that his fiancée, Miss Bennet, was abducted by Mr Darcy when under his protection.'

'And receiving treatment from my physician,' Carandini added.

Darcy snorted. 'Treatment! You mean, she was tricked into taking an opiate, to secure her compliance.'

Graf held up a hand. 'Gentlemen! Please understand that my duty here is to administer justice, and this can be done only if we confine ourselves to what can be *proved*, through evidence. Mr Darcy, I see no reason to doubt Signor Carandini's testimony on this point. It is conceded that Miss Bennet was given laudanum. For all you know, this was done for valid medical reasons. Your allegation is therefore speculation.'

Darcy shook his head. 'Miss Bennet's health has *improved* since her rescue. This shows that she was never ill in the first place. Her symptoms were merely those of withdrawal from the opiate.'

'It could be argued that her recovery testifies to the success of the treatment.'

'The balance of probability favours my interpretation.'

Graf smiled. 'In other words, you are not sure.' He turned to Carandini. 'Signor, what is it that you want?'

Carandini looked longingly at Elizabeth. 'I would like my fiancée to be returned to my household, so that we might proceed with the wedding. As for Signor Darcy, I assume the appropriate penalties will be applied.'

'Miss Bennet is not your fiancée,' Darcy said.

Carandini pointed to the desk. 'I have documentary evidence of her consent.'

'Forged,' Darcy snapped.

'Stop!' Graf raised a palm. 'Again, Mr Darcy, how can

you possibly support such an assertion? You were not present. You have no idea what happened.'

'I have Miss Bennet's testimony.'

'Very well, let us hear from the lady herself.' He faced Elizabeth, speaking as if to a child. 'Enlighten us. Did you sign this document?'

Darcy tensed, anticipating her denial, but after what seemed a struggle she said only, 'I cannot be sure.'

Graf raised his eyebrows. 'Really? Perhaps I am out of date, but I would have expected a young lady to react to a proposal of marriage with greater attention.'

'I was so tired. Signor Carandini kept telling me that I had to sign. I did not know what the document meant. He said it made no difference, since I had already signed it, and he only needed a copy …'

Graf turned to Carandini. 'Is this true?'

'No.' Carandini's voice rose to a nasal whine. 'Signorina Bennet signed the agreement in full knowledge of its import.' He looked at Elizabeth with forced magnanimity. 'I forgive my fiancée her error. No doubt Signor Darcy has worked on her since the abduction, confusing what was once a clear memory.'

'Signor!' Graf was incisive. 'This time, it is *you* that I must hold to the evidence. You have no knowledge of what passed between Mr Darcy and Miss Bennet after she left your house. Your assertion is speculation.'

'I have the signed document,' Carandini insisted.

'Indeed.' Graf spread his arms. 'I have no evidence to counter your assertion that Miss Bennet signed a betrothal agreement. There does, however, seem doubt as to her mental state at the time. You have admitted she was being treated with an opiate. I believe our best course is therefore to ascertain her feelings *now*.' He turned to Elizabeth. 'Miss Bennet, having witnessed your performance this evening, may I assume you have recovered from the side-effects of the drug, and can express your wishes clearly?'

She replied quietly but firmly. 'Yes.'

'I'm delighted to hear it. Pardon the blunt query, but it must be asked. Do you wish to marry Signor Carandini?'

'I do not.'

'You are definite on this point?'

'Yes.'

'Has there ever been a time when you felt differently?'

'Never.'

Graf turned to Carandini with a gesture of resignation. 'That seems clear enough.'

Carandini's face had darkened to purple. 'This is non-sense,' he spluttered. 'Signor Darcy has seduced my fian-cée and poisoned her against me.'

'Please.' Graf gently hushed him. 'I understand that you have acted in good faith, as has Mr Darcy, but I beg you once more to refrain from speculation. You say Mr Darcy has manipulated Miss Bennet's feelings. How do you know? The only direct evidence available is the testi-mony of Miss Bennet herself.'

Carandini looked imploringly at Elizabeth. 'No-one could doubt our attachment. I vividly recall her smiling face, her joy in making music together. Ask my mother, my sister …'

'Such signals can be misinterpreted, especially when two people come from different cultures.' Graf faced Ca-randini and lowered his voice. 'Signor, I am persuaded that we have here a misunderstanding, and that you, like Mr Darcy, have acted out of genuine concern for Miss Bennet's welfare. Your disappointment is understandable, and you have my sympathy. I must ask you, however, to make your peace with Mr Darcy, and withdraw your claim to Miss Bennet's hand.'

Carandini looked at Elizabeth once more, his face suffused with pain, then tore himself away and said petulantly, 'So you are giving my fiancée to Darcy, even though he has broken into my house, removed her by force, and fled using a false identity?'

The commander frowned. 'I am going to be lenient and overlook your accusatory tone. But let us be clear. Miss Bennet is *not* your fiancée, and her future is as yet undecided. All that has been established is that she is no longer under *your* protection. As to the other points you raise—' He turned to Darcy. 'Mr Darcy, do you admit breaking into Signor Carandini's property, and would you be willing to compensate him for any expenses incurred?'

Darcy thought for a while. 'Yes, if for instance there has been damage to the balustrade.'

'One must consider also the cost of hiring men to go after the intruders.'

Darcy sighed. 'I am willing to discuss it.'

Graf made a note. 'Good. Now, the question of travel documents. This is a clear offence, as you are doubtless aware. I am persuaded that you acted out of concern for Miss Bennet, but even so there must be redress. I am not going to question your account of how these papers came into your possession. However, I cannot sanction their illegitimate use. There will be a fine, let us say of a hundred ducats, and I ask your word of honour that it will be paid as soon as is practically feasible.'

'You have it.'

Another note. 'Finally, we come to the matter of Miss Bennet's future.' He turned to Carandini. 'You may leave now, Signor. I will inform you of my decision over any financial compensation due to you.'

Carandini rose, glowering at Darcy with unmistakeable hatred, and walked slowly to the door.

Graf waited, listening for departing footsteps, before turning back to Darcy. 'Let us go straight to the point. I understand from Fraulein Edelmann that you have been living as man and wife.'

'A pretence only, necessary for our escape.'

'I accept your assurances. Still, it cannot be denied that the situation is compromising. Miss Bennet came to Italy with the Carandini family. She has been under Signor Carandini's protection; now it would seem she is under yours. Before allowing you to go free, I need to ascertain the nature of your connection.'

Darcy looked at Elizabeth, who accepted this as a cue to speak up. 'Mr Darcy is a long-standing friend of the family, and his best friend is engaged to my sister.'

'And as to your own relationship?' He faced Darcy. 'If it were generally known what has occurred, would you be prepared to marry Miss Bennet?'

'Gladly, if she will have me.'

Graf turned to Elizabeth. 'Miss Bennet?'

She hesitated. 'May I ask the tendency of this question?'

'To prevent any contingency in which you are constrained to marry against your wishes.'

Elizabeth looked at Darcy. 'Very well. If it were necessary to marry Mr Darcy, I would be honoured to do so.'

'Good.' Commander Graf paused. 'I need your word, Mr Darcy, that there will be no further use of the Ashley papers, and that they will be returned as soon as possible to their owners. Otherwise you are free to go.' He sighed. 'I hope one day we can meet under more propitious circumstances.'

Darcy bowed. 'I am indebted to your diplomacy.'

Graf hesitated again, then smiled. 'Then indulge me. Honour apart, Mr Darcy, do you have feelings for Miss

Bennet?'

'I love her.'

He turned to Elizabeth. 'And you, madam?'

Darcy gaped at her as she replied, without hesitation, 'I love him.'

30

What have I done?

Elizabeth blinked. She was in bed, at the Pavonis. No, the Zambonis. They were in Verona. Darcy was no longer next door. He had been assigned a room at the other end of the house. They were no longer passing as the Ashleys. Hilda had informed Signor Zamboni and his family of the pretence. Once again they were Mr Darcy and Miss Bennet—both single.

For now.

She rolled out of bed and mechanically went through the motions of washing and dressing. She noticed the blonde wig incongruously perched on a chair and put it away in a drawer.

'I love him.'

Had Darcy believed her?

She rallied. Perhaps he realised that there was nothing else she could say. Yes, Commander Graf was apparently willing to let them go in any case. But might he not have changed his mind? The commander had a tenderness for her, she had sensed. He had spoken to her as if to a favourite daughter or niece. He would not wish her to be compromised into a loveless union.

What a mess!

She recalled the embarrassment of the previous evening, after their return from the *Castelvecchio*. The relief that she had evaded Carandini, and Darcy had escaped with a fine. Their awkward reception at the Zamboni residence, where Professor Pavoni had already explained their predicament to the family, and Fraulein Edelmann had retired early, professing tiredness. Strangely, her admission to Graf had not worried her then. After a bowl of soup she had gone to her room, and fallen asleep directly.

She put on a plain muslin dress and went downstairs.

'So, madam.' Hilda Edelmann was alone at the breakfast table, Darcy having left to withdraw funds from a bank. 'What are we to call you today?'

'Elizabeth. Or Miss Bennet if you feel we are no longer friends.'

'Then it will have to be Miss Bennet.' Fraulein Edelmann spoke in a monotone, as if struggling to hide her outrage. 'Friends confide in one another, do they not?'

A maid passed and Elizabeth requested coffee and two boiled eggs. She took a *brioche* from a basket and tore off an end to check the filling. 'We thought it would be easier for everyone if there was no need to dissimulate.'

'So, you judged me less intelligent than you and hence incapable of sustaining the deception?'

Was this aggressive, or some kind of ponderous humour? In either case, Elizabeth was in no mood to apologise. If Hilda wanted a fight, she could have one.

'Perhaps you are. How could I tell?'

A stifled guffaw suggested she was on the right track. They ate awhile in silence, before Elizabeth asked:

'What happened yesterday? After the constables took us away?'

Fraulein Edelmann drew herself up, folded her napkin, and clasped her hands demurely together. 'I was naturally alarmed that my esteemed accompanist had been arrested.

From Professor Pavoni I learned that the charges would be serious, including impersonation and abduction. Had I had any sense I would have left you to your fate. Instead I went to the castle to plead with Commander Graf, who had come over to wish me well before the recital. He was sympathetic, but made no promise. He would listen to the evidence and seek an equitable conclusion. A messenger was dispatched, and you know the rest.'

Elizabeth extended a hand across the table. 'You saved us, Hilda.'

Fraulein Edelmann smiled regally, ignoring the hand. 'You may thank me if you wish.'

'I would if you didn't look so satisfied with yourself.'

'As you please.' Another regal look, this time without the smile. 'In all honesty, I cannot approve.'

'Of what?'

'I understand that you had to conceal your identities. But why play the roles of man and wife?'

Elizabeth waited as the maid served her breakfast. 'We had papers only for a married couple.'

'Adjacent rooms? *Dearest* Giles? Was it essential to be quite so intimate?'

Elizabeth hesitated, appreciating the force of this. At the same time, she was in no mood for an inquisition. 'You may believe of me what you like, Hilda. It is none of your business anyway.'

Fraulein Edelmann looked away, with the hint of a smile at the corners of her mouth. She regarded Elizabeth again with a tilt of the head. 'Mr Darcy is certainly a fine gentleman.'

'He would be flattered to hear you say so.'

'Are you not of the same mind?'

Elizabeth took a deep breath, and exhaled slowly. 'He is an honourable man and has been a good friend to my family. Since in your opinion we are not friends any more, I will keep my personal feelings to myself.'

'Yes?' Fraulein Edelmann raised her eyebrows. 'Then so shall I.'

In a coffee house overlooking the Roman amphitheatre, Darcy sat opposite Brigade Commander Graf. The Austrian had a sweet tooth: as well as stirring three spoonfuls of sugar into his coffee, he ordered a plate of *Krapfen*, iced doughnuts filled with apricot jam. He was evidently a familiar customer, ushered to a corner table that offered the most comfort and privacy.

'Have you chosen your route?' Graf asked.

'North, through Tyrol.'

'Ah.' Graf licked jam from his doughnut. 'West would be shorter, but you are wise to avoid France.'

'Have you news of Bonaparte?'

'Almost daily. I cannot reveal details, but as you will imagine, coalition armies are mobilising, and converging on France from all directions.' He paused. 'I wonder …'

'Yes?'

'Will you travel with Fraulein Edelmann?'

'I hope so. The arrangement has been useful.' Darcy sighed. 'Provided she can forgive our deception.'

'I would count it as a favour if you did. I have known Hilda since she was a child, and it would concern me if she had to travel alone over such difficult territory.'

'We can follow main roads,' Darcy said. 'Trent, Bozen, Brenner pass to Innsbruck. I am assuming, of course, no further pursuit by Carandini or his agents.'

'You will carry fresh letters of safe conduct with my signature,' Graf said. 'As to Carandini, I believe caution is still advisable. I have warned him that any attempt to detain Miss Bennet will result in his immediate arrest. There remains however a possibility that he will seek revenge against *you*. I do not see him as a man with the stomach for direct combat. He might, however, hire an assassin. It is unlikely, I know, but I have seen cases where an attack has been ordered through intermediaries so as to conceal the source.'

Darcy frowned. 'Do you really see this as a risk? If so, I ought to take steps to protect Miss Bennet, and also Fraulein Edelmann if she accompanies us.'

'Perhaps I exaggerate. However, jealous lovers are notoriously irrational, and Carandini impressed me as a man who is—how can I say—*obsessive.*'

'I will employ guards.'

'It would be wise, especially until you reach the border with Austria.' He smiled wryly. 'This is proving an expensive tour for you, Mr Darcy.'

'My credit is certainly running down, but it should be sufficient.'

Graf looked away, munching through another doughnut. 'Unfortunately this is not a safe time to travel in any part of Europe. Officers are seconded to the forthcoming war, leaving depleted forces to maintain order.' He sat up suddenly and slapped the table. 'Listen. Two corporal guards from my brigade have been summoned to Austria, departing tomorrow. Shall I instruct them to accompany you?'

'By all means.' Darcy hesitated. 'I would of course pay for their services.'

Graf shook his head. 'Count this as a favour for me. I could not face my friend Oberstleutnant Edelmann again if I allowed his daughter to come to harm.' He glanced at a clock on the opposite wall. 'I must leave now. Have we any more to discuss?'

'Only the settlement with Carandini.'

Graf dismissed this with a wave of the hand. 'Leave it with me. I have your 100 ducats for the fine, and will subtract any expenses for Carandini from that. I will tell the guards to call later today to make arrangements. *Auf Wiedersehen*, sir, and my best regards to Miss Bennet.' He took a few steps, then turned back with a smile. 'If it is not out of place to say so, I hope for a happy outcome there too.'

With plenty to assimilate, Darcy remained for a second cup of coffee. Through Fraulein Edelmann's mediation they had gained the support of the regional commander, and could now travel on with an armed guard. Carandini had been forced to retreat, his claims dismissed. Most miraculous of all, Graf had elicited a declaration from Elizabeth so precious that he hardly dared believe it. *I love him.* Was she dissimulating, to ensure their safe passage? It was possible of course, but her tone had been heartfelt. He could have sworn that she really meant it.

How to proceed? He could seek a private meeting later that day, to clarify her meaning. But his instinct was to let matters lie. It was safer to focus on the practical necessities of the journey, and give Elizabeth time to reassess her feelings. He smiled, enjoying the unfamiliar sensation of hope, and recognising the true reason for his reticence. *He was afraid that if pressed, she might recant.* He had heard the words he always dreamed of hearing; for now, that was enough.

PART II

31

April 1815, one week later

On a sunny morning, with a breeze so warm that it caressed the skin, Elizabeth took breakfast outside an inn overlooking the *Duomo* in Bozen. Seated opposite, Darcy was discussing the cathedral with Fraulein Edelmann. It was apparently very old, 12th century, with subsequent modifications in the Gothic style including a six-cornered ascent to the belfry. Elizabeth leaned back, sipping tea, and let the technicalities pass her by as she took in the beauty of the square which, according to the all-knowing Hilda, had been completed just a few years ago on the orders of King Massimiliano—whoever he might be. On an island in the centre, a flower market was doing brisk business: it would be delightful to pay a visit later. After all they had been through, such simple pleasures were a welcome reminder of normal life.

Their journey from Verona had soon fallen into a regular pattern. Darcy had hired a new *vetturino*, familiar with the Tyrol, and a robust carriage with plenty of space outside for luggage and servants as well as comfortable seating for four. Their route followed the River Adige north along the right bank. As they progressed, the valley became narrower and deeper, with orchards and vineyards nearby, and jagged foothills beyond.

Having parted with Professor Pavoni they had gained

two guards, both Austrian soldiers of the rank of *Unteroffizier*, which according to Hilda meant an experienced soldier permitted to command a squadron. Their names were Bloch and Reithoffer, and in their light grey uniforms and brass helmets it was hard to tell them apart: both were tall and straight-backed, with dark sideburns, long impassive faces, and thick moustaches. They rode behind the carriage on horseback, and were armed with sabres in addition to pistols and rifles. At the start of every stage they arrived punctually and bowed before mounting; otherwise they kept to themselves. She wondered whether they would trouble Hilda's pretty maid, Gretchen, but they stayed aloof, leaving Burgess and Hilda's manservant to compete for the maid's attention.

The *vetturino* drove unerringly to the best inn at each stage, and they ordered two good-sized rooms, Elizabeth sharing with Hilda. As they moved into Austrian territory the inns were neat and clean, with polite service and wholesome food—the bread and wine in particular were excellent.

To her relief there were no problems at the border. According to Darcy their names had been listed for detention, but since a letter from Graf countermanded this request explicitly, they passed through with fulsome apologies for the delay. Finally they were outside the Kingdom of Italy and hence, she hoped, beyond Carandini's clutches.

As her earlier troubles faded, new ones took their place. She had still had no opportunity to talk privately with Darcy—nor had he made any effort to create one. After their declarations of love at the *Castelvecchio* this omission felt unnatural. He was considerate and attentive, as ever, and their conversations had been friendly, especially since she had recovered from the laudanum and no longer suffered vagaries of mood. But she missed the excitement and intimacy of their flight from Venice, when they had pretended to be married and even shared a bedroom. *She wanted that intimacy back*, more than anything she had ever wanted in her life. *That* was the truth she was resisting. She yearned to become his wife in reality, yet recognised that this was precisely what she ought *not* do, for both their sakes.

As to Fraulein Edelmann, a rivalry had developed as the quiet-mannered singer revealed her sharper side. It still rankled with Hilda that Elizabeth had sought her friendship under a false name; her objective now was to expose anything else that the former Mrs Ashley might be hiding. In the bedroom they talked long into the night, with Hilda deploying every trick to induce confidences; during the day, Elizabeth was side-lined as the Fraulein provocatively monopolised Darcy.

'So, Miss Bennet.' Fraulein Edelmann pushed away a half-eaten slice of strudel. 'We are boring you, I think.'

'On the contrary, I have been listening with avid attention,' Elizabeth smiled. 'The cathedral holds no mysteries for me now. You have illuminated every inch.'

Hilda Edelmann snorted. 'Ha! The English humour. You say the opposite to what you believe.'

'Perhaps my mind did wander for a moment or two,' Elizabeth admitted. 'Still, your knowledge is impressive.'

'This is not my first visit. My father and I stayed several days while travelling down to Florence.' She paused. 'Are you interested in playing again?'

'You mean, in public?'

'Why not?' Fraulein Edelmann leaned forward. 'Near here is a building called the *Merkantilgebäude* or Mercantile Court. Merchants meet there to organise trade fairs and markets. They have a grand hall with room for a hundred seats. I gave an impromptu recital there last time, and we could organise another now.' She looked at Darcy. 'If you think it is safe.'

'I see no danger from Carandini,' Darcy said. 'But we should not delay our journey. War can be only months away, and we must try to reach England before it starts.'

'Have you a special reason for performing here?' Elizabeth asked.

Hilda rubbed thumb against forefinger in the Neapolitan gesture for money. 'Music is my livelihood, and the burghers will pay generously to hear a concert.'

Elizabeth frowned. 'I will try, if you wish; we owe you that much. But can you not find a better accompanist?'

'Not at such short notice. Anyway, you know the pieces, and I like performing with you. If the hall is free we could rehearse today and announce the recital for tomorrow.'

Elizabeth looked at Darcy. 'Can we stay an extra day?'

'A rest will restore our energies.' He paused. 'But Fraulein, if you are short of money, I can help.'

Elizabeth laughed. 'That cannot be true, at the rate you have been spending. Your credit must be almost exhausted.' She grinned at Hilda. 'I assume half of the receipts of this concert will come to me?'

Hilda straightened her back. 'Ten per cent, Miss Bennet, is the rate due an accompanist. In case you have forgotten, I have to work my passage to Salzburg.'

'A mere hop, compared with our journey.' Elizabeth addressed Darcy. 'Seriously, how much credit is left?'

He frowned, as if annoyed by her probing. 'Sufficient, I hope, provided we spend carefully.'

'You see, Fraulein? Mr Darcy and I are also pressed for cash, and deserve our share of the spoils.'

Hilda sighed, and Elizabeth was on the point of relenting when the singer said, with a sly grin: 'Very well, but as an amateur you cannot claim the full ten per cent. Five at most.'

Elizabeth snorted. 'As an amateur, I deserve a higher rate as compensation for the strain on my nerves. Twenty per cent.'

'I see. English humour again. Out of the question.'

'Very well, no concert.'

'I will find another accompanist, far more proficient than you.'

'In twenty-four hours? Go ahead.'

Fraulein Edelmann fluttered her eyelashes at Darcy. 'I beg you, sir, protect me from this woman. She is a monster.'

Darcy looked bewildered, as if unsure whether they were joking, or engaged in a genuine battle. 'Perhaps we should first ascertain whether the hall is available. If not, the division is immaterial.'

Fraulein Edelmann clapped her hands. 'I will go directly!' She pointed a finger at Elizabeth. 'Let it never be said that I am uncharitable to the needy. Fifteen per cent and not a *kreuzer* more.'

32

'So, Mr Darcy, the mountain air is fresh, no?'

Darcy suppressed a sigh, wearying of Fraulein Edelmann's continuous efforts to engage him in conversation.

'Invigorating.' He turned away to study the road, now veering away from the River Eisack, which they had followed since Bozen. They were climbing now, in a deep valley that rose steeply on the other side of the river, but flattened on their side to a forested plain.

He glanced at Elizabeth, who was dozing with a book open on her lap. There could be no doubt now of her recovery. She was stronger, her skin glowed, and best of all, her lively charm was once more in evidence. He pictured her in the Mercantile Court Hall taking on the challenge of another concert, with much the same outcome. She shone in the silk dress, now contrasting with her natural dark hair; her absorbed expression at the pianoforte was captivating; she played calmly, unflustered by the occasional slip. Nobody could upstage Fraulein Edelmann's wonderful voice, but paired together they were a feast for the eye as well as the ear, the vivacious Englishwoman in cream-gold a perfect foil for the tall blonde Austrian in light blue.

The applause, as before, had been enthusiastic, with two encores in addition to several demands for repeats—all graciously accepted. Moreover, to his relief, there had been no unpleasant sequel. As a precaution he had asked Bloch and Reithoffer to stand at the back of the hall and watch out for anyone behaving suspiciously. Fortunately they performed the duty discreetly and even enjoyed the recital.

'How far to Brixen?' Fraulein Edelmann asked.

'We can rest the horses at a village half an hour away. Brixen is one stage further on. We should be there by early evening.'

'It is a fine old town with a long cultural tradition.' She flashed him a smile. 'We could give another recital.'

'I would prefer not to lose another day.'

'Yes, I know, you must hasten to England.' She sighed, then suddenly brightened. 'But your tour has been so limited. Why not come to Salzburg with me, and thence to Vienna? It will be safer too. You can wait for the coalition armies to defeat Bonaparte and only then return home.'

Darcy glanced again at Elizabeth, who showed no sign of following the conversation. 'I would be delighted one day to visit Austria, especially Vienna. However …' He broke off as there was a cry from the driver, and Bloch rapped on the window.

'*Achtung! Räuberbande!*'

Fraulein Edelmann gasped. 'Take care! Brigands!'

As the carriage jerked to a halt, Darcy unwrapped the pistol he had kept in readiness at his side, and buckled on his sword.

'What is happening?' Elizabeth was awake, looking frantically out of the window. 'Was that a pistol shot?'

'Stay inside and keep your heads down.' Darcy opened the door and descended. The track was soft, with grassy verges and thick pine forest on both sides. Peering into the blackness of the trees, he saw no assailants. Ahead,

Bloch and Reithoffer rode towards a bend where the back of a carriage was just visible. Darcy exhaled with relief. *They* were not under attack. The Austrian guards had gone to the aid of another party.

He called up to the manservants. 'Burgess, you have your pistol? And a rifle? Help Gretchen inside, then stay here and guard the women. I will return shortly.'

Darcy's instincts were to remain behind as well, but with the guards outnumbered it was his duty to join the fray. He heard another exchange of pistol fire as one of the guards galloped at a band of four or five men. The brigands scattered, and two of them ran back in Darcy's direction. He kneeled, took aim, and felled one of them with a shot to the leg. The other ran alarmingly towards their own carriage, but veered off into the trees on receiving a fusillade from Burgess and the other manservant.

A scrabbling noise alerted him to the brigand he had shot, who was reaching for the butt of his rifle. Darcy kicked at the grasping hand, sending the rifle spinning off into the undergrowth, before drawing his sword. The brigand spread his arms submissively and stared back, revealing a scarred weather-beaten complexion and tangled beard. He was dressed to cut a dashing figure, with an embroidered vest over dark green tunic, blue breeches, boots, and a conical feathered hat which had rolled off as he fell.

Darcy removed a knife on the man's belt and threw it after the rifle. The brigand stayed down, grimacing as he explored a dark stain on his breeches, just above the knee. Looking down the road, Darcy acknowledged a thumbs-up from Burgess, then turned to see Reithoffer approaching, still mounted, with his sabre drawn.

'*Bravo! Gut gemacht!*' Reithoffer pointed at the injured brigand, then to the carriage that had been attacked. '*Ein.*

Zwei.'

'You got one as well?' Darcy asked in Italian.

'Ja.'

'Watch him.' He left the Austrian soldier on guard and ran back to their own carriage, where Elizabeth was leaning out of the window, talking to Burgess, while Fraulein Edelmann tended Gretchen.

'You are well?' Elizabeth cried.

'Fine. It was bandits robbing the coach in front. Two are down and the rest have fled. I must join the other party now, to make sure they are safe.'

33

Her heart still thudding, Elizabeth leaned out to watch as Darcy ran ahead. She noticed one of the Austrian guards trussing a prisoner. Further along, the other guard roped a brigand to the back of a coach. Darcy joined a fashion-ably-dressed gentleman who was helping servants repack scattered valuables in a trunk. He turned, waved to her, and ran back.

'Ladies, can you help? We have a Bavarian family here travelling to Munich with a driver and two servants. The bandits were searching their belongings when we inter-vened. Herr von Essen is clearing up, but his wife Anja and their children are in distress ...'

Fraulein Edelmann, busy bandaging Gretchen's leg, dismissed Elizabeth with a wave. 'Go. I will follow.'

Darcy helped her descend. 'What happened to the maid?'

'She landed awkwardly when getting down from the carriage, and twisted her ankle.'

'I told Burgess to help her down.'

'He tried, but she panicked and jumped before he was ready. Are the family hurt?'

'The mother took a scratch.' He opened the side of the coach and Elizabeth saw a small plump woman in a plain blue gown and cap studying her face in a hand-mirror, while two small children picked pieces of coral from the floor. The woman stared at her as if she were a ghost and spoke frantically in German.

Elizabeth took the seat opposite. '*Guten Tag.* Fraulein Bennet. Do you understand English?'

'*Englisch? Nein.*'

'*Italiano?*'

The woman nodded, and pointed to her neck. '*La collana …*'

In fragments the story emerged. A bandit had wanted Frau von Essen's necklace. She was unfastening the clasp when there was a cry that soldiers were approaching. The bandit had grabbed the necklace and tugged, snapping the cord and showering the coach with coral. She pointed to a line at her throat where the cord had rasped.

Elizabeth took her hand and examined the wound. 'It is grazed, but not deeply. There will be no scar. I have balm in my reticule which may ease the discomfort.'

She found a small tub containing a preparation made from lanolin and beeswax, and rubbed the pomade gently over the folds of Frau von Essen's throat.

'Better?'

'*Ja. Danke.*'

The effect might be negligible, but merely receiving treatment calmed the woman down. Elizabeth pointed to the children, who had been watching wide-eyed as she applied the cream. 'Are they well?'

It seemed to dawn on Frau von Essen that she had been fussing over a trivial injury while ignoring her possibly traumatised son and daughter. 'Markus. Erika. Both seven years old.'

'Twins!' Elizabeth ruffled the boy's hair. 'Look, you've collected all the pieces. The necklace will be good as new.'

Erika inched closer and showed her a wooden doll, ten inches long, with hair painted on the small head, and a tuck comb carved on the crown. As Elizabeth helped her thread the arms though the sleeves of an evening gown, she noticed that all the limbs were jointed.

'Erika, what a lovely doll!'

The girl showed no sign of understanding Italian, but Frau von Essen said, 'Not Erika's doll. A sample belonging to my husband.'

'He sells them?'

She nodded eagerly. 'Traditional *Grodner Tal* dolls from Bavaria. Wood, many sizes. We trade in Milan, and now return to Munich.'

Elizabeth smiled, imagining the bandits' confusion at encountering this unusual booty.

Two hours later, Elizabeth sat opposite Darcy as they left the small town of Klausen. Ahead, in the other carriage, Fraulein Edelmann had joined the von Essen family. The brigands had been left at a *Gendarmerie* in Klausen, and a surgeon sent for.

'What will happen to them?' Elizabeth asked.

Darcy shrugged. 'If their injuries are treated they will live to face trial. In Britain they would be hung or deported. Here I assume they will be hung—or guillotined if French penalties are still applied.'

Elizabeth nodded, appreciating that he had answered her query without prevarication. 'I was in such fear as you ran towards the bandits.'

'Luckily most of them dispersed as soon as Bloch and Reithoffer rode into them.'

'I suppose you had to shoot that man?'

'He was armed, and running in the direction of our carriage. If he had turned towards the forest I would have let him go.'

Elizabeth glanced at Gretchen, whom Fraulein Edelmann had left behind for chaperonage. The maid showed no sign of following the conversation. 'Much as I admire Hilda, it is a relief to be alone with you again.'

He smiled. 'Fraulein Edelmann has certainly been talkative these last days.'

'She obviously enjoys *your* company.'

'I wish she would desist, but have tried to be polite. After all, we owe our safety to her.'

'But it must be flattering to be cajoled by such a beautiful and talented woman. Only a general's daughter, of course, but we know how little you care about social rank. I am fully expecting you to abandon me and follow the lovely Hilda to Salzburg.'

He hesitated, as if longing to contradict her, but reluctant to submit to such overt manipulation. 'Jealousy does not become you.'

She looked down, flushing. 'I'm not jealous. I feel unworthy, that is all.'

He sighed. 'I meant what I said at the *Castelvecchio*.'

She raised her eyes, preferring to keep silence so that his words hung in the air. He was studying her eagerly, no doubt hoping for a similar assurance from her. He had spoken truly; *had she?*

Eventually, almost in tears, she said, 'I am so afraid.'

'Of what?'

'Of my feelings. Of making a terrible mistake.'

They both glanced at Gretchen, who was looking out of the window and apparently paying no attention. Darcy leaned forward, lowering his voice. 'Let us be clear. Are you implying that you too meant what you said?'

She looked away, unable to meet his eye, and said in a strangled whisper, 'Yes.'

He also looked away, and for a while they remained silent. She wondered whether he too was loathe to disturb the echo of her declaration. Certainly he had relaxed, and when he spoke, his voice had a deeper resonance.

'Elizabeth, if I may use your name, please let me know what it is that you fear. If we truly love one another, why may we not marry? Why do you fear a mistake?'

'Because I have never felt this way in my life. I understand now what it was that drove you, against all rationality, to propose in Kent.'

He managed a smile. 'Perhaps for both our sakes that conversation is best forgotten.'

'But do you not see?' She faced him more confidently, encouraged that they could talk openly. 'Yes, our manners left much to be desired, yet as we have both admitted, *almost everything we said was true.* Not about Wickham, but the rest. You *were* proud and sometimes inconsiderate when we first met in Hertfordshire. My family *is* a significant obstacle. If you erred, it was on the side of generosity, in supposing that Jane and I are so different from the others. The truth is that we were brought up by an unworldly over-lenient father and foolish mother, with not even a governess to teach us a modicum of good sense. Yes, I have learned to dance, play, and sing to a moderate standard, and to bluff my way in society by an impertinent brand of repartee that some people charitably mistake for wit. But at root I am like Kitty, Lydia and the others: superficial and silly. All this, I am convinced, you had already seen at the time. *In vain have I struggled. My feelings will not be repressed.* What were you struggling against? The rational conviction that I was not a suitable partner for a man in your position. You were blinded by love—and apparently still are, the only difference being that now I am blinded too.'

She was pleased that he thought for a while, absorbing her meaning rather than issuing an immediate rebuttal.

'So you are not concerned with the disparity in our connections? Rather, you fear we are ill-suited as companions. You think that once passion has faded, I will see you as you imagine yourself to be—superficial and the rest—and lose respect for you.'

She smiled affectionately. 'You say it far better than I did.'

'You are not daunted by the social and practical duties of becoming mistress of Pemberley?'

'Yes, but I believe I might carry them off by a mixture of improvisation and bluff, which have kept me afloat in the humbler waters of Hertfordshire.'

He returned her smile. 'So the problem, if it exists, lies between ourselves. In time, I will see you as you truly are, a superficially charming scatterbrain …'

She laughed. 'And I will you see you as a highfalutin snob. Which *you* truly are.'

'If we are both so bad, we deserve one another.'

'True, I hadn't thought of that.' She calmed down. 'Of course there are other factors. You would have to stomach the mortification of Wickham as a brother-in-law.'

He looked away with an anguished expression, as if recalling a distressing memory. 'I would prefer not to invite your sister to Pemberley, with or without her husband.'

'On that point I could not agree more.' She sighed. 'Am I fretting too much?'

'On the contrary, there is much in what you say. Love can indeed be blind, and marriage should be approached as the Book of Common Prayer demands: reverently, discreetly, advisedly, soberly …'

Elizabeth nodded, relaxing. 'We are of one mind, then. A lengthy trip to England awaits. We will take our time, and see what develops.'

34

May 1815

Darcy sat opposite Elizabeth at a coffee house, just a short walk from the Maximilian Hotel on the river Inn at Innsbruck. Fraulein Edelmann was away visiting a musician friend, Herr Doktor Straub, who was to accompany her at a recital that evening. They had said farewell to the von Essens, their companions on the trail through Brixen and Brenner. Now it was time for a parting of the ways: Fraulein Edelmann would travel east to Salzburg; the von Essens north to Munich; and he and Elizabeth would go west to Lake Constance, the source of the Rhine.

The day was warm. They sat outside under sun shades with a view of the Golden Roof, a construction of gilded copper tiles overhanging a balcony, ordered over 300 years before by Emperor Maximilian I, and now the city's most famous landmark. Elizabeth, looking rested after a night at the comfortable Maximilian, was enjoying strudel with coffee—very much the speciality of the house, and Darcy's choice as well.

'Such a fragrance.' She breathed deeply. 'It makes me question whether the coffee we drink at home is worthy of the name. You should hear Hilda on the subject.'

'Is that what you talk of during the night?'

She smiled. 'No, except as a supporting argument for her main theme: the superiority of Austria over all other countries. Pick any domain—art, music, literature, food, and Vienna is pre-eminent, with Salzburg a close runner-up. The Viennese coffee house is the apex of social refinement. Indeed, her *only* quarrel with Bonaparte is that he put coffee houses out of business by blocking the importation of beans from the British Isles. Otherwise, like many people we have met on our travels, she grudgingly admires him.'

'With some reason,' Darcy said. 'In many countries he has left behind better roads and a better system of law.'

She regarded him teasingly. 'You would not dare say that in England.'

'Do not mistake me; I believe Napoleon must be overthrown. But his story is in a sense a tragedy. A man who could have advanced European civilisation is destroyed by over-ambition and nepotism.'

'And blocking imports of coffee beans.'

He smiled, enjoying the miracle of a conversation with Elizabeth in which was no undercurrent of discord. 'Are you disappointed not to be playing tonight?'

She shook her head. 'It will be a pleasure to sit back and enjoy the performance. I want to hear how an expert plays the pieces I have learned.' She made a moue. 'Pity about the money.'

'Have you been paid for the others?'

'Not yet, but Hilda has kept records and will settle up tonight. I am to receive 24 ducats.'

'We can use every coin.'

'May I ask exactly how we are placed?'

'I wrote down a budget last night after consulting Herr von Essen, who has travelled extensively in the German Confederation. I can show you the figures later, but the outcome is that we have enough to reach Brussels if we travel by chaise to Lake Constance then by boat along the

Rhine.'

'And after Brussels?'

'I have written to my bank in London instructing them to send a further letter of credit, to await collection at the main Brussels post office. We can then hire a carriage and proceed in greater comfort to Ostend, where ferries leave for the Kent coast.'

'Still a long way from home.'

'With an early start we could reach Rosings by dusk.'

Elizabeth blinked, her eyes moist. 'And thence, Gracechurch Street, and Longbourn. But I fear Lady Catherine will not wish Rosings to be polluted by persons such as myself.'

'You could stay overnight with Mrs Collins.'

'Not if her ladyship disapproves.'

'Then let us go directly to London.'

She brightened. 'Let us do that.'

'So, our last night,' Fraulein Edelmann said.

Elizabeth sponged her arms as Gretchen helped Hilda out of the silk dress she had worn for the concert. 'Perhaps from tomorrow I'll be able to get some sleep at last.'

Ja?' Hilda drew herself up haughtily. 'And what is your problem? Do I snore?'

'You talk.'

'And what about you, English madam?'

Elizabeth smiled. In the privacy of their room, Fraulein Edelmann's normally dignified manner gave way to an impertinent banter that bordered on rudeness. 'I know, I talk too. I never said it was your fault.'

'So you are fussing over nothing. As usual.' Hilda gave instructions in German to the maid, who curtseyed and left.

Elizabeth carried a candle to her bedside table as Hilda

climbed in the other side. 'Do you want to read?'

'Blow it out. My mind is buzzing from the recital.'

'I loved the new piece from *Don Giovanni*.'

'*Or sai chi l'onore*. It means, now you know who stole my honour.'

'Where is *stole*?'

'Next line. The sentence is shuffled to fit the rhyme.'

'I see why you didn't include it before. The piano part was too fast for my fingers.'

'The aria isn't suitable for me either. It needs a stronger voice.' Hilda hesitated. 'I hope you were not upset that Herr Straub took over as accompanist.'

Elizabeth sat up a little, shaking her head. 'It was instructive. I could play them better now.'

'Of course he is more accomplished, but I have liked performing with you. You listen, and adapt to what I am doing. I shall miss you.' She lowered her voice to a whisper. 'Both of you.'

'You mean, Elizabeth Bennet and Rebecca Ashley?'

'No, idiot. I mean your Mr Darcy.'

Elizabeth fell silent, wondering what lay behind this declaration. 'Why do you say *my* Mr Darcy?'

'Because I am not blind.'

'I have been wondering …' She turned to face Hilda. 'You have been very attentive to Mr Darcy, since Verona.'

'You think I am your rival?' She waved a hand. 'Allow me to reassure you. Mr Darcy is an intelligent man. I talk with him because I like intelligent conversation.'

'Which apparently you cannot get from me.'

Hilda strangled a laugh. 'You said it, *liebchen*.'

'You must have admirers among your musical friends. Herr Schubert for instance.'

'Oh, nonsense,' Hilda snapped. She turned away, as if offended, then continued reflectively, 'One point I would grant you, and it is this. I don't expect the gentlemen to fall at my feet, but I do like to be *noticed*. I am young, I can sing, I can afford elegant dresses—why should they *not* notice me? It disturbed me, when we first met, that Mr Darcy had eyes only for you. It occurred to me later that he might be making a special effort, since you were passing yourselves off as a married couple. After Verona, having at last learned your identity, I did my best to gain his attention. He enjoyed my singing, I believe, and also our conversations—but there his interest ended. It is you that he has always wanted. In your company he comes alive, as do you, in his.' She sighed. 'There is no accounting for tastes. Who in his right mind could overlook a gifted Austrian mezzo-soprano in favour of an Englishwoman who plays wrong notes?'

Elizabeth snorted. 'Spare us the crocodile tears. You never sought Mr Darcy's affections. You wanted only to tease me. As for *that gentleman* and myself, it is true that we have become somewhat, ah, *closer* these last days.'

'You have always been close.'

'If so, I could not bring myself to acknowledge it.' Elizabeth spread her arms. 'I feel so—unworthy.'

'It's not a feeling, it's a fact.' Hilda dived under the covers with a cackle. 'You *are* unworthy.'

'Most amusing.' Elizabeth aimed a punch at the hump under the bedclothes. 'Anyway, why quarrel over a mere gentleman? Have you no sisterly instincts? Surely it is the *gentlemen* who are unworthy of *us*.'

Hilda peeped out. 'Even a paragon like Mr Darcy?'

Elizabeth fell back against her pillow. 'To be honest, he *is* daunting. Massive estate. £10000 pounds a year. House in town. And his family! Lady this, Earl that. Even his sister is known for her exquisite performance on the piano.'

'Better than you?'

'Undoubtedly.'

'Have you heard her play?'

Elizabeth sighed. 'We have never met.'

'Then how do you know?' Hilda sat up and faced her. 'You've improved a lot during our rehearsals. You probably learned even more from the obsessive Carandini.'

Elizabeth yawned, feeling suddenly exhausted. 'All this is conjecture anyway. I'm not sure I *ought* to marry Mr Darcy, even assuming he still wants me by the time we get home.'

'It will work out. You will see.'

Elizabeth said goodnight and rolled onto her side, but it was a long time before sleep came.

35

They were travelling west at last, through the Fernpass, a route named *Via Claudia Augusta* after its Roman founder, the Emperor Claudius. In deference to his budget, Darcy had opted for the stagecoach rather than hiring a chaise. They had set off early with two horses, then two more were added for the climb to Lake Blindsee. Other travellers joined, all seemingly local; except for nods and bows there was no communication. Fraulein Edelmann would be on her way to her beloved Salzburg; the von Essens, to Munich. Except for Burgess, now perched on the roof, he was alone with Elizabeth.

They rounded a corner and Elizabeth, who was facing forward, pointed out of the window.

'Is it not wondrous?'

Darcy leaned over and saw an expanse of gleaming water far beneath them, much of it hidden by precipitous slopes forested with pine. He looked back at Elizabeth's excited face, and felt for a moment completely happy.

'Never have I seen a deeper blue.'

'Turquoise too, in the shallows. Is it Lake Brindsee?'

'It should be. We have been travelling four hours.'

She pointed into the distance. 'Snow on the peaks.'

'There are high mountains hereabouts. Some I believe have never been scaled.'

'To think that Roman legions once passed.'

He smiled. 'Not long ago so did Napoleon, on his way to conquering Italy.'

She sniffed. 'No doubt the innkeepers sing his praises for improvements to the road.'

'We will find out soon enough: there is a retreat overlooking the lake.'

While the horses were changed for the stage to Reutte, where they would seek rooms for the night, Darcy accompanied Elizabeth into the hostel, where a dozen local travellers were lunching. They surveyed the fare, which consisted mostly of sausage meat and potatoes swimming in grease, and Elizabeth winced.

'I would rather go hungry.'

'We have an hour.' Darcy turned, looking for Burgess. 'If you are agreeable, Miss Bennet, I believe we have ingredients for a picnic.'

They found a bench, on pastureland a few yards from the road, and Burgess opened a small hamper and drew out rolls, cheese, and fruit from the Innsbruck market, and a half-bottle of Tyrolese Riesling wine. The air at this elevation was cool and scented with pine; the meadow was lush and filled with flowers both familiar and strange. He noticed buttercups and forget-me-nots, and clumps of a thin blue-purple plant which Elizabeth identified as Alpine Honeysuckle. Beneath them, the meadow fell sharply to the lake; beyond was a series of sharp peaks, lined up in a row like teeth.

'Heavenly.' Elizabeth bit into a cheese roll. 'How clever of you to bring provisions.'

'Thank Burgess.' Darcy glanced round at the servant, now returning to the hostel in pursuit of sausage and ale.

Alone now, they ate in silence before he continued:

'Are you comfortable travelling with no maid or companion?'

'What else can we do? The priority is to cross the continent before war starts, or we run out of money.'

'I'm sorry to leave you in this situation.'

She touched his arm. 'Do not worry on my account. In truth, I am grateful for the opportunity to talk alone.'

He nodded. 'Of course we will usually remain in the company of strangers. I wonder what they make of us.'

'They probably believe us married.'

'What if our fellow-travellers speak English? We need to decide what account to give of ourselves.'

She smiled, as if at a pleasurable memory. 'We could pass again as Mr and Mrs Ashley.'

'I gave Commander Graf my word of honour.'

She smiled. 'Of course your honour must be preserved at all costs.'

'I wonder …' He paused, afraid of going too far. 'If pressed, we might say we were engaged.'

To his relief, she laughed, taking his suggestion lightly. 'Remember, I have not agreed to marry you.'

'I know. I am the last man in the world …'

She buried her face in her hands. 'Am I to be tormented by that blunder until the end of my days?'

'Believe me, the torment was mutual.'

She met his eye, suddenly serious. 'I suppose it must have been. And yet, when I look back, I am embarrassed mostly by my own folly, not by the pain I caused. Is that not curious? We blurt words out unthinkingly, unaware of their power.'

'I made a similar mistake when Charles pressed me to dance with you at the Meryton ball.'

She laughed. 'Only *tolerable!* I shan't allow you to forget that in a hurry.'

He sighed. 'Can we please leave the past alone and return to the topic? I appreciate that we cannot truly be engaged. For one thing, you prefer to wait; for another, we are not in a position to ask your father's consent. However, if our relationship is questioned, it might be simpler to bend the truth a little.'

She thought for a moment, then nodded. 'I think that would be justified, among people that we will never meet again.'

They fell silent, and Darcy breathed deeply as his eyes explored the play of light and shade across the peaks. He took a corkscrew and two cut-glass tumblers from the hamper, opened the Riesling, and offered a glass to Elizabeth.

'What is the toast?' she smiled.

'To the people back home.'

She clinked glasses. 'Yes, may we see them soon. And yet ...' She faced him. 'Despite all that has happened, I am happy. To be here, in this majestic place, and to be with you.'

Overwhelmed, he scarcely dared reply.

36

Two weeks later

A bump woke her. Her bunk rocked from side to side as the boat settled. Outside it was light, and men were shouting in German. Elizabeth sat up and surveyed the cabin. It was small, no more than ten feet by six, but cleverly appointed, with the bunk facing a narrow wardrobe and wicker divan, a locker overhead, and a dresser with a marble bowl and tap. Darcy had pressed her to accept a luxury cabin, but she had declined, realising that money was tight. Their trunks were below in steerage, where Burgess would have laid his pallet.

They had joined the *Sankt Goar* at Basel, after bypassing the turbulent stretch of the Rhine at Lake Constance and taking the main stagecoach route via Zurich. From Basel the Rhine was calmer, and riverboats drifted with the current across Germany and the Netherlands to Rotterdam, assisted when necessary by oars or sail. The boat had ten cabins laid out in two rows, each ending in a narrow staircase leading to the upper deck, where meals were served in an enclosed lounge.

Excited, Elizabeth dressed quickly and followed a central corridor to the front deck. It was an overcast morning which might turn to rain, and they were docked beside a row of warehouses to take on provisions. On the upper deck people were already breakfasting, and she spotted

Darcy seated at the back reading a newspaper.

She joined him, acknowledging stiff bows from two men in military uniform at the next table. 'Good morning. Where are we?'

'Strasbourg.' He handed her the newspaper. 'Can you make sense of this?'

She glanced at the headline, understanding only the word *Napoleon*, and put the paper aside. 'I know three German words, and I answer with one of them. *Nein.*'

'I've been trying to fathom it this last half-hour, with help from the gentlemen on my left. It seems a *timetable* has been drawn up. Armies are assembling like chessmen laid out on a board. French troops are stationed at the borders, awaiting an invasion.' He pointed towards the dock. 'The French *Armée du Rhin* is quartered just a few miles west of here. On the opposite bank we will soon pass the Austrian and Bavarian forces. Their numbers grow daily and may rise to 100,000 men.'

Elizabeth accepted coffee, and a basket of bread and pastries, marvelling that these refinements of civilisation continued as they navigated the ribbon of territory separating the armies. 'You must guide me, Mr Darcy, for I understand little of war. Should we not be alarmed?'

He smiled, taking a refill of coffee. 'No, because as I mentioned before, *there is a timetable*. First the forces assemble, then they wait patiently until the date for hostilities to begin. And that will be roughly two months from now, in July. By which time …' He looked up to meet her eye. 'We will be safely home.'

She smiled back, warmed by his optimism. 'We still have to reach Brussels, remember, which is only 50 miles from the French border.'

He nodded. 'True, but there too fortune should favour us. British forces are assembling in that very area, ready to invade France from the north. We will travel under the protection of our own army.'

She breathed deeply, allowing herself to hope. In just a month they might be home.

They were moving again, past streets with inns and shops where Bavarian infantry in blue coats and white breeches mingled with the locals.

Elizabeth turned back to Darcy. 'Tell me something about yourself. Your family, for instance.'

'You have met the principals, except for my sister.'

'But the history.' She reddened, recalling that his parents, unlike hers, had both passed away. 'If the memory is not painful.'

He smiled. 'I should have expected this. Before accepting my hand, you demand to check my credentials.' He thought for a few seconds. 'It is really a story of three families, the Fitzwilliams, the Darcys, and the de Bourghs. The old Earl Fitzwilliam had two daughters, Anne and Catherine, and a son who is the current Earl. Their estate is at Matlock, near the Peaks. My mother Lady Anne was shy as a girl, but her beauty and sweet nature drew many admirers in her first season, amongst them Mr Darcy of Pemberley. Lady Catherine, as you can imagine, was neither shy nor sweet-natured, but her determination produced a similar outcome, and before long she too found a husband. Last to marry was my uncle, who has two sons: the future earl, and Colonel Fitzwilliam.' He spread his arms. 'The result is that I spend much time in transit between four places: Pemberley, of course; my house in town; Rosings; and Matlock.'

'And your childhood?'

'Idyllic, when I was a small boy. But sadness intruded with the death of my brother from sour throat, and two other siblings stillborn. Physicians advised that my mother was too weak to tolerate another confinement, but she wished to try, and to our delight Georgiana was born. But happiness was short-lived, for soon afterwards my mother's health faded, while I was sent away to school.'

Elizabeth extended her hand towards his. 'How cruel to leave home at such a time.'

'It was usual. Expected.'

'Which school?'

'Harrow.' He looked away, as if in recollection. 'Not a long journey from our house in town. I arrived in 1798, two years before a boy named Robert Peel, of whom you may have heard.'

'Was it through your misbehaviour that he perceived the need for a professional constabulary?'

'By no means, madam. But the school was undeniably rough in those days. Fighting, swearing and drinking were rampant, even among the aspiring Dukes and Earls in the headmaster's house. In fact their behaviour was worse than ours.' He smiled. 'Byron was a case in point.'

She gasped. 'You knew the poet?'

'He was two years below me, but what an impression he made! Such a dishevelled trouble-maker, and a club foot to boot, yet he soon had a loyal following.'

She shook her head, overwhelmed by the disparity between the rich variety of his experience and the poverty of hers. 'So what did you *do* there?'

'In the morning, lessons. Latin. Greek. History. Some mathematics. Construing. Writing verse.'

'Science? Religion?'

'Very little of either. Which was strange, since almost all the teachers had taken holy orders. We attended the parish church on Sundays, but there was no insistence on piety, and many boys merely gossiped.'

'And after lessons?'

'Sport was popular. Swimming, fencing, boxing, skating in the winter. Older boys raced horses, or went rat-catching with ferrets. Many fished or shot.'

'Were you happy there? Did you make friends?'

He considered. 'It was austere and traditional, and for many a preparation for the army. But with such a variety of companions, I did find some who were congenial.'

'How were you regarded?'

'Oh, as a sobersides, since I studied diligently and took no part in gambling and drinking. Luckily I was tall and strongly built, so the bullies learned early on to leave me alone.'

She regarded him teasingly. 'No wonder those bandits ran away. Shall we take a turn on the deck?'

They descended and walked round to the bow, still talking.

37

By mid-afternoon a continuous drizzle was falling, almost obscuring the outskirts of Karlsruhe. After lunch Elizabeth had retired to her cabin to rest, leaving Darcy at a loose end. He had struggled through a polite conversation with one of the officers, who appeared interested only in lauding the Bavarian infantry and abusing the French. A beaker of mulled wine raised his spirits momentarily, but he had no wish to dull his brain by over-indulging, especially in the company of Elizabeth. He opened one of the few books he had brought from England, Robert Owen's *A New View of Society*.

The author was a mill owner who had bought land in Lanarkshire, not far from Glasgow, and used it to carry out what was in effect a social experiment, demonstrating that a mill could be run to the benefit of its workers as well as its owners. His ideas were challenged by his partners, who believed that welfare reforms cost money that might have been better diverted to their own pockets; but instead of giving way Owen bought them out, found new partners, and continued as before. Interspersed with this narrative were philosophical claims about human nature: for instance, that character was not inborn, but shaped by experience.

He heard footsteps, and Elizabeth joined him.

'Aha.' She pointed to the wine glass. 'As soon as my

back is turned you return to your cups.'

'You think I behave myself only in your presence?'

She waved this away. 'I am talking gammon as usual. Good wine?'

'Mulled with cinnamon and sugar. Warming on such a dreary day.'

'I will order coffee to clear my head.' She pointed to the book. 'Don't stop on my account.'

'Have you anything to read?'

'All my books were left behind in Venice.'

'I have a recent novel by Sir Walter Scott, if you are interested in the Jacobite rebellion. *Waverley.*'

She shook her head. 'Thank you for your kind offer, but after weeks viewing soldiers on the march I am weary of such pursuits. Have you nothing more suited to my feminine sensibilities? Fanny Burney?'

'I admire Mrs Burney and bought her latest novel, but left it at my town house for Georgiana's benefit.'

'What you are reading now?'

He held up the book, and she nodded immediately. 'My father showed me a review in a literary magazine. It caused quite a stir.' She smiled affectionately. 'One thing I like about you is that your tastes are so wide-ranging. I can never be sure what you will think about anything.'

'Many would consider that a reason to mistrust me.'

'To me it is a delight. But of course that is because I have such faith in your dependability. I could scarcely feel any other way, given all you have done for my family.'

He looked away, gratified but embarrassed. 'Some compensation for my addiction to the grape?'

She looked round to order coffee from a waiter. 'Do you think well of the author?'

He duplicated her order. 'I would have to confess a general prejudice against men of his kind. Owen is, after all, a factory owner, a breed normally concerned only in accumulating vast wealth so that they can afford country estates and the other trappings of rank.'

'Indeed?' She squared up to him, her eyes glinting with challenge. 'They might retort that they seek through effort that which you have obtained merely through birth.'

'True, but there is a difference. Having been raised as a gentleman, I have been taught to exercise responsibilities as well as privileges. I see my relationship with my tenants as a trade, to our mutual benefit. In return for their work, I not only pay them fairly but do my best to protect them, especially when they fall on hard times. This cannot be said of most factory owners. They desire the rewards, but offer nothing but a pittance in return. Children are forced to work long hours. Men too sick to work are discarded, and their families left to starve.'

She frowned, reluctant to concede the point. 'I suspect you are painting with too broad a brush. I can believe that Pemberley is a well-run estate where the poor are treated charitably. This cannot be said for all estates; nor is it plausible that *all* factory-owners are as voracious as you claim.'

'Most are.' He waved this aside. 'But not Robert Owen. He has provided good housing for his mill workers, and schools for their children. They work fewer hours, leaving time for rest and diversion; as a result they are healthier, and perform their duties more efficiently.'

She looked out of the window as a column of soldiers came into view. 'Reminiscent of Thomas More's *Utopia*.'

He gaped, not for the first time amazed by her pockets of eclectic learning. 'I cannot wait to show you the library at Pemberley.'

She smiled. 'Aha. An added inducement.'

'I must play all the cards in my hand.'

'I see your ruse, Mr Darcy. You hope to mould me into your paradigm of the *accomplished woman*. My poor little mind is to be improved by *extensive reading*.'

He pushed the book across the table. 'Why not begin with this? I need to stretch my legs.'

He finished his coffee and left her to read alone.

38

Elizabeth explored the stationery section of a bookshop near the *Paradeplatz* in Mannheim. Having spent much of the previous afternoon with *A New View of Society*, and even tried some chapters of *Waverley*, she had decided to forgo Darcy's book collection and dedicate herself instead to writing. In retrospect, she wondered why this idea had not occurred to her before. Yes, she had described some of the people and places encountered during her travels, but only in letters to Jane—which might, for all she knew, go astray. How much better to keep a journal.

They had docked at Mannheim that morning to change boat, from the *Sankt Goar* to the *Eisvogel*, which would take them along the so-called 'heroic' Rhine to the city of Bonn. Since the *Eisvogel* would depart in the afternoon, they had left Burgess to supervise the change-over, and taken the opportunity to pass some time on dry land. The old part of the city, set in the triangle between the Rhine and the river Necker, could be reached by a five-minute walk across wooded parkland. They had proceeded first to a money-changer, where she had handed over two of her precious ducats for a bag of silver *thaler*, and thence to the post office. The cobbled streets were laid out in a regular grid, framing residential blocks and grand open squares; before long they had reached the fashionable shops and restaurants of the *Paradeplatz*.

Darcy arrived at her side carrying maps of their route through the German states and Kingdom of the Netherlands. 'These may help. No recent books in English, unfortunately. Have you had better luck?'

She showed him a leather-bound notebook, octavo size, with fine-quality paper watermarked with the manufacturer and year. 'It's an indulgence, but I would like this one. Light, portable, yet robust enough to withstand the journey.'

'I spotted a coffee house across the square where we can sit outside.'

She smiled, warmed to see him in such good spirits.

'You wrote to Georgiana?' she asked.

Darcy stirred sugar into his coffee. 'Yes, in London, although I cannot be sure she is still there. I hoped she would remain with Colonel Fitzwilliam, but with the war restarting he will almost certainly be called away. I should have news when we reach Brussels.' He regarded her anxiously. 'Did you remember ...'

She raised her eyes as if seeking divine help. 'Yes! I gave specific instructions, just as you advised, and have more faith in Jane than you obviously have in me.'

'I only hope our letters get through.'

'Some must.' Elizabeth looked away across the square, wondering when her family would receive the letters dispatched from Innsbruck and Basel. 'At least we know for sure that they have been *posted*. Not misappropriated by Signor Carandini.'

They watched as two elegant women strode past carrying parasols and arguing in shrill voices. Darcy smiled, and said gently, 'You were going to tell me more of your childhood.'

'You have the essence already,' Elizabeth said. 'Three

families, Bennet, Gardiner, Phillips, that have bestridden our nation's history like a colossus. Plus Collins, but I did not encounter that branch until later.'

'I was wondering what happened after Lydia put a frog in the piano stool.'

'Oh, Mary opened it, you know, to take out some music books, and was not amused at all.'

'Did she scream?'

'No. She replaced the frog in the garden and lectured Lydia on kindness to dumb animals.' Elizabeth sighed. 'I wish I could paint a more laudable picture, Mr Darcy, but in truth we were then what we are now: five very silly and indulged young ladies.'

He smiled. 'Your wiles do not deceive me, Elizabeth. You exaggerate your family's eccentricities so as to deter me from marrying you.'

'I merely seek to give you a fair chance.'

'You will not change my feelings.'

She waved this away. 'Tell me of your career at Cambridge. I have always wondered what it was like to attend a university.'

He sipped coffee, thinking. 'At first it seemed like a continuation of school by other means.'

'To paraphrase Clausewitz.'

'Ah, so now you change tactics and try to scare me off by a daunting display of learning.'

'Keep to the point, sir.'

'The point? Oh, university. Yes, at St John's College, as in Harrow, our day comprised a long morning of study, then exercise, then dinner at four o'clock. Evenings were usually passed in local taverns, drinking, gambling, and debating. Late suppers were popular. Boar's head, ham and game pie, a bowl of punch to share.'

'Did you study the same subjects?'

'Yes, except that divinity was included. In fact, that was the most striking difference. At Harrow, religion was marginal; at Cambridge most graduates took holy orders. Only Anglicans were allowed to study for a degree. When I applied to St John's, I had to pass a test of religious orthodoxy, which so far as I know is still required.'

'Such piety hardly accords with the merry debauchery that you were describing earlier. I mean, the drinking and gambling.'

He sighed. 'Indeed, and matters were often far worse. Drunken undergraduates would roam the streets after the taverns closed, getting into fights with the townspeople, and disrespecting women.'

'*Disrespecting women.*' She laughed. 'I wonder what that means.'

'I leave it to your imagination.'

'I assume the upright young Darcy abstained from these deplorable activities?'

'Yes.' He fell silent, looking far into the distance. 'But more than once I was obliged to clear up after the misadventures of others. Who should be nameless.'

'Not Byron again?'

'No, he arrived later and was a Trinity man.'

'Who then?'

He hesitated. 'A gentleman with whom you are, unfortunately, already acquainted.'

She stared at him, open-mouthed. Surely not Colonel Fitzwilliam? Or Mr Collins? Amused at the thought of the obsequious clergyman having a misspent youth, she stifled her laugh as the truth dawned.

'Mr Wickham?' she whispered.

'The same.'

'Oh.' She waited in case he wished to elaborate, but his lips remained pressed together.

Eventually she continued: 'No wonder you were so angry when I foolishly defended him.'

'Not your fault.' He lowered his voice. 'I had another reason, even more compelling.'

Again she waited. 'May I ask ...'

'I explained in my letter.'

She coloured. 'The one I refused to read?'

He nodded. 'It concerns Georgiana.'

She froze, and listened in horror as he unfolded the story of Wickham's attempted elopement.

Instinctively she covered his hand with hers. 'Please rest assured that I will mention this to no-one. Not Jane, and of course not your sister should we ever meet.'

As they walked back to the dock, she was struck by an awful thought. She had always seen Wickham's marriage to Lydia as an impediment: for how could Darcy tolerate such an in-law? But now she understood that the situation was far worse. *Georgiana's feelings had to be considered too.* That her trusted and revered brother should become the brother-in-law of the very man who had treated her so ill! Such a betrayal would be unbearable. Unthinkable. In his right mind, Darcy would never contemplate it ...

She uncoupled her arm, and stared at the ground ahead, evading his eye. Her sympathy was now replaced by anger. *Why had he not told her before?* Why allow her to dream of a union that could never be?

39

Darcy paced the deck of the *Eisvogel*, too agitated to sit in the lounge cabin and read. They were approaching Koblenz, and the scenery was spectacular, with hills on the right and a gorge on the left. He had never seen such a concentration of castles, many of them dating from medieval times and elaborated over the centuries. In the distance he saw the outline of what must be Rheinstein Castle, which according to his map had been built in 1316 and was now a ruin. In the late afternoon sun, a more romantic spectacle could hardly be imagined—yet romance appeared far from Elizabeth's mind. After a silent breakfast she had pleaded tiredness and shut herself away in her cabin.

On reflection, he traced her sullen mood to the walk back from the Mannheim *Paradeplatz*, where he had spoken of his university years, and disclosed Wickham's attempt to elope with Georgiana. Had he upset Elizabeth by reminding her of Lydia's indiscretion? There was no way of knowing: he had never had much success in understanding her thinking, or predicting her reactions.

Weary of the uncertainty, he passed along the central corridor and tapped on her door.

'One moment.' After some frantic activity within, she appeared in the doorway. 'Oh. I expected a servant. What do you want?'

He flinched at her unyielding tone. 'To make sure you are well, and to invite you to view a castle against the setting sun.'

She made as if to close the door. 'I am busy.'

Gently he asked, 'Elizabeth, what is the matter?'

'I'm not sure you should make free with my name.'

He stared at her. 'We agreed to behave as if …'

'Yes, yes.' She exhaled irritably. 'But that was before.'

'Before what?'

'Surely that is obvious.'

'I am not a mind-reader, Miss Bennet.' He retreated a step, losing patience with her. 'However, my senses are sufficiently acute to tell when I am not wanted. Good day madam.'

He bowed, and was halfway along the corridor when she called after him, 'Wait! I will come.'

He turned, gratified to have won this little battle—whatever it was. Elizabeth emerged, buttoning a spencer jacket.

'Good idea. The air cools in the evening.'

'I should apologise.' She came to join him. 'I believe I have reason to be upset, but that is no excuse for rudeness. If I was rude.'

He said nothing, and she stamped her foot. 'Well?'

'Were you rude? Yes.'

She glared at him. 'Whatever happened to gallantry?'

'With people I respect, I prefer honesty.'

'A back-handed compliment, but I will be grateful for small mercies. Shall we see this splendid vista before the sun goes down?'

Elizabeth stood close beside him, the wind flapping the ribbons of her bonnet. 'You are right, as usual. A beautiful sight. Why so many castles here?'

'I assume the older ones were built for military purposes in locations that afford a long view while being difficult to attack. More recently, princes added parodies of the old castles as symbols of their stature.'

'Thank you for dragging me from my cabin. It would be folly to miss this.'

He looked down, and was surprised to see her eyes moist. 'My dear Miss Bennet ...'

'You can say *Elizabeth*. I was in a sulk.'

He hazarded a smile. 'I would like to ask why, but it seems this is forbidden by the rules. I have to guess.'

She smiled back. 'In which case, making allowance for your limited powers of discernment, I will explain. I am upset because I want to marry you more than I have ever wanted anything, and now discover that you have courted me these last weeks in full knowledge that a union between us is impossible.'

He stared at her. 'Impossible? What do you mean?'

She threw up her hands. 'Is it not obvious?'

'Not to me.' He lowered his voice, afraid that their exchange would attract notice. 'I beg you, Elizabeth. Place no more reliance on thought transference. Just tell me.'

She leaned across and whispered, 'Because of your sister. Imagine! After all that she has endured, to learn of your intention to marry *Mr Wickham's sister-in-law.*'

He hesitated, wondering how this point had escaped him. Eventually he replied, 'It is certainly an announcement that would have to be presented with delicacy.'

'You mean, one that should never be made at all.'

He looked away at the sky, now deep red behind the silhouette of the castle. After a long silence, he replied:

'Let us think about it. I understand your concern, but perhaps the impediment is less troubling than you fear. I do try to protect my sister, but one cannot insulate people entirely from life's travails. An embarrassment that might be only temporary should not override the desire of two people to spend their lives together.'

To his relief, Elizabeth received this thoughtfully, rather than launching an immediate rebuttal.

'Agreed,' she said slowly. She slapped the rail, as if in irritable exhaustion. 'Why is life always so difficult?'

'I believe it's called the human condition.'

She sighed. 'If only Mr Wickham and his kind could be erased from the surface of the earth.'

'Do you really believe that?'

'Yes.' She took a deep breath. 'All right, no. Anyway, such interventions are beyond my power, so it makes no difference what I believe.'

'Remember, we cannot be sure that there is any problem at all. Perhaps there is, but we are only guessing. We can discuss how the situation should be presented to my sister, see how she reacts, then think again.'

Elizabeth shivered, and wrapped her arms around her jacket. 'I haven't eaten since breakfast.'

'I assumed you had taken luncheon in your room.'

She shook her head. 'I was confiding my anxieties to the new journal.'

'Then let us dine, and talk of other things.'

She took his arm as the boat rocked in the wind, and he guided her to the steps leading to the upper deck.

40

June 1815

After a week of maddeningly slow progress, including a two-day wait in Koblenz for a gale to pass, they had disembarked finally at Cologne. The landscape was now flat, and suitable for fast transit by road—if one could find a carriage. They had taken rooms at a hotel, and with the help of the manager booked places on a stagecoach heading to Brussels via Aachen and Liège. The carriage was shared with a Prussian officer, Kapitaan von Staufen, and his wife Mathilde, travelling further south to Ligny where the captain was joining his brigade.

They set off in the late morning on the leg to Düren. The day was overcast, but fortunately for Burgess, who sat outside with two drivers and Frau von Staufen's maid, the rain held off, and there was little wind. Elizabeth, exhausted after an uncomfortable night, dozed while Darcy made conversation with the captain. To follow von Staufen's laboured English closely was beyond her powers of concentration, but the essence was reassuring. The *timetable* of which Darcy had spoken was still in operation. Coalition forces were building up around France in preparation for an invasion in July—by which time, all going well, she and Darcy would be across the channel and restored to their homes and families.

Elizabeth had been surprised at first to see the captain

accompanied by his wife. He was a genial man in his mid-forties, with a round face and strong-looking body running to fat. Frau von Straufen was of similar age and build, but displayed a more determined countenance and was perhaps the driving force in the partnership. When Darcy tactfully asked whether it was safe for *Elizabeth* to travel so near to the French border, he was told in no uncertain terms that it was *perfectly* safe, and normal practice, for the wives of officers to join their husbands at the front. In the event of an attack, wives and servants would retreat northwards, ready to tend to their husbands after the battle and accompany them on the journey home.

After the first stop at a hostelry, von Staufen produced a flask of brandy and poured a tot for his wife, followed by a larger ration for himself. Frau von Straufen explained to Elizabeth that the liquor was *medicinal*, and would keep them warm on a chilly day. Hospitably the flask was offered to Darcy, but he, like Elizabeth, politely declined. Frau von Straufen commented that cognac was particularly efficacious as a remedy for hangover. Ten minutes later, both the captain and his wife were asleep, and Elizabeth felt able to speak freely.

'Did they ask about us?' she whispered.

He shook his head. 'Only where we were bound.'

'Where is Ligny?'

'Near the border. They will change coaches at Liège.'

'How fortunate the captain speaks English. Do you think his information is reliable?'

'It confirms what the newspapers have been saying. British and Prussian troops are assembled below Brussels, waiting for the other coalition forces to arrive on France's eastern and southern borders. Until mobilisation is complete, there will be no invasion.'

'The captain would hardly bring his wife to Ligny if it

were unsafe.'

'Indeed.'

They relaxed, and talked of other things.

'I have been puzzling over the first essay in *A New View of Society*.' Elizabeth said. 'Owen says that in principle one could order society so that people had *any* desired character. We are thus virtuous, or ignorant, or venal, in consequence of our *training*.'

Darcy nodded. 'It is a striking claim.'

'And surely false. Take any family—my own for example. My sisters Mary and Lydia grew up in very similar circumstances, yet their characters are opposite.'

'At least some attributes must depend on how an individual is treated. You can make a child ignorant by withholding teaching. A puppy beaten by a cruel master is more likely to bite.'

Elizabeth smiled. 'I overheard once an argument between my father and the Vicar of Meryton. It seems that as Anglicans, we believe that every person inherits a *disposition for evil* which stems from Adam's disobedience in the Garden of Eden. My father claimed this was poppycock, since a baby knows nothing of Adam and Eve and therefore cannot be influenced by their supposed misdeed.'

Darcy raised his eyebrows. 'How did the vicar reply?'

'He turned purple and said in a roundabout way that a small child may experience temptation without being able to articulate the cause. I think my father was winding him up for amusement.'

Darcy looked out of the window at flat fields planted with wheat. 'Still, I see some merit in the idea that we are born with desires that must be curbed through training. We are greedy; we try to get our own way without considering others.'

'But if our church is correct, training is not enough. We must be saved from damnation through baptism and instruction in the true faith.' She grinned. 'Which is unfortunate for children reared by heathens.'

'None of this contradicts Robert Owen,' Darcy said. 'He says that circumstances shape character. Baptism and religious instruction are merely examples of such circumstances.'

'I imagine a baby.' Suddenly serious, Elizabeth met his eye, and continued in a whisper. 'Ours. A boy, let us say. The heir to Pemberley. We see him in his cradle, gurgling, his arms reaching although there is nothing to grasp, his features midway between yours and mine. Must we really see him as a bundle of sinful urges that can be curtailed only through baptism into a particular creed?'

Darcy blinked, moved by the image. 'I doubt I would see him in that way.'

'Yet that is what we are enjoined to do.'

'I would not take the dogmas so seriously, Elizabeth. These are traditional ceremonies that can be interpreted in a variety of ways.'

She tilted her head, challenging him. 'And how do you interpret them?'

He glanced at the von Staufens, who were still sleeping off their earlier indulgences. 'I accept that there must be a God who created the world and populated it with life. As to the various denominations, I cannot say with any confidence which, if any, is correct. Most people conform to the religion in which they grew up, and I see no reason not to do the same. As for children, my experience has been that if raised with firmness and kindness most turn out well, while a few do not. Why that should be I have no idea.'

She smiled teasingly. 'Is that what you said when you

enrolled at the University of Cambridge?'

'You mean the religious test?' He suppressed a laugh. 'I thought it best to confine myself to the 39 articles.'

'Ha! And I thought you an honest man.'

There was a stirring on her left, and Frau von Staufen said in carefully correct English, 'Please, what are the 39 articles?'

Elizabeth reddened as she wondered how much of their conversation had been overheard.

Darcy answered. 'Paragraphs, dating from Queen Elizabeth's reign, which summarise the doctrine of the Anglican church.'

'Ah.' Frau von Staufen glanced at her husband, who was still snoring. 'Perhaps a shorter version of the 95 theses which Martin Luther nailed to the door of All Saints' Church in Wittenberg?'

Elizabeth, out of her depth, waited for Darcy to reply.

'No, although I believe there was some overlap.'

The captain's wife turned to Elizabeth. 'Excuse me, you are sceptical of the significance of baptism?'

Elizabeth blinked, not wishing to get into a dispute. 'I see no harm in the ceremony, which serves to welcome a new arrival into the community.'

'Ah!' Frau von Staufen raised a finger. 'But there are people who say that babies just a few weeks old are not ready to choose which religious community they wish to join.'

'That is why we have confirmation,' Darcy said.

'In Prussia we have Anabaptists,' Frau von Staufen continued. 'Also called Mennonites. They originated in Switzerland and the Tyrol, and to escape persecution migrated to Prussia and the Netherlands, even to America. They believe that baptism should be delayed until adulthood. Also, that violence is always wrong, even in self-defence.'

Elizabeth glanced at the sleeping captain. 'I assume no Anabaptists follow your husband's profession.'

In the corner of her eye she noticed Darcy smile at this remark, but Frau von Staufen remained impassive. 'That is right. We are *Reformed Church*. Calvinist. But I have Mennonite friends and they are good people. They take their lead from the Gospels, especially the Sermon on the Mount.'

'Do we have Mennonites in Britain?' Elizabeth asked Darcy.

'Very few, I imagine. Most Englishmen are practical, and accept war as a necessary evil.'

'Still, I admire the Mennonites for their consistency.'

Darcy nodded. 'They do no harm, which is more than can be said for most people.'

'How cruel to persecute innocuous people who refuse to fight back.'

'*Ja.*' Frau von Staufen waggled a finger. 'But not in Prussia. Our king, Frederick William III, is working for a union of all Protestant churches. He is Calvinist, like us, but his wife Queen Louise, now sadly no more, was Lutheran. We have many traditions under, how do you say, the same *umbrella*, and no more persecutions.'

There was a grunt from the seat opposite, and the captain yawned, and nodded genially to the gathering. Frau von Staufen fell silent, as if conversation were no longer possible while her husband was awake. Elizabeth turned back to Darcy, wondering what he thought about such a bewildering array of religious viewpoints.

41

Wednesday 14th June

On an afternoon warmed by white hazy sunshine they at last reached Brussels. The stagecoach halted at the *Place Royale*, a cobbled square more imposing than attractive, but Darcy asked the driver to continue a little further to the Royal Park, where they made a temporary base on benches shaded by evenly spaced lime trees.

From conversation on the coach, Darcy knew that accommodation in Brussels would be hard to find: the city abounded with officers, enjoying its many pleasures while awaiting the call to action. His plan was to replenish funds, then hire a chaise that would convey them towards the coast. All depended on whether his bank in London had received his request for a fresh letter of credit.

After leaving Burgess to guard their luggage, they followed a side-road into the old centre, where the *Bureau de Poste* was a fifteen-minute walk. They queued, their eyes sometimes meeting in excited anticipation, then endured further suspense as the *employée des postes* searched a back room. Darcy looked down at Elizabeth as she took his arm, holding her breath. She gasped and clapped her hands together as the girl returned with two bundles.

'Excellent.' He led her into the street. 'Shall we find a lounge where we can sit in comfort? I believe the Hotel Metropole is round the corner.'

'Oh yes! I can scarcely wait another minute.'

The Metropole was imposing, its foyer regal in red and gold. It was also a social hub, milling with officers and their elegant wives. Darcy found a quiet tea-room where a booth was free, and they sank into crimson high-backed armchairs to open their mail.

He knew already that his bank had replied—he had recognised its stamp in the post office. He slit the envelope and found as expected a letter of credit for £1500, more than enough for his purposes. Three plump packages were addressed in Georgiana's hand; he opened the latest, and scanned it to confirm she was in good health, had received his letters, and was finding plenty to amuse herself in London. A note from his steward announced a good crop of rhubarb, and no problems except for an outbreak of sheep rustling which had obliged him to employ another shepherd. Finally, at the bottom of the pile, Darcy found a folded sheet, and with a start recognised the handwriting of his cousin.

Elizabeth touched his arm, radiant. 'It is wonderful! See, I have two letters from Jane, with such news! She is still engaged to Mr Bingley, who has not quitted Netherfield. None of my sisters has run off with an officer. My father spends every day in his study and complains that he has no intelligent conversation. My mother is well except that her nerves are aflutter through fear that I will be ravaged by French soldiers. In short, all is normal.'

'I'm gratified to hear it.' He waved his bundle. 'I also have reassuring news. Georgiana is well, and we have the funds. But I ought to read this last message.' He unfolded the note, and whistled. 'My goodness!'

'Who is it from?'

'Colonel Fitzwilliam. He is here, in Brussels, billeted at the house of Viscount de Crécy in Rue de la Violette.'

Elizabeth gasped. 'What does he say?'

'That we should call on him directly.'

'Let us find a hackney.'

He hesitated. 'You should read your letters first.'

'They can wait. I have read Jane's latest, and my mind is at rest.'

Darcy thought for a few seconds. 'Then I agree. Let's return to the park and collect our luggage.'

The hackney turned into Rue de la Violette, a cobbled street just a few paces across. It seemed so modest that Darcy feared that they had been misdirected, but the road broadened and a gateway led to a fair-sized quadrangle. The driver summoned a servant, who swung the gates open so that after unloading their trunk from the roof they could drive through. Two grand houses shared the forecourt, one belonging to the *Vicomte*.

They had found a hackney immediately as it dropped off a customer at the Metropole, but on the way to the park had stopped at a bank for ten minutes so that he could fill two bags with Dutch *guilder* and French *louis d'or*.

The servant spoke little English, but on hearing the name *Fitzwilliam* nodded enthusiastically and invited them into the hallway. Darcy was settling up with the driver when a familiar figure ran down the steps.

After greeting his cousin, Darcy extended a hand towards Elizabeth. 'You remember Miss Bennet?'

Colonel Fitzwilliam bowed. 'How could I not, after spending such jolly times together in Kent?'

'Sorry to trouble you, cuz, but we have nowhere to stay in Brussels, and the hotels are all full. Is there a store-room where we can keep our luggage?'

Colonel Fitzwilliam opened his arms. 'Of course! What is more, you will stay here. The *Vicomte* has spare chambers. There is space in the attic for Burgess.' He spoke in French to the servant, who went off to summon help.

Darcy drew Elizabeth aside. 'What do you think? Shall we stay one night and leave tomorrow morning?'

'It would be a pleasure,' Elizabeth beamed. 'We need rest after our coach journey, and you cannot miss such an opportunity to exchange your news.'

'Well said!' cried Colonel Fitzwilliam, rejoining them. 'Now, all is in train here. Let us go upstairs and take some refreshment.'

Feeling like a trespasser, Elizabeth accompanied Darcy up the broad staircase and through to a spacious lounge furnished in classical French style, and lit by three grand chandeliers. She was unconvinced by Colonel Fitzwilliam's assumption that the Viscount would offer hospitality to strangers, but it turned out that the possibility had already been discussed, and arrangements made.

The *Vicomte* rose to greet them, and introduced his daughter, the honourable Lorraine de Crécy. He was tall, and so thin that he seemed taller than Darcy even though their heads were actually on a level. Both in stature and character, the word that fitted him was *upright*: he carried himself well; he obviously abstained from excess in food and drink; his manner was courtly and correct. All these traits had passed to his daughter, a slender elegant woman in her early twenties, with severely pinned dark hair and a long face that was striking in spite of plain features.

Mademoiselle de Crécy took Elizabeth aside as the men began talking of the campaign. 'Pleasure to have you here. May I show you the house?'

They viewed a parlour, a dining room, the Viscount's study, and two drawing rooms which had been converted for use as offices. On the upper floor they visited Mademoiselle de Crécy's *boudoir* and *salle de bains*, which adjoined a small chamber which had been allocated to Elizabeth.

'This room is used for guests,' Mademoiselle de Crécy said. 'We thought you could share the *salle de bains* with me, if that is convenient.'

Elizabeth admired the bathroom, which held a flushing lavatory and bidet of latest design, in addition to the bath and dressing table. 'I'm overwhelmed that your family should go to so much trouble.'

'It is no more than an expression of our gratitude to England for defending Wallonia against Bonaparte. My father is among many nobles who have offered accommodation to British officers. Colonel Fitzwilliam has become a valued friend.'

'These considerations hardly apply to Mr Darcy—or myself.'

'Colonel Fitzwilliam has letters from Miss Darcy describing your adventures.' Mademoiselle de Crécy smiled. 'Although not in enough detail to satisfy *my* curiosity.'

Elizabeth coloured. 'The story is not entirely edifying.'

'These are difficult times, Miss Bennet, and we all cope as best we can. Colonel Fitzwilliam speaks of you in the warmest terms, and that is enough for me.'

Elizabeth's eyes moistened at this kindness, and she realised how much she had feared ostracism if their unconventional and often unchaperoned trip across Europe became generally known. Still, she was unsure as yet how much had been confided …

A maid passed carrying Elizabeth's clothes, and they followed her into the small chamber.

'Perhaps you would like to wash and change after your journey,' Mademoiselle de Crécy said. 'At noon we take a light luncheon. Dinner is later than usual in these parts, at six o'clock.'

She spoke as if accustomed to organise, her calm confidence daunting. But there was affection in her eyes, and Elizabeth hoped she had found a new friend.

'So cuz, what are your duties here?' Darcy demanded.

The Viscount had withdrawn to his study, leaving the cousins alone with instructions to help themselves from a decanter of wine on the sideboard.

Colonel Fitzwilliam shrugged. 'Office work. I coordinate a team that procures supplies for my regiment. We receive reports on the state of our armaments, uniforms, and other equipment, and intercede with the suppliers. Also with the War Office, which foots the bill.'

'And when the regiment marches to fight the French?'

'I will ride with them. Liaise with headquarters and the battalion leaders. Take part in hand-to-hand fighting if the need arises.' He clapped Darcy on the shoulder. 'Don't look so glum! I have survived such encounters in the past, and with reasonable luck will do so again. Enough of me. How do matters stand between yourself and the charming Miss Bennet?'

Darcy hesitated. 'There is no, ah, formal arrangement.'

Colonel Fitzwilliam laughed. 'Come on, Darce. I could not help noticing how she looks at you. At Rosings the claws were out. Now she purrs.'

'Certainly her feelings have—altered.' Darcy sipped claret as he studied a portrait of the Viscount's late wife. 'But Elizabeth is troubled. That ghastly Italian family has undermined her confidence. She feels unworthy, she fears our family will reject her. Above all, she is ashamed that a certain gentleman of ill repute has become her brother-in-law.'

'Hmm.' Colonel Fitzwilliam frowned. 'More your doing than hers, I should have thought.'

'She believes our marriage would distress Georgiana.'

Colonel Fitzwilliam was incisive. 'Georgiana will love her.'

'Elizabeth, yes.' Darcy lowered his voice. 'But not her family tie with Wickham.'

'Oh.' Colonel Fitzwilliam reflected. 'I see what Miss Bennet means, but no, I will not have it. The Wickhams are settled 150 miles to the north, and I wager that you will be in no hurry to invite them to Pemberley.'

Darcy harrumphed. 'A safe bet if ever I heard one.'

'Listen.' Colonel Fitzwilliam stepped closer, and lowered his voice. 'Why not stay a few days? The family is hospitable, and Mademoiselle Lorraine will make a fine companion for Miss Bennet. If you need occupation, I could benefit from some assistance in the office—figures were never my strong point.' He raised a finger. 'And yes, I nearly forgot. The Duchess of Richmond is hosting a ball tomorrow evening, to which all senior officers and their wives are invited. Ladies will be in short supply, especially ones that speak English. Absolutely Miss Bennet must attend, and you too as my guest.'

42

Thursday 15ᵗʰ June

The barouche turned into Rue de Minimes, a cobbled street just five minutes drive from the *Place Royale*. Elizabeth sat beside Mademoiselle de Crécy, who was keeping an appointment at a hospital of which she was patroness.

It had been a busy afternoon, the first order of business being the vital question of their dresses for the ball. There was no time to measure up for a new gown. Elizabeth had taken her cream-gold silk dress to the modiste, so that a fashionable sash might be added at the back; Mademoiselle de Crécy ordered similar alterations in a white gown ornamented with pink borders and crimson ribbons. Their dresses would be delivered by early evening so that they could leave at eight o'clock.

At the Minimes hospital they were taken on a tour of inspection, and Elizabeth stayed in the background as her companion paused to speak with people at all levels—not just doctors but nurses, patients, cooks, cleaners. So far as she could tell, the hospital was well run, mostly by nuns in white habits and starched wimples, large cloths shaped into hats called *cornettes*.

At length they were shown to the chief surgeon's office, where Mademoiselle de Crécy held a meeting with senior staff. Unable to follow—she had learned only the rudiments of French as a child—Elizabeth waited in an armchair in the corner and thought about her new friend.

They had gone to their rooms after supper and cards; Elizabeth had been in her nightdress loosening her hair when the door from the dressing room opened an inch.

'Mademoiselle Bennet?'

'Come in.'

Mademoiselle de Crécy entered, also in her nightdress. 'I wanted to check you have everything you need. Shall I ask my maid to brush out your hair?'

'I can manage alone.' Elizabeth held up her mother-of-pearl brush. 'You should know that I am a thief. This heirloom was pilfered from Villa Foscari near Venice.'

Mademoiselle de Crécy raised her eyebrows. 'We had better count the spoons before you leave.'

'The villa had been abandoned for decades. It was the most beautiful building I have ever seen, left for use as a storehouse for a local farmer.'

'What adventures you must have had. Are you tired?'

'More excited than tired, with the ball tomorrow.'

'Why not come to my room and talk?'

They made themselves comfortable on Mademoiselle de Crécy's broad four-poster, with the window ajar to let in a cooling breeze. Cautiously Elizabeth described her abduction by Carandini, Darcy's rescue mission, and their flight across the Venice lagoon. She feared that the Viscount's daughter, with her noble birth and strict Catholic upbringing, would shudder at the impropriety of it all, but Mademoiselle de Crécy was enthralled, even envious.

'More, more!' she cried. 'What happened next?'

Elizabeth swallowed, and provided an edited version of their encounter with Gerard Hanson and Alice Dill.

'Oh, it is *romantique*, *scandaleux!* And did you like this artist, Mademoiselle Alice?'

'I confess I did.'

'*Bien dit*, Elizabeth.' Mademoiselle de Crécy clapped a hand to her mouth. 'Pardon me …'

Elizabeth smiled. 'If I am to confide such intimacies, we may as well use first names.'

She continued, omitting only the embarrassing episode in the small riverside town of Oriago where she and Darcy had shared a bedroom.

'*Alors.*' Mademoiselle de Crécy leaned back against her pillow. 'You enjoyed being Madame Rebecca Ashley?'

'Yes.' Elizabeth met her eye. 'And what are you smiling at, mademoiselle?'

'I think you will also enjoy being Madame D—'

'That's quite enough.'

'No need to be missish and deny the obvious.'

Elizabeth looked away. Mademoiselle de Crécy leaned over and touched her arm. 'Pardon me.'

'It's all right. I'm not angry.' She turned back. 'What did Colonel Fitzwilliam say about us?'

'Only that Mr Darcy had found you in Venice and helped extricate you from a difficult situation.'

'That is all?'

Mademoiselle de Crécy frowned. 'That was all he *said*, but he did look at my father *in a certain way*, as if there was something else …'

'I see.' Elizabeth sighed. 'I should return to my room.'

'Sleep here if you like.' Mademoiselle de Crécy smiled. 'Unlike your Fraulein Edelmann I am quiet as a mouse.'

Returning from the hospital to Rue de la Violette, they found Darcy and Colonel Fitzwilliam in the lounge, talking in hushed voices with the *Vicomte*.

'Come!' Lorraine de Crécy gestured her to follow. 'We will leave the men undisturbed and go to the parlour.'

'Is something amiss?'

'My father looks worried.'

Some minutes later, Darcy entered and bowed.

'Mademoiselle, your father asks to see you in the study. I need to speak in private with Miss Bennet.'

When they were alone he sat beside her and said, with forced calm: 'There is a disturbing report which we must discuss. Bonaparte's army has overrun the border guards near Charleroi and is advancing towards the Prussian position at Ligny.'

Elizabeth gasped. 'Is that not where Captain von Staufen and his wife were bound?'

'I'm afraid so, and I wish them every fortune. But we must also consider our own safety. The general feeling is that this is a feint. Headquarters has decided that the ball is to go ahead, and that all officers may attend.'

Elizabeth felt a tingle of fear and excitement. 'What is your cousin's opinion?'

'He will go. So will the Viscount and, I presume, his daughter.' He spread his hands. 'There can be no imminent threat. The only question is whether we should proceed with our current plan, or find a carriage and leave today. The trouble is that flight provides no guarantee of safety. With French troops rampaging over Wallonia I believe we would do better to stay put until Bonaparte's intentions are revealed. At least here we enjoy secure accommodation and the protection of the British army.'

Elizabeth nodded. 'Let us remain with our friends.'

43

At the end of Rue della Blanchisserie was such a crush of carriages that the Viscount instructed his driver to halt, so that the party could proceed on foot. Colonel Fitzwilliam led off, clearing a path for his hosts; Darcy followed with Elizabeth on his arm. The Duke of Richmond's residence was easily located: Gordon Highlanders were playing the bagpipes at the entrance, attended by red-coated officers, some mounted, as well as the cream of Brussels society.

Viscount de Crécy presented their invitations, and they passed through to a ground-floor coach house which had been transformed into a huge ballroom. Elizabeth gasped, released Darcy's arm, and stepped forward to survey the scene. Never in her life had she seen so many people at a ball: already there must be hundreds, and the arena was still filling. The opulence took her breath away. The walls had been newly papered in a rose trellis design, and were adorned with huge drapes, and clusters of flags representing countries of the coalition. Pillars bordering the dance floor were bedecked in ribbons and flowers; behind them, in the alcoves, divans, chairs and drinks tables were set out on rugs. Overhead hung rows of magnificent chandeliers.

Lorraine de Crécy came to join her. 'Impressive, no?'

'Splendid beyond words.'

'The duchess is not what one might call *frugal*. Perhaps

the duke's fortune could be better spent, and yet …' She swept her arm around the hall. 'These men are about to risk their lives, and deserve the best farewell party we can give them.'

'All officers are invited?' Elizabeth asked.

'Yes, as well as nobles from home and abroad. William, Prince of Orange will be attending. Also his brother Prince Frederick. Numberless dukes and counts with their wives and daughters.'

The *Vicomte* led them to an alcove where they joined a group centred around the Duc and Duchesse de Beaufort and their daughter, who jumped up to greet Lorraine. The young women conversed in rapid French, leaving Elizabeth beside an Englishwoman who had sunk into a sofa looking pale and exhausted. Her husband, it emerged, was a general who had left her alone while joining a discussion about the campaign. Darcy, like the other gentlemen, remained standing. The noise was deafening, with excited voices raised so that they could be heard against the bagpipes and general clatter.

Lorraine de Crécy leaned close to her ear. 'Everyone is talking about the French advance. Some say it is just a border skirmish; others say Bonaparte is already engaging our Prussian allies. All rumour, but since Field Marshall Wellesley urged that the ball go ahead, my friend thinks the situation cannot be too grave.'

'Is the Field Marshall here?'

'Not yet. Normally he would never miss such an event, so it will be a bad sign if he stays away. But it is early, so we should not be concerned.'

'Miss Bennet!' Elizabeth looked up to see Darcy kneel beside her. 'Might I make so bold as to reserve a couple of dances? The first, and the supper set?'

'*Two* sets!' She grinned. 'You do me great honour, sir,

but I warn you: tongues will wag.'

'Tonight they have plenty else to wag about.'

She marked her card, while Darcy requested a set also from Mademoiselle de Crécy.

Lorraine bowed graciously. '*Enchanté*. The second set?'

'We are paid a great compliment,' Elizabeth said, with a sly glance at Darcy. 'As a rule Mr Darcy does not dance at all. Three sets are exceptional.'

'And sufficient for one evening,' Darcy said. 'The party is mainly for the officers.'

Looking around, Elizabeth saw that the redcoats did indeed outnumber the ladies present—and that Lorraine and herself were attracting the attention of British cavalry officers. But the room hushed as the Master of Ceremonies announced a Quadrille, and Darcy came to claim her hand.

Several sets later, Elizabeth returned with Colonel Fitzwilliam to a seat near the *Vicomte*, having just danced an Allemande.

'You look tired.' Lorraine de Crécy joined her on the sofa. 'Take some refreshment. A glass of wine.'

She waved to a servant, who poured from a decanter.

'The toast?' Lorraine asked.

'To our brave soldiers,' Elizabeth said. 'May they return unscathed; and may they tire of dancing before I am utterly exhausted.'

Lorraine clinked glasses with a smile. 'Perdition to Bonaparte.'

'May the rain fall upon his armies so that they stick in the mud.'

'Is your card marked for the next?'

'I hope to sit this one out so that I have energy left for the supper set.'

They continued talking through the interval, until an officer came to claim the next dance with Mademoiselle de Crécy. Elizabeth exchanged a few words with the Viscount, but they were interrupted by a buzz at the entrance, followed by cheering and clapping as a group of men in red-gold coats and white breeches entered the ballroom.

'*Hourra! A la bonne heure!*' The Viscount pointed to the leader. 'Field Marshall Wellesley, latterly Duke of Wellington.'

'He has come after all!' Impulsively Elizabeth jumped up and advanced a few steps for a better view, almost colliding with two officers who appeared suddenly from behind a column. One of them turned, and with a gasp she froze, unable to believe her eyes.

He stared at her with equal shock. 'Miss Bennet?'

She managed a bow. 'Mr Wickham.'

He floundered, for once lost for words. 'I hardly expected to meet *you* here.'

'Nor I you.'

'I am now in the regulars you know. First Yorkshires. Since …'

She nodded. 'Since your marriage to my sister.'

'A pity you were away and could not attend the wedding. It was arranged hastily, of course, in town. Mr and Mrs Gardiner represented your family.'

Elizabeth frowned. 'I was relieved to learn it had taken place at all.'

'Certainly it did not happen in the best way …' His cheeks reddened and he blustered on, 'Miss Bennet, if you are free may I ask for the supper set?'

'I'm sorry, I am already engaged.'

'Perhaps the second dance of *this* set?'

Elizabeth hesitated, casting round for an excuse, but

he looked so eager, so lost, that she could not bring herself to refuse: after all, he might shortly be risking his life on the battlefield.

'I should be delighted.'

'Excellent. Your group is …'

Elizabeth flinched, recalling that she had given no account of her presence in so unlikely a location. *What did Wickham know?* He would have learned from the Gardiners of her expedition to Italy in the company of Sir Ambrose and Lady Havers; and perhaps of Sir Ambrose's death from cholera. But the rest, including Darcy's rescue mission? Probably not …

Her gaze wandered to the opposite alcove, where Darcy had joined a group of officers after dancing with Lorraine. She had spotted him several times in earnest conversation, probably seeking advice on their journey to the coast; for once, he had felt no necessity to keep her under observation.

'Miss Bennet?' Wickham prompted.

'Sorry, I was distracted.' She had to decide: mention Darcy, or not? With a sigh, she pointed at the sofa where the *Vicomte* was conversing with the Duchess de Beaufort. 'I am with the Viscount de Crécy's party.'

'Good. Until later!'

They bowed, and she returned trembling to the alcove. As she took her seat, she realised at last the folly of what she had done. Wickham's presence at the ball could not be concealed from Darcy: Colonel Fitzwilliam was still dancing, and sure to see them. What was worse, the next dance was not a traditional Cotillion or Boulangere. It was the latest trend, still shocking in London society, in which the gentleman might rest his hand on the lady's waist …

Wickham stood before her, his earlier confusion replaced

by his usual supercilious charm.

'I had forgotten that this dance was a waltz,' Elizabeth said as they walked to the floor.

'Have you danced it before?'

'Yes, at a ball in Venice. My friend Lady Havers taught me the steps.'

The music started and they circled slowly. He held her gently, with practised confidence, and gradually she relaxed and felt able to talk.

'How is my sister?'

'Well, so far as I know.' He smiled wryly. 'Lydia is not one to write often.'

'Have you been in Brussels long?'

'We have been encamped west of the city for just over two weeks.'

'Could Lydia have accompanied you here?'

'Since I am an ensign that would be rare, and we could not afford the accommodation.' He grimaced. 'Financially we are placed somewhat ill.'

'And where is your new home?'

'We have a town house in Newcastle.' He wrinkled his nose. 'Passable, but a far cry from the parsonage at Kympton that I should have had, if a certain gentleman had honoured his father's wishes.'

'You would have enjoyed preaching sermons?'

'Exceedingly: a quiet life would have been much to my taste.'

Elizabeth raised her eyebrows. 'Strange, for I have it on good authority that you were not always set on becoming a clergyman, so much so that you renounced the living, accepting a considerable sum as compensation.'

He forced a smile. 'Well, there is truth in that too—indeed, I said as much when we first met, you may recall.'

'It must have slipped my mind. Still, we need not dispute over the past …'

Elizabeth froze, almost tripping as a tall familiar figure emerged from the alcove and regarded them with thunderous rage. As they turned, Wickham saw him too and stared at her in shock.

'My God, was that …'

'Yes. Mr Darcy. I forgot to mention that he is visiting Colonel Fitzwilliam.'

He guided her to the other side of the floor as the music sped to its conclusion. 'Pardon me, Miss Bennet, but I ought to re-join my party. The order to march may come at any moment. To see you again has been a delight. Pray convey my best wishes to your family when you return to Longbourn.'

'Thank you sir, and I wish you every good fortune.'

He blinked, as if moved, and they parted.

44

As the waltz ended, Darcy lost sight of Elizabeth, who had been manoeuvred—deliberately he suspected—to the other side of the ballroom. So agitated that he could feel his heart pulsing, he crossed the floor to the seating area where the Viscount de Crécy and Duke de Beaufort were in conversation with Colonel Fitzwilliam. Mademoiselle de Crécy had returned, but not Elizabeth.

Darcy leaned over his cousin. 'Have you seen Miss Bennet?'

Colonel Fitzwilliam shook his head. 'The *Vicomte* said she had been dancing. Should be back soon. I say, Darce, have you heard …'

'Later.' Darcy stood tall, peering over the crowd. 'Ah! I see her.'

Without waiting for a reply he threaded his way along the alcove and blocked her path.

Elizabeth stared at him. 'Mr Darcy! Are you well?'

'Where is that—fiend?'

She recoiled. 'How dare you accost me so!'

'I asked you a question, madam.'

'Which I refuse to answer, until you approach me in a more gentlemanlike manner.'

He flinched at hearing again a phrase that had haunted him, and struggled to control his voice. 'Pardon me. I am not myself. I beg you Elizabeth, where is he?'

'Mr Wickham has just left.'

Darcy screwed up his face in distaste. 'Just like him to take the coward's way out.'

She rolled her eyes contemptuously. 'The *coward* of whom you speak is re-joining his regiment to fight a battle in which he will quite probably be injured, or worse.'

'What could possibly have come over you? Why agree to dance with a scoundrel who has wronged your sister and mine, and cost me a fortune correcting his misdeeds and clearing his debts?'

Elizabeth held up a palm, glancing at a party nearby. 'If you are determined to shout at me, can we seek a more private spot?'

He lowered his voice. 'That is unnecessary.'

'I think not: after all, I am dealing with a man who *dare not vouch for his temper*!' She turned with a toss of the head and set off towards an open window at the back.

'That's better.' She breathed deeply. 'The ballroom has become so hot.'

'My question stands, Elizabeth.'

She sighed. 'I am not going to accept any more abuse, Mr Darcy, but if you try to calm down I will explain what happened. Of course I had no idea that Mr Wickham was here. We met by chance during the first dance of the last set. As you presumably know, he is an ensign in a northern regiment; in consequence he is now encamped outside Brussels and expecting any day to move against the French. You can imagine my shock on bumping into him. When he asked to dance, my first impulse, naturally, was to refuse. But somehow I could not. After all, *the reason we are here* is to provide solace and entertainment to our soldiers before their ordeal. What is more, like it or not, we are now kin: he is husband of my sister.'

'So you agreed to dance the waltz.'

'In my confusion I forgot which dance came next.' She threw up her hands. 'Even so, what harm was done?'

'You could have warned me.'

'I did not wish to disturb you.'

'Be honest, Elizabeth. You knew your decision would anger me, and hoped to conceal it.'

She looked up, eyes flashing. 'Certainly I feared an intemperate reaction, and with good reason.'

'To see that devil smirk with satisfaction as you shared that most intimate of dances.' Darcy looked away, unable to meet her eye. 'I cannot believe you would do this to me.'

'It is done, and I have nothing further to say.'

She whirled round and returned to her seat.

Darcy remained at the window, welcoming the opportunity to collect his thoughts. The fresh air cleared his head, and as his anger receded he noticed a buzz in the ballroom. People were huddling in groups, whispering excitedly; a woman nearby wailed openly in dismay.

He hurried back to the alcove, where Elizabeth was talking earnestly with Mademoiselle de Crécy. Colonel Fitzwilliam jumped up and drew him aside.

'Rumours of a French advance are confirmed. The Duchess of Richmond's daughter asked Wellington openly and he said yes, our army would be marching tomorrow. Or today, since it has now gone midnight. Some officers have already left, with instructions to return to their camps by three o'clock in the morning.'

Darcy frowned, recalling his ill-advised comment on Wickham's departure. Perhaps Wickham had been *ordered* to leave, in which case cowardice had nothing to do with it—quite the contrary.

'Has Wellington also left?'

Colonel Fitzwilliam smiled. 'Not him—he prides himself on his insouciance, and continues dancing and talking to the ladies to show his contempt for the enemy.'

'And so the ball goes on.'

'As it should: there can be no immediate threat.'

The supper dance was called, and Darcy uneasily approached Elizabeth.

'Shall we take the floor?'

She whispered a final word to Mademoiselle de Crécy and rose wearily to join him.

'We could sit it out if you are tired.'

'No. I will come.'

Their eyes met, and he realised she was more sad than angry. 'Miss Bennet, not for the first time, I owe you an apology.'

'The famous Darcy temper.' She forced a smile. 'If we could only set you before Bonaparte's troops they would take fright and scuttle back to France.'

'Have you heard that men are already leaving, in case they have to march tomorrow?'

'Yes.' Her face clouded over. 'It is truly horrible. I fear for your cousin, and for Mr Wickham too, whatever we may think of him.'

'You are right. May fortune protect them both.'

Couples were forming up in a ring, and Elizabeth said, 'This is unexpected. The *gallopade* usually comes last.'

'A signal, perhaps, that there will be no more dancing after supper. Are you familiar with the steps?'

'I tried it once in Venice. Similar to a waltz, but in two time rather than three.'

Elizabeth held out her right hand, and he held it gently as he placed his own right hand above her waist. She rested her left hand on his arm, looking up with a challenging grin, and as he smiled back he recalled a couplet from Byron's satire on the waltz as a mutual embrace: *Hands which may freely range in public sight where ne'er before …*

The dancers circled, slowly at first. Always light on her feet, Elizabeth guided him gracefully through the gallop phases and the turns. *Endearing waltz, to thy more melting tune.* Not a waltz exactly, but the phrase still applied, and he did feel his limbs melt at the intimacy of their clinch.

The sequence was soon learned: four bars in the waltz hold; change sides and repeat; separate and face; join right hands and spin; return to the waltz hold and gallop. It was if a barrier had dissolved; two had become one. Their eyes met and he saw that she too was relaxed and immersed in the dance.

As the wheel of couples turned at a stately pace, Darcy observed the intensity of feeling on the dance floor. Men in red coats danced with wives in the knowledge that they would shortly be parted, and might never see one another again. There was little jollity, more a quiet tenderness, a savouring of these last precious moments.

The orchestra picked up the beat, and the melancholy mood dispelled as the dance became a romp. Some couples collided; others, unable to keep up, left the circle. Elizabeth's embrace tightened in the turns; she whooped as they finally parted.

'Wonderful! I am quite out of breath.'

He guided her to a seat. 'I cannot recall enjoying a dance more. And yet how tinged with sadness.'

'I know. Look—' She pointed to Colonel Fitzwilliam, who was partnering Mademoiselle de Crécy. 'Your cousin is waving.'

Colonel Fitzwilliam bowed to Elizabeth before drawing Darcy aside.

'More news, not good. During the gallopade a message arrived for the Prince of Orange. The French have advanced faster than expected, engaged the Prussian armies near Charleroi, and forced them to retreat. Field Marshall Wellesley is remaining for the supper, but the Prince and his entourage have left for his headquarters.'

Darcy glanced at Elizabeth and Mademoiselle de Crécy who had edged across to hear. 'Have you received orders for tonight?'

'We can stay for the supper. After that I should return to my office at the Viscount's home, ready to leave early in the morning.'

Darcy shook his head in wonder. 'So we must make merry while these grave events are unfolding just a two-hour ride away.'

Colonel Fitzwilliam shrugged. 'It is our custom. Drake finishing his game of bowls …'

At the supper, Darcy had a good view of the Field Marshall, seated on an opposite table beside the Duchess's daughter. On the other side sat a woman he had met earlier in the evening, accompanying her husband who was a lieutenant in the 9th Dragoons. Around him people chatted inconsequentially, in a poignant effort to stay cheerful in the teeth of anxiety.

'So what happened to the *timetable*?' Elizabeth asked. 'I thought it had been agreed that hostilities would not start until July.'

Darcy smiled. 'It seems Bonaparte has opted for a pre-emptive strike against his most dangerous adversary. Perhaps it was naive of the coalition to expect anything else.' He brushed Elizabeth's arm and pointed discreetly at the opposite table. 'You recall my schooldays at Harrow?'

'Don't tell me you fagged for the Field Marshall?'

'No, but I knew the lieutenant on his left, James Webster. The lady sitting next to Wellington is Sir James's wife

Lady Frances.'

'How beautiful she looks.'

'Many have thought so.' He lowered his voice. 'James was in Byron's set, a renowned fighter and gambler proud of his nickname *Bold Webster*. The union is said to be one of convenience. Lady Frances married him aged but 17 to escape her family; he was glad to wed the daughter of an earl.'

Elizabeth smiled. 'I see what you are about, Mr Darcy. You wish to educate me in the realities of matrimony.'

'They seem happy in their way. James has always been interested in promoting prize-fighters. He loves to attend bouts and bet on the outcome.'

'And Lady Frances?'

'I don't know her well, but it is said she has cultivated *close friendships* with Lord Byron and others.'

'She appears on close terms with the Field Marshal.'

'Indeed.' Darcy turned as Colonel Fitzwilliam tapped his arm and pointed to a tall man in black and gold striding to the main table.

'The Prince of Orange is back!'

The man leaned over Wellington, whispering, and the Field Marshal sat up with a jerk as if taken by surprise.

'Urgent news!' Colonel Fitzwilliam hissed.

Wellington withdrew for a private conference with the Prince, but returned to the table and concluded his conversation with Lady Frances before announcing that he would retire to bed. The room hushed as he leaned across to the Duke of Richmond, asked to see a map, then followed his host into the house.

'What can this signify?' Elizabeth said.

'I don't know, but I mean to find out.'

Darcy jumped up, rounded the table, and kneeled beside Sir James Webster. 'What did you hear?'

'The French are nearly at Quatre Bras,' Sir James said. 'A crossroads less than 20 miles away.'

Darcy hastened back to Colonel Fitzwilliam, who was in conversation with another officer, and whispered the news.

Colonel Fitzwilliam extended an arm to his companion. 'Captain Bowles here has spoken with the Duke of Richmond. Wellington admits Bonaparte has tricked him. He will try to stop the French at Quatre Bras, but failing that, plans to retreat to a town further along the road to Brussels. It is called Waterloo.'

They stood beside their seats in the alcove, preparing to leave. The news had gone round; there would be no more dancing. Elizabeth, shivering, held his arm as they stared at the extraordinary scene. All around the ballroom people stood in groups saying farewell to their friends and kin. Mothers and wives wept unashamedly as they parted with their menfolk; all jollity had gone, replaced by grief and dread.

The Viscount joined them. '*Mes amis*, we must go now and get some sleep. Tomorrow morning I will rise early, and we will make plans.'

Darcy's mind raced as they walked over the cobbles towards their carriage. What *plans* did the Viscount have in mind? Elizabeth and the other ladies would have to flee Brussels—that much was obvious. But himself? His instinct, of course, was to remain with Elizabeth, but as an Englishman, and Colonel Fitzwilliam's cousin, other responsibilities had to be considered.

He sighed wearily. First they must sleep.

45

A hand touched her shoulder. Elizabeth rolled over to see Lorraine de Crécy at her side.

'Sorry, I must wake you.'

Elizabeth sat up, her stomach churning as she recalled their predicament. 'News?'

'It is confirmed that our armies have been marching to Quatre Bras to support the Prussians, and will engage the French today.' Lorraine sighed. 'The men are already up, studying the latest messages. Shall I ask my maid to attend you?'

Elizabeth dressed and hastened downstairs to find the others assembled in the dining room, talking over coffee and rolls.

She sat beside Darcy. 'Has anything been decided?'

Colonel Fitzwilliam answered. 'My orders just arrived. I am to join my regiment at their camp for an inspection, then report to headquarters.'

'The 52nd is still encamped west of Brussels?' Elizabeth asked.

'Yes. You see, on first hearing of the French advance, the Field Marshall believed it might be a feint, with the main attack coming from the west. He therefore split the army in two parts, one to intercept the enemy at Quatre Bras, the other, including my regiment, to wait near the city. It is now too late to join our comrades, so for the time being we can only wait and hope.'

Lorraine frowned. 'But with only half an army against Bonaparte's entire force, what can be done?'

Colonel Fitzwilliam spread his palms. 'Nothing is sure. The French may have committed only part of their army. Also we are not alone: the Prussians will be joining from the east. But you are probably right. If we cannot hold them we must conserve our troops and retreat.'

'In which case,' said the Vicomte, 'Brussels may fall within a few days.' He turned to his daughter. 'You must leave, *ma chère*, for Antwerp. Mademoiselle Bennet too.'

'Why Antwerp?' Elizabeth asked.

'It is 25 miles to the north,' Darcy said, 'well fortified, and located on a river not far from the sea.'

Mademoiselle de Crécy turned to her father. '*Papa*, I wish to remain where I can be of use in the hospital. If what we fear comes to pass, the *Minimes* will be overwhelmed.'

The Vicomte shook his head. 'Out of the question. If Bonaparte enters Brussels, none of us will be safe. People are already destroying newspapers that carry insulting cartoons of the self-styled Emperor. His spies know we have aided the British. I cannot leave ladies here in the path of a rampaging French army.'

Darcy nodded. 'I agree.'

Lorraine de Crécy glanced at Elizabeth, then faced her father again. 'And the nuns and other nurses? If they stay, then as patron so should I.'

'It would be a meaningless gesture,' the Vicomte said.

Bristling, Lorraine cried, 'Outrageous! You know that I understand the administration of the hospital intimately and can help in many ways.'

The Vicomte looked away, more in sadness than anger. 'I am not going to argue. A decision has been taken, and you will leave this morning at eight o'clock.'

'And the gentlemen?' Elizabeth asked.

'I must remain one more day,' the Vicomte said. 'If Mr Darcy agrees, I would be vastly reassured if he accompanied you to Antwerp.'

Elizabeth turned to Darcy, expecting an immediate confirmation, but he hesitated. 'I need to confer with my cousin.'

She felt a pain like a stab to the heart. 'But surely you can do nothing here? It is a matter for the military.'

Colonel Fitzwilliam said gently, 'That is not altogether true, Miss Bennet. The fighting is for trained soldiers, but there are jobs behind the lines for any fit man, especially one that can read and write.'

'Or any fit *woman*,' Lorraine de Crécy said pointedly.

The Vicomte slapped the table. 'I am not going to put the ladies in the way of French soldiers,' he said. 'That is final.'

Elizabeth took Darcy's arm. 'I beg you …'

He said kindly, 'I must do my duty, Elizabeth. Whether that lies in protecting you, or serving my country, remains uncertain.'

She longed to press him, but intuited that this was not the time. 'I will support whatever you decide.'

Elizabeth sorted through a case in which she was keeping Jane's letters and other treasured mementos of her journey. A trunk had been packed with essential clothing, and she looked longingly at her silk dress, wondering if she would ever come back to reclaim it.

There was a tap on the door, and Lorraine entered and sat beside her on the edge of her bed.

'It is sad to leave our precious things behind, no?'

Elizabeth smiled sadly. 'And people.'

'But surely your Mr Darcy will come.'

Elizabeth's eyes filled with tears. 'He will see it as his duty to remain with his cousin.'

Lorraine squeezed her hand. 'But *chérie*, he loves you.'

'Even so.' Elizabeth wiped her eyes impatiently on her cuff. 'I wish *we* could stay as well.'

'I too.' Lorraine pointed at the case. 'What are you taking?'

Elizabeth showed her some of the items, handling them with reverent care as the memories returned. The blonde wig was admired, and they both tried it on. Alice Dill's drawings. Copies of two songs by Schubert. Two Bavarian wooden dolls with jointed limbs.

'But your lovely silk dress, which you wore to the ball!' Lorraine protested. 'Absolutely you must bring it too.'

'I doubt I will feel like dancing in Antwerp.'

'Never mind. It is now part of you, essential for the morale.'

'I suppose we could make room for it.'

'You must! I will call the servant.'

When they re-joined the men in the lounge, Elizabeth knew immediately that her fears were justified. Darcy regarded her stony-faced as the Vicomte explained the latest developments. Colonel Fitzwilliam believed that Mr Darcy could usefully be co-opted as an adjutant to assist the 52nd behind the lines. To explore this possibility, Mr Darcy, like the Vicomte, would stay one more day. This left the ladies to depart alone; fortunately, the Duke and Duchess de Beaufort were also leaving, and had space in their carriage.

Elizabeth had expected Lorraine to object, but instead she went to her father and embraced him. Darcy, his expression still grave, motioned Elizabeth to a corner where they could talk in privacy.

He met her eye and sighed. 'I beg you, Elizabeth, have no fear on my account. In all probability, the Viscount and I will join you in Antwerp. But I cannot in conscience leave now. Fate has led us into the centre of this conflict, and I could not live with myself if I fled when I could have been of service. Remember that as an adjutant I would play no part in the fighting.'

She stared at him, her face twisted with pain. 'And this is the man who *abhors disguise of any sort?* The *Viscount*, perhaps, will join us later, but not *you*. Well, fine. Be the hero, if you must, but let us call a spade a spade. Even behind the lines, you will be in range of enemy artillery, or fall prey to their soldiers if they break through. By remaining, you place yourself in mortal peril, so please let us have no nonsense about *having no fear*. I will be sick with anxiety for you, and your cousin, and that is an end to it.'

His face darkened. 'I am shocked that you speak thus. *Be the hero*, indeed. As if my actions were motivated by egotism. Nor do I apologize for trying to reassure you. In such times, it does no good to focus on possible disasters. Far better to keep hope alive.'

She took both his hands, her eyes wet. 'I am just so— afraid.'

He stroked her hand, as if comforting a child, and they parted.

46

Saturday 17th June

Darcy opened his bedroom shutters and inhaled moist warm air. Heavy rain had fallen during the night, accompanied by thunder, and the sky remained overcast with the threat of showers.

He was alone in the house except for Colonel Fitzwilliam, Burgess, and a skeleton staff. The Viscount, having completed his business, had left just a few hours after his daughter on the Friday; Darcy had caught up on lost sleep while waiting for his cousin to return from the tour of inspection. The result left little room for doubt. The regiment was preparing to march to its battle station north-west of the Mont St Jean ridge, and needed urgently to re-provision from Brussels. With some command of French, and access to funds, Darcy was ideally placed to help.

The rest of the day he spent touring the city with Burgess and another servant, buying beer, biscuits, salt pork, dried peas, lint and other medical materials, and hiring carters to carry them to the new camp. It was frustrating work, the roads often blocked by fleeing families, or soldiers, or quartermasters from other regiments also seeking supplies. But it was conducted against a background of artillery, audible even twenty miles away: a reminder, if one were needed, of the urgency of their preparations.

On the Friday evening the oppressive heat broke as

the rain and thunder came, and by dark the guns had fallen silent. News arrived of an indecisive battle. Bonaparte had tried to drive a wedge between the Prussians at Ligny, and the British at Quatre Bras. French forces led by Marshal Ney had bombarded the British positions and gained ground, but in the shelter of a wood the British had regrouped and driven the enemy back.

Darcy breakfasted alone, recalling his parting with Elizabeth. He had written her a note, treading a fine line between honesty and reassurance; so far no post had arrived from Antwerp. The cannon were silent. He was on his second cup of coffee when Colonel Fitzwilliam lumbered in and slumped into a chair.

'Morning, Darce. I could sleep for a month.'

'Any news of the battle?'

Colonel Fitzwilliam chuckled. 'It seems we have at last outwitted the Corsican. Our men, and the Prussians too, slipped away in the night and retreated on parallel routes to Brussels. They arrived early this morning, soaked to the skin but in good spirits. When the French resume their advance they will find the battlefield empty.'

Darcy frowned. 'Is that such good news? It is a blessing that we have preserved the army, but if Quatre Bras has been abandoned with impunity, why fight for it in the first place?'

'We were taken by surprise, and could not bring all our forces to the battle. Yes, leaving Quatre Bras is a concession, but far better to re-unify the army and confront the French on ground of our own choosing.'

'What is the plan for today?'

Colonel Fitzwilliam took a list from his coat pocket. 'There will be no battle. Bonaparte needs time to regroup and march. We will fortify our positions along the ridge, and set up camps and field hospitals on the north slope. I have a fresh list of provisions. We should also get you an adjutant uniform for tomorrow ...'

Elizabeth accompanied Mademoiselle de Crécy along the promenade beside the wide Scheldt river.

'So many boats,' she said, pointing.

'Yes, Antwerp has pretensions to become the largest port in Europe,' Lorraine said. 'The docks have been extended, and the river bed deepened to allow large ships to pass. You can probably guess who was responsible.'

'Bonaparte again?'

'I'm afraid so.'

'Wherever I go, his name crops up. A bridge here, a road there, now a dock. It is intolerable.'

'He wished to weaken Britain, by building up Antwerp into a port that would rival London as a trading centre.'

'Of course there would be some nefarious motive. Did you sleep well?'

Lorraine smiled. 'Yes, despite the rain and your fidgeting.'

'I was distressed.'

'Understandably, with your friends in danger.'

'Yes, but I was mostly upset with myself, as usual.'

'For agreeing to leave Brussels?'

Elizabeth sighed. 'No, for my treatment of Mr Darcy. What is it about that man? Always he brings out the worst in me.'

'Surely you did not quarrel at such a time? I was angry with father for insisting that I left, but our parting was affectionate.'

'I wanted so much for him to come with us.' Elizabeth looked away, struggling to compose herself. 'When your father's carriage arrived yesterday I thought for a moment that Mr Darcy had relented. But no. Always *he* is the one that must solve the world's problems, regardless of the cost to himself.'

'Is that not admirable?'

'Of course!'

'Then why quarrel with him?'

Elizabeth threw up her hands. 'Why indeed? Because I am a child. I have been pampered all my life, and have never taken responsibility for anything. If the world is not to my liking, I sulk like a little girl deprived of her doll. I am only here now because Mr Darcy spent a fortune and risked his life to rescue me. Now he devotes himself to a cause far more deserving than myself, and how do I react? Instead of giving unqualified support, I pick holes in his attempts to reassure me, and even imply that he is acting out of vanity.' She covered her face. 'The look of contempt on his face as we parted! I could feel his respect for me draining away.'

Mademoiselle de Crécy made no reply, and they proceeded in silence. Eventually she said, 'Shall we return and find a place for breakfast?'

They turned from the river, and a five-minute walk brought them to a grand square opposite the Cathedral of Our Lady. The weather was warm, although overcast, and they sat outside in the square and ordered coffee and waffles.

'You exaggerate, Elizabeth.' Lorraine took a bite from the grid-shaped pastry, garnished with strawberries and crushed sugar. 'Perhaps in your anxiety you spoke carelessly, but I cannot believe Mr Darcy regarded you with disrespect. He might even have been heartened that you pleaded with him to leave. It shows the depth of your affection.'

Elizabeth sighed. 'Have you heard the artillery?'

'Not since yesterday evening.'

'If only they could be safe.' Instinctively, Elizabeth put her hands together, then looked self-consciously at Lorraine. 'Do you trust the efficacy of prayer?'

Mademoiselle de Crécy raised her eyebrows. 'Unfortunately our enemies pray to the same God.'

'It is kind of the Duke and Duchess to take us in.'

'Our families have been friends for generations.'

They ate in silence, listening to a frantic conversation on the next table about Quatre Bras.

'What are they saying?' Elizabeth asked.

'That the Prussians are incompetent, and the British and Dutch outnumbered.'

Elizabeth looked into the distance, towards the cathedral facade. 'What will happen to us, if Bonaparte wins?'

'You, I imagine, will flee by boat to England. Here, in Wallonia, we will return to our former status as a region of France rather than the Netherlands.'

Elizabeth studied her friend, marvelling at the stoicism with which people on the European mainland accepted these perpetual upheavals and shifting sovereignties.

'How many languages do you speak?'

Lorraine counted on her fingers. 'French, in the Walloon dialect, of course. English, studied since childhood. Quite good Flemish. A few words of German and Italian. Yourself?'

Elizabeth raised a single finger. 'English. Plus whatever I picked up on this trip—mostly Italian.'

Lorraine smiled. 'It is because you live on an island.'

And because we are arrogant and lazy, Elizabeth thought. She recalled cartoons in the English newspapers, with their pretentions of superiority, and their portrayal of foreigners as comical numskulls.

'Shall we look inside the cathedral?'

'Why not?' Lorraine stood up. 'We could say a prayer.'
'For victory?'
'Or for sanity.'
Elizabeth agreed, and took her arm as they left.

47

Sunday 18th June, 7.00 am

Darcy rode with Colonel Fitzwilliam along the edge of a cornfield, to the west of Waterloo. They had risen at dawn, after overnighting in Brussels, and taken a road due south for an hour. Heavy rain on Saturday evening left the ground so mired that the roads near Waterloo were blocked, obliging them to detour into the adjoining fields to avoid a queue of carts struggling through the mud. The rain stopped during their ride, but with mist rising from the sodden corn, visibility remained poor.

After discussion they had left Burgess in Brussels, with the Viscount's servants; his instructions were to await news of the battle, and if the French won, to go immediately to Antwerp, ready to accompany Elizabeth by boat to England if the French advanced further north, or if Darcy for whatever reason was unable to join them.

The British had taken their stand on the north side of the Mont St Jean ridge, just below Waterloo. To reach them coming from the south, the French would have to march uphill through pastures and fields of rye. Three outposts near the top of this slope had been fortified. To the west was the chateau of Hougoumont, a large country house concealed by trees. In the centre stood a walled farmhouse called La Haye Sainte, adjoining the main road to Brussels, and hence a vital position. Finally, to the east, lay a hamlet where troops could easily be garrisoned. Darcy had memorised these locations the evening before, from a detailed local map, but for the 52nd regiment the key area was the reverse slope behind Hougoumont, for it was here, hidden from the advancing enemy, that they were encamped.

As they crossed another field, Darcy caught his first sight of their objective, a mass of tents looming out of the mist. He quivered with foreboding as they approached, and the reality of the situation hit home. The camp had been pitched near farm buildings at the foot of the slope, and included stores of food and weaponry, a field hospital, and improvised accommodation for camp followers.

They tethered their horses and walked to a cluster of tents, mounted side by side to enclose a large area. Inside, officers milled around talking, while others sat at folding tables writing messages. Colonel Fitzwilliam took an empty desk in a corner, and shifted two barrels for use as chairs.

'Darce, I must leave now to confer with the Lieutenant General. For the next few hours we will probably be kicking our heels, so I suggest you look around, and introduce yourself to the surgeons and other duty officers.'

Darcy swallowed, reminded incongruously of his first day at Harrow.

To begin with, Darcy checked paperwork, which included names of the officers in the regiment and the men in each battalion. After the battle they would have to log the casualties, and prepare statistics for headquarters and letters for the families. He put the registers aside and walked to a hospital area where surgeons were setting out instruments amid stacks of blankets, stretchers, and bandaging.

Like the surgeons, Darcy wore a scarlet uniform with

red piping; his cylindrical cap held a cockade—the black ribbon shaped into the wheel that marked medical staff. During the battle, his main duty was to organise convoys that would transport supplies to the dressing stations further up the ridge, and bring back wounded soldiers. He had not realised that these tasks would be left to an unofficial band of camp-followers, often wives and other relatives of the men. Another duty was to organise the transfer of seriously injured men to local villages or hospitals in Brussels; for this purpose, a motley collection of carriages and bullock carts was assembling beside the road, including some he had hired himself the previous day.

Strolling to the edge of the encampment he found a group out of uniform, mostly women, their small children running around the makeshift tents. One or two had set up stalls where soldiers queued to buy tobacco or brandy. Outside he spotted a man in gentleman's attire, who was seated on a rock scribbling in a notebook.

'Good morning.' Darcy bowed and introduced himself. 'I was co-opted at the last minute as an adjutant.'

'James Herrick.' The man slipped a pencil into the spine of the notebook. 'I work for the *Times* of London. Have you news from the front?'

'No. You?'

'We had a report half an hour ago that Wellington is visiting our positions at the front, after staying up most of the night writing letters to other commanders. He is relying on the Prussians to protect our left flank, while the Dutch help us hold the right. The problem is whether the Prussians will arrive in time. Luckily Bonaparte is not yet marching. Our spies say he slept in a house three miles away, and is still there.'

'I will leave you to your work.'

They nodded to one another and Darcy moved on.

Two hours later, Darcy was back at his desk when the artillery opened fire. He had met some of the officers, and accompanied one up a path to the nearest dressing station, even venturing to the crest of the ridge where they saw British infantry garrisoned inside the walls of the chateau of Hougoumont, and several lines of reinforcement behind. In the distance, in the clearing mist, he could just make out a vast mass of dark blue as the French armies began their advance.

Colonel Fitzwilliam had returned from headquarters with the news that the right and centre were now firm, allowing a retreat seawards if necessary, but the left flank would remain weak until the Prussians arrived. It was expected that Bonaparte would attack down the centre, so as to separate the British from the Prussians and control the main road into Brussels.

The explosions of cannon were shockingly loud, but still distant. The men remained calm, but a buzz went round when news came of a French advance towards the chateau. Darcy joined a group of officers discussing the significance of this move. Why attack Wellington's right flank instead of the centre? Was it the main target, or was this a diversion?

There was a collective gasp as a thunderous roar came from nearby.

'Our guns,' Colonel Fitzwilliam shouted. 'The French infantry must be in range.'

The deafening clatter continued, making it difficult to speak or even think. An officer grabbed Darcy's arm.

'Can you help? An overturned cart is blocking the path to the dressing station.'

'Shall I go?' Colonel Fitzwilliam shouted.

'You are needed here,' Darcy shouted back.

Darcy rounded up a dozen camp followers and rode ahead up the track. Just a hundred yards from the dressing station, a bullock cart had hit a deep rut in the mud and twisted on its side, spilling three wounded men who now lay at the verge. Two soldiers and a local driver had unyoked the ox, but were struggling to shift the cart. When Darcy added his weight, the cart moved a little, then fell back. He told them to save their energy, and attended to the men. All had musket wounds, roughly bandaged. One man with a head injury was unconscious; one had taken a ball in his ribs; the other, in his shoulder.

There were cries from below as camp followers joined them, and cheerfully swarmed around the cart. A massive heave not only righted the cart but nearly tipped it over the other way. The soldiers carefully reloaded their comrades, while Darcy inspected the rut which had caused the accident.

'Stop!' He ran down the hill, yelling at the retreating camp followers. 'Come here!'

They trooped back, and he counted six men, two boys, and five women, one of them pregnant.

'We must repair the path!' He jumped over a ditch into the adjoining field, and scooped up an armful of clay and stones from the border. 'Pack the hole until it is level and firm.'

The boys caught on, and set to work with enthusiasm. Striding downhill, Darcy noticed other spots where the track would become impassable. *They should have thought of this before!* But there was still time. He snapped off posts from a rotting fence and dug them into the roadside to mark ruts that needed filling.

48

Sunday 18th June, 6.00 pm

Darcy stumbled into the officers' tent, breathless from another sortie to the forward dressing station. He spotted his cousin buckling on his sabre and went to meet him.

'News?'

'The first and second waves have done their best. Now it's our turn.'

'What are your orders?'

'The French have almost gained La Haye Sainte farmhouse and are advancing up the centre. We are to form squares ready to attack from the flank.'

Darcy slapped his arm lightly. 'Good luck, cuz.'

'You look dead beat. Get a drink and sit down.'

Darcy scooped a mug of tea from an urn and sat on the straw, leaning his back against a barrel. From the next tent came screams as surgeons performed their gruesome work. Attacks against Hougoumont had continued the whole day, yet miraculously it had held. On one occasion French infantry had broken through a gate into the courtyard, only to be trapped and cut down when British soldiers swarmed to the breach and re-secured it.

But the main battle had shifted to the centre. In early afternoon, a massive infantry attack up the Brussels road threatened La Haye Sainte. This was repulsed temporarily when British cavalry charged over the ridge and down the hill. But the French reformed, and responded two hours later with a cavalry charge of their own. Wave after wave attacked; the British could only defend and hope that the Prussians would get past the French in the east, and come to their aid.

Among the departing officers, the mood was sombre. Despite heroic resistance by the troops at the front, the battle was almost lost. During the next hour the French would probably overrun the British centre, after which there would be a rout.

There was no more news, but judging from the numbers of wounded, the fighting was still intense. Carts moved in convoys up and down the slope, and as the path dried out, fewer repairs to the road were needed.

'Sir!' Darcy saw the Times correspondent Mr Herrick approaching. 'May I accompany you on this run?'

Darcy pointed to a pile of stretchers. 'Give me a hand with these.'

The journalist pocketed his notebook and they finished loading the cart.

Darcy yelled, 'Have you a horse?'

'At the back.'

'Catch us up.'

Darcy mounted, and rode ahead of the convoy to ensure the path was clear. At the dressing station, twenty men waited. Carefully he helped load three soldiers with grapeshot wounds.

Herrick arrived at his side. 'Can we go further up?'

'Too risky.'

Darcy was on the point of remounting when a woman ran screaming towards him. 'Sir! Help!'

He recognised the pregnant wife who had helped repair the road. 'What is it?'

'My Harold.' She pointed to the crest. 'Hit by cannon. Left 'im at the top.'

Darcy called out to Herrick. 'Here's your chance!'

They grabbed a stretcher, and followed the woman along the border of a field. Half a mile to their left, above the farmhouse of La Haye Sainte, Darcy saw a British position apparently abandoned, only a handful of men still standing. Hundreds of bodies lay in the long grass, victims, he assumed, of French artillery.

He tasted bile, and thought for a moment he would be sick, but managed to choke it back and press on. They passed a clump of bushes, climbed a steep bank of rough grass, and suddenly the whole valley spread before them.

Herrick gasped as they looked down on Armageddon.

Peering through the smoke, Darcy strove to take in the scene. The French had taken La Haye Sainte and were climbing towards the abandoned ridge. Below him, west of Hougoumont, squares of British infantry were waiting.

'They are ours!' Herrick shouted. 'The 52nd.'

Darcy looked again, but at this distance there would be no way of making out his cousin.

Herrick pointed past the chateau. 'The French are deploying the Imperial Guard!'

There was firing on their left, and Darcy swivelled to witness an astonishing sight. In the field he had presumed abandoned, the bodies in the long grass suddenly came to life, leapt up, and discharged lethal fire into the French infantry cresting the ridge.

He grasped Herrick's arm, and pointed. 'Look!'

The French were retreating, taking heavy casualties as they stumbled in shock down the hill. Herrick glanced at the carnage, but pulled away, intent on the massed ranks in dark blue further back.

The French infantry attacking the ridge had reformed

near the farm buildings, and Darcy switched his gaze to the Imperial Guard, which had veered west as if aiming to break through nearer the chateau.

'My God, they're coming our way!' Herrick shouted.

Darcy turned, looking for the woman. 'Let's go!'

They spotted her waving frantically, having located her husband. Darcy sprinted across the ridge to her side, and with Herrick's help lifted the man on to the stretcher. The ball had struck a glancing blow on the chest, leaving him with crushed ribs and probable damage to the lungs.

'Name?' Darcy asked, to check he was responsive.

'Corporal Dunne.' The wheezing voice was barely audible.

'We'll have you to a doctor in no time.'

With a final glance at the battlefield, Darcy saw the 52nd wheel round to approach the Guard on their flank, under cover of the trees around the chateau. Tearing himself away, he took the front of the stretcher, and with Herrick's help hastened back to the dressing station.

The convoy had left. They set Corporal Dunne beside a regimental surgeon, who had a quick look at the wound and waved them down the slope.

'Can you do nothing?' Darcy demanded.

'Surgery won't help. Get him to a bed where his wife can look after him.'

It would be simplest to leave Dunne for the next convoy, but the thought of abandoning him to a bullock cart, where his broken ribs would be horribly jarred, was unbearable.

'Shall we take him now, Mr Herrick? We can pick up the horses later.'

At the camp, duty officers were organising further transfers of the wounded to the village of Merbe Braine, where they would be attended by local doctors and women. Mrs Dunne, after running beside them all the way, bent over her husband while getting her breath back. His condition had worsened; he lay inert with his eyes closed, only the rise and fall of his chest signalling life. Darcy was about to leave when Mrs Dunne double-backed with a screech.

'Oh my God! Me waters!'

Darcy stared at her. 'Pardon?'

'The babe, bless it. It's coming.'

Darcy called out to a surgeon. 'We have a lady here in childbirth.'

'Too busy.' The man pointed towards the area where the camp followers had set their tents. 'Take her to the women.'

Darcy returned to Mrs Dunne. 'Can you walk?'

'I'm not leaving Harold.'

'Stay here, with the women. We'll take your husband to the village, and you can join him later.'

'No. I'm coming with you!'

Darcy looked at Herrick, who had remained to observe the drama. Having left so many injured men at the field hospital, it was disproportionate to devote so much effort to this couple, yet he felt impelled to carry the task through.

'Herrick! Let's carry the corporal to a carriage at the back.' Darcy looked at Mrs Dunne, and sighed. 'All right. Come if you must.'

49

Monday 19ᵗʰ June

In the Duchesse de Beaufort's parlour, Elizabeth sat quietly beside Lorraine de Crécy. After staying up half the night talking they were subdued, and having breakfasted, there was nothing to do anyway but wait.

The previous day had been the most fearful of her life—worse even than abduction by the Carandinis. From mid-morning until evening, the rumble of cannon had been constant; if it could be heard 30 miles away, what must it be like on the battlefield? A note from Darcy confirmed that he would be helping behind the lines, and would send news as soon as possible. At church she met army wives also waiting and hoping; one had lost her brother at Quatre Bras and was anxious for her husband; others had arranged to flee Antwerp by boat.

Late on Sunday they had heard shouting in the streets as a report spread that the French had been forced back and routed. The Vicomte gave it little credence, pointing out that contrary rumours had been circulating all day.

Excited voices rang out from the hall, and the Duchess looked into the parlour. 'Lorraine, Miss Bennet, please join us in the *salon*. Captain Marshall from the 52ⁿᵈ has called with a message for the Vicomte, and the news is good. Quickly now!'

Elizabeth's heart jumped—*they are safe, please let it be that they are safe*—and she ran after Lorraine to the living room where a stocky red-coated young man was addressing the Viscount.

'… seemed all was up,' he was saying, 'but as the Imperial Guard advanced to break through our centre, the Prussians arrived to defend our left flank, while the 52nd lined up on the other side and poured fire into the Guard. The *Chasseurs* resisted of course. It is said they have never retreated in their history. But eventually they ran, and our lads raced after them. On seeing this, the other French forces panicked and also scattered.'

'Wonderful!' The Vicomte clapped his hands. 'And what of our friend Colonel Fitzwilliam?'

'I heard he was at a village near Waterloo called Merbe Braine. Wounded, but should recover.'

Elizabeth stepped forward. 'And Mr Darcy?'

Captain Marshall frowned. 'Pardon, ma'am …'

'The colonel's cousin,' Elizabeth said, her heart thudding. 'He was to help behind the lines.'

'Now that you mention it, I was introduced to a cousin at the field hospital, doing useful work transporting the wounded. I have no news of what befell him.'

'Have you details of Colonel Fitzwilliam's injuries?' the Viscount asked.

Captain Marshall consulted a pocket-book. 'He was concussed, and took a bayonet slash in the leg, but with help was able to walk off the battlefield.'

Elizabeth moved to the captain's side. 'You are certain there is no mention of Mr Darcy? May I check?'

He showed her the page, which listed names of officers with shorthand codes representing outcomes ranging from death to minor injury. 'Sorry, ma'am.'

Lorraine took her arm and whispered, 'Elizabeth, we have no reason to think Mr Darcy has come to harm.'

Elizabeth grimaced. 'I want to know *where he is.*'

By midday there was no further news, and Elizabeth had formed a resolution: *she had to reach Brussels.* The Viscount politely but firmly declined. There were reports of chaos as deserters and locals clashed with soldiers struggling to keep order. Elizabeth was reluctant to press her hosts, but had an ally in Lorraine, who was incensed at remaining offstage in Antwerp when there was work to be done at the Minimes hospital.

A compromise was reached. A servant would ride to their house in Brussels, seek news of Darcy and the colonel, and report back on the state of the roads. They waited, expecting this mission to take four hours at least, but in under an hour the footman returned, having been interrogated by a Prussian officer and refused passage.

Next morning at dawn, the servant rode out again, and found that the confusion had eased. By now the Viscount was weary of arguing, and on learning that Captain Marshall was riding back, and willing to accompany them, he agreed to make the attempt. Abandoning their personal effects, they loaded two trunks with food and medical supplies and set off, taking Lorraine's maid as well as the driver and footman.

It was a slow and harrowing journey. The road was often blocked with wagons, guarded by short-tempered soldiers who refused to move out of the way. At one point, while they were overtaking an almost stationary wagon, a Prussian officer waved his sword in their driver's face and ordered him back; fortunately, Captain Marshall managed to restore calm. As they neared Brussels the smell of gunpowder was overwhelming, and the heat oppressive. At this point Captain Marshall had to gallop ahead—he had promised to report in by midday—but at last they could deviate into familiar side-streets, and progress was easier.

Elizabeth's heart hammered as they clattered up *Rue de la Violette* to the Viscount's forecourt. As the gate opened she recognised a manservant, with Burgess following behind. But no Darcy.

'You have heard nothing?' Elizabeth pressed.

Burgess raised his broad frame to its full height. 'Not a word, madam. My instructions were specific. Remain here until the master returned, or sent further orders. Or, if I heard he was, ah, …'

'Indisposed?'

'Exactly. Indisposed. Then join you in Antwerp and arrange transport to England.'

'So two days have passed since you parted.'

'I was told to remain here, madam.'

'You did well.' She tried to appear authoritative. 'But now the situation has changed. We have the colonel's address, where we can obtain news of Mr Darcy.'

Burgess faced her stubbornly. 'What if Colonel Fitzwilliam is no longer at Merbe Braine?'

'Then we will ask where he has been moved.'

Predictably the Viscount opposed her plan, this time with Lorraine's support. But matters took a new twist when Captain Marshall returned, and offered to escort Elizabeth and Burgess to Waterloo. A small, manoeuvrable carriage was prepared, and they departed directly, first to the Minimes hospital where Lorraine and her maid got off, unloading most of the medical supplies, and then along the road south, with Burgess driving and Captain Marshall riding ahead.

Conditions were now far worse. Soldiers blocked their path; the captain had to wave his sword and shout their business before they were allowed to proceed. As they painstakingly approached Waterloo the air stank with rotting flesh, and their horses howled and strained as if impelled by an instinct to flee. They turned towards Merbe Braine, the village to the west where most wounded officers from the 52nd had been taken. Elizabeth could hardly bear to look. Mutilated bodies were abandoned in piles beside the road—men, mostly British and Dutch by the uniforms, and horses too. She drew the curtains, put her head in her hands, and wept.

The carriage halted, Captain Marshall asked directions, and they turned into a row of cottages.

'Here, madam.'

Burgess helped her down. A petite woman in her thirties approached and introduced herself as Madame Villeneuve.

'Villagers have offered hospitality,' the captain said.

Elizabeth followed the woman to a tiny room, where a board had been affixed to the wall and covered with a straw pallet to make a bed. For a moment she trembled, thinking it was Darcy, but a closer look revealed the similar features of his cousin.

He stared at her. 'Miss Bennet? What …'

She pulled up a stool. 'How are you?'

'I'll pull through.' He pointed to the bandage on his head. 'Ran into the butt of a French bayonet. Confounded silly of me. Not satisfied with giving me a headache, the blighter slashed my leg just above the knee. Luckily he was cut down himself before he could finish the job.'

'And Mr Darcy?'

'Haven't seen him since he dropped by this morning.'

'So he is well?' She blinked, fighting tears. 'Pardon me. I have been in such anxiety.'

'As well as a man can be if he never sleeps.'

A shape appeared in the doorway and she span round,

only to see Captain Marshall accompanied by a stranger in army medical uniform.

'How is my patient?' the physician asked.

'Bored,' Colonel Fitzwilliam said.

The man bowed to Elizabeth. 'Good afternoon, madam. Mr Harrison.' He felt the colonel's brow. 'The fever should abate soon. Sleep. I'll bleed you again tomorrow if the wound festers.'

Colonel Fitzwilliam grunted. 'The Frenchie has already bled me enough for one lifetime. Have you seen Darcy?'

'He's still at the field hospital.'

'Tell him Miss Bennet is here.'

'No.' Elizabeth rose and addressed the captain. 'Take me to him.'

'Better remain here, ma'am. There are hundreds of injured men at the hospital. It's a most distressing sight.'

'If I ask Mr Darcy to come here, he will be distracted from his work. I would prefer to help.' She appealed to the colonel. 'I have brought provisions. Hard biscuit, oats and lint.'

'It's true that we're overwhelmed,' Colonel Fitzwilliam said. 'If you really think you can face it, go ahead. But you must be prepared for the most horrible scenes.'

She swallowed, reminded of her impulsive decision to accompany Fraulein Edelmann at the recital in Verona. Was this hubris? Was she taking on a task that she was incapable of performing?

'I will try.'

'Captain, can you go with Miss Bennet to the camp?'

Marshall shook his head. 'Impossible to get a carriage through. The track is jammed with carts in both directions. I will ride.'

Harrison, the physician, spoke up. 'I am walking back across the fields. I can accompany Miss Bennet if she is determined to go.'

Colonel Fitzwilliam looked at Elizabeth. 'I'm not sure Darcy will forgive me for this, but you may leave with Mr Harrison. The captain will find men to go with you and carry the provisions. Take care to remember the path, in case you need to return.'

50

Arrangements had been made. Burgess remained behind to watch the carriage, and send word if the colonel's condition worsened. Three soldiers were tasked to carry boxes of provisions. The physician led the little party down a lane to the edge of a farm.

'How far, Mr Harrison?' Elizabeth asked.

'Fifteen minutes using the short-cut.'

They crossed a makeshift bridge into an open cornfield. 'When did you last see Mr Darcy?'

'This morning. He was organising a new convoy for the troops that defended La Haye Sainte.' He pointed left. 'It was our central fortification, so most of the fighting took place there.'

'Was he well?'

'Exhausted. He worked through the night Sunday and Monday, with scarcely a pause.'

She sighed: how like Darcy. 'Important work?'

'Very. He organised recovery of the wounded, made sure the roads were kept in good repair, and paid carters to bring mattresses and blankets. They are trying now to set up a large field hospital at Mont St Jean, but ours grew so quickly that we have accepted men from other regiments.'

She swallowed, imagining the horror and enormity of

the task, and pointed back at the men carrying supplies. 'This will be a drop in the ocean.'

'It helps, believe me. We were so short of bandaging this morning that women were tearing strips from their petticoats.'

They passed through a copse, and suddenly there were soldiers everywhere. She glanced at a paddock where redcoats were wearily digging, and her stomach lurched when she saw a pile of bodies beyond. The physician hastened past stables into a courtyard, where women and children, lined up in a chain, were passing water from the well.

'This way.' Harrison guided her to a canvas-roofed enclosure and spoke to an officer. 'Where is Mr Darcy?'

'Who?'

'Colonel Fitzwilliam's cousin,' Elizabeth said.

'The Lieutenant-Colonel ordered him to sleep. Try the barn.'

He lay under a haystack on a red coat, his head supported by an empty sack folded double. She kept away, afraid of waking him, but he moaned and twisted his head, irritated by a stalk poking through the sackcloth. Carefully Elizabeth kneeled and pulled the stalk out, but he sniffed, as if catching her scent, and opened his eyes.

'Elizabeth? What …'

She took his hand. 'I didn't mean to disturb you. Sleep now.'

He blinked and edged himself up a little. 'Did you get my messages?'

'Only the first. We had news of your cousin from Captain Marshall, so I came to the village.'

'This is no place for you, Elizabeth.'

'It is no place for anyone, but I have seen women and children doing their best to help, and so shall I.'

He clenched his fists, as if intending to contradict her, then exhaled, his expression changing from alarm to resignation. 'As you wish.'

She guided him to the pillow and stroked his hair back, her hand brushing several days' growth of stubble. 'Sleep. I will come by in an hour and hope to find you still here.'

He looked up at her, and his eyes moistened. 'I have seen terrible things.'

'We will talk of them another time.' She leaned over, kissed his brow, and left him.

The hospital centred on the cowsheds, the largest covered area, but overflowed into stables and tents. After leaving her bonnet, reticule and jacket in the officers' tent, Elizabeth was introduced to Soeur Gabrielle, one of two local nuns who had taken charge of nursing. The sister spoke no English, but from gestures, and her smattering of French, Elizabeth understood that she was to follow the nun and help her apply bandages.

They began in the cowsheds, where only a curtain separated rows of makeshift beds from the tables where amputations were performed. Elizabeth saw straight away that she was not the only untrained helper. A surgeon toured, calling out instructions, but most of the work was done by women, including English wives and daughters from the camp followers. On the adjoining line a little girl of perhaps nine or ten was carefully tearing lint into strips and passing them to her mother.

They kneeled beside a man lying on an improvised straw mattress; Soeur Gabrielle lifted a blanket to reveal white woollen breeches shredded up one side and stained with mud and gore. Elizabeth winced as the impassive sister cut away the tatters around the wound. The man screamed, and Soeur Gabrielle thrust the scissors to Elizabeth, gesturing that she should cut from the cuff.

Elizabeth took a deep breath. Adapting dresses had given her experience of tailoring; *surely she could do this*. She managed to cut through a hard ridge at the bottom, after which the material parted easily to reveal a sickening mess of mangled flesh and dried blood. Soeur Gabrielle peeled the edges back, and cleaned the leg with a wet sponge. She waved to an assistant surgeon who peered into the wound, muttered 'Grape shot', and told them to keep the patient still while he probed with forceps. Kneeling at the head of the mattress, Elizabeth took the man's arm and felt him tremble as metal balls were removed from his leg. Through gritted teeth he grinned and muttered something that might have been *'You're a pretty'un'*. His face ran with sweat. She touched his brow, and spoke to the surgeon.

'He's feverish.'

The surgeon nodded. 'Apply a light camphor dressing for now. Don't think leeches will help. Probably have to come off later in any case.'

Elizabeth looked at the sister, who pointed to a bucket and said, *'Camphre.'*

'First wet the bandage,' the surgeon said. 'You'll soon get the hang of it.'

Elizabeth turned to thank him, but he was already on his way. The sister dipped a strip of lint into the camphor water and wrung it out.

'Élever!' She motioned Elizabeth to lift the injured leg so that she could wind the bandage around it.

Gently Elizabeth replaced the leg. *Probably have to come off later.* Which meant amputation, presumably. She shivered as they passed to the next bed.

Hours must have passed, and the horrific had become routine. Now working alone, Elizabeth had been sent to an open tent where a new consignment was laid in the dirt, cushioned only by a layer of straw. She had evolved a formula, repeated for each case. Try talking to the patient to classify the injury. Expose the affected parts, sponge them down, and unless the wounds were superficial, call a physician. Follow instructions, and pass to the next.

She was treating a man who had been struck by a cannon ball. Normally such an impact would be fatal, but since he had suffered a glancing blow on an area well layered in muscle, he had escaped with severe bruising and a hip fracture. The assistant surgeon suggested rubbing on *eau de vie*, a liquor which smelled of pears. The soldier had banged his head on a rock while falling; he observed her with a friendly smile as she sponged and bandaged the graze.

'Bless you, ma'am. What's the stuff you rubbed on?'

'A spirit similar to brandy.'

'Any left over? I could fancy a drink.'

'I can bring water later. Mixed with wine if the pain is unbearable.'

'I can wait. There's men worse than me.'

'Where are you from, sir?'

'First Yorkshires.'

She gasped. 'Do you know an Ensign Wickham?'

He nodded immediately. 'He took over as our platoon leader after the Lieutenant bought it. Good fellow. Liked a drink and a game of cards.'

She flinched at the past tense. 'What happened?'

'We was lying behind the crest, see, when the Frenchies was climbing up from La Haye farm. We jumped up and fired straight into 'em. George was near me in the second line, and got four or five of the blighters before falling. Never saw him after that. They turned and ran, we chased 'em down the hill, and I was on me way back when the ball hit me.'

Elizabeth tried to control tears. 'He died bravely, then.'

'Sorry ma'am. Relative, was he?'

'A distant one.' She frowned. 'Why have you only just arrived here?'

'Spent a night on the battlefield, didn't I, followed by another night waiting at La Haye.'

'You were left alone? No food? No medical care?'

'Couple of local lasses passed with bread and ale. Angels.' He held up a finger with blood near the knuckle. 'Unlike the hag what done this.'

'You should have told me!' She sponged the injury, but it was merely a graze. 'She scratched you?'

'Dug her nails in, didn't she, trying to rip off the ring while I was asleep. Probably thought I'd bought it.'

'How disgraceful!'

'They do worse than that. Pull teeth, even cut off fingers if they can't get the ring off ...'

Elizabeth winced, sickened by the thought that Wickham might have suffered this fate. 'I must move on now. Good luck to you, sir, and thanks for your information.'

Dusk was falling; inside the tents, lamps flickered. More and more carts arrived, and with fewer women now available to help, Elizabeth forced herself to keep going. At the back of her mind, thoughts of Wickham intruded. Was he really dead, or only injured? Was it even possible that he had fallen *deliberately*, playing dead to escape enemy fire? She dismissed the unkind thought. If Wickham had intended such a trick, he would surely have fallen *immediately* rather than firing several rounds first. No, people were a mixture of good and bad: a scoundrel could show heroism in war. She wondered what Darcy would say ...

Darcy! She had promised to look for him during the

afternoon—was he now fretting over her safety? She finished bandaging a sabre cut and made her way past the cowsheds towards the barn. A nun approached, and she recognised Soeur Gabrielle, still hard at work. The sister regarded her impassively.

'*Tout va bien?*'

'*Oui.*'

'*Reposez-vous!*'

Without smiling, Soeur Gabrielle embraced her before walking on. Moved, Elizabeth paused, watching the nun's weary tread, before hastening to the barn. There were still men resting, but Darcy had gone.

She went to the officers' tent, took a mug of tea from an urn, and sat on an empty barrel, chewing a biscuit. An officer's wife, also helping, waved to her, and they talked. An uncomfortable realisation had surfaced. She had seen Lydia's marriage to Wickham as an obstacle to her own hopes. But suppose Wickham were dead! Lydia would grieve; everyone would mourn Wickham and commend his bravery; *but the barrier would be removed.*

Instantly this thought intruded, she rejected it, hating herself. No! There should be no silver lining to a man's death. A marriage based on such a premise would turn sour, like a river poisoned at its source.

'Elizabeth!' She rose, dismissing these musings as Darcy approached with outstretched arms and took both her hands. 'Taking a well-earned rest, I see.'

'The nurse advised it.' She peered through the gloom at his face. 'Did you sleep long?'

'A couple of hours.'

'I'm sorry, I meant to look for you …'

'You were busy. I saw you while I passed the stables, but decided not to disturb you.'

'I must tell you something.' She pointed to another

barrel and they both sat. 'I met a private from the First Yorkshires who was in Mr Wickham's platoon …' She repeated what she had heard, wondering what feelings lay behind Darcy's grave countenance. 'Tragic, is it not?'

'Indeed.' He studied her closely. 'But is it certain?'

'This man knew Mr Wickham well. He talked of him as a friend.'

'For your sister's sake, I hope the soldier is mistaken.'

'I hope so too.' She puzzled over the implication of his words. Did he mean that Wickham's death would be a misfortune *only for Lydia*? Or was he merely expressing the truism that Lydia would be the person most affected?

Not wishing to discuss the matter now, she asked: 'Do you mean to work through the night again?'

He looked down a moment, thinking. 'Our intake will fall to a trickle soon since they are ready to open a hospital at Mont St Jean with superior facilities. We have already cared for the casualties from the 52nd, which were in any case relatively light. I understand from Captain Marshall that Burgess is waiting at the village, with a carriage.'

'Yes. He was told to stay there, and send word if the colonel's condition altered.'

'Can you continue another two hours? Then, if you agree, we might walk back to Merbe Braine and find out whether my cousin can be moved to Brussels.'

51

The bells of the St Michael and Gudula cathedral chimed two in the morning as their carriage at last turned into *Rue de la Violette*. Darcy sat up front beside Burgess; on his left, Elizabeth clung to his arm, a blanket draped over her shoulders and her head resting on his shoulder. Inside, on the cushioned seats, Colonel Fitzwilliam lay next to another officer, more seriously wounded, to be transferred to the Minimes hospital if there was room.

The forecourt was busy, even at this late hour. Burgess manoeuvred into a spot opposite the coach-house, which like the stables had been adapted as a hospital extension. A footman was still awake, and with his help they carried Colonel Fitzwilliam inside, while a maid was roused to attend Elizabeth.

Their arrival also woke the Viscount, who joined Darcy in the lounge and offered a restorative brandy.

'We have brought another officer from the 52nd,' Darcy explained. 'He has grape-shot wounds down his right leg, and the physician advised bringing him to a hospital in town where an amputation can be performed in greater safety. My plan was to take him to the Minimes.'

The Viscount shook his head. 'The Minimes is already overwhelmed; that is why my daughter has opened a new ward in the coach-house. Let the officer rest here tonight, and I'll ask my personal physician to see him tomorrow.

Perhaps after all the leg can be saved.'

'But have you room?'

The Viscount paced the carpet, thinking. 'We had to accommodate a surgeon in the room which Miss Bennet used before. Your room is still free, but not large enough for two. We could move a mattress into the colonel's bedroom.'

'Why not put the injured officer in my room? I will move in with my cousin.'

'Very well,' The Viscount called a servant and issued rapid instructions. 'If you can overlook the discomfort.'

'I'm so tired that I would sleep soundly on the kitchen table. But what of Miss Bennet?'

'She will share with Lorraine.'

'A pity your daughter must be disturbed.'

The Viscount spread his hands helplessly. 'She is still at work in the coach-house. I tell her repeatedly to rest, but she will not hear of it.'

Darcy sighed. 'I wish I could report that the crisis will ease, but in truth it is only starting. The numbers of the wounded are staggering, and as they are transferred from field hospitals to Brussels, the city will bear most of the strain.'

'It is a small price to pay.' The Viscount refilled their glasses. 'These fine men have ended Bonaparte's regime for ever. King Louis will be restored, and with God's help these perpetual wars will cease, and we can all return to normal co-existence.'

Elizabeth stirred as the bed creaked and someone slid under the covers. Confused, she believed for a moment that she was back at the hotel in Oriago—a scene that had provoked strange dreams more than once.

'Who ...'

'*C'est moi*,' Lorraine de Crécy whispered. 'Did I wake you?'

'No. I mean, yes, but it doesn't matter.' Lorraine had extinguished her candle, but Elizabeth could see her dimly in the moonlight. 'What time is it?'

'Past three.' Lorraine touched her arm. 'I'm so relieved that you and your friends are safe.'

'Have you been working all this time?'

'It is hard to stop when men are arriving day and night. The nuns cannot cope. We have to recruit volunteers and train them by example.' She stretched, and groaned. 'My back is killing me. Father said you helped at the field hospital.'

'Yes, washing and dressing wounds.'

'Conditions must be appalling there. Worse than in the city hospitals …' Lorraine paused. 'What are your plans?'

Elizabeth lay back, recalling a discussion with Darcy on the coach. 'It will depend on Colonel Fitzwilliam. We hope to bring him to England. Until he is fit to travel, we must stay here.'

'Will you return to the field hospital?'

'No. Mr Darcy may pass by Merbe Braine to organise transport to the city, but they have less need for nurses.'

Lorraine smiled. 'So, my dear Elizabeth, we may find work for you here!'

52

Thursday 22nd June

On a humid afternoon, Elizabeth toured a stables in *Rue du Lombard* which had been converted to a ward for men recovering from head wounds. Her role had shifted from direct nursing to supervision, as the improvised hospitals recruited servant girls capable of performing practical tasks more deftly than she could. Her value now lay partly in translating; she had acquired a vocabulary of French medical terms by late-night study with Lorraine. Additionally, she had examined such a wide range of injuries that she could judge when a physician had to be called urgently, and prescribe simple treatments on her own. Like Lorraine, she was wearing the uniform used at the Minimes for lay nurses.

Darcy's role was also changing. While Burgess plied the roads between Waterloo and Brussels, ferrying urgent cases to the city, Darcy took over Colonel Fitzwilliam's duties in recording casualties and writing to families. This still required travel, not only to Merbe Braine but to Mont St Jean, where some men from the 52nd had ended up after chasing the Imperial Guard into the centre of the battlefield. But much of it could be done in the office, allowing Darcy to spend time with his cousin, and consult him when necessary.

A new batch had arrived, and the ward at *Rue du Lom-*

bard was filling up. Elizabeth had trained two maids from the owner's household to perform the simple tasks she had learned from Soeur Gabrielle, and taught them English words for body parts, weapons, and symptoms such as pain, fever and thirst. What the maids could *not* manage was conversation: asking how the injury had been sustained, how it had been treated at the field hospital, and whether the patient had special requests. Elizabeth passed along the row, checking for cases that might be particularly urgent, then froze with shock.

Could it be?

The man was barely conscious, and much of his scalp was hidden by a rough bandage, but *those features*, that impudent smirk engrained at the corners of the mouth …

She leaned over him and whispered: 'Mr Wickham?'

He opened an eye, and flinched. 'You?'

She knelt beside him. 'I'm overjoyed to find you alive, sir. Can you talk?'

He blinked, as if absorbing her words was a huge effort. 'Darcy?'

'Do you want to see him?'

He shivered. 'No. Drink?'

She called in French to a maid, who brought a glass of wine diluted in water. Afraid of choking him, she scooped a small amount with a spoon, and held it between his lips.

'You'll like this. The owner keeps a good cellar.'

He slurped it down, with the hint of a grin. 'More.'

Patiently she continued spooning the liquid. 'Are you in bad pain?'

'Just weak.'

'May I examine your wound?'

He flinched, and she pulled her hand back. 'I'll be very gentle.'

He grunted. 'Not a pretty sight.'

'I'm used to that. Hold still.'

Very carefully she unwound the dirty linen, so stained in blood that she suspected it had been re-used from another patient. The blood was coming from a deep groove on the right side of the head, where a musket ball or piece of grapeshot must have ploughed into the skull, perhaps lodging there.

She wiped with a sponge to get a clearer look. 'What caused this?'

'Musket.'

'Is the ball still inside?'

He shook his head. 'Surgeon took it out.'

'Listen, I'm going to get a doctor. I should be back in twenty minutes.'

He nodded, and she called a maid over to apply a clean bandage.

An assistant surgeon named Lebrun was touring external wards. Elizabeth caught up with him at one of the largest venues, a count's coach house, and he agreed to pass by as soon as he was finished there.

She returned at leisure, enjoying the fresh air—a welcome change from the disgusting smells of the ward. Her first thought had been to send a servant, but she was glad now that she had come herself. The original motive had been practical: she believed her personal plea would yield a quicker response. Escaping the stables, even for a few minutes, was icing on the cake.

By the time she had reviewed the other new cases, Monsieur Lebrun arrived, with an orderly. Elizabeth sat with Wickham, trying to divert him with gossip from Jane's letters, while Lebrun examined another patient. Finally Lebrun came over and spoke to Wickham.

'How are you feeling?'

'Dizzy. Sick.'

'Can you recall where you fell?'

'Only what I was told. Later.'

Lebrun raised fingers. 'How many?'

'Three.'

'You recognised Miss Bennet straight away?'

He nodded, eyes losing focus as he submitted to the surgeon's examination.

Lebrun drew Elizabeth aside and lowered his voice. 'I think with good care he should pull through. He must lie still, and sleep as much as possible, to conserve energy. As you see, there is a hole and some cracking in the skull. This can be repaired later by fitting a silver plate.'

She found Darcy in Colonel Fitzwilliam's office, writing letters. In a trembling voice, fearing his reaction, she told him what had happened.

He received the news in silence, a deep frown suggesting either that he was dismayed, or simply thinking: she could not tell which.

Eventually he asked, 'What level of care is he receiving at present?'

'Rudimentary.'

'Then we should intervene. Whatever we may think of Mr Wickham, he is your sister's husband, and has by all accounts fought bravely. Can you take me to him?'

She hesitated. 'I think he fears you.'

'That is one reason I would like to see him.'

As they walked the short distance to *Rue du Lombard*, she asked Darcy about his desk work.

'I've been writing letters for families of those who fell in the 52nd. So far we have the names of 38 officers and men.'

She thought of the hundreds of men she had treated. 'It sounds a large number, but perhaps it is not.'

'That is correct. In a regiment of over a thousand men our casualties were relatively light, since the 52nd took the field later in the battle.'

'What can you say to the families?'

'We express regret, of course, but I have tried also to include details of what these men did, and how they died. I spent much of yesterday touring hospitals to talk with our wounded, to get their reports. Of course some editing is necessary. Then I take the letters to my cousin, who signs them.'

Elizabeth observed as Darcy carried a stool to the bedside. Wickham, who had been dozing, opened an eye, and flinched.

'So, George.' Darcy spoke gently. 'We meet again.'

'It was just a dance,' Wickham muttered.

Darcy smiled. 'I hardly expected you of all people to turn up in Brussels.'

'Like the proverbial bad penny ...'

Elizabeth stepped forward, encouraged by Wickham's fluency—perhaps he was recovering from the pounding in the wagon. 'I was glad to dance with Mr Wickham, and his behaviour was gentlemanlike.'

'Hear that, Darcy?' Wickham looked away, reddening, and muttered, 'What's the use? You'll never give me a fair chance.'

Darcy snorted. 'Fair chance? Who paid compensation when you renounced the living? Who arranged your marriage and paid off your debts? Who did all this and more, *despite* your abuse of ... my family?' Darcy held up a palm, forestalling objections. 'You know, in your heart, that all this is so. But one more thing needs to be said. What you do *not* know is that just before the battle was decided, I found myself on the hill above the chateau, and saw the French infantry climbing to the ridge where you and your comrades were hiding. Of course I could not identify individuals, but I spoke later to a man in your platoon who confirmed that you were there. I watched as you and your comrades rose, formed into lines, and poured round after round into the French ranks, keeping your discipline even as they returned fire. It was the bravest action I ever saw, and quite possibly turned the battle.'

Wickham stared at him. After a long silence, he cleared his throat and said in a creaking voice, 'I cannot remember any of it.'

'You fell, but only after standing your ground for four or five rounds, and downing several of the enemy.'

Elizabeth had expected Wickham to gloat at receiving such praise, from such a source, but instead he scowled, as if ashamed at his own heroism. 'We had no choice.'

'Pardon?'

'They shoot runaways.'

Darcy touched his arm. 'Come, George, accept that for once you acted honourably, and let us discuss what is to be done. Miss Bennet and I are lodged nearby with a family that has taken in a number of patients, including my cousin. I believe that you would be more comfortable there, and receive superior treatment. If you agree, I will ask for you to be moved.'

Wickham looked anxiously at Elizabeth, as if seeking confirmation that this could be true.

'It will be best,' she said. 'We can arrange it.'

His face softened. 'Then I am in your debt.'

53

Monday 26th June

Darcy rode south, paying a final visit to the village of Merbe Braine. Burgess had left with the carriage earlier in the morning, with instructions to wait there. Before closing down the operation, Darcy wanted to ensure that all patients had been transferred to the city—excepting those who could not safely be moved.

The huge task of clearing up after the battle was continuing. By comparing statistics with officers from other regiments, they estimated British losses as 3000 dead and 10000 wounded; another 2000 were unaccounted. These casualties added up to a quarter of Wellington's army; the other three-quarters were now advancing on Paris. Bonaparte was still at large, but it was rumoured that he would shortly abdicate and go into hiding. All coalition armies, including the Prussians and Dutch, were now occupied with the invasion of France, leaving it to the Walloons to cope with the aftermath of the battle.

Convoys of wounded still came from the field hospital at Mont St Jean, keeping Lorraine de Crécy and Elizabeth busy until late into the evening. However, the days of two or three hours sleep were over. More and more wards had been set up in private houses; servants had been trained in simple nursing; surgeons had come from Antwerp, Mons and Ghent. Elizabeth had recovered her strength, and performed the daunting work calmly. Late at night, sipping brandy with the de Crécys, she looked fulfilled, even radiant. Their conversation too had changed. There was no sarcasm, quarrelling, or teasing, and only sporadic flashes of wit or erudition. It was as if, now that they had genuinely important things to say, they had less need for these embellishments—just as wholesome food had less need for spice. Nobody needed to be clever, personalities retreated into the background, and they simply talked.

The patients, too, were on the mend. Colonel Fitzwilliam's concussion had passed, except for a slight headache, and his wound was clearing up after a course with maggots. Wickham had been moved to a small bed in the Vicomte's box room, and examined by a specialist in head injuries. The treatment was simply to lie still, so that the skull could re-knit, then affix a plate. The physician removed a few fragments of bone with tweezers. Without a deep cut there was no call for leeches; a little honey was smeared on, to reduce festering, and a clean bandage applied. Of course with Wickham there would be problems. Often bored, he did his best to charm the maids, and pester the footmen into playing cards; luckily, he passed much of the day asleep.

Darcy had asked Madame Villeneuve to take in Corporal Harold Dunne, hoping that his condition might improve under her excellent care. The trip from the field hospital, during the battle, had been so rough that it was surprising the corporal had survived the day. Since then, he had lain in constant discomfort from a cough, as well as difficulty in breathing. His wife, also badly shaken up, had spent two long days in labour, becoming so weak that she had sadly passed away after delivery of a baby boy.

Reaching Merbe Braine, Darcy learned that the situation had taken another turn for the worse: he found Madame Villeneuve distressed, and her patient dead.

Darcy went to the tiny bedroom, once occupied by his cousin, and saw the corporal laid out. He asked what had happened, his French now good enough to follow the answer. Corporal Dunne had always wanted a boy, planning to hand down his own name, Harold; but news of his wife's death had soured what should have been a happy event, and he had faded rapidly.

Arrangements were made. Two patients could be taken to Brussels; the villagers would bury Corporal Dunne and his wife in a brief ceremony. The baby was brought out—a plump little fellow with a square wrinkled face—and consigned to Darcy's care. Luckily Burgess was ferrying another wife back to the city; she agreed to take the baby so that Darcy could ride ahead.

Elizabeth cradled the baby, now wrapped in a clean white shawl. 'So sad. What can we do?'

It was nearly six o'clock—dinner hour in the de Crécy household—and they were in the *salon*. Darcy poured two glasses of sherry from a decanter. 'Responsibility is not ours, since Corporal Dunne was in the 71st Foot. However, it was I that brought Dunne to Merbe Braine, and he hailed from a village named Rodmersham in Kent—no great distance from our route into London. If you agree, I would like to take the infant there, and search for relatives who might adopt him.'

Elizabeth nodded. 'I will be happy to look after him.'

'We can find a nursemaid to accompany us.'

'How?'

'I know of several Englishwomen who find themselves stranded here after their menfolk left, or fell in the battle. For instance, among the camp followers in the 52nd was a woman named Martha Briggs, who helped with repairing the road as well as nursing.'

Elizabeth looked up. 'Rosie's mother! I met her at the field hospital. What happened to her husband?'

'He marched off unscathed towards Paris. Mrs Briggs stayed behind because she wanted to return home. She is working in Brussels while the 52nd organises her transport. Burgess has her address.'

'Perfect! Let us ask her immediately.'

'I'll put Burgess on the job.' Darcy watched her dandle the baby, moved by the domesticity of the scene. 'I hope that in a few days we can leave for Ostend. Colonel Fitzwilliam is fast improving.'

'And Mr Wickham?'

'Will have to stay several weeks longer. The Viscount offered to keep him here until there is room at the Minimes. After that, the First Yorkshires can look after him.'

Elizabeth looked away, her eyes moist. 'It is an absurd thing to say, but I shall be sorry to go.'

He nodded. 'The experience of a lifetime.'

'Yes.' She regarded him earnestly. 'I am so grateful that you allowed me to play my part.'

'We were desperately short. Whatever my misgivings, it was necessary. For the men.'

She whispered, 'For me too.'

54

Tuesday 4ᵗʰ July 5pm

Elizabeth dozed as their hired carriage passed through the Kentish countryside towards Rodmersham, home of Corporal and Mrs Dunne. The crossing from Ostend to Ramsgate had taken 24 hours, during which she had suffered continuously from seasickness and not slept at all. Opposite, Martha Briggs and Rosie also looked pale, and Colonel Fitzwilliam weary, although he had not been sick. Only Darcy and Burgess seemed unaffected—and also, thankfully, the baby.

They had set off on Friday morning after an emotional parting from the de Crécys. The dramatic aftermath of the battle had forged a bond strong as a family tie, especially with Lorraine, whom she now counted as one of her closest friends. She thought often of the tall, graceful, plain young woman, not gifted like Alice Dill or Hilda Edelmann, but kind and courageous—and such fun when she let her hair down in private. Lorraine had agreed to write, and also to visit, once teasing Elizabeth that they might meet up in Derbyshire …

There had been no more discussion of marriage. So far as the Viscount and Colonel Fitzwilliam were concerned, she and Darcy were presumed betrothed. Between themselves, matters had not advanced since their conversation in the Tyrol: it was acknowledged that they were in love, but they would display *discretion* and *sobriety*, as demanded by the Book of Common Prayer, and reconsider their future after the journey. Well, they should talk it over before reaching London—if they could only find a calm moment of privacy.

At Rodmersham they stopped at St Nicholas Church, and Elizabeth accompanied Darcy to enquire at the Vicarage. The housekeeper perked up as soon as they mentioned the Dunnes. Of course, at Baker Cottage. Near the green. Yes, there was a son, Harold, in the army. Married to Kitty Farr last year. No children, one on the way. Why ...

Darcy replied noncommittally that he needed to speak with the parents on a private matter.

At Baker cottage they found Mrs Dunne and confided the sad news. The corporal's mother was a sturdy down-to-earth woman, and her initial reaction was stoical: having received no letter since before the battle, she already feared the worst. But her restraint dissolved in tears when Elizabeth brought forward the child, and placed it in her arms. Darcy stayed to talk with her, satisfying himself that she was the person best placed to take over responsibility.

As they left, a storm broke; luckily there was an inn yards away across the village green with a comfy interior, and aromas of mutton pie from the kitchen. As they ate, Darcy leaned over and whispered: 'Elizabeth, we will not reach London tonight in such weather.'

'Perhaps it will clear.'

'I see no sign of it. We are also tired after the crossing. I know you have misgivings, but I think it best that we stay overnight at Rosings.'

She stared at him. Darcy had informed Lady Catherine by letter that he and Colonel Fitzwilliam were well, and on their way back to England; he had omitted any reference to Elizabeth.

'*Misgivings* hardly covers it. We both know how your aunt would react if she knew what had passed between us these last months. I cannot ask hospitality of her.'

'You can stay with the Collinses.'

'And when her ladyship finds out? Her wrath will descend on poor Charlotte like the seven last plagues.'

Darcy sighed. 'I'm afraid my aunt's ire must be faced by all of us, sooner or later.' He touched her arm. 'Come, after all we have endured, we can survive the rants of Lady Catherine.'

They reached Rosings two hours after sundown. The rain had abated, but with the sky still overcast there was no moonlight. Reluctantly Elizabeth accepted that Darcy was right: navigating the lane to Hunsford was hard enough, let alone the road to London.

At last she recognised the laurel hedge and the familiar garden sloping up to the parsonage, where candlelight still glowed in a front room. A maid-of-all-work stood in the doorway, peering anxiously through the gloom; on recognising Elizabeth she gasped, and disappeared within to summon Mrs Collins.

'Lizzy, what a surprise!' Charlotte pointed to the upper floor, continuing in a whisper. 'Mr Collins is abed; he rises early, you know.' She saw Darcy coming up the path, and bowed. 'Good evening, sir.'

'Good evening, Mrs Collins, and forgive our sudden intrusion.' Darcy also kept his voice low. 'It is a lot to ask, but can you offer Miss Bennet a bed for the night? I will proceed with Colonel Fitzwilliam to Rosings.'

Charlotte looked back and forth from Darcy to Elizabeth, in great confusion. 'You are always welcome here, Lizzy. But how …'

Darcy smiled. 'Have no fear, Mrs Collins: Lady Catherine will approve. I shall see to that.' He turned to Elizabeth. 'I will call late tomorrow morning. We all need to catch up on sleep.'

The carriage left, and Elizabeth followed Charlotte to the parlour while the maid prepared refreshment.

'Lizzy, what can this mean? There are rumours you have been seen *at a ball in Brussels* with Mr Darcy and the colonel. Lady Catherine was *beside herself* and demanded that I should explain! I had only your letter ...'

'From Verona?'

'Exactly! You said you had joined a party returning to England, attended concerts, toured Roman ruins. Was Mr Darcy in the party?'

'It's a long story.' Elizabeth sighed. 'Dear Charlotte, it is wrong for me to remain here tonight ...'

Charlotte shook her head firmly. 'Why? Mr Darcy has assured me that her ladyship will raise no objection. Anyway, where else can you go?'

'Should we inform Mr Collins?'

'Wake him now? Certainly not.' Charlotte kneeled at her side. 'Lizzy, you are exhausted. Ellen is preparing hot toddies with brandy and honey. The chamber you used before is made up; she will bring your drink there. We can talk in the morning.'

55

Breakfast at Rosings was an ample meal served at nine thirty. The table was laid with boiled eggs, kept warm by woollen caps, dishes of bacon and cold meats, smoked haddock, rolls and other breads, preserves, tea, coffee and hot chocolate. It was Lady Catherine's habit to enter at *exactly* the time ordained—and Darcy's to arrive earlier, so that he could pass an agreeable ten minutes in conversation with Anne or Colonel Fitzwilliam, without constant interruption from her ladyship.

Anne de Bourgh was in her late twenties, just a year younger than Darcy. She looked as she usually did: pale, thin, a little puffy. With every passing year, a look of defeat etched deeper in her once pretty features. He felt a certain guilt: perhaps he should have forced the issue of their so-called *betrothal* into the open long ago, leaving Lady Catherine no alternative but to seek another suitor. He had hoped that this would be achieved by his own marriage. Unfortunately the years had slipped by in fruitless search, and when he had at last fallen in love, he had been rejected ...

Anne's best chance, he believed, was that fate would separate her from her mother. He asked what she was reading, when she had last been in town, whether she had made new friends. Every question was met with the briefest possible answer. He kept trying, but it was almost a relief when Lady Catherine swept in.

'The wanderers have returned.' She sat at the end of the table, opposite Colonel Fitzwilliam. 'Johnson, where are the brown rolls? I asked particularly that we should have a choice of white or brown. Have the eggs been boiled four minutes?'

The servant bowed. 'Yes ma'am.'

'We shall see. It is of the utmost importance that the timing be precise. Well Darcy! I have been hearing most disturbing reports.'

Darcy raised his eyebrows. 'Good morning, aunt. You refer no doubt to the injuries my cousin sustained in the battle. He is too modest to say so, but you should know that his regiment performed magnificently against Bonaparte's elite troops.'

Colonel Fitzwilliam waved this away. 'Let us not alarm the ladies, Darce.' He turned to Anne. 'My wounds were minor, and I am now fully recovered.'

'I am gratified to hear it.' Lady Catherine cried. 'But I was speaking of quite another matter. I suppose you realise, Darcy, that your indiscretions are openly discussed in the *ton*. I heard from Lady Frances Webster, who is such a gossip that by now everyone will know. I tried my best to limit the damage, but ...' She threw up her hands. 'There is only one remedy. We must announce your engagement to Anne in *The Times* immediately.'

Darcy broke the top of an egg, taking his time so as to conceal his irritation. 'I have not the pleasure of understanding you. We met Lady Webster at a ball in Brussels, and enjoyed a pleasant conversation. I have known her husband since our schooldays.'

'I refer, as you well know, to Mr Collins's cousin, Miss Elizabeth Bennet, to whom I showed such gracious condescension during her visit last year, considering that she is a young lady of no consequence. Imagine my shock on learning that you had not only accompanied Miss Bennet to a ball, but danced with her *twice!* To pay *such* attentions, to *such* a woman, when betrothed to another!' She shivered, as if insects were crawling over her skin. 'I told Lady Webster that she must be mistaken. But no, she was quite sure; she regarded me with that supercilious smile of hers, revelling in her superior information. For shame, sir! That I should have to *humiliate* myself before that *frightful* woman, that *shameless wanton*, to undo the harm you have done, and preserve the good name of the family.'

Darcy sipped coffee, allowing this intemperate outburst to hang in the air, its absurdity, he hoped, manifest. 'You will excuse me if my sympathy is muted, aunt. It is embarrassing, I know, when an acquaintance is better informed on family affairs than you are. However, a little embarrassment is easily borne.' He turned to indicate Colonel Fitzwilliam. 'Your nephew fought bravely at Waterloo and survived only by luck. Miss Bennet, whom you hold in such low esteem, worked for over a week tending to wounded officers and men. She is a remarkable and lovely woman, and her husband, when she marries, will be fortunate indeed. As to whether I shall be that man …' He sighed. 'I cannot say. When I know, you will be told.'

Lady Catherine stared at him, her mouth wide open as if frozen in the act of speaking. Eventually she spluttered, 'Miss Bennet … worked … as a *nurse?*'

'Yes.'

'Were there no *servants* in Brussels?'

Colonel Fitzwilliam coughed. 'You should understand, aunt, that after a major battle thousands of men need urgent treatment. Hospitals are overwhelmed. Local servants, if available at all, speak no English. Miss Bennet, like Darce, threw herself into the breach, earning our admiration as well as our gratitude.'

Lady Catherine shook her head, momentarily speechless. 'I never heard anything more disgraceful.'

There was a frosty silence. Darcy observed Anne, following intently and obviously shocked. Perhaps they had been too explicit in describing the horrors of war—or perhaps a dose of reality would help Anne grow up: who could tell?

Lady Catherine slapped the table. 'Where is Miss Bennet now? Has she returned to Hertfordshire?'

'She spent the night at Hunsford.'

'Indeed!' Lady Catherine summoned a servant. 'Tell Mr and Mrs Collins that they are to come here immediately. You hear? *Immediately*. Not Miss Bennet. She is to remain behind. I will *not* have her at Rosings.'

Darcy made no protest. He had finally made his feelings plain to Anne. Lady Catherine had never listened to reason in her life, and would scarcely begin now. If the Collinses came to Rosings, an opportunity presented itself. It was time to talk with Elizabeth in private.

56

He walked the half-mile to Hunsford in the morning sunshine. The park railings, laurel hedge, gate, door-bell, all reminded him of a similar mission 15 months before. A maid, the same one, answered the door. Of course, Elizabeth might not be in. She would be tempted to take advantage of the weather and roam the park. But no: he was led to the same room, and announced.

Elizabeth was seated at a window, writing in her journal. She rose as he entered, and they waited in silence as the maid's footsteps receded.

She smiled, breaking the spell. 'Disturbing, is it not?'

'The stage is unchanged; the players, I hope, have advanced in understanding.'

'Did you pass Mr and Mrs Collins on your way here?'

'I left just as they were arriving.'

'Mr Collins is in such a flap! I fear they are about to suffer the sharp edge of her ladyship's tongue—and on my account.'

'I'm sorry, Elizabeth. This is my fault.'

'Did you speak with your aunt?'

He nodded. 'News of the ball has reached London, and her reaction, as you may imagine, was abusive. I concealed nothing. She knows we have been travelling together. She knows my feelings in your regard; and so does Miss de Bourgh.'

She eyed him impishly. 'Are you going to tell me too?'

He looked doubtfully around the room. 'We must talk. But not here.'

'How about the park?'

After strolling through a copse, talking inconsequentially, they reached a clearing where a bench, partially shaded, overlooked a pond. Elizabeth closed her parasol, and they sat side by side.

'We must leave today for London,' Darcy said. 'All of us, Colonel Fitzwilliam too. Despite his protestations, he needs to convalesce in a peaceful well-ordered household, and he will not find that here with my aunt in a frenzy.'

'And once we reach London? I assume I will stay with my Uncle and Aunt Gardiner, and leave for Longbourn the next day.'

'I was hoping you would come first to Darcy House, so that I could introduce you to my sister.'

'I am eager to meet her.'

'She will be curious as to the, ah, relationship between us.' He smiled. 'I must admit to an interest in that very point myself.'

'Aha!' She dealt him a sly grin. 'You are about to reveal those *feelings* that you have already admitted to Lady Catherine.'

'My feelings are as they were last year, except that now they are based on secure knowledge rather than early impressions.'

'You have found out how scatter-brained I am?'

He smiled. 'Perhaps, but also that you are courageous, conscientious, compassionate, and remarkably well-read. My only doubt is whether I am worthy of you.'

She gave a little shiver, her eyes filling, and reached for his hand.

'Have no worries on that score, my dearest. We are going to marry. Is it not plain to you?'

Relief spread through him. He breathed deeply, before replying: 'You seemed quiet these last days, even downcast. Perhaps it was the rigours of the journey.'

She shook her head. 'It has been a reaction, I believe, to the period we passed in Brussels after the battle. I have never experienced such excitement and comradeship before. I cannot say how much it meant to me. For the first time in my life I contributed to something worthwhile. I longed to return home, but still it was a wrench to leave Lorraine and the others.'

He nodded, understanding what she meant. 'You have not been in anxiety over—our future.'

'Not at all. Before, while we sailed down the Rhine, I had doubts. In Brussels I was too immersed in nursing to have any thoughts about myself. And when it was over, I knew, without further reflection, that our destiny was decided. Perhaps it is perverse, but I feel in spirit we are *already* married. The ceremony will merely confirm it.'

'Because we pretended to be man and wife in Italy?'

She laughed. 'No. Because of what happened later. I was so proud of what you had achieved at the camp, and longed to help, like you and Lorraine. To my surprise and relief I found that I really *could* do it. I could face terrible wounds, disgusting chores, life-and-death decisions, and care for those poor men. And I was proud that we were both *overjoyed* to find Mr Wickham alive; and that without a second thought you secured him the best treatment. I recalled with shame my panic on the boat when you told me of Mr Wickham's designs on your sister. How *inconvenient* for me that such a scoundrel should prevent me from marrying the man I loved! But the truth is ...' She faced him, taking a breath. 'The truth is that the world was not created for our convenience. We fear Georgiana's distress that my sister is now Mrs Wickham, but as you pointed out, is it so awful that she should be upset for a while? Must everything be perfect? I am flawed, so are you, so will our marriage be. No matter. We both know we belong together, and that is that.'

They were silent a long time, until Darcy said, with a smile, 'So imperfection is the human condition.'

She laughed. 'It took me a long time to say that.'

'Yet some *moments* are perfect, and this is one of them.' He raised her hand to his lips.

She faced him, radiating confidence, delight, certainty. 'You could kiss me even better if we stood up.'

They rose, and observing the protruding edges of her bonnet, he began slowly to unlace it.

'You seem in no hurry, sir,' she complained.

'I am savouring the moment.'

She coloured, her whole body trembling in anticipation as his arms went around her.

57

St Margaret's Church struck six as they crossed Westminster Bridge, festooned with flags to celebrate Wellington's victory. Elizabeth sat opposite the gentlemen, with Rosie Briggs at her side playing with one of Herr von Essen's wooden dolls. They were not far now from Brompton, where Martha lived with Corporal Briggs's mother; however, Darcy preferred to proceed first to his town house in Mayfair, so that driver and horses could be changed before taking Mrs Briggs and daughter to their home.

They traversed the parkland around St James's Palace and Buckingham House—now Queen Charlotte's residence—and before long entered Park Lane, with Hyde Park and the Serpentine on their left, and grand town houses on their right. A turn into Grosvenor Street, and the carriage at last stopped outside a broad terraced house with three stories plus basement and attic.

Darcy handed Elizabeth down, and she took in a well-kept facade with black-painted railings overhanging the basement area, and pillars framing three steps leading to the main entrance, also black, with brass fittings. A footman ushered them to a palatial drawing room papered in crimson, with a parquet floor, Indian rug, and comfortable chairs and divans in unobtrusive good taste.

A young woman appeared in the doorway, looked shyly at the party, then cried out and ran to Darcy with arms outstretched.

'William! Home at last!'

Elizabeth observed the girl with curiosity. The family resemblance was clear: she was quite tall, with a straight nose and intelligent blue-grey eyes. However, unlike Darcy her colouring was fair, with very pale skin, and blonde hair carefully pinned.

'Miss Bennet.' Darcy led the girl towards her. 'May I introduce my sister, Miss Georgiana Darcy.'

Georgiana regarded her with a mixture of shyness and avid interest, but seemed lost for words.

Elizabeth smiled. 'You must be relieved to have your brother back safe.'

'Oh yes. I had his letters of course.'

'And Colonel Fitzwilliam too. You have been left quite alone.'

'Well, I have had Mrs Annesley. Also, since last week, Mr Bingley is in town. I believe you are acquainted?' She put a hand to her mouth. 'But how foolish of me! He is betrothed to your sister.'

'I *have* heard the good news, but the post has been so unreliable that one can take nothing for granted. I hear you are fond of music, Miss Darcy.'

'Oh yes. It is my favourite pastime.' Again she stopped abruptly. 'But I am forgetting! My brother said in a letter that you had accompanied a famous singer at a concert in Italy. I'm sure you play far better than I.'

Elizabeth laughed. 'You will be disabused of *that* idea directly you hear me play. Perhaps we can try a duet this evening.'

'I would love that.'

Darcy clapped his hands and addressed the whole gathering. 'Welcome to our London home. Dinner will be served in half an hour. Meanwhile, permit us to show you your rooms. Miss Bennet, perhaps Georgiana can escort you, since your chamber is next to hers.'

'You are all kindness, sir.' She met his eye with an arch smile, and then looked away, realising how closely Georgiana was observing them.

'Shall we go immediately?' Georgiana asked.

'One moment.' Elizabeth drew Darcy aside. 'I ought to call on my uncle and aunt Gardiner to reassure them I am well. However, it is getting late and I am tired of sitting in carriages.'

'Why not send a message? I can invite them to visit us tomorrow morning, if that is convenient.'

Elizabeth smiled her relief. 'Perfect. I will feel so much better if they are informed.'

With a glance at Georgiana, now talking to Colonel Fitzwilliam, Darcy whispered: 'My sister too should be informed, of what we agreed earlier.'

'Certainly,' Elizabeth whispered. 'But can you wait until tomorrow? Let me get to know her first.'

At eleven o'clock, Elizabeth accompanied Georgiana to their corridor on the second floor. She was tired, but not *quite* ready to sleep: with the gentlemen enjoying brandy and cigars in Darcy's study, no doubt exchanging tales of the war or some such masculine topic, it was time for a private chat with the lady of the house.

The evening had passed in an atmosphere of relaxed contentment, as she reacquainted herself with the routines of English life. Familiar brands of rouge and cream were laid out in her dressing room. Instead of challenging continental dishes, they had enjoyed Irish stew, still fashionable in the *ton*. She had sight-read duets with Georgiana in the music room, happily trilling out handfuls of wrong notes that would have shocked Carandini. It also served her purpose that Georgiana knew these pieces while she did not: after their session, the girl was no longer daunted.

They shared Georgiana's maid, and when they were in their dressing gowns, Elizabeth suggested cocoa before retiring.

'I would like that. We can go to my boudoir.'

The maid left for the kitchen, and they made themselves comfortable in the cosy retreat, furnished like a miniature salon, which adjoined Georgiana's bedroom. While waiting for their drinks they talked of safe topics, but sooner or later the nettle would have to be grasped. *How much did Georgiana know?* Had Darcy told her, in person or in his letters, of his feelings for the woman that had shared his Grand Tour?

'You find your brother well?' Elizabeth asked.

'Oh yes! So much more content than formerly.' Georgiana flushed, as if unsure how to continue, and sipped cocoa to occupy the silence. 'You see, Miss Bennet, last year William was not himself. He had been preoccupied for some months, then in the spring returned from Kent in the darkest mood. I have never seen him so low.' Her eyes moistened. 'It is unpleasant to contemplate, for I believe his distress was *my fault.*'

Elizabeth stared at her. 'My dear Miss Darcy, what do you mean?'

Georgiana hung her head, biting her lip. 'I ought not to speak of it. You see ...' She looked up, as if in supplication. 'I made a mistake. A bad mistake, which upset my brother exceedingly, and gave him no end of trouble. It was resolved, covered up anyway, but it took him a long time to get over it. He was often away in those months, visiting Mr Bingley in Hertfordshire. I believe he found it painful to remain in my company.'

Elizabeth's heart went out to the girl as she struggled to retain her poise. Impulsively she moved to the divan and took her hand. 'Listen. I happen to know why your brother returned from Rosings in a black mood, and the reason is not what you imagine. Your, ah, *mistake* was far from his mind. The person who angered him was—me.'

Georgiana gaped at her.

'I will explain.' Elizabeth smiled. 'And you will discover that you are not the only person who makes mistakes. I met your brother in Hertfordshire, and then by chance at Rosings, while visiting a friend who had married the parson. Mr Darcy, much to my surprise, *offered me his hand in marriage*, whereupon I made my first mistake. I rejected his offer in the rudest fashion imaginable.'

Georgiana gasped. 'No! I cannot believe …'

'Wait. There is more. Not only was I rude, but I justified my refusal by accusations that proved entirely false. Mistake number two. Still more: when he wrote a letter explaining my errors, *I refused to read it.* Three!'

'But Miss Bennet …'

'I have not finished! Having rejected the finest man I had ever met, I befriended an unscrupulous Italian woman, allowed her deranged brother to believe I would marry him, and ended up a prisoner in Venice. Four! Were it not for Mr Darcy I would probably be there still, the victim of a forced marriage.'

'So that is why …' Georgiana's eyes were like saucers. 'Is that all the mistakes?'

Elizabeth laughed. 'On my side, yes. However, earlier today your brother committed the ultimate folly of asking me *again* to marry him …'

'Oh, Miss Bennet!' Georgiana faced her with a radiant smile. 'I see it all now. That is why William is so changed, so relaxed and happy …'

Elizabeth nodded. 'Just so. Perhaps the stars were in a favourable configuration, perhaps divine providence came to our aid, but for once in my life *I did the right thing*. I accepted, and unless he comes to his senses and quickly changes his mind, we are to be married.'

Georgiana hesitated, perhaps nonplussed by so many twists and turns, but her warm smile returned. 'I am overjoyed and wish you every happiness.'

'Thank you.' Elizabeth relaxed a little: the first hurdle was crossed. But she had to go further. 'Miss Darcy, being serious for once, I am aware of my good fortune in marrying your brother. However, a concern remains.' She leaned closer and lowered her voice. 'You may have heard that my youngest sister, Lydia, was recently wed.'

Georgiana coloured, and nodded assent.

'To a man we are both acquainted with. Mr Wickham.'

She flinched, and managed another tiny nod.

Elizabeth swallowed. 'I am now going to distress you, but I see no alternative. For a very special reason, your brother has explained what passed between you and Mr Wickham at Ramsgate, when you were fifteen. Let me assure you that he has confided in myself *alone*, after I, like you, had been deceived by Mr Wickham, and accused Mr Darcy of maltreating *him*. Thus I am already aware, in outline, of the *mistake* you referred to before.' She took a deep breath. 'Could you bear the thought of your brother marrying a woman who now finds herself, much to her distaste, that gentleman's *sister-in-law*?'

Georgiana fell silent, biting her lip in concentration. 'I see no difficulty, except ...' She coloured. 'I would be discomfited if the Wickhams were to visit Pemberely.'

'They will never be invited. You have my word, as well as Mr Darcy's.'

Georgiana looked away dreamily. 'You will think me

foolish, but I feel no hatred towards George—I mean, Mr Wickham. I know he is unprincipled. But he was kind to me when I was a small girl, and our ... *indiscretion* was as much my fault as his. I hope he will mend his ways, and find joy in his marriage to your sister.'

Elizabeth thought for a while, before replying: 'Then I should acquaint you with the latest developments.' And Georgiana listened open-mouthed as she told of Wickham's heroism in the battle, and the injury from which he was now recovering.'

'So William actually *helped* him!' Georgiana said.

'He did, and without my prompting.'

'William is so good.' Georgiana pressed her hands together, as if in prayer. 'And to think that George was so heroic! Do you believe in redemption, Miss Bennet?'

Elizabeth pressed her lips together. 'Not really. Yes, a scoundrel may act nobly once in a while, but I fear the habits of cheating and excess will re-emerge.'

'You think I am innocent?'

'I don't know you well enough to draw any such conclusion. What I do think is that none of us is perfect. After all, you have made one mistake, and I have just admitted to four. Mr Wickham may justifiably lay claim to a far greater number. But at root we are all flawed, and must get on with one another as best we can.'

Georgiana shook her head. '*William* is always honourable.'

Elizabeth smiled. 'To tease him I sometimes claim he is without flaw, but that is not really true. Why, at the ball where we met, he disdained to dance even though gentlemen were scarce, and told everyone within earshot that my appearance was barely tolerable.' She put a hand to her mouth. 'Never tell him I said that!'

'I cannot believe William would insult a lady in that

manner.'

'You think I made it up?'

Georgiana reddened, but seemed to realise she was being teased, and smiled shyly. 'You have confused me so much that I don't know what to think.'

Elizabeth took a final sip of cocoa. 'Then we had better retire before I reveal more than I should.'

'Very well, but sometime I want to hear all about your journey. William's letters were vague on many points.'

'So you shall.' Elizabeth rose and stretched. 'We shall be good friends, and conspire to outwit your brother as often as may be.'

58

They came. Waiting at the window, Elizabeth recognised the carriage she had occupied just over a year ago, on the day she had met Giuseppe and Regina Carandini.

As Mr Gardiner helped down his wife, Elizabeth spotted behind them another woman, familiar blonde curls framed by a familiar bonnet …

She turned to Darcy, who had also heard the carriage. 'It is Jane!'

He raised his eyebrows. 'Indeed?'

'You knew!' She confronted him, hands on hips. 'My uncle must have told the messenger last night.'

'It slipped my mind.'

'What nonsense! You wanted to surprise me. Oh, what does it matter?' She ran to the door, and stood with arms outstretched as Jane mounted the steps.

'Lizzy! At last!' Jane's normally composed countenance crumpled as she took Elizabeth's hands and burst into tears. 'I was afraid I might never see you again.'

The Gardiners came through, and Elizabeth greeted them warmly before leading Jane away in search of a more private place to talk. At the back of the hall Georgiana stood in readiness, and Elizabeth performed the introduction.

'Miss Bennet, what a pleasure,' Georgiana said earnestly. 'Ever since Mr Bingley told me of your engagement, I have been hoping you would come to London so that we could meet.'

Elizabeth was gratified by this confident speech: she had wondered whether Georgiana *herself* had feelings for Mr Bingley, and might see Jane as a victorious rival.

Jane, still struggling to compose herself, regarded the elegant, unpretentious girl with evident admiration. 'I also have longed to meet you, having heard from Mr Bingley and Mr Darcy of your many accomplishments. Excuse my agitation.' She dabbed her eyes. 'I have not seen Lizzy for a year. I can scarce believe she is really back.'

'Truly I understand, Miss Bennet; I felt the same when my brother returned yesterday. But you will want to catch up on your news. May I show you to the parlour?'

'So Jane, you must confess all,' Elizabeth said. 'What did Mr Bingley have to say for himself last autumn after his return to Netherfield?'

They had been served coffee in the parlour while the others congregated in the drawing room. Jane, now her usual calm self, took a modest bite from a jam tart. 'It was after Lydia and her husband visited us, you know, on their way north.' Jane grimaced—Elizabeth had told her of Wickham's injury in the battle. 'Poor Mr Wickham, I do hope he makes a full recovery.'

'As do we all, dear Jane, but you are digressing.'

'Oh. Mr Bingley. Well, he said he had recently learned of my presence in London the previous winter, and was distraught not to have known at the time, since otherwise he would have called on me; but he hoped he could make amends now by calling *very* often, provided of course that such attentions would be welcome ...'

'Did he say *who told him* you had been in London?'

'No. Miss Bingley, I imagine.'

'Hmm.' Elizabeth decided to keep silent on this point. 'And why did he tarry so long before returning to Netherfield, loving you as he did?'

'He believed me indifferent.' Jane put head in hands. 'It is really my own fault, Lizzy. I am too timid in expressing my feelings.'

Elizabeth snorted. 'He called often enough when he first leased Netherfield, so you must have given him ample encouragement then.'

'He may have been dissuaded by his sisters.'

Again Elizabeth opted for discretion: this was not the time to expose Darcy's role. 'You must have been under severe strain when Lydia absconded. I wish I could have been there to support you.'

'It was a hard time, with father away and mother in a frenzy. Luckily Mr Darcy heard of our disgrace through his aunt, who learned of it from Mr Collins, and assumed responsibility for finding the runaways. Father still has no idea to whom we are indebted. I was sworn to secrecy by Aunt Gardiner.'

Elizabeth nodded. 'I have managed to wring some of the story from Mr Darcy, but it was hard work. I gather he learned of Mr Gardiner from Colonel Forster, and felt more able to approach him than father. Also Mr Gardiner was in London, of course.'

Jane smiled. 'But the true mystery, Lizzy, is why Mr Darcy should go to such trouble to help our family, and on that topic I was hoping *you* might enlighten us.'

Elizabeth hesitated. 'What are people saying?'

'Your exploits are widely reported.' Jane grinned. 'Mr Gardiner may have a surprise for you there.'

'And father?'

'Most of all he's relieved to learn you are safe. As to Mr Darcy, father naturally appreciates his help in bringing you home.' She lowered her voice. 'But he fears you will feel obliged to marry against your will.' She looked down. 'As do I.'

'Then let me reassure you.' Elizabeth took her hand. 'We *will* marry, and I am the happiest creature alive.'

'But Lizzy, you disliked him so much …'

'All that is forgotten. We have travelled together many months, and lived through experiences I would have never believed possible.' Suddenly overwhelmed, she fought tears. 'Jane, I have learned so much, about the world, and also about myself. I will tell all … but gradually.'

'Mr Bingley and I discussed the possibility. We hoped you might finally have come to a good understanding. But after you rejected him before … is it not remarkable?'

'Mr Darcy is certainly persistent.' Elizabeth looked up, smiling. 'Have you and Mr Bingley set a date?'

'We have been awaiting your safe return.'

'Then let's have a double wedding! Mother will be beside herself.'

As they entered the drawing room, Mrs Gardiner jumped up. 'Lizzy! I understand congratulations are in order.'

Elizabeth smiled at Darcy. 'It would appear you have passed on our news.'

'Should I have waited?'

'No, but you realise now that you cannot change your mind?'

Colonel Fitzwilliam handed her a sheet from a newspaper, with a passage marked. 'You should know, Miss Elizabeth, that my cousin was put on the spot. You are both now celebrities.'

With a severe glance at Jane, Elizabeth retreated to a corner chair and began to read.

From our war correspondent, James Herrick

During the battle I was approached again by Mr
Fitzwilliam Darcy, who was organising the camp
followers to transport the wounded. Despite
confusion and treacherous terrain, this little
band of wives, brothers, even children, kept
the carts moving hour upon hour as the valiant
British fortress at Hougoumont held out under
successive assaults. At the climax of the
French attack, when Marshal Ney unleashed the
elite soldiers of the Imperial Guard, we ventured to the crest to save an injured corporal,
and witnessed the grand sight of the 52nd Foot
preparing to engage from the flank; minutes
later, as Mr Darcy and I carried the corporal
downhill, the 52nd turned the battle by forcing
the Imperial Guard to retreat in panic.

It is with pride that I report the work of Mr
Darcy and other followers in caring for our
soldiers. After victory was secured, Mr Darcy
worked tirelessly bringing injured men to the
field hospital or to local villages. Mrs Henri-
etta Smith left the safety of Antwerp to sit at
her husband's bedside, and ministered to other
officers. Women made their way to the field
hospital, where they assisted our surgeons under the most appalling conditions. Miss Elizabeth Bennet, Mr Darcy's fiancée, laboured long
into the night tending to the wounded with un-
flinching good humour. These helpers were not
present in any official capacity. They came to
accompany relatives or friends, and assisted
others out of patriotism and compassion. I have
named some individuals whom I met while following the 52nd; their service was matched by
countless others across our whole army, and I
salute them all.

Darcy joined her, and whispered: 'I'm sorry that you
should be embarrassed in this way. Mr Herrick saw us
together and asked whether you were my wife; I told him,
as we agreed, that we were engaged. It never occurred to

me that he would use our names in his reports.'

Elizabeth cringed, her face still red. 'Could Lady Catherine have seen this?'

'Unlikely. It came out just two days ago, and my aunt never reads newspapers on principle. Of course she is bound to hear eventually, from other sources.'

'It is so out of proportion. Soldiers like Colonel Fitzwilliam and Mr Wickham risked their lives. We worked for a few days in relative safety.'

'My sentiments exactly. Still, newspapers are soon forgotten, and fortunately we have not been forced to marry against our wishes.'

Mr Gardiner approached, and bowed. 'A remarkable tribute, Lizzy. I am proud of you both.'

She grimaced. 'Thank you, uncle, but the credit for our victory belongs to others. Let us talk of it no more.'

After lunch the Gardiners returned home, leaving Jane at Darcy House with Elizabeth so that she would be present when the Bingleys called in the evening.

'Miss Elizabeth.' Darcy hovered beside a corner of the drawing room, where Elizabeth was talking with Jane and Georgiana. 'May I have a word?'

He led her to his study, closed the door, and kissed her. She stood on tip-toe to kiss him back, before retreating with a smile. 'Is that what you meant by *having a word?*'

'No, merely an overture. We need to make plans, and I have a question. Do you feel you must go straight away to your family at Longbourn, or can we remain a few days in London first?'

She raised her eyebrows. 'You wish to come to Longbourn?'

'There is a matter to discuss with your father.'

'Hmm.' She walked across the room, thinking. 'Since

Jane has just arrived, I think it would be better to stay here this week. You should spend more time with your sister. I will visit Gracechurch Street and see the children. The Bingleys will be here.'

Darcy nodded. 'I should also call on Edward Havers to check that he and Céline got back safely.'

'Of course!' Elizabeth recalled their last meeting, in Venice, when her mind had been blurred by laudanum. How long ago it seemed. She looked up at Darcy's grave, reassuring presence, and moved to his side, as if to remind herself that she was now safe among true friends, and with good fortune always would be.

59

Darcy sat in his study facing Charles Bingley, who had arrived with his sisters and Mr Hurst for dinner. Their leather armchairs were separated by a coffee table holding a decanter of sherry and two glasses. Bingley was his usual cheerful self, relieved that his friends had returned safely, and eager to set a date for the wedding. Or *weddings*, since Darcy had confirmed what everyone capable of reading a newspaper could now discover for themselves.

'Why are you in London?' Darcy asked. 'It must be an urgent matter, to tear you away from Hertfordshire.'

'Business. A friend in the city has advised me to sell some stock.'

'May one ask for details?'

Bingley grinned. 'War is a terrible thing, but it can be dashed profitable. I invested a large sum in a government bearer bond called Omnium when the price collapsed after the du Bourg hoax. Do you remember?'

'Remind me.'

'A man posing as Colonel du Bourg arrived at Dover with news that Bonaparte had been killed, and the French monarchy restored. All nonsense: he made it up. When the rumour reached London, government stocks soared until the story was officially denied, whereupon they fell to the floor. Perfect time to buy.'

'Aha.' Darcy, whose grip on matters financial was tentative, hazarded an inference. 'So now that Bonaparte has finally been defeated, the stocks are riding high again?'

'Just so. I stand to make a tidy profit.'

'Why sell now, if the stock is so valuable?'

'My adviser believes markets over-react. In the euphoria over our victory, it is forgotten that the government is still heavily in debt, and faces other uncertainties abroad.'

Darcy nodded, and sipped sherry. 'How long will it take to perform this lucrative operation?'

'I'll be finished by the weekend. The problem is what to do with the money. Jane suggests I should consult Mr Gardiner, who is busy rebuilding his trading contacts now that Europe is returning to sanity.'

'Then let it be Saturday. Would it suit you if I came to Netherfield with Georgiana, and proceeded from there to Pemberley?'

'Excellent. It will be a jolly party, and I shall host a ball to celebrate.'

In many ways it was a familiar dinner at Darcy House. At the head of the table, Darcy sat opposite Georgiana; Mr Hurst joined Colonel Fitzwilliam and Mr Bingley on one side, facing Mrs Hurst and Caroline Bingley on the other. But now there were two newcomers, the Miss Bennets, seated between Georgiana and Bingley's sisters.

During the soup, the guests talked quietly in small huddles. Darcy fended off enquiries from Miss Bingley on his adventures on the continent, while keeping an eye on the far corner, where Elizabeth was entertaining Jane and Georgiana with an anecdote. Bingley was conversing with Colonel Fitzwilliam, who was looking stronger and had begun to revisit his old haunts in town. Only the Hursts were left out; still, Louisa seemed happy enough listening to her sister, while Mr Hurst gave his full attention to the wine.

The fish came, and Miss Bingley faced the whole table. 'So, Miss Eliza, you have deserted us and lived among foreigners for a whole year! Pray, is it true what they say of the French and Italians, that they subsist mainly on garlic?'

Elizabeth met Darcy's eye, with the hint of a wink. '*Au contraire*, Miss Bingley, I found them uncommonly civilised both in cuisine and dress: indeed, they often create fashions that arrive here years later.'

'I wonder you troubled to return to our modest little island, if you think them so superior.'

'I rejoice to be back home, Miss Bingley, but it is true that I made wonderful friends on my journey, and will miss them.'

'Your sisters have certainly kept busy during your absence.' Miss Bingley threw a forced smile at Jane. 'To my great delight, Miss Bennet is betrothed to Charles, while Miss Lydia is now Mrs Wickham. A most worthy match, would you not agree, Mr Darcy?'

Darcy observed Georgiana out of the corner of his eye, while struggling to control his anger. Caroline knew nothing of Georgiana's lapse; she was aware however that Wickham was held in low regard, and obviously hoped to embarrass Elizabeth. To his surprise, Georgiana seemed unperturbed, and after exchanging a glance with Elizabeth, replied on his behalf.

'Your praise of Mr Wickham is timely, Miss Bingley, for William has told me of his bravery in the recent battle, where he received serious injuries from which he is now recovering.'

'Indeed!' Miss Bingley fell silent, while her brother tactfully changed the subject and spoke of the ball he planned to hold at Netherfield. Darcy hardly listened, so amazed was he at Georgiana's composure: it was as if the ghost of Wickham's infamy was finally laid to rest. He recalled Elizabeth's words shortly after their arrival: *let me get to know her first*. There must have been a heart-to-heart in which Elizabeth had succeeded in dissipating the trauma. Or had Georgiana simply matured while he had been away?

The roast was served, and Colonel Fitzwilliam tapped the table. 'I have an announcement!'

All conversation stopped, and with a sly smile at Darcy, the colonel continued. 'I paid a visit to my club this afternoon, where I met my old chum Major Harry Percy. He it was that carried Wellington's news of our victory to London. He told me how his ship was becalmed in the channel, obliging his men to row the last 20 miles to Broadstairs. He arrived in town bloodied from the battle, for he had not paused one second, and went straight to a dinner party in St James's Square to deliver the letter to the Prince Regent.'

'I hope Major Percy has had time to wash since then,' Bingley remarked.

'I found him in excellent form. Now, to the nub. The major celebration will await the return of Wellington, who is still with the army in France. However, the Regent is hosting a party tomorrow at Carlton House, for officers like Major Percy and myself who fought at Waterloo.' He turned to Darcy. 'Your schoolmate Sir James Webster will attend, with Lady Frances. I hardly needed to mention your help. Major Percy has read the piece in the Times, and remembers meeting you at the Duchess of Richmond's ball. He insists that you accompany me, and bring Miss Elizabeth as well.'

There was a collective gasp.

'Darcy, this is a great honour,' Bingley said. 'Absolutely you must go.'

Cries of agreement rang around the table, except for Miss Bingley, who glowered in silence. Darcy was surprised to feel a twinge of pity. He hoped that after the weddings, Caroline would accept reality and try to make herself interesting to another man.

60

'Lizzy, this is exquisite.' Jane ran a finger over the silk of Elizabeth's dress, and studied the nets that overlaid the sleeves.

'Shall I keep the sash? I added it for the Duchess of Richmond's ball, since that was the fashion in Brussels.'

'Why not? There will be women at the dinner who attended the same ball.'

Elizabeth sighed, recalling the sombre scene as the ball in Brussels broke up. 'The Prince Regent may see this as a victory party, but I doubt many of his guests will feel like celebrating. We are relieved to have won—but at what a cost.'

'It is an honour to attend.'

'True. I have been melancholy today, since Mr Darcy and I visited Montagu Square.'

'Were your friends not well? You said the little girl, Céline, was thriving under Sir Edward's guardianship.'

Elizabeth nodded. 'He is a kind man, and a magnet for the ladies now that he is the baronet. No, I was affected by the news from Venice. Sir Edward has written regularly to Lady Havers, and received only a single brief reply. He hardly expects to receive another. She did not trouble to enquire after Céline—or me for that matter. It would seem she has bigger fish to fry, for Regina will shortly become a countess!'

'A new title! So she will not take up the dower?'

'Not her! What an amazing woman. So charming and handsome on the outside, so sly on the inside.'

Jane smiled. 'Like a certain gentleman of our acquaintance?'

'Mr Wickham? Just so—and I was taken in by them both, dupe that I am.'

'Did Lady Havers send news of her brother?'

Elizabeth shivered from the dark memory. 'Gabriele has quarrelled with his cousin Mario, for helping Mr Darcy trace my whereabouts, and barred him from family reunions.'

'Signor Mario still runs the business?'

'Yes, according to Mr Gardiner. But there will be no further imports of glass beads—not at least through our uncle, whom Gabriele has blacklisted. I suppose he wants to block out all reminders of the ungrateful woman who jilted him. How he must hate me.'

Extending between Pall Mall and the Mall, Carlton House was the grandest town residence Elizabeth had ever seen. The front reminded her of Villa Foscari, with its Greek columns and central balcony, but on a larger scale. The prince had extended the property over several decades; now that he was Regent, it was in essence a royal palace.

After Colonel Fitzwilliam had presented their invitations they were ushered into a hall of vast height, leading to an octagonal room which served as a crossroads: on one side the grand staircase, on another a courtyard. Yet another route led to a blue-carpeted drawing room with rose satin walls, where dignitaries, officers, and their elegant wives waited to be announced.

'Is it not ironic,' Elizabeth whispered to Darcy. 'We celebrate our victory in a palace built, decorated and furnished in the French style.'

He smiled, his eyes wandering over the assembly. 'It will be some minutes before our turn comes. Meanwhile, I already recognise several couples from the ball.'

'What wonderful pictures.' Elizabeth left him with the colonel, and walked past paintings by Old Masters including Rembrandt and Rubens, as well as more recent pieces by Reynolds and Gainsborough.

She returned to find Darcy in conversation with Major Percy, who proceeded to take them under his wing. They were escorted to the dining room, where at the entrance a white-wigged man of immense girth reclined on an equally wide armchair, flanked by a grand lady with silver hair.

'Your highness.' Major Percy bowed. 'Lady Hertford. May I present Colonel Fitzwilliam of the 52nd Foot. He is accompanied by Mr Fitzwilliam Darcy and Miss Elizabeth Bennet, who were present after the battle and organised care for hundreds of our men.'

Elizabeth curtsied, trembling with awe as she faced the man who had served as regent since his father, George III, had been declared insane. He was dressed in military colours, with a red waistcoat stretching across his massive paunch, cream breaches, and a dark blue coat with gold buttons. His left hand held a cigar, and his small eyes, peering from beneath folds of flesh, were lascivious as they probed her up and down.

'Charming,' he grunted.

She retreated, her cheeks flaming, as Darcy bowed in his turn, and said pointedly: 'Miss Bennet is my fiancée.'

The royal eyebrows went up. 'Dashed good show. Enjoy the dinner.'

Elizabeth curtsied to the prince's companion, whom she knew from the gossip columns to be his current mistress; to her surprise the lady was in her sixties, some ten years older than the prince. Lady Hertford acknowledged her with a nod, tilting her head with a knowing smile.

'I have read of your service, Miss Bennet, and wish you an enjoyable evening. You deserve it.'

Elizabeth thanked her, and swallowed as Darcy led her away. 'Oh my goodness! I would rather face Bonaparte's cavalry.'

'The prince took a shine to you.' Darcy smiled, but she detected a note of anxiety.

'I hope not. If embraced by such a mound of flesh, I doubt I would find my way out.'

'Take care, my love, if he approaches you again.'

'It is hardly likely, with so many alluring ladies to distract him. Anyway, I wager I can run faster.'

'The secret,' Colonel Fitzwilliam advised, 'is to bide your time.'

As the banquet progressed, Elizabeth appreciated his good sense. The dishes, in conformity with the decor, were French: consommé, purée, two kinds of fish, duck, dumplings, lamb, beef, pheasant, vegetables, accompanied by a succession of fine wines. The soups and fish dishes were so delicious that she would gladly have asked for seconds, but she followed the colonel's example and ate a half portion of her favourites, and a taste of anything else.

The dining room was lined with ornate carvings painted in gold, extending across the marble-coloured ceiling to chains supporting low-hanging chandeliers. A long table ran down the middle, so broad that conversation was possible only with your neighbours. While Colonel Fitzwilliam caught up with a fellow-officer, Darcy sat beside Sir James Webster, back from Brussels with Lady Frances Webster, whom Elizabeth had last seen flirting with Wellington. Soon bored with the officer on her right, Lady

Frances applied to Darcy to change places, so that she could talk with Elizabeth. She was heavily pregnant, and sank into the red-and-gold upholstered chair with a tired groan.

'Saw you at the ball,' Lady Frances said. 'Lovely dress.'

'How long have you been back?'

'A week.' She sighed. 'We should have let Bonaparte win, so that he would dig a tunnel under that confounded English Channel.'

Elizabeth laughed. 'It was brave of you to accompany your husband in your, ah, condition.'

She regretted this intimate remark immediately, realising that she had already drunk too much wine, but Lady Frances was unoffended. 'One more month. I hope for a son this time, much as I love my daughter.'

'May I ask if you have a name in mind?'

'Charles Byron if we get a boy.' She glanced across at her husband, who was holding forth on his favourite topic of prize fighting, and winked at Elizabeth. 'Lord Byron is a close friend—of my husband's.'

And of yours, Elizabeth thought, but this time managed to hold her tongue.

'Mr Darcy is a fine man.' Lady Frances lowered her voice. 'Yours is a love match, I wager.'

'With my tiny dowry I hope so, for his sake.'

Lady Frances laughed, and leaned over to whisper. 'Do enjoy the first few years. Children are a blessing but you can keep them for later. It is easily managed if you lock your bedroom door at certain times of the month.'

Elizabeth struggled to keep a straight face. 'I see I have much to learn from you.'

'We are granted only one life, and may as well enjoy it.' She whispered again. 'My husband and I are good friends, and he is a loving father to my daughter.'

Elizabeth hesitated, before asking: 'You were talking with the Duke of Wellington at the supper. What sort of man is he?'

'Abstemious and self-disciplined in most things. Even at home he prefers to dine on plain food and sleep on a bunk. He has just two indulgences: wine, and women.' She leaned closer. 'Not that I had much success in Brussels.' She patted Elizabeth's arm with a conspiratorial wink. 'I'll try again once little Charles Byron is out in the world.'

Elizabeth shook her head, amazed at such indiscretion. 'I fear my life is less, ah, *interesting* than yours.'

Lady Webster smiled. 'You are charming, *cherie*, but I think you disapprove of me.'

'I disapprove of myself because I *don't* disapprove of you.'

'Ah!' Her face lit up in a smile of genuine friendliness. 'One of the tragedies of life, Miss Elizabeth, is that entertaining people are usually untrustworthy, while honourable people are dull. I believe you are an exception.'

'You mean I am both untrustworthy *and* dull?'

Lady Webster guffawed, spraying wine across the table. 'Will you visit us in London? James is always happy to see old schoolmates, and Mr Darcy must be one of the few men in the *ton* polite enough to take an interest in his absurd pursuits.'

'I would love to visit you, Lady Webster. How about in the autumn, when with luck I will be married, and little Charles, or perhaps Charlotte, has been safely delivered?'

It was time for the sweet courses. Huge silver platters of profiteroles and tartlets were brought, along with bowls of exotic fruits. The Websters had gone to greet another couple, and Elizabeth was about to compare notes with

Darcy when a distinguished gentleman dressed in a dark evening coat and white neck scarf approached them.

'Mr Darcy? Bathurst. Major Percy pointed you out to me. Excuse me, madam. May I have a word?'

She observed with curiosity as Lord Bathurst took the empty chair beside Darcy. He was tall, with alert eyes, a strong chin, and close-cropped dark grey hair. 'This is in my official capacity, since as you may know, I am Secretary of State for War and the Colonies. It has been drawn to my attention that you served as an adjutant in the 52nd Foot, and observed at close quarters the transport and care of the wounded.'

'Transport, yes.' Darcy glanced at Elizabeth. 'Miss Bennet was more directly concerned with care.'

'Ah.' Lord Bathurst beamed at her as if complimenting a child. 'Admirable. Let me come to the point. I have long felt that insufficient attention is given to the management of such tasks after a major battle. We have reports from surgeons, but these are incomplete because they focus on issues of treatment, such as—' He glanced awkwardly at Elizabeth. 'Such as the best moment to operate. What I would appreciate, sir, if you have the time and inclination, is your impression of the whole process. Conveyance to field hospitals. Nursing. Surgery. Transfer to hospitals in nearby towns. A written report would be best. As long or short as you like.' He looked at Elizabeth. 'No doubt Miss Bennet can provide valuable testimony.'

Darcy glanced at her again, with a slight raise of the eyebrows. He turned back to Lord Bathurst. 'For my part, I would be glad to accept. If what I observed is typical, the transport and care of the wounded is performed mostly by camp-followers and local people, whose viewpoint is never canvassed.'

'Excellent!' Lord Bathurst lowered his voice. 'I am asking this as a favour, Mr Darcy, not a paid assignment. It should be mentioned, however, that I have the ear of the regent, who is aware of your contribution, and may see fit to acknowledge it in the annual list. Of course I cannot promise. It is his highness's decision alone.'

Darcy frowned, as if in distaste. 'I agree that payment is out of the question: what you ask is not demanding, and would bring its own satisfaction. As for *alternative* forms of recognition, I believe others have a far stronger claim.'

Lord Bathurst was silent a moment, then nodded. 'I understand. A pleasure to have met you, sir, and I look forward to receiving your report in due time.' He bowed to Elizabeth. 'Madam. My sincere appreciation again for your service.'

She thanked him, and managed to keep a straight face until he was out of earshot. Darcy met her eye severely, and she dissolved into laughter.

'I'm sorry!' She looked down, red-faced. 'I have had too much wine. Why are these people so absurd?'

'Because they are exactly as we expect. Caricatures of themselves.'

'Still, a good idea, is it not? The report?'

'Will you help?'

'Naturally.' She grinned. 'What award do *I* get?'

'You want a title? How about Mrs Darcy?'

'That will do nicely for now.'

61

Saturday 8th July 2pm

On a clear summer day—breezy, with cumulus clouds interrupting spells of sunshine—two carriages rounded the church and turned towards Longbourn. Darcy sat facing Georgiana and Mrs Annesley, while Elizabeth chattered excitedly with Jane; Bingley's party followed in the carriage behind.

As they rolled into the forecourt there was a huge commotion. Darcy recognised Mrs Bennet's squawking as she called Mrs Hill; Kitty Bennet rushed out, followed by two maids and a footman; Mary Bennet's face appeared in a window. No sign of Mr Bennet; Darcy hoped he was not sick or away from home.

He smiled at his sister, who was observing the boisterous scene with alarm. 'Bear up, Georgiana. One gets used to it in time.'

Elizabeth threw him a disdainful glance, but made no comment. In the other carriage, Bingley had already got down and advanced to greet the family.

Georgiana's nerves were as nothing compared with the reaction of Mrs Bennet, once she realised that the Darcys were in the party. Bingley had written to confirm that his friend would again be staying at Netherfield—but without any clarification of his intentions towards Elizabeth. Mrs Bennet stumbled down the step, squawked again, and ran straight back inside with renewed appeals to Mrs Hill.

Darcy handed down the ladies, and held back with his sister while Elizabeth ran to embrace Kitty and Mary. As always it amused him to observe other families. Nobody could accuse the Bennets of being elegant or proper; still, there were compensations. Small quarrels sprang up constantly, but their affection was plain to see.

Mrs Annesley joined Bingley's sisters and Mr Hurst, who sent compliments but declined to enter; their carriage set off for Netherfield. Alone with Georgiana, Darcy swallowed and led her to the doorway. It was time to confront Mrs Bennet.

Darcy waited in the parlour, recalling his last visit in the winter. Kitty as before was silent, overawed. Bingley sat beside his fiancée, relaxed and content now that a date could be announced. Mrs Bennet was unusually quiet, her eyes flicking between Elizabeth and himself as if she were trying to divine their feelings. Her countenance was oddly asymmetric, as if the left and right sides expressed different emotions—one anxious, the other hopeful. Mary had taken Georgiana away to the drawing room to view her sheet music. Only Bingley kept the conversation going, with occasional light interjections from Elizabeth.

Mr Bennet appeared at the door, looking distracted as if he had been reading, or pondering some deep matter; Darcy rose immediately to greet him.

'Good afternoon, sir.' Mr Bennet returned his bow. 'A word, if you would be so good. In my study.'

Darcy left, exchanging a grimace with Elizabeth, and entered the familiar study, with its piles of books, and the coffee table holding a bottle of port and two glasses. On the desk he noticed a newspaper, with a passage marked. He could not tell whether it was the *same* passage, but Mr

Bennet must know: Mr Gardiner would have alerted him by letter.

Mr Bennet indicated an armchair. 'Refreshment?'

'Later, perhaps.' Darcy tried to keep his voice calm. 'I can imagine how you must …'

Mr Bennet held up a hand. 'Please. Allow me the satisfaction of having my say, even if you have already guessed my import. I should like, first of all, to thank you, from the bottom of my heart, for bringing our beloved daughter to safety. Any reservations on other matters are a pinprick in comparison.'

'Thank you. It has been a complex journey, and as you will know, my choice of route proved unfortunate, and exposed Miss Elizabeth to danger.'

'Indeed.' He pressed his lips together. 'Was there *really* no alternative?'

'In the weeks leading up to the battle, Brussels seemed the safest option. It was protected by British troops, and provided a relatively short crossing via Ostend.'

Mr Bennet nodded. 'I realise it is easy to be wise after the event. But having seen the newspaper reports, I am at a loss to understand your decision, after the battle, to stay near Waterloo rather than sailing immediately from Antwerp. That my daughter should be exposed to the horrors of a field hospital after such slaughter! What could have possessed you?'

'I saw it as my duty to remain near my cousin. As for Miss Elizabeth, I concur fully with your viewpoint. I sent her to Antwerp with a trustworthy local family, and there she stayed until news came that my cousin was wounded, and my whereabouts unknown. My instructions were that she should wait for some days, then leave for England. Instead, with remarkable courage, she made her way to the field hospital to confirm that I was well, then insisted on helping.'

'You made no attempt to dissuade her?'

Darcy leaned forward. 'Sir, had you been present, you would have understood. Casualties from the battlefield were arriving in their hundreds, with just a handful of camp-followers and nuns to feed them, bandage their wounds, and arrange transport to local villages. I care profoundly for your daughter, and under normal circumstances would shield her from such atrocities, but her sensibilities were of minor importance compared with her value as a dedicated, intelligent helper. I judged she was in no danger. Nor were the other women at the camp. The men depended on them, even worshipped them. It would have been far riskier to take her away, along roads swarming with runaways and soldiers of many nationalities.'

Mr Bennet blinked, and it was a while before he spoke again.

'My Lizzy.' He looked up, as if coming out of a dream. 'So. What is this talk of *betrothal?* I was under the impression that as her father, I had some say in the matter.' Mr Bennet jumped up to retrieve the newspaper from his desk. 'Here! Your *fiancée.*'

'At times during our journey, we had to explain why an unmarried man and woman travelled unchaperoned. We agreed that when necessary, we would pretend an engagement that did not exist.' He took a deep breath. 'Yet.'

'You wish to marry Lizzy?'

'More than I have ever wished anything.'

'And does she return this feeling?'

'Yes. That has been our understanding since we left Italy.'

'Forgive me, Mr Darcy, but it has been my impression that she does not see you in this light at all.'

'She has changed. As have I.'

'Why?' Mr Bennet poured port, and drank a sizeable draught. 'My daughter has no dowry or connections to speak of. Why should a man of your standing go to such lengths to secure her hand?'

Darcy regarded him provocatively. 'You believe Miss Elizabeth unworthy of me?'

He bristled. 'I most certainly do not, sir!'

'And nor do I.'

It was early evening. Darcy and Bingley had left for Netherfield. Elizabeth sat in her chamber, surrounded by mementoes of her journey: a wooden doll (she had given the other to Rosie Briggs), Alice's sketches, and the rest.

The main business of the day was accomplished. Her father had demanded whether she had taken leave of her senses in accepting this man. Had she not always hated him? She had explained their history at length, including as an incentive Darcy's role in rescuing Lydia. The change in Mr Bennet's countenance had been comical, as if a balloon had deflated. Belligerence was replaced by relief, and then by astonishment as she told him of their subsequent meetings with Wickham in Brussels. The good news had been announced to the whole assembly. Bingley was affable; Mrs Bennet, hysterical; everyone else, overjoyed. Finally, adding a cherry to the cake, Bingley made Kitty's day by inviting them to a ball at Netherfield.

The familiar bedroom embraced Elizabeth in a cocoon of security. Here she had been a ten-year-old tearaway, fond of climbing trees, a fifteen-year-old girl in the shadow of Jane's beauty, a twenty-year-old flirting with Wickham and needling Darcy. She returned to the letters that had awaited her at Longbourn, from Céline, Alice, Hilda, Maria Grazia, and others. Nothing from Regina. Smiling, she pulled out Fraulein Edelmann's offering to read again.

Lieber Fraulein Bennet!

So, Elizabeth Bennet, Mrs Ashley, Mrs Darcy, or
whatever you call yourself these days, I hope
this finds you well, and that you still play
the pianoforte (and make fewer mistakes).

I am back in Salzburg, among cultured people
and fine coffee houses and accompanists who
know what they are doing.

Herr Schubert came last week. He wants to marry
a certain Fraulein Grob, daughter of a silk
maker, but has been denied since he has insufficient means to support her. I exposed him to
the full radiance of my charm without success.
Men are truly fools.

Please put my mind at rest and confirm by return of post that my esteemed musical partner
is restored safely to her homeland!

I cannot believe I paid 24 ducats for your per-
formances at the concerts. I must have been de-
mented.

Good-bye liebchen, from your friend

Hilda Edelmann

Elizabeth folded the letter and put it away, tears filling her
eyes. An intense nostalgia overcame her as she reviewed,
as if from a mountain top, all she had experienced—the
people, the places, the adventures. Now a new chapter
would open. She would be mistress of Pemberley. Jane
would live at Netherfield, or perhaps nearer, in Derbyshire, if Bingley bought an estate there. But she would
return to mainland Europe. She would sample again its
variety of languages, religions, fashions, cuisines, land-
scapes, entertainments. They would see Salzburg. Her
children would thrill at the Rhine, the Dolomites, the his-

toric cities. She would keep in touch with Hilda and Lorraine, and one day they would meet again.

The door creaked and Mrs Bennet entered. *The dress, they must order the dress!* Such finery she would have, and such jewels! Jane's would be nothing in comparison. How handsome was Mr Darcy! How elegant his sister! How could they have believed him ill-natured? Three daughters married! If only such husbands could be found for Mary and Kitty …

Elizabeth smiled, agreed when she could, and accompanied her mother downstairs to join the others.

Epilogue

August 1825, ten years later

Elizabeth relaxed in her favourite wicker chair in the conservatory at Pemberley, taking afternoon tea. She was alone: Darcy had joined Colonel Fitzwilliam in London to petition the government over the formation of an Army Medical Corps, a cause they had been promoting for a decade. The outcome, she had little doubt, would be the same as before. Yes, it was a worthy concept. No, it could not be implemented *at this precise moment*. Still, they kept pressing, and with Darcy's schoolmate Robert Peel a rising star in the cabinet, the future might bring better luck.

A maid asked whether she needed a fresh pot of tea.

'No, Bertha. The scones were delicious.'

'Thank you, your ladyship. Oh!' The maid, a pleasant girl but forgetful, stopped in her tracks. 'A party asked to see the park. Mrs Horton said they talked foreign, like.'

'Very well.' Elizabeth sighed. She needed to speak with the housekeeper about preparations for the following day, the 10th anniversary of their wedding. But that could wait for now.

She leaned back, enjoying the warmth and fragrance of the glass-domed room. Darcy would be on his way back; he planned to break the journey at Bingley's estate, twenty miles south of Pemberley, so that they could travel up together in the morning. No doubt he would bring a *present*, purchased in town: an art work, she hoped, rather than jewellery, which she already had in abundance.

Marriage had brought them joy, their mutual fascination as lively as ever. It had brought children too: the heir William, and Charles, followed by Alice. The boys were outside now, fishing, while the little girl sketched with the governess. Elizabeth smiled proudly, wondering whether the girl would emulate her namesake. Mrs Gerard Hanson, known professionally as Alice Dill, was an artist and botanist of rising reputation; her delicate watercolours in the Pemberley gallery provided welcome relief from portraits of Darcy's ancestors.

Fortune had favoured Elizabeth's family. Mr Bennet still lived, passing each day in much the same manner, and growing ever more eccentric and outspoken. Mrs Bennet achieved the satisfaction of settling *all* her daughters after a sea captain carried off Kitty, and Mary accepted a proposal from a clergyman twice her age; unfortunately Mary's marriage ended after only six months with the untimely death of her husband, and although left well provided for, she had returned to Longbourn. Wickham had recovered well from his wound, but lost his taste for soldiering. He remained in the north, trying one unlikely career after another, and paying little attention to Lydia except as a means of begging funds from her sisters.

Darcy's family too had flourished. Georgiana married well and lived in town, where she frequented concerts. The scandalous Lady Webster, now a family friend, had introduced Colonel Fitzwilliam to a plain but charming young lady with an ample dowry. Only at Rosings had misfortune struck, with the death from apoplexy of Lady Catherine de Bourgh. Mr Collins sent Darcy a long letter of condolence, enclosing a sermon, written for the occasion, on how God calls to His presence those He loves best. But there was a silver lining: far from being crushed by her mother's death, Anne de Bourgh grew in health and confidence, married a distant cousin, and was now expecting their first child.

'Ma'am, you have a visitor.' Bertha leaned over to collect the tray. 'A lady from the group touring the park. She said she knew you long ago. I think her name was *Fontana*.'

'Can you show her to the parlour?'

Elizabeth passed by her dressing room to check her hair and powder. *Who could this be?* Her thoughts returned, as they often did, to friends encountered during their journey across Europe. Hilda Edelmann, who wrote every Christmas, had married a friend of Franz Schubert's—so solving definitively the problem of finding an accompanist for her recitals. Lorraine de Crécy had visited Elizabeth at Darcy House just two months ago; she was also married, to the editor of a journal promoting the independence of Belgium from the Netherlands.

But *Fontana* sounded Italian …

In the parlour, a dark elfin woman in her early twenties rose to greet her.

'Lady Darcy?' The young woman smiled shyly. *'Non vi ricordate di me?'*

Elizabeth stared at her, then gasped. 'Maddalena?'

'The very same! I am with my husband Professor Fontana, and his sister's family, bound for the Lakes. We have been in London, where we visited Mr Gardiner; he said we should on no account miss the park at Pemberley.'

'But this is wonderful!' Elizabeth stepped forward and kissed cheeks, in the Italian manner. 'Have you been married long?'

'Three months. This is a sort of extended honeymoon. My husband is Professor of English Literature, and admires your poets. We are bound for Ambleside, where he hopes to visit Mr Wordsworth.'

'What a treat awaits you—we also passed our honeymoon there. Now, let us go to the conservatory, which is lovely at this time of day. You must take some refreshment. Coffee? Wine?'

'A glass of *vino rosso* would restore me.'

Comfortably installed among the orchids and climbing plants, with a decanter of wine and two glasses, Elizabeth beamed at her guest. 'You must tell me all! We have heard nothing since your family broke off contact with my uncle in 1815. Our last news of your sister was that she was marrying a count.'

'We learned of your marriage from Mr Gardiner, but nothing after that. I had not realised that Mr Darcy would inherit a title.'

Elizabeth shook her head. 'Not inherited. He received a knighthood for services to the War Office.'

'Our news is mixed.' Maddalena sighed. 'Mother died five years ago, and her loss hit my brother hard. Regina had already left home, so he was left alone—except for a sister he hated.'

'Why should he hate you?'

'Because I saw what he was. Insecure. Aware of others only as a means of feeding his own vanity.'

Elizabeth blinked, as memories returned. 'I hope I did not make your life more difficult.'

'Gabriele and I were enemies long before you came.' Maddalena touched Elizabeth's arm. 'But it is true that your loss devastated him. He became a recluse, interested only in his violin. He had a portrait of you painted from a sketch. Do you remember the artist who visited and took your likeness?'

'An exercise in flattery if ever there was one.'

'Well, that was it. The portrait remained at Gabriele's bedside until his death.'

Elizabeth gasped. 'When?'

'Last year, around the time I met my future husband. There was an outbreak of typhoid fever in Venice, and Gabriele succumbed.'

'I'm sorry.' Elizabeth recalled Carandini's dominating personality, his opinions fixed in stone, his obsessional striving for perfection. How hard to imagine that such a force was no more. 'He was never a happy man.'

'His treatment of you was outrageous. Had it not been for Mr Darcy, he would have forced you to marry him.'

'I am told we have a certain 12-year-old girl to thank for that,' Elizabeth smiled. 'Did you not help Mr Darcy come to my rescue?'

'I threw my doll into the garden!' Maddalena smiled. 'Poor dolly! She was never the same again.'

Elizabeth laughed—but with a twinge of alarm. Had her future hung on this slender strand? Surely not: Darcy would have found another way. 'Does Regina own the business?'

'No, Mario does. The inheritance followed the Roman tradition of favouring the nearest male relative. I am happy. Mario is a good man, and looks after everyone.' She finished her wine. 'In a way it is for the best. My brother is at peace, and our family flourishes as it did when my father was alive.' She walked to the window. 'Lady Darcy, I should go now. My companions are waiting.'

'But Maddalena, you must *all* stay! At least until to-morrow, when Sir William arrives.' She smiled. 'Or Mr Darcy, as you knew him.'

'I wish I could accept, but my husband is eager to progress while the weather holds.' Maddalena raised a finger. 'I have a present, from my sister!' She withdrew a parcel from her bag. 'Fragile. Take care!'

Elizabeth removed the paper to reveal a framed portrait, an exquisite vignette of herself at the age of twenty-one. 'Oh Maddalena! Is this the painting …'

She nodded. 'There is a message.'

Elizabeth turned the frame over and saw a folded note fixed to the back. Opening it, she found just three words, written in Regina's hand.

Cara Elisabetta, Perdonami. R.

Forgive me …

From her treacherous friend.

Maddalena had left. Elizabeth, her mind abuzz, could not bear to remain seated. She paced, thinking of those traumatic days in Venice, and of the journey in which she had learned to appreciate and love Darcy—as well as regaining her own self-respect.

She had remained too long in the settled contentment of Pemberley, their house in town, their families. Gabriele and his manipulative mother were no more. They could visit Brussels, Salzburg, now even Venice …

Next year. In the spring. All of them, the children too.

It was time for another journey.

Afterword

Darcy's Journey diverges from *Pride and Prejudice* after Darcy's proposal at Hunsford, dated here in 1814. Elizabeth refuses to read Darcy's letter, the Gardiners cancel their summer trip, and she goes to Venice instead of Derbyshire. Such a journey could have happened only after Napoleon's exile to Elba in April 1814, which led to a brief interval of peace until his escape in February 1815.

As will be obvious, many people, places, and events in *Darcy's Journey* are historical. They include not only Wellington, Waterloo, and the Prince Regent, but references that are less well-known. I list below the main ones, in the order in which they appear in the novel; most are the subject of Wikipedia entries.

In Venice, the British consul Richard Hoppner and his wife Isabelle are historical; Hoppner later became a friend of Lord Byron. The opera house La Fenice is of course a real place, opened in 1792. So is Caffè Florian, which has occupied its current site in St Mark's Square since 1720. Palazzo Gritti is now a hotel.

On the route from Venice to Padua, all places are real except for Hotel Petrarca in Oriago. Villa Foscari is a 16th century Palladian villa. It had been abandoned by the start of the 19th century, but is now restored and open to the public.

In Padua and Verona most locations are real, including

the Basilica of Saint Anthony, the Roman Amphitheatre, Palazzo Maffei, the Prefettura, and Castelvecchio; the people are fictional (Gerard Hanson, Alice Dill, Pavoni, Zamboni, Fraulein Edelmann, Commander Graf). The same applies to the onward journey across Europe to Brussels: most places are real, people fictional.

In Brussels the de Crécy and de Beaufort families are fictional, but there are well-known historical events starting with the Duchess of Richmond's ball on 15th June 1815. In her biography of Wellington, Elizabeth Longford described this as 'the most famous ball in history'. It was attended, as described in the novel, by the Duke of Wellington and the Prince of Orange. Sir James Webster and his wife Frances are historical people who attended the ball; gossips speculated whether Lady Frances was having an affair with Wellington, or only flirting. Many participants wrote recollections of the ball (see *Duchess of Richmond's ball* in Wikipedia for details); it also inspired writers such as Thackeray and Byron. Actions by Wellington and the Prince of Orange are taken from these memoirs.

The other major historical event, obviously, is the Battle of Waterloo (and engagements like Quatre Bras that preceded it). In outline the novel conforms to historical accounts, although these are debated: some have claimed, for instance, that Wellington exaggerated the role of British forces in turning the battle. General descriptions of the aftermath were taken from the article *British medical services at the Battle of Waterloo* by M.R. Howard (British Medical Journal, 1988). This covers the main types of injury, treatments used by surgeons, and the role of camp followers (especially women) in transporting and caring for the wounded. The regiments existed, although it is uncertain what roles they played in the fighting.

For an eye-witness account, I relied especially on the memoir *A Week at Waterloo in 1815* by Lady Magdalene de Lancey, wife of Sir William de Lancey (freely available from Project Gutenberg). Charles Dickens wrote in 1841 that reading it had been an 'epoch in his life': 'I shall never forget the lightest word of it from this hour to the hour of my death'. Lady de Lancey describes how she was sent to Antwerp before the fighting began, learned of her husband's possibly mortal injury, made her way to the village where he lay, and nursed him until his death a week later. I used events from this memoir in describing Elizabeth's perspective on the battle and its aftermath.

Finally, it was indeed Major Harry Percy who brought news of Wellington's victory to the Prince Regent, whose main residence was Carlton House. Lady Hertford—or to give her full title, Isabella Anne Seymour-Conway, Marchioness of Hertford—was the Prince Regent's mistress, and Lord Bathurst was Secretary of State for War and the Colonies. However, the dinner party at Carlton House is fictional.

M.A. Sandiford, April 2016

Made in the USA
San Bernardino, CA
15 May 2016